Praise for Love Story, With Murders

'*Love Story, With Murders* boasts what must be the most startling protagonist in modern crime fiction . . . Brutal, freakish and totally original' *Sunday Times*

'This compelling crime novel . . . amply proves the freshness and flair that he [Bingham] has brought to the police procedural. Written with unexpected warmth and wry observation, it brings its gruesome story to life without turning the stomach . . . Surprisingly delicate, it weaves a sinuous, seductive spell and confirms we have a new crime talent to treasure' *Daily Mail*

'Superbly compulsive!' *Peterborough Evening Telegraph*

'There is a complex and very clever double mystery here, and what makes the story unique is the parallel unravelling of Fiona's own mystery, and it's her voice, established precisely in the first book but given even freer rein here, that makes it so compelling' *Tangled Web*

'DC Fiona Griffiths is ditsy, funny, stubborn and sharp . . . Bingham provides a spirited Welsh response to the Scottish domination of British crime fiction' *The Times*

'In Bingham's hands she [Fiona Griffiths] comes exuberantly to life and his tale of the investigation into the death of an exotic dancer . . . is richly enjoyable' *Daily Telegraph*

'Bingham's superb second police procedural featuring Det. Constable Fiona Griffiths delivers an even more intense plot and richer cha-- -- -- -- -- his first' *Publisher's Weekly*

Harry Bingham is an author of fiction and non-fiction. When he isn't writing, he's either walking the dogs or running The Writers' Workshop, a leading editorial consultancy. He lives in Oxfordshire with his wife and two children.

If you want to find out more, join the Fiona Griffiths Readers Club now at www.harrybingham.com/lev-in-glasgow

By Harry Bingham

FIONA GRIFFITHS CRIME THRILLER SERIES
Talking to the Dead
Love Story, With Murders
The Strange Death of Fiona Griffiths
This Thing of Darkness
The Dead House

OTHER NOVELS
The Money Makers
Sweet Talking Money
The Sons of Adam
Glory Boys
The Lieutenant's Lover

NON-FICTION
This Little Britain
Stuff Matters
Getting Published
How to Write

LOVE STORY, WITH MURDERS

HARRY BINGHAM

An Orion paperback

First published in Great Britain in 2013
by Orion Books
This paperback edition published in 2014
by Orion Books,
an imprint of The Orion Publishing Group Ltd.
Carmelite House, 50 Victoria Embankment
London EC4Y 0DZ

An Hachette UK company

3 5 7 9 10 8 6 4 2

ISBN 978-1-4091-3723-8

Typeset by Input Data Services Ltd, Bridgwater, Somerset

Printed and bound by CPI Group (UK) Ltd, Croydon, CR0 4YY

The Orion Publishing Group's policy is to use papers that
are natural, renewable and recyclable products and
made from wood grown in sustainable forests. The logging
and manufacturing processes are expected to conform to
the environmental regulations of the country of origin.

www.orionbooks.co.uk

To N., as ever

(i do not know what it is about you that closes
and opens; only something in me understands
the voice of your eyes is deeper than all roses)
nobody, not even the rain, has such small hands

E. E. Cummings
From 'somewhere i have never travelled,
gladly beyond' (1931)

1

Cardiff Prison. September 2010.
'Welcome.'

Penry opens his hands in what's meant to be a spreading gesture, only they never get more than about eight inches apart. It's as though the ghosts of his handcuffs are still there.

'Nice place,' I tell him.

Formica tables with metal legs. Overhead fluorescent lighting. No daylight. Official notices on the wall and a couple of prison warders watching everything. Seven hundred and eighty-five other prisoners, ninety-four of them lifers. Nice.

'Well, you know, I was going to repaint. Freshen things up a bit. But ...' He shrugs. 'You know how it is.'

'Will you manage it?'

The time, not the paintwork. The court handed down a four year sentence, every minute of it deserved. I helped put Penry behind bars – Brian Penry, a bent ex-copper with a line in fraud and one or two worse things besides – and I shouldn't like him, but I do.

'Four years, serve two. Yeah, I'll manage.' His face goes through a few different expressions before settling on something blandly generic. 'My first week here, a guy in the same wing as me kills himself. Piece of broken glass.' He makes a gesture along the inside of both wrists. 'They only noticed when there was blood leaking out from the door. Fucking ...' He shakes his head instead of finishing, but I get the drift.

'Bugger was only in for eighteen months and didn't even seem depressed, apparently.'

I remember the story, but vaguely, the way you do when it concerns something on the inside. What I do remember well was the arrest. A young father. Worked for a precision engineering company. Nice lad, doing well. Done for trying to import cocaine from southern Spain in a shipment of steel tubing. Loses job, loses wife, loses kids, goes to jail. Life over.

'You'll be okay, Brian,' I tell him.

'Yeah. Yeah, once I get the place freshened up, eh?'

We talk for another thirty minutes and it feels like a century. When I leave the building, I find I'm almost running.

2

Cardiff. Late October 2010.
It's a Friday afternoon. October in Wales, but you wouldn't think so. High clouds scudding in from the west and plenty of sunshine. The last shreds of summer and never mind the falling leaves.

I'm in a patrol car with a PC Adrian Condon, on the way back from a wasted five hours going house-to-house in Rumney. We'd been trying to find anyone who could tell us about a street fight that injured one female bystander and two men, one of whom is in hospital with a fractured skull. We'd got nothing useful, but hadn't expected to. Our bosses hadn't expected us to. It was one of those box-ticking things. You do it because you have to.

We're in end-of-shift mode, talking shop, thinking about the weekend, when Condon's radio squawks. Incident called in in Cyncoed. Something to do with illegal rubbish found during a house clearance. Condon looks at me. We could duck this one or we could be good little soldiers. I shrug. I don't care. Illegal rubbish in Cyncoed, what I came into policing for.

Condon shrugs as well. He's already swinging the car around as I reach for the radio.

The dispatcher gives us an address on the Rhyd-y-penau Road, up by the reservoir. Not the sort of address that generally gives us trouble. It's a place of clipped privet, tidy front gardens and net curtains. Bungalows and china dogs.

3

We're there in ten minutes. A big blue van, doors banging open in the wind, marks the target. Condon whirls the car into the vacant scrap of driveway, parks under a bare-branched cherry tree.

We get out. Condon's in uniform and I'm not, and he's a man, which I'm not. So although I'm technically the senior officer, it's him the house clearance guys defer to as they pull off their gloves and shake hands with those big masculine grips.

I don't care, just stand back and watch the clouds scud. Illegal rubbish. How tough can the assignment be? I hear fragments only. Bungalow belonged to an old lady, died two months back, next of kin in Australia. Blah blah. The blue van is piled with old-lady furniture. Curved mahogany legs, green velour trim. Beige cushions with pale gold tassels. I can't see more because of the van door, still banging in the wind.

Condon moves off toward the garage with the clearance guys. I follow. The garage door is raised and there's a skip in front of it, half full. Old garden junk, gummed-up paintpots, bristleless brooms, a spidery fold-out deck chair. Inside, the garage is half cleared, half full.

Teak garden furniture. The sort that's good enough you store it indoors over winter and in bad weather. Take outside when it's warm.

And there's a chest freezer. Capacious. As big as two bathtubs. The sort of thing that nice little old ladies who live with their net curtains and china dogs up by the Llanishen Reservoir fill with stewed apple compotes in autumn and bits of lamb when it's on sale at the local butcher. Of course, there hasn't been any power here for a month or two, so the packaged lamb and stewed apples aren't as good as they were. A wheelie bin, stinking, holds the first layer of bags excavated from the freezer. A pile of plastic wrapped packages lies on the ground, the greyish-yellow colour of meat turned bad and condensation dripping from the inside of each bag.

4

That's not what catches the eye, though. What catches the eye lies in front of the lamb and the pork belly on the concrete floor. A polythene bag more than a metre long. More meat turning bad. The same yellowy grey. Same condensation, same smell. Only this meat looks a hell of a lot like a human leg. That, plus it's wearing a high-heeled shoe.

Condon sees it a moment before I do and, like a good copper, he knows he needs to puke outside. Keep the crime scene tidy. Me, I don't puke at corpses. As Condon is decorating the flower bed, I approach the bag, feeling the flesh through the thick polythene. It feels like old, cold steak. I squat down by the dead girl, keeping her company, letting the peace flow out of the bag and into me.

Condon and the clearance guys are silhouettes moving in the garage doorway. With my hand still on the girl's thigh, I call the office. Rhiannon Watkins, the only DI I know to be on duty. I give her the gist. Condon will probably be getting something going with the dispatcher too, but this will be a CID case from here on. A sweet little murder. I feel a deep sigh of relaxation pass through me. Of pleasure. I didn't have much planned for the weekend. And whatever there might have been, this will be better.

I give the thigh a last, long affectionate squeeze and stand up so I can see down into the depths of the freezer. I'm expecting more of the same. Arms, head, the other leg. Chunks of torso sawn up and stored. But there's nothing. Squidgy apple puree. Bags of beans, unusable now. A few Tupperware containers with handwritten labels and dates, no longer legible in the dark and wet. Nothing that looks like body parts. Nothing that looks like the rest of this stinky jigsaw.

In the doorway to the garage, the clearance men are beginning to realise that they're going to need to make different plans for the evening. We're going to need statements from them. We'll need their van, if it comes to that. It's part of the crime scene now, a lorryload of evidence. In Cathays Park, the word will be spreading, shift patterns reallocated, people bundling into cars and blazing up here, lights flashing, sirens wailing.

I like all that, but I'm not ready for it yet. While Condon is still busy at the front, I walk through the garage door into the house itself. Get a feel of it before it's invaded. The clocks haven't gone back yet, so there's still plenty of light. The house is more or less empty. A shag pile carpet in yellow and brown, dents where the furniture once stood. In the living room, a mantelpiece not yet cleared of photos.

Not many photos, probably because there isn't much family. There's a wedding photo, of the widow presumably and her late husband. He's in an army uniform and the photo looks like it's Second World War vintage. That makes the widow late eighties or early nineties, even if she was young when she married. A pretty bride, half-smiling, unsure whether to look at the camera or her new husband.

There are other photos besides this one. The same pair, older. With a baby. With a young daughter. With the same daughter as a teenager, then as a young woman, then as a bride herself – now the Australian next of kin, I imagine. The last photo of the widow's husband shows him in his late forties, maybe fifties, with a cigarette in his hand. No evidence that he survived into his sixties even.

The shoe on the dead girl's leg was pink suede, platform sole, skinny wedge heels, round toe, and an ankle strap. I'm hardly the world's first authority on fashion, but the shoe looked to me neither brand-new nor ancient history. Christina Aguilera vintage, approximately.

I line up the photos with my thumbnail. Not much of a rogues' gallery: an elderly widow, a dead husband, an Australian daughter. All that, and a murder victim who consists of only a leg and a Christina Aguilera taste in shoes.

I'm smiling like an idiot. Weekends don't come any better.

6

3

Mayhem rides up the hill and takes possession. The queen of the carnival is Rhiannon Watkins. Rhiannon bloody Watkins. Watkins the badge. Rhiannon Watkins, the youngest woman ever appointed DI in Cardiff and currently the longest-serving officer of that rank. One whose ability could have made her DCI, or even Chief Constable, yet whose capacity to make herself disliked could have made her the first murder victim with over a million plausible suspects. A group that would include every one of her CID colleagues.

Typically, Watkins is in the lead car. Typically, she's the first out. Typically, there's a black-jacketed army spreading out behind her. Taping off the crime scene. Starting to talk to neighbours. Getting the removals van moved to a police pound, to safeguard our chain of evidence. Starting to interview the removals men. Separately, so their statements can be compared. And all the time, phone and radio constantly on the go back to Cathays Park.

I'm fooling around on my phone, trying to keep my head down, but I can hear Watkins criticizing the Scene of Crime boys for their slowness. Probably for other things too, when she gets the chance. Lack of moral fibre. Inattention to detail. Off-centre trouser creases. Having once smiled.

Condon also gets lacerated for something. I don't know what, but he stalks past me looking ashen. Then my turn.

Watkins – severe black suit, white shirt, the uptight-lezza look – beckons me over.

'You entered the house. Why?'

I give her my full-beam smile. One of the good things about my crazy brain: these stupid mind games don't particularly faze me, so I quite like playing them.

'We didn't know if there was further evidence inside the property, and if so whether that evidence was appropriately secured. I made it my business to check.'

'The interior of the house is a crime scene and –'

'I touched nothing. I didn't want to confuse the picture for the SOCOs. I assume you noticed the shoe?'

DI Watkins likes that. She likes it the way a snake would like it if a vole popped up to ask if anyone was hungry. Strike, swallow, digest.

She smiles at me, so I smile back. Sharing the joy.

'Did I notice the shoe?' This said slowly, lingeringly.

'Yes, ma'am. The leg we found was wearing a shoe.'

'Well, yes, I did take a look at the leg, and my twenty-eight years of experience in the CID helped me notice, even through the polythene, that –'

'Sorry, ma'am. I wasn't clear. That shoe is not a contemporary style.' I show her my phone and the pictures I've just downloaded from the Internet. 'I've only had a few moments, but I'd place the shoe as being approximately 2001, 2002. That suggests any crime could be as much as ten years old. I assume that you've got people back at Cathays searching for investigations where no body was ever fully recovered. You might wish to direct those team members to focus their efforts on the first few years of the last decade.'

I give her my loveliest smile. We're standing in the property's little forecourt and the last of the sun is going down in a boil of cloud to the northwest. Watkins wants to bite my head off, but she can't. Worse still, she has to stand there and let me watch as she calls Cathays to relay my information.

Behind us, I can see other cars start to darken the street. Flash photography. The print media are normally first to these things, but this story could be big enough to attract a film crew before long.

Watkins rings off. She's seen what I've seen. I don't know what her take on it is. No senior officer is indifferent to media attention. Some love it. Some loathe it. I don't know Watkins well enough to know which way she swings. But even though her attention is refocusing on the press guys, she hasn't forgotten that she needs to be horrible to me.

She tells me, icily, that that was useful information about the shoe and, since I was obviously alert to such things, would I kindly go to back to Cathays to join the research team there. I could present a summary of our conclusions to her in the morning.

She thinks she's been a pain in the arse, because I'll have to work half the night. I'm feeling happy, because I wanted to do that anyway, and go skipping off to find Condon so he can run me down into town.

I find him on the road outside. He's talking to one of the guys, who wants to know when he's going to get his van back. Condon is handling the situation the way we're trained to, but I can see that he's still vibrating internally from his encounter with the Ice Queen.

'Hey, Adrian.' I pat his upper arm in what's meant to be a supportive but professionally acceptable way. To the clearance guy, I say, 'You'll get your van back when DI Watkins says. And she's a bitch, so it could be a while. Sorry.'

The guy laughs at my frankness, and I continue into the laughter. 'When you found the leg, where was it stored, exactly? I mean, in the freezer, I know, but lying exactly where? At the front, back? Deep down? On top?'

When he understands my question, the clearance guy – who

has a name it turns out, Geoff – is helpful. The leg was lying along the back wall of the freezer, not quite at the bottom but almost.

'And neatly?' I ask. 'Like it had been tidily packed away, not leaving any gaps? Or more like it had just been dropped in a hurry?'

'Oh no, quite tidy, like. If you, if . . .'

Geoff is turning green, not that I can really tell in the ebbing daylight and the first sodium glow of the streetlamps. There are, strictly speaking, two reservoirs at Llanishen. The smaller, upper reservoir still has water in it, but the other one – the one people still mean when they talk about *the* reservoir – was drained earlier this year. Drained, fenced off, studded with black and yellow security notices. Some company wants to redevelop the site as upmarket housing, which I wouldn't mind except that Llanishen used to shelter grass snakes and toads and slowworms and waxcap fungi, and I like all those things more than tarmac and luxury homes.

Skins like silver pebbles and a soft slither into the dark.

I tell Geoff not to worry, that he's been helpful. Take his phone number just in case, then cadge a lift from Condon, telling him I'll just be a moment.

I run back up to the house. My version of running, I mean, which doesn't always involve actual running. Back to the garage. A SOCO photographer is there, wearing one of those white polypropylene suits with elasticated hood and cuffs, setting up lighting.

I ask him to give me some dates from the packages still in the bottom of the freezer. He's not sure whether to be helpful, because somewhere along the way he's eaten a training manual which is telling him to do things in a different order. I ask him if he wants me to pass his professional reservations along to DI Watkins and he decides to get helpful, bending down into the freezer with a torch.

As he does so, I inspect the packages lying loose on the floor. Not all of them are dated, but some are. There's a whole pile of thin little freezer bags of apple compote, dating from 2005. Some butcher's packages dated 2006, 2007, 2008, and 2009. One package of I'm not sure what is dated 1984, but in such wavering handwriting that I'm inclined to suspect the old lady's mind had wandered.

The SOCO pulls out of the freezer. He has a mask on, which I don't, but even so it must have stunk in there.

'Can't see 'em all, and I won't move anything till we're done with the imaging. But what I can see – oldest is '96, newest maybe 2002. Possibly 2003, because the ink has run and …' He shrugs. 'We'll know once we can start moving them and get a proper look.'

I take some pictures of the dead girl's shoe with my phone, and the SOCO promises to email some better-quality shots through to me when he's got to that stage.

I give him the thumbs-up and head back to Condon, ready for my ride.

4

Home.

I asked Condon to bring me here, not Cathays. If it's going to be a long weekend, I might as well get ready. Swap skirt for jeans, shoes for my most comfortable pair of boots. Jumper. Put a toothbrush and toothpaste into my bag, along with a change of knickers and tights. I think about eating, but I'm not hungry, so I don't. Think about taking a shower, but can't be bothered.

I don't put any lights on. Just let the house grow dark around me, seeing what I need to from the streetlamps outside.

Somebody cut a young woman into pieces and put her left leg into a suburban freezer in Cyncoed.

Up by the reservoir, it's as dark as it is here. The voles and the snakes and the toads and the bats are either going to bed or coming out to hunt. And we're coming out to hunt too. Me, Watkins the Badge, and the might of South Wales's finest.

For me, these things aren't only about finding the killers, but about giving peace to the dead. It's not primarily a question of justice. The dead don't care about that. The murder investigation, arrest, and conviction are just part of the funeral rite, the final acts of completion. Gifts I bring the dead in exchange for the peace they bring me.

The peace of the dead, which passeth all understanding.

I'm moving slowly now. No reason. Just waiting for my

energies to gather. When they do, I find a cereal bar in my dark and silent kitchen and start chomping it on the way to my car.

I should drive straight to Cathays. I *do* drive straight to Cathays, only when I get there, I find myself driving straight on through, over the river to Pontcanna.

Big Victorian houses. Over-ornamented. High-ceilinged and respectable. I stop at a house in Plasturton Gardens. Home of Piers Ivor Harris, MP. One of his homes, I should say. He also has a house in Chelsea in London and a place in France.

I'm in luck. His car is here, a silver Jag. His wife's car too, a cream and black Mini. Lights on inside the house, curtains drawn.

I wander up and down the road, noting down number-plates. Most of them I recognise – this isn't exactly the first time I've done this, to put it mildly – but some of which are new. Of the new ones, none look immediately interesting. The cars either not posh enough or not parked close enough to the house to suggest that they're connected with the Harrises. I note the registrations anyway.

Then back to my car. Then up to Whitchurch. Same thing again. The object of my interest: Galton Evans, an agricultural insurance guy, who made a packet of money ten years ago when he sold his business to a private equity buyer, then decided to devote the rest of his life to becoming a major-league arsehole.

That's my theory anyway. Maybe Evans is a nice guy. I wouldn't know. I've never met him.

I don't think I've got anything useful from the trip, but that's why you have to do these things as often as you can. Fishing takes patience. One of my fortes.

I wonder about hitting some of my other targets, but my mood has changed and Cathays is calling me now. I send a text to DS David Brydon, David 'Buzz' Brydon, my official-as-anything boyfriend, to let him know where I am and what I'm up to. Truth is, he'll already have heard about the case and will know that I've probably been sucked into it, but I'm working hard to be Girlfriend of the Year and good girlfriends text their boyfriends to tell them about changes of plan, so that's what I do too. It's how we behave on Planet Normal.

I zoom back into Cathays, ready for a long night hunting corpses.

5

At four in the morning, I get my corpse.

Mary Jane Langton. Disappeared August 2005. A student at Swansea University, twenty-two years old. Reported missing. Media hoohah. Investigated as well as these things can be. No leads of consequence. The case never closed. Rhiannon Watkins the officer in charge of that one too.

I know Langton's our girl because one of the photos we have of her shows her at some kind of party. Slightly plump, short dress, reasonably good looks, blonde hair. And the shoes. Pink suede things with round toes and narrow wedge heels. She probably bought them two or three years before her death. Liked them so much, she wore them through the passing fashions. Is wearing them still, in death and beyond. In a stinking freezer by an empty reservoir.

I'm the last person in the office. The other people researching went home around midnight. Late enough that even Watkins couldn't reprimand them for slacking. The ceiling lights are off, so it's just me and a desk light and the tiny rectangular LEDs of phones and printers, glimmering like fireflies in the dark.

I should tell someone about Langton, but I flip rapidly through the file first. An MA in English literature. She was working on a dissertation on Dylan Thomas. A good Welsh choice for an English girl. Parents lived in Bath. Him, a solicitor. Her, a charity worker. Two siblings, a brother and a sister.

Langton's files showed nothing strange. A bit of dope found in her student room. An ordinary number of boyfriends. Okay grades as a student. Not brilliant, but good enough. Thinking about maybe a career in publishing, but nothing definite. Just a girl who liked shoes.

Except for one thing.

The press reports we have on file, and the notes from our own investigation, state that Langton supported herself as a student through 'exotic' dancing.

A stupid phrase, that. For one thing, you can hardly get less exotic than a slightly plump English girl cavorting round a scaffolding pole. For another, it's not about dancing. It's about flesh, men and money. The files includes photos of Langton as a dancer. A tiny spangled mini-skirt in one picture. A sequinned bikini in another. A grin on her face in both, cow-toothed, more schoolgirlish than sexy.

Fuck.

This is the nightmare scenario, the one thing I hoped would never happen in my policing career. Something I stupidly thought wouldn't ever happen and consequently don't know how to handle now that it has.

Fuck.

I want to get up, leave, go for a drive, give myself room to think, but I don't have the time. If I were at home, I'd go for a quick smoke in the garden to clear my head, but that's not an option here.

There probably isn't a problem, I tell myself. And I'm right. There *probably* isn't. Trouble is, there *possibly* is, and if so the problem is of a magnitude that's off-the-scale bad. So, even though I told myself I would never do this, I find myself picking up a phone and calling home.

I get Mam. Sleepy-voiced, worried.

'Mam, it's me. Everything's okay, so don't worry. But is Dad there?'

He is. The phone is passed over.

'Hello, Fi, love.'

'Dad, something's come up, it's probably fine, but can you give me a call back from a private number?'

A moment's hesitation, or not even. Half a moment. A nanosecond. Then, 'Course I can, love, just give me a moment.'

Two minutes later my mobile bleats. Caller details withheld.

'Dad.'

'Fi, love?'

'Look, I expect this doesn't matter, but I don't know if you've heard the news about the discovery of human remains up by Llanishen.'

'Up by the reservoir, love? No. Sounds horrible, though. You never really think of Cyncoed as being that sort of place.'

I digest that a moment, then say, 'The dead girl was Mary Langton.' I leave a pause in case Dad wants to say anything, then, before he can fill it with his usual white noise, continue. 'Disappeared August 2005. She was a pole dancer. Well, a student really, but did some pole dancing to make a little extra cash. Mary Langton.'

Dad listens without interrupting, then says, 'Poor girl. Awful, that sort of thing, isn't it? At that age, I mean, her whole life in front of her. And then – bang, gone. Just think of her poor parents. Lord, if anything ever happened to you or the other girls, your mam and I –'

'Dad, was she a–? Did she dance at one of your clubs?'

'Gosh, love, you do ask questions. You know how it is, though. Middle of the night. Some poor lass that vanished five years ago now. And, you know, we've had so many dancers over the years. I couldn't possibly remember each one. Course, there'll be records, we could look at them. If it's helpful, I could get Emrys to take a look. Me, I'm not really the man for paper. But Emrys, he'll find anything. Do you want me to call him? I mean, if it's important, I can get him out

17

of bed, no problem at all. And after all, if it's a police matter, he can afford to lose a little sleep. We're both up, aren't we, love?'

He's all set to go wittering on, but I interrupt. I tell him it's fine. I just wanted to check. I tell him to go back to bed, sorry for waking him, sorry for worrying Mam. He tells me to look after myself, tells me to come over tomorrow for dinner, 'and bring your young man, we'd love to see more of him'.

We ring off.

Back to the silence. Desks stretching out into the darkness. Small rectangular fireflies. The hum of dormant electronics. Four twenty-five.

He's good, Dad is. Very good. That's something I've only recently started to understand and the knowledge frightens me. Things you thought you know changing shape the more you look at them.

Part of his trick is that torrent of patter. His readiness to talk, that total unstrategised openness. Anyone listening to the call would have sworn that my dad was the ultimate WYSIWYG man: what you see is what you get. Friendly, concerned, open, helpful.

Except then you start to look at the whole thing differently. Picking up on tiny clues. I said we'd discovered human remains up by Llanishen. That doesn't necessarily mean the reservoir, but even if that's how you understand it, the reservoir has two sides. The Cyncoed side and the side which is Llanishen proper.

Dad changed my word 'Llanishen' to 'Cyncoed'. That could just be an assumption. A middle-of-the-night thing, said by someone thinking blurrily. Or it could be a signal that he knew everything already, that things were under control. And if he was signalling like that, is that because he had nothing to hide? Or because everything was already sufficiently hidden? Or because, although something dangerous had been

18

exposed, he was already working to neutralise the threat?

I don't know.

I don't need to know, except that I am a serving police officer and I made a phone call which alerted, what, a possible informant? a possible suspect? I'd always told myself that I wouldn't use my position to shelter my father, and now the very first time there's a possible collision between my role as daughter and my role as detective, I choose the former with no more than a few minutes' hesitation. Does that mean that if push came to shove, I'd make the same choice? Or that the point of my phone call was to make as sure as dammit that push never would come to shove?

I don't know. Problems for another day. Fireflies and dead girls' shoes.

I spend a moment tuning in to my heartbeat, my breathing. Finding my body. Feeling myself. I press my knuckles down on the wooden desk until I feel the pain. I can't quite feel my feet fully, but that's not unusual for me, and I have, after all, been awake for almost twenty-four hours. I realise I'm feeling tired. A good feeling. Appropriate, normal.

I take my boots off and bundle my papers together. Rhiannon Watkins's office is on the floor above me, and I take the lift in silence from my floor to hers. Swipe my card through the security door. Find the right office. Open the door, ready to leave everything on her desk with a note.

I haven't put any lights on, because at this stage of the night, I prefer the dark. But inside Watkins's office there's a pool of light from her desk lamp. A small, intense pool because the lamp has been bent right down over the desk. And behind the desk, Watkins the badge, looking more like a grandmother than the ferocious Queen Bitch of the Cardiff CID, asleep in her chair.

I'm wondering how best to wake her when she wakes up of her own accord. Focuses her gaze. Takes some time to

19

remember where she is, who I am, why we're here. Her short grey hair is messed up and her suit is rumpled. Not really the kind of clothing item to look good after being worn all day and slept in half the night.

I hold up the file.

'Mary Jane Langton,' I say. 'Our victim. I've matched the shoes.'

I give her the file, pulling out the shoe photo and showing her that first, matching it against my own photos of the murder scene.

Watkins looks carefully at the photos, then very briefly at the file, then says, 'Good. Look, just give me a moment.'

She rubs her face, and gropes around under her desk for her shoes, which aren't there but set neatly beside each other to her right. She finds them, yawns, stands up, grimaces at me – a kind of 'good job, stick around' face – then leaves the room.

I can't help but contrast the slowness with which she gathers herself with the speed of my father's own process. I wonder whether Watkins and my father are on opposite sides of this investigation or whether, as I hope, they have nothing at all to do with each other.

Some minutes go by. I practise my breathing. *In*-two-three-four-five. *Out*-two-three-four-five. A habit now. A good one. I can feel my toes, my heels. I feel one of those moments of gratitude. A moment of thankfulness for it all: a boyfriend who loves me, a family, a job. Bodily sensations that I can feel, emotions that often now approach me normally, leave me safe when they leave. Thankfulness, with a thin splash of alarm at how precarious it still is. How easily I could lose it.

I hear Watkins outside and turn to the door with my office face on. She sticks her head inside.

'I need some coffee. You?'

Watkins the Badge in Junior Detective Coffee Offer Shock. I nod in surprise, then hastily amend my acceptance. 'Yes, please, only not coffee. Tea? If that's okay. Milk, no sugar.'

Her head vanishes, leaving something grumpy in the air. Was I meant to have offered to go instead? I wonder about that for a moment, then stop. If someone offers me a drink, they can bloody well get it without grumping at me.

I sit down. Make myself at home. Shift the chairs around. Change the lighting. Massage my feet.

When Watkins comes back, she isn't grumpy. Gives me my tea in a mug that I think belongs to DCI Jackson. I don't usually trust myself with caffeine, but these days I sometimes go crazy and risk life on the edge. Live fast, die young.

Watkins studies the file silently for a few moments, then calls the lab.

The lab doesn't normally work through the night, but it does when it has to. Most murders are solved within forty-eight hours or not solved at all, and that means we push the lab for very quick results in cases like this. Watkins tells whoever she's talking to that we think we've identified the murder victim, and gives the necessary details. We have Langton's DNA on record from the previous investigation, so it'll be a swift business making the match. Watkins ends the call with her normal curtness.

'They'll have something by eight this morning.'

I nod. Truth is, the lab would have got there anyway. My truffling through the night has saved us a few hours, nothing more. Probably irrelevant, but Watkins has a lose-not-a-minute philosophy, which I like. I'm the same.

Watkins: 'When did you come on duty, Constable?'

'Yesterday. In the morning.'

'Right. You need to sleep. Get yourself home. I want you to –'

'You'll be seeing the parents?' I interrupt.

A pause. I'm not sure if that's because she's angry at my interruption or because she hasn't yet thought ahead to the

21

business of informing next of kin. Most DIs don't do the next-of-kin bit themselves, but some do.

Watkins nods and says, 'Yes.'

'If possible, I'd like to come.'

'You've been working all week? Monday to Friday?'

I nod.

Another pause, then, 'Okay. We'll leave as soon as the lab comes back with confirmation.' She digs around in a cupboard and comes out with something that looks like a tartan picnic blanket. 'Dennis Jackson has a sofa in his office. You can use that.' She scrutinises me a moment or two longer, then nods again.

I'm dismissed.

If I was a good little officer, I'd say something like 'Thank you, ma'am,' but if anyone should thank anyone, she should thank me, because she went to sleep without a victim ID and woke up with one. So I just take the blanket, the tea, and myself off to DCI Jackson's sofa. It's fake black leather. Sticky and synthetic.

Through the thin office walls, I can hear Watkins starting to make calls. Alerting people to come in early, starting to hand out assignments, checking back with the lab. Getting the machinery of investigation ready for its next clanking advance.

It takes me twenty minutes or more, but then sleep comes to me like night over the reservoir. Swift, silent, and total. A snake vanishing under rocks.

I dream of nothing.

6

Dream of nothing and wake with nice Bev Rowland bringing me a cup of peppermint tea and a look of anxiety.

I unstick myself from the sofa. My mouth feels like someone's been using it to boil up connective tissue for glue.

I take the tea. 'Thanks, Bev. You're a gem.'

'Were you here all night?'

Bev is awed, partly because I've been asleep on a DCI's sofa, but mostly because I've spent a night working with *la* Watkins and am still alive to tell the tale.

It's seven thirty-five. The lab results are due at eight. Watkins will leave without me if I'm not ready. She sent Bev to tell me so.

I prevail on Bev to go and scavenge some food, while I go to the Ladies to see what warm water can do for me. I brush my teeth, wash my face, change my underwear and do a sort-of cleanup job on other parts by using handfuls of paper towels and that pink liquid soap that never really rinses off properly. By the end of my endeavours, I don't feel properly clean but at least I'm lightly fragranced with whatever icky scent they put into the soap. Bev comes to find me with a pre-packed chicken salad sandwich, all she could lay her hands on. We go to hunt down my boots, which are still by my desk.

Seven fifty-two.

'I wish I could get ready as fast as that.'

'Ready-ish.' I give her a lame grin.

I sit on the edge of my desk, getting my computer to print off whatever data has come in overnight. I tell Bev about finding Watkins asleep and her making me tea. Bev thinks my jumper and jeans don't look smart enough for a next-of-kin visit, so she gets me her black jacket, the one she always wears when she has to be a bit formal. It's a size too big but I take it anyway and wear it over everything else.

Seven fifty-nine.

Eight minutes later, we're in a car heading out of town. Watkins's car, a BMW. Uniform police driver, because Watkins needs to make calls and she doesn't trust me to drive. The lab has confirmed the Langton ID.

I eat my chicken sandwich and read the papers I've printed off.

The widow in Cyncoed was called Elsie Williams. Died following a stroke at the age of eighty-five. Five foot three. Medical records showed a succession of minor health problems: arthritis, raised cholesterol, sleeping issues.

Husband died twenty years previously, lung cancer. The best of alibis.

Daughter, Karen Johnston, now living permanently in Australia, married to an Aussie husband, job in food processing. The couple seem to have visited Elsie Williams for two or three weeks each summer. Indeed, but for distance, the family seemed close and supportive. Regular phone calls. The Johnstons supplementing the old lady's pension. Paying to upgrade her conservatory when the last one started to look tired.

No information yet on whether they were in the U.K. for the relevant dates in August 2005, but every chance.

Inventory of items found at the house is still incomplete, but it includes everything you might need to dismember a corpse: a small electric saw, a handsaw, knives. On the other hand, plenty of houses would keep the same tools. Nothing either suspicious or unsuspicious.

Numerous stains, including probable biological stains, have been found in the garage and to a lesser degree in the house. Analysis ongoing. No other body parts yet located.

Neighbours include no known criminals or sex offenders. A number had petty quarrels with Mrs Williams, who seems to have been anti-cat, anti-dog, also anti-music, shirtlessness and children on bicycles.

Nothing obvious to link anyone in the area to Mary Langton. Langton's own excursion into exotic dancing seemed a fairly temporary thing. As far as we can tell, her first encounter with the industry was Easter 2004 and had more or less ended up by early 2005 – that is to say, several months before her death. So maybe the lap dancing had nothing to do with it.

Remarkably, Mrs Williams had an official caution on her record: she had jammed her walking stick into the spokes of a child's bicycle, while a boy was riding it. The boy had fallen and started crying. An altercation ensued, which led to the boy's mother being warned for using abusive language to a police officer. The officer in question subsequently also issued Mrs Williams with an official caution. The incident took place in 2007 and wouldn't appear to have any direct link to Mary Langton's leg, except insofar as the episode shed some light as to Mrs Williams's general character and outlook. Which does not seem to have been sunny.

I think of saying something to Watkins, but she's busy, so I don't.

I finish my reading and let the countryside slide by. It's wet and the wipers are going all the time. The police driver keeps the car at a precise seventy miles an hour, moving out from the slow lane when he needs to overtake, moving back again as soon as he can. Indicators on and off every time.

Watkins is on her BlackBerry. Making calls, checking and sending emails. Handling media, forensics, neighbourhood inquiries, public information appeals. Progress reports to

Robert Kirby, the Detective Superintendent who has overall supervision of this investigation and is, in effect, Watkins's boss for the duration. There's also Interpol liaison, because of the Aussie angle. Getting updates on anyone whose names cropped up in the first, 2005, phase of the Langton investigation.

A communications blizzard. The nature of command.

But eventually she's done. She hasn't had any more sleep than I have, and she has that pink soap smell about her too. She looks at my jeans with taut disapproval but doesn't say anything. She's wearing a grey woollen dress that she must have had ready in her office.

'The leg was at the back of the freezer,' I say, because it's weird not saying anything.

She looks at me, waiting, so I continue.

'Mrs Williams was only an inch or so taller than me and arthritic. The freezer was almost a metre high and two feet deep. If I had to bundle a leg in there, I could probably manage it, but I don't think I could have laid it neatly along the bottom of the back wall unless I virtually climbed into the thing.'

'No.'

'And the polythene didn't match any of the other packages.'

'I don't think Elsie Williams is our killer.'

'Do we know if she left her garage unlocked? Or if any of the neighbours had a key?'

Watkins raises a chin to acknowledge the questions. Those things might have been on her to-do list anyway.

We're off the motorway now, in the hills above Bath. Farmhouses and villages glimmering through the rain, then the long plunge downhill into the city.

The driver lets the satnav guide him to an address just west of Victoria Park. Ordinary, pleasant streets. Watkins puts her BlackBerry away, braces herself for the brutal moment.

She says nothing about how she wants to conduct the

interview, but when she gets out of the car, I follow. She rings the doorbell. Lights on inside. Noise. A shape moves behind the door, then it opens. A woman. Langton's mother, dark hair, jeans, rugby top. Her face is composed in a 'how can I help' look, which collapses completely the moment she recognises Watkins.

'Oh.'

Nothing else. Just 'Oh'. She takes us on wordlessly through to the kitchen. Same thing with her husband. The collapsing face, the wordlessness. A telly on in the background, which he mutes.

We sit down and Watkins says what she has to say.

'I'm sorry. Yesterday evening, DC Griffiths here was called to a house in Cardiff. We found some human remains, your daughter. We've been able to identify her from clothing and DNA. I'm very sorry.'

The husband has that numbed look. That thing where you're only partly present in the room, where feelings and sounds and sensations all feel deadened, as if glimpsed through a glass wall. That's the place where I've spent so much of my life: behind that wall, watching it thicken and cloud till I could hardly see through it at all.

The wife, Mrs Langton, isn't like that. She's crying without sound, tears falling like sand. She has some instinct toward hospitality, and keeps starting to offer us a drink, but never quite gets there. In the end, I get up, power off the TV and put the kettle on, then just stand behind her with my hands resting on her shoulders.

I'm good in these situations because I don't have normal feelings. I operate the way I usually do, relying on my brain more than my heart or instinct. Mrs Langton is sobbing now. Noisy, juddering sobs. The sort you're supposed to have at this kind of moment. I don't intervene, just stand there and let her cry. Watkins and the husband make tea.

When things are calmer, Watkins continues. Tells the truth. That we have a leg, not a daughter. That we can't say how she died. That we can't offer any comfort or close off any awful possibility. That the worst of those possibilities are all too likely. Some sexual, sadistic, long-drawn-out weirdness ending in a macabre death. Watkins doesn't say that last bit, of course, but it's there, present in the room, as real as the rain.

Finally, we're through the tears. Mrs Langton says that they'd never really given up, that they'd always hoped, that her daughter's room is still ready for her upstairs.

I ask to see it.

My request is unexpected. Not what I'm meant to do, either from Watkins's point of view or the Langtons'. But still. Mrs Langton says all right, because that's easier than saying no. I go upstairs behind her. Beige carpets. A willow tree beyond the landing window. Then the room. Scrupulously tidy. Student books. A revision chart. A poster with a Dylan Thomas poem on it.

I sit on the bed, Mrs Langton on the desk chair.

'I'm really sorry, Mrs Langton –'

'Oh, call me Rosemary, dear.'

'I'm Fiona. Fi. Whichever.'

'Fiona. My niece is Fiona.'

'This is how her room was? This tidy?'

'Oh, she was always tidy.'

I look in a wardrobe. Her clothes are still there. Not night-clubby, spangly miniskirt things either. Just normal student stuff. If anything, a bit tame, a bit dorky.

'Sorry, is it okay to look around? I always like to get the feel of someone.'

'I know it looks strange. Keeping it like this. But we're not … I mean, we use it as a spare room too. It's just nice keeping her things around.'

There are photos on the desk. No pole-dancing ones. A formal school one. A family shot. One of her on a pony. Another of her playing field hockey, red-faced, in pursuit of an invisible ball.

We sit for a while. I try imagining myself as Mary Langton, Rosemary as my mother. I'm about the right age. Hockey and Dylan Thomas. That isn't me, but it could have been. Some parallel life.

'You'll be okay, will you?' I say.

'You know, it never leaves you, but life has to go on. We have two others, a boy and a girl. Twenty-three and twenty-seven.'

She wants to show me their rooms, their photos, but I'm not interested.

I say, 'Inspector Watkins is very good, you know. She's a bit scary, but she's the best investigator we have.'

'Oh, I'm sure. That's nice to know, actually. Thank you.'

We sit a bit longer, then go downstairs.

Watkins is pissed off with me for going AWOL, but she can't say anything with the Langtons there. We say goodbye. On our way to the car, I say, 'She needed a hug. I thought she might be better off doing that one-on-one. She had a good cry, then felt better.'

Watkins looks at me with one of her speciality looks, storm clouds over glaciers. But she doesn't say anything and we simply drive off in silence.

Back through the city centre, up the hill, through the rainy countryside, back to the motorway. Only once we're there, and the driver is doing a hypnotically exact seventy miles an hour, wipers going like a metronome and the indicators blinking on and off each time we change lanes, does she wave her BlackBerry at me.

'They've found a hand.'

'Ah!'

I wait further news.

'A right hand. Three hundred yards from the house. On the banks of the reservoir.'

I keep waiting. This should be good news. Important. A step forward. But something's hanging out of sight, something wrong.

I wait for her to tell me more and she does.

'It's a man's hand. Dark-skinned. Arab, Mediterranean, something like that. And fresh. It's completely fresh.'

7

Home.

I didn't want to come, but Watkins ignored my protests and had the driver drop me at my door on our way back in to Cathays. When we arrived and I had the one door open ready to get out, she said coldly, 'If you want to investigate a bedroom, then do so. Don't lie to me about hugging Rosemary Langton.'

'Yes, ma'am,' I say, wondering how she knew.

'Does she still have that poster up?'

'The Dylan Thomas one? "The force that through the green fuse drives the flower"? That's still there.'

'Weird poem.'

I shrug. I don't know if the poem is weird or not. But I don't care. Nor, all of a sudden, does Watkins. She slams the door, has the driver drive off. I go inside.

I'm feeling tired, but I find it hard to sleep when it's daylight outside. I run a bath, but don't get into it straightaway. Think about rolling a joint, but can't be bothered to do even that.

Instead I make peppermint tea and drink it slowly, watching the rain fall. I like the rain. When I was ill, I always felt less ill when it was raining. I used to go outside to get wet. It was one of the things I could almost always feel: the cold, the wet, that sense of falling.

Eventually I finish my tea, have a bath, wash that icky pink soap smell away, and sleep for a couple of hours. Not good sleep, though. It feels like it's raining body parts. A hand. A leg. An ear or two. A drizzle of humanity.

Eventually I wake up, feeling worse than I did when I went to bed. Make more tea, look out at the rain, think about a smoke.

I call Buzz.

He takes the call with his voice set to formal, then walks away from wherever he is and says, in his intimate voice, 'Hey, babe, have a nice time with Watkins?'

I tell him about my night, except not the bit about going down to Pontcanna or up to Whitchurch, or the bit about calling my dad, or the bit about going into the dead girl's room, or the drizzle of body parts, or the joint which I thought about twice but didn't have. Apart from that, I'm as open as sunshine.

Buzz fills me in on the investigation, because he knows I won't let it go until he tells me.

They've found another hand, a foot, and a forearm, all apparently belonging to the same dark-skinned male body as the original hand. 'Better fresh than frozen, eh?' he says. The inevitable policeish joke.

'On public land, or in gardens, or where?'

'One of the hands and the foot in that little bit of wood just down from the Williams house. Public access land. The other hand and the forearm in back gardens no more than three hundred yards from the Williams house. The hand maybe could have been lobbed in there from the open land behind the garden. The forearm looked placed, not thrown.'

'No ideas who yet?'

'Nothing. Not a clue. Too early for DNA, but we might have something by this evening. No one on the MisPer register who looks likely. No one local, anyway.'

I know what he means. At a national level, the missing persons register is always well stocked, not least with Londoners

32

of every possible ethnic background. That doesn't mean we'd be smart to go chasing after every missing Arab-Londoner, Mediterranean-Londoner, or whatever. The DNA may reveal more once it's analysed.

'You're up at Llanishen now?' I ask.

'Me and every other officer in South Wales. A *fingertip* search.' More policeish humour, a thing I dearly love.

We chat a bit more, or try to. Any room we might have found for personal chitchat feels drowned out by what we've just talked about. My fault. Buzz is better at switching his police mode on and off. Me, if I'm on the hunt for something, I can never really let it drop. In my mind, I'm already up there in Llanishen, walking across the sodden slopes, examining every tussock of grass, hoping always to find something – a foot, an ear, a pair of fingers – shining in the mud like an autumn mushroom. So though we try having a personal moment, and sort of do, it's not great. It'll be better when we can spend an evening together.

We ring off.

I wish I was better at those little intimacies. I'm lucky Buzz is patient.

There's been a thumping noise in my head for some time and I now realise I'm hearing the beat of a chopper overhead. I live only a couple of miles from Llanishen – eight minutes by road, five if no one's watching – and the helicopter, presumably, is part of the operation.

Partly that'll be for aerial observation. Looking for a change in the vegetation, discolouration in the soil. But shallow graves are the hardest to find. They don't disturb the earth enough. In a drought, maybe, a corpse will be revealed by the moisture it holds, but not in Wales, not in Llanishen, and certainly not at the dead end of a wet October. So the chopper is also there as a warning to nutcases. We're watching you. Stay away. Hunker down. Be good.

I try to think of some positive ways to spend time – ironing, food shopping, hoovering, gym – but I already know what I'm going to do.

I go upstairs. The spare room, as I used to call it. Then Buzz took to calling it, disapprovingly, the operations room, so it's been that, or just the ops room, ever since. A good name. Military. One that handles like a gun, serviceable and clean.

I swing the door open. There's a desk, a table, and a cupboard, all from IKEA. Also a bed, covered by a sheet of plywood, and a felt-covered corkboard on the wall.

Papers. Photos. Files. Lists.

Also a laptop, a PC, a printer, wireless router, automatic data storage backup. Not me who connected all that lot. One of Dad's friends. A Tony somebody. From here I can access the PNC, the Police National Computer, and most of its databases, the ones you don't have to be a PNC analyst to get into. This is also where my Google alerts come into. Also where I keep my subscriptions to things like LexisNexis, the news and business service.

I keep the curtains drawn, because it's hard to reach them across all papers on the bed. But I prefer the room dark anyway. It smells of toner cartridges and warm electronics. In a locked desk drawer, I have 460 bullets and no gun.

The ops room.

When we broke the Rattigan case – located Fletcher, the trafficked girls, those charming boys from Kaliningrad – my major concern was that the principal bad guy, Brendan Rattigan himself, was already dead, his bones rattling under two hundred feet of seawater. But Rattigan had friends. And some of those friends liked what Rattigan liked, fucked what he fucked, took advantage of his whole deluxe fuck-an-Albanian conveyor belt. As far as I'm concerned, they were just as guilty as he was, just as deserving of punishment.

And that's the operation.

Find out who Rattigan's fuck buddies were. Then destroy them.

I log my latest sheaf of number plates. I can't track everyone who knew Rattigan, so I've limited myself to his closest associates. Those connected to him in multiple ways: company directorships, racing syndicates, dining clubs, yachting holidays, weddings, investment partnerships, charitable boards, political donations. I've picked six names, local ones, from a much longer possible list, so I can give them the proper focus.

Ivor Harris. Mostly seems to hang out with other wealthy, politically connected people. Spends more time in London than Wales. I haven't been able to connect Harris to any obviously suspicious types: drug suspects, pimps, prostitutes. No obviously odd patterns to his movements.

Galton Evans. Worth thirty million quid or so. A playboy, if you can still be a playboy at the age of fifty-two. According to the car registrations I've collected – easier in his case, as visitors park on his drive – Evans gets visited by plenty of younger women, a couple of whom have minor possession offences. Trivial stuff. Hard to detect any pattern to his movements, because playboys do whatever they want whenever they want to do it.

And so on. Other names. *Trevor Yergin. Huw Allsop. Ben Rossiter. David Marr-Phillips.*

I've got a B-list too. People who knew Rattigan fairly well, but whose links weren't quite as close. I'd be willing to bet that a fair few of my B-list knew at least something about Rattigan's proclivities, which makes them culpable too. *Idris Prothero. Joe Johnson. Owain Owen.* A dozen others.

The latest batch of plates I've collected for Harris don't yield anything new. I've got a new plate for Evans, which I'll check when I get into the office. Check my Google alerts for the names. Check some of the databases that I have access to via the PNC, the ANPR one – automatic number plate recognition – particularly. Some data that seems worth recording, but nothing much. I log it anyway.

I don't know what I'm looking for exactly. Just that if there is anything to find, I hope I'll notice it before anyone else does. Notice, and find a way to use it.

On the back of the door, there is a small pink dress with a white bow. Next to it, on a shelf, some shiny black shoes, a hair grip, a camera. On the corkboard, held up by four neat red drawing pins, is a photo.

The photo is of me.

The dress is my dress.

In August 1986, I was found by Tom and Kathleen Griffiths sitting peacefully in the back of their open-top Jag. Wearing this dress, those shoes. I was about two and a half – give or take – and nobody knew who I was or where I'd come from.

Tom and Kathleen, my beloved new mam and dad, adopted me. They asked me every question you would naturally ask a little girl in these circumstances, and for eighteen months I said nothing. I was mute, unspeaking, silent. Then one day, I said, 'Mam, can I have some more cheese, please?' and my life began again. My puzzling, fractured life that has no beginning.

I can't look at that dress without feeling dizzy. It's as though I find myself standing on the lip of a very deep well. No idea of how I came to be there, but weak at the knees and looking down.

My dress. My life.

Buzz doesn't know it, but the ops room has two missions, not one. Find Rattigan's fuck-buddies. Find out who I am.

No progress on either front, but I can't keep from looking.

I'm tired, the ironing still refuses to do itself, and it's raining. Before I know it, I'm in my car on the Ty-draw Road, heading for the muddy delights of Llanishen.

I break the speed limit all the way. I'm there in six minutes.

8

I'm on garden duty. Out in the fields and woods by the reservoir – where I'd sooner be – a long line of coppers, in wellies and fluorescent jackets, inches forward. Shoulder to shoulder. The pace just five yards a minute, even less than that in the woods.

Our haul of body parts is growing all the time. Nothing more of Mary Langton, but the male corpse has now yielded a harvest of both hands, both feet, a forearm, a liver, a calf, and a thigh. A Labrador retriever was spotted with the liver in its mouth half a mile away, toward the upper reservoir, the one with water still in it, so the search is now covering an area at least a mile square, and possibly much more than that if the search ends up reaching to the Saint Mellons Road.

Nor is it just bits of corpse that we're looking for. The forensics team want everything of possible interest marked. A straggle of fibre, a boot print, a single hair even. The whole area is now tagged with a small forest of bamboo wands, marked with luminous paint. The space-suited SOCOs are travelling from wand to wand, photographing, bagging, collecting.

Even with all that, the public land is the easy bit. At least the access is easy, even when the ground itself is overgrown and difficult. The gardens that back onto the reservoir make for a far more difficult search. Flower beds, sheds, greenhouses, garages. Complicated spaces that come with complicated owners, fretting, watching, asking, needing.

I'm assigned to a team with three officers, all uniformed constables, two from Swansea, one from Newport.

We do five gardens. We're asked seven times if we want tea, and are told six times to be careful of various tedious-looking plants, which I make a point of standing on when no one's looking. The rain is intermittent now, but water still flashes from every hard surface, still fills every boot print with a curl of silver.

I'm finding my temporary colleagues as annoying as the owners, and when we get to the next couple of properties – two newly built houses, with bland lawns and new brickwork – I tell them I'll make a start on the next one and hop over the fence to do just that.

Garden eight. A proper old-fashioned plot, framed by a lattice of espaliered fruit trees. Within, a patchwork of vegetable beds. Pegs, string, bean sticks. Marrows going over, the leeks just coming. Runner beans. Some unhappy-looking spinach, defeated by the turning weather. A tiny greenhouse, a wooden compost bin, a shed. Smells of sodden wood, wet leaves and creosote.

The owner, an old man, comes out to introduce himself. Arthur Price. Soft grey suit and tie. The national service generation. He invites me to check everything, then shoots back into the house, keen to show how little he intends to interfere. 'Shout if you want me,' he calls.

The light is starting to die. A violent orange sunset, tangled in trees. A flock of geese, V-shaped like a squadron of bombers, makes its noisy descent toward the reservoir mud. The helicopter is long gone.

I do the shed first, because of the fading light. I have a torch with me, but don't use it. Just push open the door, walk inside, and stand there, letting the space and silence settle.

I realise I've been searching the wrong way. Systematic and

disciplined. The police way, not mine. As though corpses had nothing to say to me.

Balls of twine, two sorts, green and undyed. Forks and spades hanging from nails. A hoe. A lawn mower. Garden chemicals. Bags of compost and sharp sand. Those lovely old-fashioned things like griddles and curved pruning saws. A pair of shears, its wooden handles polished from use.

And peace. Far too much peace for a tiny end-of-October shed.

I lean up against the workbench. If I had a joint with me, I'd smoke it now. Melting into the moment, as the geese fly overhead and my colleagues march shoulder-to-shoulder outside.

In the corner, there's the bottom half of a plastic barrel, filled with dark liquid. I'd initially thought it was water, but realise it's not. Do lawn mowers need their oil changed? Presumably they do. The barrel smells of old oil, collecting year after year, down there with the cobwebs and the dead wasps. How many summers have added their oil to that barrel?

There's laughter around me now. A shared and silent joke. I'm not exactly laughing, but I am smiling. It's impossible not to. There's a kind of joy in the air, vibrating over into mirth. A gift, really.

I share the joke until the silence grows too strong, then kneel down by the barrel and thrust both hands in. They come out with Mary Langton's blonde and dripping head.

9

Monday ends a weekend of mayhem. More searching in weather which has turned windy as well as wet, an ever-increasing collection of body parts, and media interest which has turned so intense it seems like Cyncoed is sprouting a television camera at the end of every road.

Bits of information pop up through the weekend. We, the searchers, only get to hear the news when we stop for a hot drink or gather something from a passing journalist or neighbour.

The male corpse has been identified: it's Ali el-Khalifi, a lecturer at the Cardiff School of Engineering.

A lung has been discovered, bobbing like a clumsy grey balloon three-quarters filled with water on the leeward side of what remains of the larger reservoir.

In Cyncoed, Mary Langton's arms, bound together with duct tape and bagged up in polythene, have been found up amongst the loose timber and sheets of fibreboard that Ryan Humphrys, a plumbers' merchant from Cyncoed, stored up in his garage roof.

PC Jen Murray has been taken to hospital with possible hypothermia after getting too wet on Sunday morning.

Watkins publicly shouted at DI Staunton for some bit of scheduling muddle on Sunday afternoon.

We hear these things, but aren't sure how much is true, how much only rumour.

Meantime, the investigation accumulates ever more information, ever less direction. It turns out that Karen Johnston and her husband were both in Wales over the relevant period in 2005. Which would be an interesting fact except that neither has a police record and, so far, we have a whiteboard listing fourteen properties where body parts have been found. There are thirty-eight people living in those properties. Including the extended families of those thirty-eight, there are at least seventy-one people potentially implicated. Adding in close friends or colleagues takes the circle of 'suspects' to more than a hundred. And corpse pieces are still being found, so that total is growing all the time. No one we've looked at so far has had any meaningful brush with the police or any serious indicator of potential for sexual violence.

We've also checked on anyone living locally who has any kind of record for sexual assault, violence, or child sex offences. There are a few such people, of course, and we've started to do the basics, but because the reservoir is a well-used beauty spot and dog-walking area, we need to consider that all of Cyncoed, Llanishen, Lisvane, Llanederyn, and Pontprennau are potentially relevant to the investigation – and, indeed, given that people come from all over Cardiff to the area, there's really no part of the city we can rule out. We have two corpses and a million suspects.

Buzz and I are both working, though on different teams, all day Sunday, but we spend the night together at his apartment. Bacon and eggs for dinner. We start off watching a Coen brothers film on the telly, only we end up talking through it and go to the bedroom to make love while George Clooney is still being a funny man in the living room. Afterward, I realise how tired I am, drag myself to the shower, then fall back into bed, while Buzz washes up and tells George Clooney to stand down. If I dream at all, it's of Arthur Price's garden and the geese flying overhead.

On Monday morning, the weekend's scattered fragments are welded together for us by Rhiannon Watkins. She's introduced by Detective Superintendent Kirby, but this is Watkins's show. The incident room is as full as I've ever seen it. Exhausted faces and strong coffee. A thick stew of conversation. Watkins has given the operation a properly formal code name – Operation Abacus, for some reason – but the office name is simpler and more memorable. Stirfry. Not a name anyone will use with the boss, but even DCI Jackson has been heard using it.

There were still people coming in late when Kirby was speaking, but Watkins calls us to order with nothing more than a look. She stands up at the front, no podium, no notes. Low-heeled black shoes, grey suit, zero humour.

Quickly, no wasted words, she summarises what we have.

Ali el-Khalifi first. It's been a week since he was last seen at work, at a seminar for grad students in materials science. Owing to the vagaries of the university timetable, Khalifi's workload this last week was very light, so although his absence was noted, no one was particularly worried. He travelled fairly extensively anyway and it was assumed he'd simply turn up again when required. When an Arab-looking corpse was reported, the university called us with their concerns. We collected DNA from his office. A match was made.

'From what we know,' says Watkins, 'Khalifi has no wife, no partner. We've spoken with his departmental head and one or two others, but we need much more. What connection did he have to Mary Langton? Who might have wanted him dead and why?'

Next we turn to Langton. Needless to say, you can't find large chunks of human remains in someone's shed or garage without pulling those people in for questioning. So on Saturday night, Arthur Price had been driven down to Cathays. The interview plan had been to hang tough for an hour or so,

42

not quite accusing the old man, but almost, and seeing if any cracks emerged. In fact, the old man was so open, so soldier-like, flirtatious and charming, that after twenty minutes the two DCs conducting the interview broke for a consultation with their team leaders, and decided to run the whole thing differently. Someone went out to get chips, and the rest of the interview was conducted over mugs of tea and plates of chips with brown sauce, with Price doing his gallant best to assist.

I know all this only because one of the DCs involved, Susan Konchesky, told me about it all. Watkins says nothing except, 'Interrogation of Price revealed no grounds for suspicion. His garden is easily accessed from the land to the rear of his property. He reports a minor squabble with Elsie Williams' – according to Konchesky: she didn't like him burning garden clippings, he called her an old harpie – 'but no real contact.' The Ice Queen doesn't say it, but we all know by now that Elsie Williams could have picked a quarrel with an empty room, so Price is hardly unique in having had a run-in with her.

And in any case, as Watkins goes on to say, there seems absolutely no connection between Elsie Williams or Arthur Price and Ryan Humphrys, the plumbers' merchant. Nor between any of them and Mary Langton.

'Price and Humphrys have supplied us with lists of friends, family, and tradesmen who have had access to their property. We are currently cross-checking those lists against address books and phone records, but so far we haven't found any significant overlap.'

Watkins grimaces at the lack of correlations. As though it's someone's fault. Then says, 'Causes of death.'

There's laughter at that. It sounds stupid – because people tend not to live long and healthy lives when they've been divided into dozens of pieces and distributed around suburban Cardiff – but Watkins is right: we don't actually know what killed either Langton or Khalifi. Were they cut up whilst still alive? If so, why? If not, then what?

More questions than answers. The corpses seemed to have been butchered reasonably proficiently, 'but a garden saw or kitchen knives could have done the job adequately. We've got no evidence so far of slashing, hacking, or even signs of struggle.' So quite likely a clean death, with butchery taking place thereafter.

Then some complex and uncertain forensic material, which Watkins summarises in her usual take-no-prisoners way.

The biggest curiosity: the condition of Mary Langton's corpse.

The leg found in the freezer was, according to the guesstimates we have so far, in roughly the condition you'd expect from a leg that had been frozen for five years, then left to rot in a wet freezer with the power off. The arms and the head were in worse condition, but probably not five years worse. The fact is that forensic science doesn't have a whole raft of statistical data on how rapidly a head decomposes when submerged in a barrel of old lawn mower oil. There are various tests currently being done to explore how far the oil has penetrated the bone and soft tissues. Those tests may or may not give us something more definite, but we're never likely to get a firm fix on the timing.

'Best estimate,' says Watkins, 'the head was in that barrel for one to three years. Maybe more, maybe less.'

A stone had been left in the mouth to keep the head below the surface. It had fallen out, with a little oily plop, when I lifted the head. In ancient Greece, corpses were buried with a coin in their mouths, so the newly dead had something with which to pay for their passage into the underworld. That falling pebble felt like Mary Langton finally making payment. Her spirit finally exiting this world.

'With the arms, it's a little clearer,' Watkins continues. 'If

44

those arms have been consistently stored at ambient temperature, the extent of the decomposition is consistent with something between two and four years. I'm told that, in the opinion of our forensics team, it is highly unlikely that the arms were stored in Ryan Humphrys's roof for the full five years.'

She emphasises those words: *highly unlikely*. I realise that nearly everyone is writing notes in their notebook. I'm not. I look keen instead.

Watkins has found a psychologist from somewhere to give a psych briefing. Those things are normally mind-numbingly stupid, amounting to little more than, 'I think your killer may not be quite right in the head.' A tedious message wrapped up in half-baked jargon and faux-scientific references. The tarot of modern criminal investigation.

This time, however, the psychologist – a tired-looking guy from Swansea – has a little more to offer. He notes that the Langton killing is odd for at least three reasons. One, the dismemberment. Two, the very wide distribution of body parts. Three, the apparent efforts made to preserve the body parts (the freezer, the barrel of oil, the airtight wrapping of the arms) may suggest some novel type of disorder or obsession.

'Naturally, it's possible,' says the psychologist, 'that the killer distributed body parts in order to confuse and deflect any criminal investigation. That could be a rational behaviour under the circumstances. But there are other ways to deflect attention and of course disposing of the corpse so that it isn't found at all might have been an even more rational course of action.' He pauses. Most of these guys are wannabe detectives, but he's aware he won't be loved for trampling on our turf. He backs off.

'What I *would* say is that the dismembering of corpses has been strongly associated in the past with offenders suffering from various personality disorders, often with possible

45

schizoid features. Speculating further, I'd suggest it's reasonably probable that the killer chose to retain at least one item for himself as a kind of memento. That kind of retentiveness is common in some offenders. Think of it as trophy hunting, if you will. But the obsession with *preserving* the corpse is a new one on me. It's as though there's a splash of compulsive hoarding in there. A refusal to give things up. A desire to retain control. I don't want to pretend there's much science I can offer here, but if you want my gut feel, I'd say we were looking for a guy who needs to hold on to things. Possibly a hoarder. At very high risk of being a repeat offender.'

One of my colleagues asks whether the Langton killer and the Khalifi killer are likely to be the same person. The psychologist thinks maybe not, though he – and everyone else here – thinks the killings are certainly linked.

A discussion, led by Watkins, ensues. But the energy which filled the room at the start, that bristling energy that had stalked the room like some giant beast, is pretty much dead now. Times like this show Watkins at her best and worst.

At her worst, because she's so taut, so devoid of humour or sympathy. She's like an order-issuing robot – rapid, precise, disapproving, relentless.

And at her best, for the same reason. An order-issuing robot is just what we need. There are search teams for Cyncoed, search teams for the reservoir, teams for database research and QUEST analysis, teams for the Khalifi interviews. Bam, bam, bam. She spits out instructions like something ejecting nails.

I think about Mary Langton. A red-cheeked English girl who chased a hockey ball and found her death. When you have a dead girl's head in your hands, a head that can't help but stare at you with sightless eyes even as it spits its black penny out, you have a connection. Like it or not, you're joined. While my colleagues scribble their notes, I remember

46

Mary. The weight of her head. The slipperiness. That feel of bone.

How did you die, Mary? I ask her. She doesn't tell me, but it's early days.

Eventually, forty minutes after starting, Watkins shuts up. I have a ringing in my ears. Her voice. Those commands. That tone. I think everyone feels the same way.

I'm on the Khalifi team, which disappoints me. I assumed I'd be on the Langton team and think about asking to be reassigned. If it were anyone but Watkins, I *would* ask, but because it's her, I just walk grumpily upstairs to a smaller conference room where pink-faced DI Owen Dunwoody assembles us.

Against the wall, there's a table laid out with ID photos, known facts, basic bio. Born Moroccan, but a longtime British resident, here since he was a student. Born Muslim, but nonpractising, nonreligious. Family in North Africa, but limited contacts with them. The intelligence databases are closed to us, but we can send in queries and have had a clean bill of health back: no known terrorist links. No hints of religious fundamentalism.

Dunwoody's team – me, Bev Rowland, Jon Breakell, Jim Davis, Angela Yorke, one or two others – start taking what we need: photos, fact sheets. Khalifi has a thin brown face. Forty-something. Neat dark hair. A kind of fussy precision in his suit, his narrow tie and white shirt. But there's something else too, something that scampers away from me before I can define it. His face isn't static. It's in motion. Half-looking away from the camera. Mouth opening into a laugh. Or perhaps opening to say something. But there's a disconnect between the eyes and the mouth. Like the eyes are saying one thing and the mouth is about to say another.

I don't know, though. The photograph eludes me. Mary Langton's photos were as plain as toast. A cow-toothed English girl who played hockey. When I found her head, her flesh was in a pretty decayed state but the cow teeth were still there. Somewhere in her eyeless stare, you could still hear the clack of a hockey ball, the smell of riding tackle.

My annoyance at being here instead of on the Langton team is already beginning to dissolve.

Who are you, Mr Khalifi? And what do you have to do with Mary Langton?

We're about to find out.

10

The Engineering Faculty is a short walk from Cathays. Never been before.

We get there at ten. Three DCs, me, and DS Jim Davis, who loves and adores me. I love and adore him too. We express our love by never talking to each other and by making sharky comments to third parties whenever we get the chance.

We're greeted by Gayle Thomas, the Head of School's assistant.

She offers three platitudes about the 'terrible tragedy.' Then gives us a list of Khalifi's students. A list of his faculty colleagues. Shows us to an 'interview space,' an underheated room with old carpet, big windows, and some books behind glass cupboards.

'Refreshments for you there,' she says, pointing to a tray of thermoses, as though we wouldn't be able to recognise them without assistance. 'We've drawn up an interview schedule to help get things organised. Obviously if you need longer with anyone, that can be arranged. All the students have been notified and they know that it's okay for them to skip a lecture if they have to.'

She gives a little smile. One of those hospitality smiles. The sort which says, *I'm professionally dressed in an inoffensive blue suit, I've put tea bags in individual sachets out on a small china saucer, I've made you some lists which are all neatly stapled, and look – I'm smiling.* Small white efficient teeth.

Through the glass pane in the door, I can see the first students assembling.

It's a well-organised setup and we do need to interview these people, but I hate the sense of being managed.

Davis does too. He starts grumbling about the tables. Privacy issues. Hospitality Thomas holds her hands in front of her like a supplicant at some Catholic shrine. She tells Davis that she'll arrange for some break-out rooms. He grumbles some more. She does prayer hands. He grumbles once more about the coffee, then drops it. The first students come in.

I interview three of them.

Three people, not all that much younger than me. Khalifi a reasonably popular lecturer. Expertise in materials science, whatever that is. Also mechanical engineering.

The third of my students, Kerry, is a mouse-haired girl who sits opposite me wearing a long gauzy scarf and pulling at it like she's dying to make some experiments in self-strangulation.

She bores me.

'Did he ever make a pass at you?' I ask.

'A pass? No. No.' She looks shocked by the idea.

'Did he have a fling with any of your fellow students? A one-night stand? Late night snog? Anything like that?'

'No.'

It's bad interview technique, but I'm bored and feeling antsy. I don't want my lovely little murder case to turn dull on me. I feel angry at these girls for being alive, when Mary Langton is dead.

'Sexual relationships with other lecturers? Drugs? Global jihad? Bondage games?'

'No.'

Kerry looks at me reproachfully, as though I'm not doing my job. Which I'm not.

'Fine,' I say. 'Could you look through these questions and note down anything that might be relevant? Thanks.'

I leave her with pen and paper going through our list of interview questions.

I walk out of the room and let the door bang shut behind me. I'm in a bland, official corridor. Blue carpeted. Student posters and notices tacked to the wall. The same blend of academic earnestness and trying-too-hard hipness I remember from Cambridge.

Where do you hide a leaf? In a forest. How do you conceal a secret? With openness. Prayer hands and efficient teeth.

I start to prowl. I'm not too sure where I'm headed, but I'm not utterly surprised when I end up on the management floor. Same blue carpets, no student posters.

I find my way to the Head of Faculty's office. Connor McKelvey. Outside his office, moored like a motorboat and freighted with an impressive amount of office hardware, is a PA's station, complete with a blondely fragile PA. An etched plastic plate tells me that she's Corinne. On the wall behind her are some photos. Prize awards for some student projects. The Head of Faculty with donors and grandees. My buddy Ivor Harris, MP, among their number.

'Hi Corinne.'

I give her my own best smile. I can't do blandly inoffensive. It's not my style. But I give good teeth, all brushed and white and shiny.

'Hello?'

She doesn't know who I am.

'I'm Fiona Griffiths, with the police.'

'Oh yes.' Corinne arranges her face in a subdued, we're-all-very-sorry-about-this-terrible-tragedy way.

'I need to see Mr McKelvey,' I tell her, and walk, without knocking, into the office she's guarding.

McKelvey looks up, surprised and a tad annoyed. He looks like you'd expect him to look, half engineer, half bureaucrat. Grey suit, grey-brown curly hair. Solid looking and slabby, as though inexpensively manufactured from some durable sheet material.

'Mr McKelvey, Corinne told me you were free. I'm Fiona Griffiths with the CID. I wonder if I could have a few minutes of your time.'

He doesn't look pleased about it, but waves a hand toward the seating area in the corner. A boxy armchair, boxy sofa, glass table.

I sit on the sofa. His normal spot. McKelvey does a momentary double take, then sits in the armchair. A red tag dangles from the arm. I reach out and read the label, which has to do with fire regulations.

'Flame retardant,' I say. 'Nice.'

'You all right downstairs?'

'Yes.'

I don't say anything more. He doesn't say anything more. He's waiting for me to start things off, which is good. I prefer it that way. I sit there saying nothing, because silence is always uncomfortable if you're not in control of it.

Eventually I say, 'Why was Khalifi killed?'

'Why? I have no idea.'

I nod at that, like he's said something sensible, and write it in my notebook, slowly.

'It wasn't the obvious things, was it?' I say. 'Sex. Drugs. Honour killings. None of the above.'

'Isn't that your job? To find out?'

I nod again. Write again. I do everything slowly. I don't know if there's a particularly annoying way to write, but if there is, I'm doing it.

'Yes. Yes, it is our job. So why was your colleague, Ali el-Khalifi, murdered? In your opinion.'

'I don't have an opinion.'

'Yes, you do. You think it wasn't sex, drugs, or honour killings.'

'I didn't say that.'

'Sorry, so you think it *was* one of those things?'

McKelvey sighs. 'Look. Ali was a diligent member of the department. We certainly weren't aware of any –'

'No. I know you weren't.'

I pause again. Not a tactical silence this time, a real one. There's an emptiness in the room, a withholding, that shouldn't be there. If McKelvey really had nothing to hide, he'd be more talkative. I know I'm being a total pain in the arse, but people are inclined to talk more under those circumstances or at least to get angry. McKelvey is being too controlled. I don't think he murdered Khalifi or even that he knows why Khalifi was killed, but there's something that he doesn't want me to know, which makes me want to know it twice over.

I try the sex angle first.

'Obviously, Mr Khalifi was a single man,' I say.

'Yes, and Ali liked to have fun. But look, we aren't here to judge our staff's private lives. What Ali did or didn't do –'

He continues a bit, but he relaxes as he talks. Whatever makes him come over all controlled, it isn't this. My guess: Khalifi was a bit of a womaniser. He was too smart to risk his job by playing fast and loose with the students. The rest of Cardiff would have been a different matter, however.

But the conversation is shifting away from whatever McKelvey is trying to guard. I want to get back to the emptiness, the withholding.

'Materials science,' I say. 'Tell me about it.'

McKelvey nods. This is home ground for him. 'That was Ali's speciality. Materials science has to do with the fundamental properties of various materials. It's at the confluence of physics, chemistry, and engineering. Nanotechnologies as well now, of course. Ali was extremely good with various types of steels. Some polymers, high-modulus polyethylenes.

Engineering plastics. That kind of thing.'

I nod, jotting down some of the terms. As I do, he goes on talking.

'You know, because we're out here in Cardiff, not a big-name university, people tend to think of us as somehow second rate. They assume we can't compete with the big boys. But you know, we've got one of the best engineering schools in the country here. And in our chosen fields, Ali's for one, we're as good as anyone. He's going to be tough to replace. We'll miss him.'

I nod, wondering how to use the flow. That's the thing about secrets, people want to talk about them. They can't help themselves.

'You'll miss him in other ways too,' I say, opting to stick with the positive.

'Yes. I wouldn't say he was the most, I don't know, popular member of the faculty. I'm not saying the opposite – just, he was happy enough to work hard, he didn't need to come to every summer barbecue. On the other hand, when it came to helping the faculty. You know, donors, tie-ups with business. Getting students into real engineering positions. Those sort of things, he was first class. Dedicated.'

I nod again. I can't see that I've got what I came for. On the other hand, I'm not sure how I can get it. Or what it is. My pencil hesitates over the page.

'I'll put that he was very helpful, shall I?'

McKelvey smirks at me patronisingly. 'Yes, you can put that.' The air has cleared up now. Like the emptiness isn't there, or is sealed off, if it is. I insist on talking a bit more, but I only do that to be annoying. I don't think I get anything more.

As I get up to leave, I say, 'Donors. What kind of money are we talking about?'

'This is an engineering faculty. It's not one of the arts,

where some donor agrees to host a poetry evening or a wine and cheese party.'

I nod, encouraging more of the same.

'Look, I've got an invoice here for a new universal electromechanical testing machine. Nothing fancy. Not one of our priciest bits of kit. But you take into account data-acquisition software, installation, everything else, and we'll have no change from forty, forty-five thousand pounds. We don't get kit like that on government budgets. It's all private-sector money. Research collaborations, product development partnerships, licensing agreements. We're going to miss Ali. He was bloody good at all that.'

McKelvey hovers over me, shuffling me towards the door. I'm small, so I'm easily shuffled.

I wonder if my sense of myself would be different if I were taller, bigger, stronger. I think it would.

'I've put that he was helpful,' I say, giving him and Corinne a final smile. 'Very helpful.'

And that's that. It really is. Except that as I go downstairs from one blue-carpeted floor to another, it doesn't feel that way at all.

I'm on the stairs. Walking down. Face to the light of the window. Thinking a bit about McKelvey, whether I could sense anything awry in his answers. Thinking too about Jim Davis. I've been AWOL for the best part of half an hour and he'll report me if he can. But mostly I'm just walking down the stairs, facing the window, doing nothing very much.

And then – I don't know. My leg twists. Or it's as though my ankle can't support my weight anymore and I just start sliding sideways. I would fall, except that I'm close enough to the bannister to be able to grab it for support. And as all this happens, I'm twisted around, as though someone has come from behind and forcibly moved me.

Indeed, that's what I assume has happened. I assume

someone has, for whatever reason, needed to move me violently, as though to protect me from some fast-moving object. Only there's no one there. No fast-moving object. No person. Nothing. I'm on the stairs, alone.

I sit down. I assume I've just experienced a bout of faintness, though I don't get faint normally. Didn't even when I was sick. I don't feel giddy or sweaty.

I *do* wonder about morning sickness. Surely to goodness *that's* not the issue. I'm on the pill and my last bleed was completely normal. I worry about the possibility, before deciding it can't be that. And it really can't be, I think. Really mustn't be, for that matter.

So it has to be my knee or ankle. I try standing, cautiously, a hand still out on the bannister, but my legs are fine. Ankles, knees, fine.

I'm fine. I'm a young, healthy adult and there is nothing wrong with me. I can feel my feet and hands normally – as normally as I ever can, anyway – and my breathing is a little flustered but basically okay. I stamp feeling down into my feet, clench and unclench my hands to get the senses moving there too.

I'm a fit and healthy adult and there is nothing wrong with me.

Walk downstairs, cautiously and with one hand on the bannister, back to Jim Davis and the team, all set for the rest of my merry little interviewing day.

11

That evening, I'm with Buzz. His place, not mine. A two-bed flat down by Atlantic Wharf. It's nice. A bit bachelor-ish. A bit IKEA-ish. But nice. Not as IKEA as my place, and at least Buzz has made an effort. There are pictures on the wall, cushions on the sofa, photos on the shelves, candles on the table.

Every time we have dinner together, I have this slightly spacy, buzzy feeling. Am I really here? Is this really me? A reasonably pretty girl, reasonably nicely dressed, sitting opposite this handsome and capable man, who moves around the room setting food on the table, dimming lights, lighting candles, arranging glasses.

I help, of course. I do what I'm meant to do, but I still feel like an actor from a TV movie, who opened the wrong door one day and stepped out into real life, and is here still, feeling the lights on her, the cameras, the invisibly watching eyes. My performance is probably good enough for a TV movie, but I'm always being caught out in little things. I remember to dim the lights, but forget to light the candles. Or I forget that there are napkins, real cloth ones, in a drawer, and don't put them out. Or sit down at the table before we're ready.

Buzz is never impatient with me. Never once, which I find a bit creepy. I'd be impatient with me all the time. Shift your bloody arse, Griffiths, this isn't a restaurant, you know. That's what I'd say.

And Buzz doesn't. He is the world's nicest man, maybe. I worry that he's too naïve to have a girlfriend like me. Shouldn't someone warn him? Shouldn't I?

Anyway. We're ready. We plate up. Buzz real-lifes himself over to the table with his plate, I TV-movie myself over. Then there's always this moment. Buzz says something like 'Well, Fi,' looks into my eyes, and chinks glasses. I do likewise. I feel spacy when I do it, but I do it.

Then we eat.

I want to talk about the case, but Buzz has these rules, good ones, about not letting the office intrude too much on the relationship. So we talk a bit about other things. Buzz plays hockey, which I used to think was mostly a girl's game, only he plays it aggressively and well, captaining the Cardiff third team, and leading his team out of whichever league they're in, into whichever league they'll be in next. Two of his players got stomach bugs after eating fast food from a van. He's angry with them because of breaches in team discipline and is unsure how to replace them for the upcoming game.

I'm silently amazed that all this is taken so seriously. Amazed that there are even multiple leagues for this kind of thing. And for grown-ups too. Adult men with jobs. But I don't say so. I try to follow the ins and outs as best I can. Say the right things. Evince the right emotions.

Then I say, 'Mary Langton played hockey. She had a photo in her room.'

Buzz looks sharply at me, then laughs.

'Okay, Fi, fair enough. Let's talk about murder.'

I laugh at myself too, but relax into shoptalk.

I say, 'Do you think it was a sex killing?'

'Which one?'

'Either.'

'Mary Langton. Must be ninety-five percent likely.'

I know the logic. The logic says that if it wasn't close family or a dodgy boyfriend – and Watkins would have caught any of those if they'd been the killer – then it had to be a sex-related thing. Partly because Langton was a twenty-something girl. Partly because of what she did – or had done – for a living. Put those two things together and the stats say it has to be a sex crime. Ninety-five percent probably undercooks it.

'And Khalifi?'

'Don't know.'

'I was with his students today.' His boring, boring students. 'No frisson from them. If he was some lecherous professor type, I reckon we'd have picked it up.'

'Right, but sex doesn't have to be like that, does it? I mean, maybe Khalifi's a perfect professional at work. Then, maybe not even that often, once a month or whatever, he goes down to a club, has a few, loses control and gets involved in something that he can't handle. Susan Konchesky has been going through his bank records and says that he's been up for a party in his time. A bit of a bad boy.'

McKelvey hinted the same thing, more or less.

'Okay,' I nod. 'Let's assume that's right. That doesn't mean there's any connection at all with Langton. She's a twenty-something girl who died five years ago. He's a late-thirties man who died on Friday.'

'True, but ...' Again, Buzz doesn't trace the logic all the way through, but he knows I know what he's thinking. He's thinking that this is Cardiff. We just don't get bodies chopped like stir-fry and scattered over town. Maybe that happens in Baltimore or Mexico City, but not here, not Cardiff. So if it does happen, it's weird, a once-in-a-century thing. If it happens twice, and in the same part of town, there must be a connection. That connection will suggest an avenue for investigation. We find the connection and investigate hard. Get a break. Get our killer.

'It could be copycatting. Could be. I mean, I know the timing's not helpful.'

'Not helpful? Honestly, what are the chances? You're a murderer. You hear about the Langton find on the radio, so you think, "That sounds fun," and, quick as anything, you grab a victim, bump him off, and scatter his body parts. You do all that the very same night that you hear the first radio or TV broadcast. Within hours, probably.'

'Or, more likely, you've already got a victim and have been wondering what to do with him.'

'Same thing, though. I mean, what are the chances? "Bloody hell, we've just killed someone, what shall we do with the body? I know what, let's listen to the wireless, see if we can pick up some tips on Radio 4." It's hardly likely, is it?'

That's true. But the coincidences cut both ways. The Langton body parts had been waiting seven years to be found. Even if both victims did have the same killer, how did that person know to kill Khalifi at essentially the same time we found the first piece of Mary Langton? Whichever way you look at it, something improbable happened.

I'd like to go on talking about it, but Buzz doesn't. He's good at switching off. Or rather, he knows that we don't yet have enough information, so he's not interested in speculating.

Not like me then.

Buzz starts asking me about my day. I tell him. About Jim Davis. The tedious students. My sense that the whole process was somehow over-managed.

'Jim told me you went AWOL.'

'Women's troubles.'

'Bullshit.' A friendly 'bullshit,' that, not a mean one.

'Okay, I went to interview the Head of Faculty.'

'Really? You just–?'

'I did it *Cagney and Lacey* style. Smashed the door down. Gun to his head. *Now start talking, punk.*'

'What's that accent meant to be? Was that Cagney or Lacey?'

'He was quite boring too, though. He didn't tell me anything.'

'Not surprising. You sounded more Pakistani than American. *Now start talking, punk.*' He does Cagney in an American-Welsh-Pakistani accent. Then says it a couple more times, perfecting the voice. Funny man.

I'm about to tell Buzz about the thing that happened on the stairs. The moment when my knee buckled. My panic about a possible pregnancy. Then I realise that I can't tell him a thing. If I said I might be pregnant, he wouldn't treat that as some awful drama. He'd be pleased. Calming. Treating it as an opportunity. I don't think he's about to propose exactly, but I realise that, if everything works out between us, Buzz sees marriage as being the ultimate destination. What this whole thing is about. The candlesticks. The glassware. The patience.

I feel suddenly panicked. More than I did on the stairs. Like TV Movie Girl has stumbled into some real-life scene which she has to play for real. She's been doing dummy fights with dummy weapons and now all of a sudden she's facing a real-life Johnny Depp with a real-life cutlass.

Sharp steel in front of her and the ocean pounding at her back.

'Are you okay, love?'

I nod.

Yes. Yes, I am okay. Nothing bad has happened. In fact, the very worst thing in my life at this moment is that a thirty-three-year-old police officer and former paratrooper, with an impeccable record in both services, happens to love me. And be committed to me. And be patient with me. That's my worst thing.

My best thing too, of course. But definitely the scariest.

Buzz waits a bit, then says, in his concerned voice, 'It's not your *stuff*, is it?'

My *stuff*. The Cotard's. My illness. And no, it isn't that. It wasn't that on the stairs either.

I mumble my way out of wherever it is we are, and the meal goes on, except that nothing's quite how it was. We have sex quite often, pretty much every night that I stay over, and this was meant to be a staying-over night. But we can both feel that's not where this evening is headed now. We finish eating. Find a little rhythm again. Have a nice cuddle on his sofa, but we both realise that I need some head space and so, before too long, I make my move and go.

Downstairs and outside.

A wet cold autumnal street. Today is the first of November. Is this the last month of autumn, or the first of winter? I don't know, but I like it. I like any weather that feels hostile.

This part of town is tidy now. Modern, functional, well designed. And yet, in comparison with the old Tiger Bay, the place is void of life. Before the developers arrived, the area was a warren of rusting docks, narrow streets, and dark, secretive little pubs. The people were different too. A stew of foreign sailors, Welsh prostitutes, and Somali-Norwegian-Yemeni-Caribbean immigrants with their maze of accents and unknowable intrigues.

That's where my Dad came from, back in the day. The place he grew up. The place that made him.

Because I can't revisit that world, I just get in my car and start driving home. No music. I don't even speed.

I'm almost there. About to turn off Eastern Avenue. Then just Pentwyn Road, Croescadarn, and home. Home to bed.

That's the theory.

Only where I should turn off, I don't. I keep going, up toward Saint Mellon's. Not too sure where I'm going. Hoping to navigate from old memories, sepia-tinted prints up in the attic of my mind. I get lost in the cul-de-sacs, swear a bit, wonder if this is a good idea – then, suddenly, I'm there. My headlights shining on hooped iron railings. The lawn. The circular flower bed, rosebushes cropped against the weather.

The house is dark. I'm looking at the dashboard clock – 11 PM and too late to knock – when I see a light come on downstairs.

A sign.

I don't believe in signs, but I do believe in light switches.

I go to the door and knock.

12

Emrys Thomas doesn't seem to have aged. Or perhaps when I was thirteen he just struck me as so amazingly old, I can't tell the difference now. Not that he is old, even. Sixty, sixty-five. White haired and courteous. A bit slow, but he was always slow.

I want to sit with him in his yellow-walled kitchen and ask some questions, but that's all too fast for him. He has to take my coat, shake it out, hang it on a peg by the door, then he decides it won't dry out there, so he moves some other coats so mine can stretch across two pegs for better drying.

'There!'

I didn't mind my coat wet.

We exchange comments about the weather. Then he sees me through to the kitchen. Then goes back to the living room to reset the heating controls. Then back to the kitchen and the kettle. Then biscuits, which I refuse but which he gets anyway. Then tea. I ask if he has herbal and, bless the man, he does, so I have herbal.

'You've grown, haven't you? A bit, anyway.'

'Not much, Em. You should see the others, though. Kay's as tall as you are, and Ant's my height. She might even be taller now.'

Emrys did some babysitting for Mam and Dad at one point. Not babysitting exactly. It was more like he acted like an honorary uncle for a while. If Mam and Dad went off to London for something, they'd drive us round to Em's for the evening. We'd sleep here even. Me in a little room next to Em's. Ant and Kay in the twin beds down the hall. It was a safe place. Boring, but in a nice way. Em and Kay and I would sit on the living room floor and play Monopoly or Cluedo, while Ant fell asleep upstairs. Then Kay would get sleepy too and I'd have an hour or so reading or watching TV with Emrys, before I too headed up. They were nice times. Normal and quiet, in a way that life with my dad never was.

Then I got a little older, and my illness muddled everything, and we stopped coming. Still saw Em at family events and the like, but far less than we used to. No big bust-up or anything like that. Just life moving on.

'I saw the light on,' I explain for the second time.

'Oh, that's all right, dear. I don't sleep as much as I used to.'

'You know – well, you know that I'm a detective now.'

Stupid question. Of course he does. Emrys and my dad go way back. Right to the beginning. You couldn't have that kind of background and not know when someone in your circle joined the CID.

Emrys waits.

I don't know quite why I'm here, except that it seems to make sense.

'There was this girl, Mary Langton. You'll have heard about her. The girl whose body keeps popping up all over Cyncoed.'

Emrys nods, but says nothing.

'She was a lap dancer. Pole dancer. According to our records, police records, she worked for the other two clubs in Cardiff, but never for Dad. Never for the Unicorn.' The Unicorn: strictly speaking the Virgin & Unicorn, but I never call it that. Dad's first club. Source of his first fortune, or his first legitimate one anyway.

65

'I don't know,' murmured Emrys. 'We must have checked at the time, but …'

'Oh, I'm sure she was never on the payroll or we'd have known about it. But presumably these girls dance for cash. If you'd needed emergency cover one night and you found a girl willing to do it for tips alone, someone might have agreed to it. I'm not saying that's how you normally operate, or would want to operate, just that if the need arose, the manager might have made his own decision.'

There's no way Dad would ever admit anything to a police officer and nor would Emrys, because he's stamped from the same mould, cut from the same cloth, hacked from the same block. Still, he tilts his head in a way that doesn't outright deny what I just said.

'And maybe if some of those managers were asked again about Langton, on the strict understanding that there'd be no comeback, they might remember things differently from the first time around. Especially if, let's say, it wasn't me asking, if there wasn't any police interest at all, if it was just you asking people what they could remember.'

Emrys doesn't say anything to that at all, but nor is he moving me onto neutral conversational territory.

'And then there's this other guy, Ali el-Khalifi. His is the other body that's keeping us busy. My colleagues are very keen to connect him to Mary Langton. Trying to see if he knew her when she was still alive. And let's just say that Mary Langton did dance a few nights at Dad's club. And let's just say that you've got credit card receipts or CCTV footage that places Khalifi in the club on one of those nights – well, wouldn't that be interesting?'

Emrys has gone very still and now, as I finish, he shakes himself alert.

'No CCTV,' he says. 'We wouldn't have that. Not that far back.'

'I haven't come here. I haven't asked you anything. I won't push for any answer at all. I don't need to know anything. Just if certain things turned out to be true, they might be interesting.'

Emrys nods. Doesn't say yes. Doesn't say no. Doesn't acknowledge anything I've said. Which is fine. I let the conversation shift off to other places. It's nice being with Emrys. I always liked him.

Then he yawns or I do, and he gets up, back to the living room to readjust the heating.

I follow.

This living room. Unchanged, pretty much. The Cluedo set is still there. Also Monopoly. A photo of Emrys and my dad, both looking younger, Emrys in a black shirt with the top three buttons undone and a spark of gold from a large signet ring. He always had this little bit of flash to him, a whiff of the gangster. He and Dad are standing proudly in front of that open-top Jag. The one where I was found.

I pick up the photo and stare at it closely. Because it's the same kind of angle, the same kind of sunny street, it feels weird to me that the car ever existed without me in it.

'When was this, Em?'

'When your dad bought it. What, eighty-four, was it? Eighty-five?'

Before me, in other words. I'm looking at life before me. Or rather: I was alive, somewhere, with someone, doing something. I just don't know where or who or what.

'It must have been strange for you. Dad finding me like that.'

It's the first time Emrys has allowed his expression to wobble at all. I guess he hasn't prepared for this particular contingency. Hasn't been instructed on how to react. But he rides the swell. 'Strange, yes. But your dad – Kathleen and him, both of them – were delighted. I've never seen your pa so happy. Quite right too, eh? He did well, didn't he?'

I shrug and put the photo back. 'I'm pleased it was him. I've never wanted any other dad.'

'You did well. You chose well.'

'Yes.' I look at the photo again. Interrogating it. 'Yes.'

An empty car.

An absent girl.

A road filled with sunshine and secrets.

'Em, can I borrow this? I'll give it back.'

'You want to borrow it? Of course you can.'

I thank him and hold on to the photo. On the shelves, below where the photo was sitting, there's a pile of magazines, some videos, and a photo album in fake burgundy leather.

'It'd be nice to spend some proper time together sometime, Em,' I say. 'A bit less last minute.'

He agrees. I think he's pleased. We promise to make a date and mean it. He sees me to the door and tells me to drive safely.

I do drive off, but don't know how safe I am. My thoughts are with that sunny street, that empty car. I've already asked the most obvious questions about my past. Asked them, and got answers that take me nowhere.

Do I, in fact, have some genetic relationship to my father? The most obvious question of them all. A man, known to be something of a rogue, finds a little girl in the back of his car. If he'd fathered me with some woman other than my mother, and if something happened to that other woman, might he not engineer it that I was 'found' in his car one sunny Sunday?

Well, the answer on this occasion is no. I've taken DNA swabs from me, my mam, and my dad – they didn't know I was taking them – and sent the material to a private laboratory for analysis. There was no genetic relationship between any of the three samples.

Do the clothes, shoes, or hair grip that I was wearing provide

68

any useful clue as to their provenance? No. All the items I've been able to trace were widely sold in the UK in the 1980s. Some may have been sold overseas too. The items were neither expensive nor cheap. The sort of thing that more or less anyone might have bought.

Are there any useful DNA traces on the clothes, shoes, or camera? Harder to check that one, but I did get them all checked at a forensics lab. No DNA showed up, except my own, my mam's, and my dad's. Which makes sense. DNA is quite easily destroyed. Sunlight, for example, can destroy a sample. Washing certainly can, and my mam would have washed my dress before putting it away. The only DNA samples that were found probably date from the very recent past: when Dad, Mam, and I were passing the items around the kitchen table.

Does the camera provide me with any other kind of clue? No. Again: it was a fairly ordinary camera. A few years old, but people back then didn't change their gadgets as often as they do now. There were no pictures on the film in it other than of me in that car.

I've looked at other questions too. I was found when my mam and dad came out of chapel. The minister could perhaps have engineered something, but I've spoken privately to him and investigated his background as much as I could and found nothing there. Him, two churchwardens, and a family friend my mam used to go to chapel with. I've tried to figure out something from the location of the chapel itself.

And got nowhere.

The investigation of my own life is not one whit further forward than it was when my dad first told me the truth about of my arrival.

I don't drive home straightaway. Drive instead to the reservoir. A thumbprint of darkness pressed down on a neon city. Muddy grass, inky trees, and that dark, aquatic mud.

Langton was at a party on the Lisvane side of the railway line, just near the Llanishen stop. She'd left the party early, before it was properly dark. The initial investigation was unable to find out whether Langton had ever boarded a train, so the inquiry was unable to restrict itself to a single geographical focus. It *had* however, been assumed that any abduction would either have taken place in Central Cardiff – Langton's intended destination – or on the streets directly connecting the party address with the railway station.

But maybe not.

Some people like twilight. Maybe the reservoir called Langton drew her away from those lighted, populated streets. There's something creepily welcoming about this place. The way it's unlike everything else.

Would you come here in a party dress, in party shoes, and at twilight? *I* wouldn't and I like darkness. But Langton: you never know. An August evening. A bad party. Maybe she came out here to clear her head. Or smoke a joint. Or pop a pill. It's only a few hundred yards from the station. Why not?

I don't know.

Home.

In the bathroom, I check the little disc with my contraceptive pills in. I haven't missed a day – I never do – and the contraceptive pill is better than 99 percent safe if you take it right. So I don't know what it was, that moment on the stairs.

In the ops room, I take Em's photo and the one of me sitting in the Jag and compare the two. It's the same car, but different times and places. Though the angle is much the same, it's still different enough that you can't just measure across from one photo to the other.

And yet, the thing I thought was there *is* there. In the earlier photo, Em's one, the Jaguar's long bonnet rises in one long, smooth curve from the radiator grille. The leaping-jaguar statuette pounces from a sloping metal bank. In the later photo, the one with me in it and one taken with a different camera, the bonnet is almost, but not quite, the same. In the left centre of the picture, the reflections don't fall quite evenly. It looks as though the smooth curve has been briefly interrupted by something linear, something flattened. I stare as hard as I can at the picture under the desk light, until I'm certain: either the Jaguar bonnet has been dented and repaired, or else the camera lens has a tiny flaw on it. A slight smudge of imperfection.

I have the camera still. It was left hanging round my neck the day Mam and Dad found me in their car. Tomorrow I'll buy film and test it out.

Another puzzle. Too many already.

Bed.

13

Days go by. Short, blustery days. Long nights. No progress.

Watkins and Kirby continue to hold well-attended briefings at the start of every working day. Kirby's presence grows increasingly less. This is Watkins's show and everyone knows it. Information accumulates, but not much wisdom.

We can't find evidence that Khalifi ever met Langton.

On the morning of his death, Khalifi withdrew two hundred pounds from a cash machine in the centre of town at 9.43 AM. CCTV has him entering a coffee shop immediately thereafter. He stayed nineteen minutes, then left. CCTV has him walking out of shot. Not hurried, not scared, not furtive, not anything. Just a man walking calmly to his death.

He made one phone call that morning: to a Midlands machine tools company about some piece of research work they were both involved in.

The coffee shop staff have been interviewed. Ditto the machine tools people. No reports of anything interesting. Nada.

I don't hear back from Emrys.

Buzz plays his hockey game and wins it, even with two boys out on the naughty step.

I do buy film for the camera I was found with. I take pictures of straight lines. Horizontal, vertical, diagonal. In grids and on their own. Get them developed – there are still places that can do that – and study the resultant pics. The answer is yes, the lens is flawed. In that spot just left of and somewhat below centre, the lens imposes a slight distortion on the image, dragging shapes a little downward and leftward. The distortion laid over the image of the Jaguar's bonnet caused that slight flattening. An effect you'd never notice unless you had two photos to compare, and even then one you'd never notice unless you were obsessed.

Which I am.

It's a rotten clue but all I have. Somewhere in the country, presumably, is a photo album that has photos in it taken with this same camera, with this same flaw. That photo album, presumably, belongs to the person who left me in that car. My mother or father presumably. My biological mother and father.

I've checked my dad's photo album and it seems normal to me: no flaws that I can find.

Meantime, I've interviewed more students, more faculty staff. On the downside, they're all still boring. On the upside, I've had no more episodes on the stairs and I'm basically certain that I'm not pregnant.

We're no longer searching for bits of Khalifi. We've recovered about 60 percent of his corpse, and we assume that dogs, crows, and foxes will by now have taken the rest. All of Khalifi's parts were found in open land, or in gardens or unlocked outbuildings backing onto open land.

We've found about 50 percent of Mary Langton. I've found a leg and a head, which puts me way out at the top of the Langton Collectors' League, but for some reason no one wants to give me a medal. Weirdly – and disturbingly – we found a chunk of her thigh, sawn up and skin removed, wrapped in an unlabelled plastic bag in somebody's garage freezer. Because of the way the chunk was packaged, it looked more or less like a joint of pork.

There's some debate in the office about whether such packages would be noticed. It seems that with smaller, kitchen freezers, people tend to know what's in them with reasonable accuracy. With larger chest-type cabinets, the sort you keep in an outbuilding, or at any rate away from the main living areas, it seems that no one really keeps accurate tabs on things. Garden vegetables get put there in season. Ditto leftovers, ditto soft fruits, ditto any cuts of meat that are on special offer locally. Sometimes these things are properly labelled, but often enough they're not, or the labels fall off, or become illegible.

No one quite wants to say it, but it's pretty clear that, for a proportion of people at any rate, there's a fair risk that mistakes could have been made. That pieces of Mary Langton could have been mistaken for something else. Mistaken, cooked, and eaten. That's not information we're keen to spread too widely, but the press is already full of snickering innuendo. The Cyncoed cannibals.

We have, of course, interviewed the lady in whose freezer the pork was found. She knew who Elsie Williams was but had never spoken to her. Her husband, now deceased, had a driveway-cleaning business – operating a pressure washer to remove bird poo, as far as I can make out – so knew plenty of people in the area, and indeed across all of Cardiff. No connection that we can find to Mary Langton. And in any case, the freezer was kept in their garage, which was left unlocked most of the summer months. So, in short, anyone at all could have placed the item in there.

One wall of the incident room is completely given over to our 'People of Interest': those people in whose homes bits of Langton or Khalifi were found, plus immediate family and close associates; also anyone living in the area with a history of sex offences or violence. We now have 167 'people of interest.' Someone, for a joke, pinned the local phone directory to the noticeboard. The directory was removed, but the point echoed.

Our investigation lacks a centre. We don't know where we ought to be looking.

By Thursday, the first reassignments begin. It's not a formal change. A burglary in Llandaff. An attempted rape in Caerau. Staff are peeled off to deal with them, and not assigned back afterward. Overtime drops back to normal levels. The leave which was cancelled is uncancelled.

Because it's Watkins, the pressure is still there. She stomps around the building, with her short iron-grey hair and dark, dykey suits, asking for lists, questioning facts, demanding notes. She distributes happiness the way a storm cloud distributes sunshine. Truth is, though, I like working for her. There's something about her bad-tempered relentlessness which appeals to me. If she's spiky with me, I'm spiky right back at her. She knows about my episode with McKelvey, because Jim Davis found a way to tell her, so she drags me into her office and asks about it.

'McKelvey wasn't on the interview list, but you went up there anyway.'

'Yes, ma'am.'

'Why?'

'Khalifi was killed because of sex or money. If it was sex, we're already covering every possible angle. If it was money, then McKelvey is the only person we know who's both connected to Khalifi and has control of large sums of cash.'

'McKelvey?'

I tell Watkins what McKelvey told me about engineering budgets. Also what I've been able to glean from public accounts. Also the public accounts of those companies with whom Khalifi struck partnership deals. The smallest of them has a turnover of twenty million pounds. The largest has revenues of more than one billion. His contacts ranged much further still.

Watkins hears me out without commenting. Then: 'Were you going to tell me any of this, Constable?'

'It's in my notes, ma'am.' Which it is. Though, admittedly,

presented in a way that hardly drew attention to the issue.

Watkins glares at me. Or rather, scrutinises me, the way an entomologist looks at a pinned butterfly. Which doesn't bother me. I like directness.

'Go on.'

'These two deaths are weird. Because they're weird, we're looking for connections. Because Langton was who she was, we assume we're looking for something sexual. But it's possible we're looking in the wrong direction. Those two aren't the only violent deaths there have been recently. And Khalifi's death has some clear connections with one of the others.'

Watkins's eyebrows are high now. Her face is angry, or I think it is.

I continue.

'Early September, a prisoner in Cardiff Prison, Mark Mortimer, committed suicide. Slashed both wrists with broken glass. He worked for a precision engineering company in Barry. His firm had an ongoing development project with the university.'

'Any money involved?'

'No. I mean yes, *some* money. But peanuts. Not slash-your-wrists-and-chop-lecturers-into-pieces money.'

Watkins does laser eyes at me to show how much she appreciates my turn of phrase, then calls up stuff on her computer. She doesn't say stay or go, so I just stand there while she taps away. I can't see what she's looking at, but if I were her I'd be looking at my notes and details of the Mortimer inquest. I've already studied the inquest files. They conclude exactly what you'd expect them to conclude. A promising young man screws up his career with a stupid drug deal. He loses his job, renders himself unemployable, sees his wife and kids bugger off back to her mum's house in the West Midlands. He can't take the mess he's made of his own life and chooses to end it.

I don't want to watch Watkins sit and read, so I say, 'Would you like some coffee?' She glowers at me and says, 'Black. No sugar.'

I make treacle for her, peppermint tea for me. Amrita, who manages the office and shares my addiction for peppermint tea, is in the kitchenette too. We chat. Amrita is the queen of office gossip and I worship before her throne for a while. Then I tell her that I'm in the middle of being bollocked by Rhiannon Watkins and better make a move.

'Oh my God, that woman.'

I shrug. 'Jim Davis complained about me.'

Amrita wants to know more and I tell her. My version. I was having my period, cramping up, having problems. Davis wouldn't believe me when I told him. Telling that stuff to Amrita is like broadcasting it on some in-house Twitter service. 'And you know his breath really stank that day. Do you think he drinks, maybe? He seemed quite, I don't know, unsteady or something.'

I leave her with that thought, and go back upstairs with the mugs, entering Watkins's room without knocking. She doesn't say thank you, just, 'The Mortimer suicide seems straightforward. And we haven't found drug traces in Khalifi's flat or anywhere else.'

'He's a plastics man.'

Watkins isn't as interested in the various uses of industrial plastics as I am and just glares at me, which I take as an invitation to educate her.

'One of his areas of expertise was high-modulus polyethylenes. That's like the stuff you use to make plastic shopping bags, only far tougher. The super-high-density stuff, Khalifi's speciality, can be used as glide rails in industrial equipment, docking gear, that kind of thing. The high, but not super-high, density plastics are what you make buckets out of, water pipes, plastic milk bottles, stuff like that.'

'Packaging. You think he created packaging systems

for drugs shipments? No smell. No leakage. Shockproof. Completely sealed.'

'It's possible. Mortimer and Khalifi probably knew each other. Khalifi worked with Mortimer's company, which has only ninety people on its payroll, and Mortimer was one of only six mechanical engineers there.

'Mortimer was busted because his packaging was amateur-ish. He had the stuff put in a steel tube and had the ends welded up. Khalifi is probably the go-to guy in Cardiff – maybe in Britain – for plastics expertise. The university doesn't have manufacturing facilities as such, but Khalifi would have known precisely where to go for that. He's the department's champion networker.'

Watkins ponders all this. Nothing that I've said is evidence. It's mere possibility. But then again, we don't have any evidence of any sexual link to Langton, so that's all speculative too.

'Why didn't you tell me all this earlier?'

'It's in my notes.'

'It's not in your notes. I've just looked. Not properly.'

'I wanted to look further before bothering you. I wanted something tangible.'

'What does that mean? *Look further*? You're a police officer. You don't conduct private investigations.'

'No, ma'am.'

'You carry out your designated tasks, Constable. You report when they're completed. Then you're assigned further tasks.'

'I *have* carried out my designated tasks.'

'You didn't answer my question.'

'I know one of the inmates in Cardiff Prison. I'm seeing him on Saturday.'

Watkins shakes her head. 'You won't get anything –'

'Brian Penry. He's a former police officer. A good one. Good apart from being an embezzler, I mean.'

'And you'll do what?'

'Ask him for gossip about the Mortimer suicide. See what he can find out.'

Watkins thinks for a bit. Her jaw moves like she's masticating something chewy or cartilaginous. If she was a man, she'd probably be clamping her jaw muscles or doing something testosteroney like that.

'Jim Davis is an idiot,' she says eventually. 'You are not an idiot. But Jim is part of a team and you are no use to me if you can't play with the team.'

I trained as a philosopher at Cambridge, and the thing about a discipline like that is you can't help but be offended by lapses of logic. In actual fact, the most useful things I've done so far have had nothing to do with team play, and all the most boring things have been because some idiot like Jim Davis asked me to do them. It seems to me the evidence strongly suggests that I'm vastly more useful to Watkins working the way I like to work and, in any case, I've hardly been working off-piste at all. Not by my standards.

But she's still doing that thing with her jaw, so I say, 'Yes, ma'am,' and look at my hands and go on saying it till she stops lecturing me.

Then she stops.

I say, 'Thank you, ma'am,' and get up to go. She says, 'Okay,' and then for no reason at all, except maybe to annoy her, I say, 'Sorry, do you mind? Can I ask where you got your suit? I just think it really works on you.'

An expression crosses her face which I can't read. Maybe it's anger – her default setting – but maybe it's not. Maybe it's something else. But anyway, she says, 'Hobbs,' and I say, 'Oh, Hobbs?' and she nods, then looks down at herself, straightens out the fabric, and says, 'Thank you.' If it weren't against the laws of physics, I'd think she reddened.

I give her a lovely big smile and walk out of her office.

14

Penry again. Same room. Same lighting. Same guards. Same paintwork.

He's in a better mood this time. Too good. Buzzy and over-energetic, the way a four-year-old is before a sugar crash.

'Bloody hell, Fi, you spend a lifetime in the police force, but it's only when you get in here you understand what's really going on. Some of the stories I've heard ...'

He starts to tell me some of them, waving his hands and laughing too loud. The tales he tells mostly sound like bullshit to me. I expect when he comes down off his high, they'll sound the same way to him. I'm not judgemental though. Penry's got to do two years inside. If this is part of his adjustment process, so be it.

I let him talk a while, then interrupt.

'Brian, can I ask a favour?'

I tell him the picture as I see it. Two murders, one suicide. 'Everyone thinks that Khalifi must somehow be linked to the Langton death, but it seems to me we ought to be looking hard at the Mortimer death too.'

Penry asks a few questions in quick succession, getting himself up to speed. His assessment of the case is rapid, decisive. I realise I'm seeing him in police mode, the way he was before his career went off the rails.

'This is real, Fi, is it? You're not just ...?'

'Trying to cheer you up? No. It's real. I mean, it is from my point of view. Watkins thinks it might be worth looking at. Everyone else thinks I'm barking mad.'

'Good enough.' He rubs his face with both hands. When he removes them, he looks older. More like himself actually, minus the sugar high. 'What's your hypothesis?'

'Don't have one. But here are the pieces. Mortimer was involved in drugs, but an idiot when it came to bringing them into the country. Khalifi has expertise in materials and access to an enormous amount of manufacturing knowhow. Plastics certainly, but general engineering too. The two men very likely knew each other. If Khalifi did something that pissed off some big-league drug dealer, then maybe Mortimer was in the firing line as well. Obviously no one snuck into Mortimer's cell to bump him off, but maybe he gets a message saying that unless he kills himself his family will be murdered. Or whatever.'

I stop. It all sounds ropey to me when I say it, but there *are* three corpses kicking around. They're real.

'Got it,' says Penry. 'I'll see what I can do.'

We talk rubbish for another ten minutes. Uncomfortable minutes. I'm always aware of the guards, of the other prisoners, the atmosphere of poverty and limits. I'm aware of the walls.

As soon as I can, I leave.

Outside the jail, I realise I'm not coping so well. My head is worse than I'd realised. As a teenager, I was ill for two years. Mental illness, as bad as it gets. For much of that time, I was kept in a secure unit. There was a courtyard garden and various common areas where we were allowed to come and go freely, but that was it. Outside access to the unit was via a porters' lodge. Staff and visitors needed to show ID to enter and leave. Patients were prohibited from leaving without written discharge papers from one of the shrinks, so we were imprisoned every bit as much as Penry is now. More so, in some ways. The courtyard garden had two wooden benches, an ornamental maple tree, a couple of cypresses, and some bedding plants which were constantly being trashed by the crazier patients. There was a metal bin for cigarettes, but we all just scattered ciggy stubs on the ground and let the nurses clear them up. We weren't allowed matches, of course – someone would have tried to burn the place down – but there was an electric lighter gadget on the side of the bin and a cigarette machine inside the building. We all smoked twenty or thirty a day, the nurses too.

Inside, some architect had designed the place to be cheerful. The common room was clad in varnished pine so it looked like some Nordic sauna. The seating was built-in with heavy leatherette cushions. The only movable items were either completely soft – beanbags and foam cushions – or too heavy to lift. The TV was screwed to the wall. The knives and forks in the canteen were plastic. Even so, never a day went by without someone trying to do something stupid. One guy, I remember, normally one of our tamer schizos, scavenged dry leaves from the garden and built a pile of them inside one of the chair seats. He didn't set fire to them straight away, because the smoke alarms would have sounded instantly, so he waited till the one day each month when fire drills were held anyway. As soon as the alarms started ringing for their regular test, he used a cigarette butt to get his leaves alight. Instead of shutting off after their test sequence was completed, the sirens just went on sounding. For a good few minutes, the staff just ignored the noise, clustering in the corridors with their coffee mugs and tutting. Not until someone noticed that the common room was filling with smoke did anyone take action. One of the seating bays was properly ablaze before the fire was brought under control. When they rebuilt everything, they drenched the place in some flame-retardant chemical that made two of the self-harmers sick for weeks. That was us: smart enough to cause destruction, crazy enough to want to.

In those two years, I spent more time in that facility than I did at home.

Cardiff jail is more like that place than anywhere else I've ever been, and I can feel some of my old self-destructive patterns starting to gather themselves, like fog patches forming in the beam of car headlights. Self-harm was never particularly one of my things – I was a little too crazy for that and the self-harmers stood well below me in the private hierarchies of the insane – but I used to like pressing kitchen knives against my forearms to see how much I could feel. The usual answer was almost nothing. I drew blood a few times. By accident mostly.

Now, standing on the road outside Cardiff Prison, I feel that old impulse again. To press some cold steel against my exposed arm. To study the blade as it whitens my skin. Hoping to feel something, terrified I won't.

I want to roll up my sleeve so I can look at my white skin and blue veins.

But those are bad thoughts. Addictive. A flight of stone stairs, leading down.

I have a plastic bag of ready-rolled joints in the boot of my car, concealed under the tyre irons, along with a cigarette lighter and a bar of chocolate. I've an impulse to stand and smoke a joint, right here outside the jail.

That's not a good idea, though. I can feel my brain send a chatter of alarmed telexes to my impulse control centres. All in capitals: DO NOT DO WHAT YOU ARE THINKING OF DOING. REPEAT. DO NOT DO WHAT YOU ARE THINKING OF DOING. The telexes are followed by lists of reasons. *Think about where you are. Remember that you're trying to cut down. Remember that you want to be a supergreat and perfect girlfriend to Buzz* – your phrase, Griffiths – *and Buzz really, really wouldn't like you being hauled in on some possession charge, now would he?*

The chatter and the lists continue, but already the impulse is waning. Buzz is tediously traditional on issues like whether it's okay for coppers to smoke weed, so I haven't told him that I do. He doesn't know that I grow it in my garden shed and would go nuts with me if he found out. He'd probably report me.

But in the end, it's not those reasons that make the difference. These days, I'm trying to do things right. To avoid escape routes. To do things in the right way for the right reasons at the right time. Sometimes, the right thing is for me to smoke dope. A comfort blanket I can't yet give up. But it's not the right thing for me now.

I stamp feeling into my legs. Jump up and down. Pump my arms. Run just far enough to feel out of breath and for one of my feet to start blistering.

I start to feel more normal. The prison feeling hasn't quite left, but it's not dangerous any more, just unpleasant, like last night's cigarette smoke in the hair. I need to wash the feeling away.

I limp back to my car, wondering how long it takes to get to Droitwich.

15

Two and a half hours is the answer. Some accident just south of Worcester blocks two lanes and I end up spending an hour in almost stationary traffic, watching long curtains of rain sweep across from the Malvern Hills. I keep switching stations on the radio, trying and failing to find music that doesn't annoy me, then end up settling for exhaust fumes and silence. I power the windows down and let the rain come in. I think about lowering the soft top, but don't.

I text Buzz to let him know I'll be late.

The farther I get from Cardiff jail, the less sure I am of what I'm doing. I mean: I think it needs to be done. I'm just not sure it'll be worth another bollocking from Watkins. When I get into Droitwich proper, I stop the car and call Watkins's mobile. She answers it in her normal snappish way. I tell her what I want to do and where I am.

'Droitwich?'

'Mortimer's wife and kids moved back here when he went to prison.'

'And you're there why?'

'I've been visiting a friend,' I say. 'So I'm in the area.'

There's a pause down the end of the line. I can't hear anything, but I bet she's doing that thing with her jaw. Then, 'Okay.'

'Okay as in, "Yes, please, go ahead and interview Sophie Mortimer"? I don't have to.'

'It's fine, Constable. You might as well, since you're there.'

That's hardly a massively positive vote, but it's good enough.

'How is it where you are?' I say. 'It's rainy here. Not too cold, though. I don't like the cold.'

Another pause, probably some jaw action involved in it, then, 'Let me know what you get from Mortimer.'

She rings off before I can say goodbye.

I drive slowly to Mortimer's house. I have the address from the inquest notes. I don't know if she's still here. I didn't call ahead.

The house is at the end of a short cul-de-sac. Pleasant, unremarkable. Patches of lawn in front of every house. A few shrubs. Tidy, clean. Lights on in the house I'm after.

I get out of the car and ring the doorbell. Nothing. I'm about to ring a second time when the door opens. It's a woman. Younger than I was expecting. Mid-thirties, which I'd known from the inquest notes, but somehow hadn't pictured. Also prettier. Slim, blonde, hair more than shoulder length, a kind of natural sulkiness around her mouth. Skinny jeans, a floral print top in dark grey and lilac, black biker jacket.

'Mrs Mortimer?' I ask.

'Not anymore. I don't use that name anymore. I'm Sophie Hinton now.'

I introduce myself, show my warrant card, ask for twenty minutes of her time. She says she doesn't have twenty minutes, she's expecting a friend to drop the kids off any moment now, then has to go straight out.

I say, 'Well, any time you've got ...'

She doesn't like it much, but she swings the door open, lets me in, and shows me through to the kitchen. The room had its last major refurbishment in the 1980s, it looks like. Country-style cabinets with limed oak doors and tiled countertops. I can't put the kitchen together with the woman, then remember I'm in her mother's house.

I sit down. Hinton doesn't. She doesn't take her jacket off. She puts her phone down on the counter, but in a place where she can still see the screen. Her car key down next to it.

There's a vibe in the room which I can't explain. Obviously there are some classes of people who exhibit an almost automatic them-versus-us hostility to the police, but a nice little cul-de-sac in Droitwich isn't somewhere I'd expect to encounter it.

I introduce myself. Say why I'm here: 'We're investigating a couple of serious crimes in Cardiff. One of the victims probably knew your husband. I just want to check if there's anything there we need to explore.'

She sits down on a stool at the breakfast bar, but there's something provisional in the way she sits, one long leg sloping all the way to the floor, as though to show she could get up and walk out at a moment's notice.

'Have you ever heard of a man named Ali el-Khalifi?' I ask. 'He was an engineering lecturer at the university.'

'Never heard of him.' Her response is instant but followed by a hesitation. She amends her answer. 'A Middle Eastern guy?'

Yes, I tell her. North African, in fact, but I don't think Hinton is after geographical exactitude.

'Met him at an office party, maybe. I didn't talk to him.'

Her leg moves as she says this. Her toes comes in under her centre of gravity, so she's even closer to standing up than she was before.

'We found him cut into about fifteen different pieces round Llanishen Reservoir. He used to work with your ex.'

Hinton's colour rises. She reaches for her phone and fiddles with it.

'We found his lung bobbing around in the water.'

Her colour hardens, but something else does too. 'Look, I don't know that person. I don't want to sound insensitive.

87

I'm very sorry and everything, but –' She shrugs. 'What was your question?'

'Do you know why your husband – your ex-husband – killed himself?'

'Because he was an idiot.'

'Did anyone ever threaten you? You or your children? Did your ex-husband ever receive threats that he told you about?'

The question doesn't get anything much more than a snort. Half laugh, half dismissal. 'No,' she says, standing up. She reaches for her phone and car key. Her colour is still high, still too bright, but there's a kind of armouring now which I don't think I'll be able to penetrate.

'Why did you leave him?'

'Why did I leave him? He was a drug dealer. He had this Saint Mark thing going. Butter wouldn't melt, and all that. Then what is he, really? A drug dealer who was busted and sent to jail. And we had two children together.'

There are tears in her eyes now, but the armour is still present, still shining.

'Your ex wasn't a dealer. Not really. He was some sort of middleman who screwed up. The person who killed Khalifi is the sort of person who would be happy to threaten wives and children too. We can't protect you if you don't tell us stuff. Sophie, have you been threatened? You or the kids? Now or in the past?'

'No.' She runs her hand hard through her hair, shaking it out. A kind of anger there. Or defiance. A running away? I can't tell.

'Or any recent contacts which struck you as odd?'

There are other questions I want to ask, but I've lost my witness. She's in some space I don't understand and can't reach.

Sophie stands over me, taller and blonder than I'll ever be, wanting me to leave. I nod, compliant and submissive. I don't want to prompt a complaint to Watkins.

'I'm going to leave you my phone number. If you need any kind of help, let me know. We *can* help, we just need you to ask.'

She nods. I write out my name and number on a sheet in my notebook, tear out the page and push it over the counter to her. As I do that, we hear a car outside, doors slamming, the sound of children's voices. Sophie doesn't take my number. Just leaves it on the counter.

We walk to the front door. The strange atmosphere is still with us, but I don't understand it.

Hinton goes out to get her kids. I hang back, because I don't know what I'm supposed to do. Hinton says something about me, because I see her gesture in my direction.

The kids spill out of the car. Theo and Ayla, I know from the inquest notes. Six and five. Ayla's in some kind of ballet costume and wants to show her mother her pirouette. The friend drives off with a wave.

I say, 'Thank you, Sophie. I'll get going.'

Hinton gives me a look that says I can't leave soon enough for her, then, abruptly, as I have my hand on the door of my car, says, 'Actually, look, I have to go out. It would be easier if I didn't have them. Can you look after them for ten minutes? My mum should be back soon.'

I say yes.

'She should be here any moment.'

I tell her that's fine.

Hinton looks at me hard. I think she's trying to imply that she has fiercely high child-care standards and she's seeking to determine if I meet those tests. I give her my best child-care face, whatever that is.

'Okay.' She nods. Takes me and the kids into the house. Gets orange juice for Theo. Puts the telly on. Says again, 'It'll be five minutes, literally.'

I don't believe her. I think Sophie takes the path of least

resistance in most situations. That she does whatever is pleasantest and most convenient and simply rearranges her mental furniture to make her own behaviour seems acceptable. Perhaps we all do the same thing, if not quite on Hinton's scale.

I say again that we'll be fine.

Hinton gives me the hard stare one last time, then whirls off.

Theo is in front of the TV already, watching an American cartoon. Things being whacked, splatted, and chased.

I say to Ayla, 'I'm Fiona, a friend of your mam's. You're Ayla, aren't you?'

Ayla nods. Her eyes are wide and serious. 'Are you a policewoman?'

'Yes.'

I assume Sophie said as much to her friend when she arrived. Ayla frowns at my answer, but I know why.

'I'm a detective, so I don't get to wear a uniform. I used to, though. It was very hot.'

Theo is watching me now, or half-watching me anyway. I'm neck-and-neck with the cartoon.

'That's why I don't have a police car either. Detectives aren't usually allowed them.'

'Do you have a gun?'

Theo: the boy's question.

I say, 'No, they don't let us have guns,' but I show him my warrant card, and he likes that.

'My daddy went to prison.'

Theo again.

Ayla's eyes travel to a photo on the windowsill. Of Mark Mortimer, with his family. I haven't noticed any other photos of him anywhere.

I mute the TV and, acknowledging Ayla's look, say, 'That's your daddy there, is it? He looks nice.' I don't know what to say.

90

Ayla nods.

I get the photo and sit on the floor with my back against the sofa. The kids sit either side of me. Ayla quite close, Theo still keeping his distance.

I bet Mark Mortimer doesn't get much airtime in this house. Not from Sophie Hinton, not from anyone else either.

'Tell me about your daddy,' I say. 'Anything you remember.'

They don't say much at first, but then Ayla volunteers something – 'He was really tall' – and then Theo does, and then both kids are talking. They're not crying exactly, but tears aren't far away.

I don't say much. Just let them keep talking. This isn't me in police mode – the children couldn't possibly have any useful evidence – but it seems fair to let them remember their father, in their way, at their pace. Whatever Mortimer did or didn't do, his children don't deserve to have him airbrushed from their lives.

Then Theo says, 'Why did he go to prison?'

Ayla, who had been saying something, shuts up completely.

'If you're in the police,' adds Theo, pushing.

'I don't know,' I whisper. 'I know what they say he did, but I don't really know. The real reason, I mean.'

'Was it a mistake?'

A very good question, as a matter of fact. *Was* it a mistake? Nothing about Mortimer shouts drug smuggler – or at least, nothing beyond a steel tube packed full of cocaine.

'Maybe,' I tell Theo. 'I don't know. We're trying to find out.'

'Is that why you're here?'

'Sort of. Yes.'

And, unexpectedly, what I say feels like the truth. Two other corpses brought me here, but Mortimer's corpse matters too. His children do. I can feel their questions plucking at me. Demanding something. Theo's a good interrogator, actually. He's done what we're trained to do: extract truths and insights that the subject had no intention of disclosing.

To myself as much as them, I repeat, 'We're trying to find out.'

Time goes by.

The kids switch their attention to other things with the alarming ease of the very young. The TV comes back on. Car chases and shouting.

No sign of Sophie Hinton or of her mum. I don't care, but I've been here twenty minutes, not the promised five.

After more time passes, we hear a car stopping outside: Hinton's mother. I go to meet her. Explain who I am and offer to see myself out. She doesn't seem all that amazed to find a stranger looking after her daughter's children.

I say, 'They seem lovely. Must be so hard for them after losing their father.'

Hinton's mother, Geraldine, tuts at that. Scowls. Another airbrusher.

I bend down to the kids. 'I'll do my best. To find out if it was a mistake.'

Theo nods, as though he's swearing some sacred oath. Ayla is wearing a little bracelet: seashells on a piece of elastic. She takes it off and holds it out to me. 'For you.'

I put it on. 'Thank you, Ayla. Thank you, sweetheart.'

I leave. Their grandmother shuffles them inside. Geraldine likes me almost as much as her daughter did.

I walk over to my car, but don't get in right away. I go to the boot and root round in the tyre irons until I find a joint and a lighter. I light up. Smoking outside the prison would have been against my rules, because it would have been a bad response to a temporary emergency. This smoke isn't like that. It's not breaking my rules.

I'm about halfway done when Sophie Hinton's red Mini sweeps down the cul-de-sac. Stops. She gets out, with something liquid in her eyes. I wonder if whatever she's been out doing involved a glass or two of white wine. I'm guessing yes.

'You're still here.'

'Just leaving. The kids are terrific. Your mam's in with them now.'

She nods brusquely.

'Sophie, that office party where you met Khalifi, who threw it? Mark's firm? The university? Or what?'

'I don't know. Some engineering thing. Circle of Welsh Engineers or something.'

'Okay. And if you remember anything else, you have my number.'

Hinton nods, heads inside.

I've got half my joint left, but don't want it now. Take one more puff, then drop the end down a storm drain.

Conflict doesn't bother me, but what I've had from Sophie Hinton wasn't conflict. Was she pissed off with me because she didn't want to be reminded of her troublesome former husband? Pissed off because she *had* been threatened and didn't want to risk any police involvement? Pissed off because she resented the police for jailing her husband? Or was she just a spoiled pretty-girl whose life wasn't running the way she'd intended and who was perfectly ready to let her bad mood spill out on anyone who got in its way?

Who knows? Not me.

I swing my car door open. Sophie Hinton glowers from the kitchen window. Skinny jeans and a biker jacket. I try to imagine myself in those clothes. Long-haired and petulant. Different look, different me.

I wave at her, then head for the motorway, head for home. Keep my shell bracelet on all the way. The journey time is eighty-three minutes.

16

The next few days, I mix it up. Do the work that Watkins and pink-faced Dunwoody want me to do. Do some more interesting things too.

So, I come in on time. Make stupid calls. Write stupid lists. Check bits of paper. Write up notes. Listen to briefings: the Stirfry morning show. For the first time since the start, Supterintendent. Kirby misses two briefings in a row. The incident room board listing our people of interest now shows a tally of 221. That's not a sign of progress, but one of failure.

I don't pick fights with Jim Davis or try to needle Rhiannon Watkins. Dunwoody notices my little worker-bee productivity and is pleased with me, albeit in a faintly patronising way. No one gives me a bollocking for anything. Susan Konchesky's work on Khalifi's bank records places him at two Cardiff lap-dancing clubs, Dad's and one other. Trouble is, Langton apparently never worked at Dad's club and the dates of Khalifi's visits to the other club all fell after Langton's disappearance. A tantalising connection: almost-but-not-quite.

And the more interesting stuff – well, that part I do the way I like it. Haunt my targets. Make checks on my six names: Ivor Harris, Galton Evans, Trevor Yergin. Huw Allsop. Ben Rossiter. David Marr-Phillips.

I add another one, Idris Prothero, to the list too. Bump him up from the B-team. He and Ivor Harris both have their thumbprints somewhere near this case.

Ivor Harris has had quite a lot to do with the university, including the engineering faculty, but you wouldn't expect anything less from a busy local MP. Not much of a thumbprint, in all honesty.

Idris Prothero is a wee bit more interesting. He was a business associate of Rattigan's more than a friend, which is why he was on my B-team, not my A-team. But Prothero has a variety of venture-capital-type investments in local businesses, including the outright ownership of the late Mark Mortimer's firm, Barry Precision. I can't really see how a financial investment in a firm that once employed a not-very-competent drug smuggler ties Prothero into anything much – and still less does it suggest that Prothero was part of Rattigan's fuck-an-Albanian circle of buddies. But if you don't seek, you don't find. So I seek.

The same logic also impels me to scratch away at that Mark Mortimer itch. I would prefer to do that solo as well, but I've already had one team-play bollocking from Watkins and I can't risk another one, not quite so soon anyway. So I run things past her. Give her notes on my interview with Hinton. Tell her, in so many words, that there was something strange in the widow's manner. A strangeness that, to a copper, suggests something being withheld.

Watkins doesn't like my theory of a possible Mortimer–Khalifi connection, but she can't quite ignore it either. It's not as though she has an obviously superior alternative. So she allows me to investigate, but I'm on a short leash. Every call, every interview, I have to run by her first. I hate the supervision, but I welcome the chance to dig.

I call Mortimer's ex-colleagues. University connections. His brother and sister. I don't get anything tangible, but I also don't get the sense I'm looking at a drug dealer. He just doesn't have that smell about him. He seems to have been a scrupulous employee, never late, seldom absent. Then too there was that 'Saint Mark' comment of Sophie Hinton's. I've got nothing that would count for anything in court. Nothing even to justify a shift in investigative resources. But I feel strongly that something is not quite right in the picture we've been presented with.

Watkins only half agrees with me, but half is enough for now. The growing feeling is that our inquiry is getting nowhere. We don't have a single useful lead on Mary Langton. Khalifi's another dead end. We've found out about a few sexual liaisons – the man was no hermit – but we've found nothing to connect with Langton, nothing to suggest a motive for his murder. The Mortimer–Khalifi link and Sophie Hinton's odd evasion is as good as anything else we have. So Watkins lets me run with it.

I have nothing tangible to show for my efforts yet, but some flowers bloom slowly. I once watched a moody cow, a big Hereford heifer, start to lean against a post-and-rail fence on my aunt Gwyn's farm. The heifer pushed, the fence resisted: nothing. But the cow didn't give up. She just kept at it. Shifting her position from time to time, but all the time leaning her nine-hundred-pound weight hard against the upper rail. And in the end, the rail broke. Just snapped into two jagged timber lances. The cow studied her work, then backed away peacefully, happy to start munching again. But it taught me a lesson, that. Apply pressure, keep going and things can snap even when they seem to be at their most static. If there's a line of weakness, sooner or later something will fracture.

And it does.

The engineering group at whose party Sophie Hinton once met Khalifi is called, rather pretentiously, the Welsh Circle of Engineering Excellence. Its chairman is a retired engineer, Arwel Adams. I call him up. He agrees to chat with me and says, if I'm in the area, I'd be welcome to pop by. He's in

Penarth, just down the coast from Cardiff proper. I hesitate briefly – I told Watkins I would *call* Adams, not *visit* him – but even Watkins surely couldn't care if I do a little more than promised. And in any case, it's getting towards the end of the day. I've had enough of desks and offices and overhead lamps. I tell Adams I'm on my way.

His house, when I get there, turns out to be right by the shore, overlooking the sea. Picture windows that frame a strip of grass, a band of scrub, then a line of grey sea and a mountainscape of grey cloud.

He offers me tea. I refuse, but add, 'What is it like all day, looking out at this?'

He says the sort of thing that people say. The light. The movement. The ceaseless change. But I think that's wrong. Isn't it the other way around? That it never changes. That you are staring at a vision of eternity, sometimes sunlit, sometimes furious, but always there. Gazing at you gazing at it.

I say something along those lines and Adams laughs. 'You could be right.' He doesn't put the lights on, so we're just there watching the light fail over water. There will be rain before long.

I say why I've come. Routine inquiry, pursuant to the murder of Ali el-Khalifi. Blah blah. Start asking questions.

Adams is helpful, a good witness. He's good on names and dates. Swift recall, documentary records, precise answers.

'Ali and Mark certainly knew each other. They were both Circle regulars. I've often seen them chatting together. I got the impression they knew each other outside these meetings too.'

'How far did their connection go back?'

Adams consults his attendance records. He has to put the lights on for this, and the sea beyond the windows recedes into the darkness. 'I've only got records for the last four years,' he says, 'but they were both booked to attend a meet in July 2006. If it helps, I could talk to my predecessor and go further back.'

I shake my head at that. Instead, I poke away at the nature of their connection. 'What were their shared interests? What did they talk about?'

'I'm not sure. Ali's passion was industrial plastics, which Mark wouldn't have had much to do with. But Ali was a university man, of course. He needed to keep abreast of the literature. Barry Precision is all about highly engineered steels. If you needed a specific part with some demanding specifications – shock resistance, heat resistance, very narrow design tolerances, that kind of thing – then Mark's outfit would take care of that. Ali didn't have a research interest in that kind of area, but he was still very well versed in it. And of course Ali was amazingly well connected. If you had a problem that Ali couldn't solve, he'd know someone who could. In a way, that was his real expertise. Ali knew everyone.'

'What about geography?' I ask.

I explain what I mean. One of the things that has niggled at me is that Khalifi was of Moroccan extraction. Mortimer tried to bring in his drugs via southern Spain, just north of Gibraltar. Now, in itself, there's nothing odd about Spain as an import route. Most cocaine enters the UK via Spain or Holland. Spain because of its Latin American connections, Holland because of Rotterdam's importance as a logistics hub. On the other hand, it's possible in this instance that there's more to Mortimer's import route than mere probabilities. Khalifi still had family in Morocco and the Spanish supplier whose steel tubing Mortimer tried to use did business all over North Africa. It's one of those tantalising almost-connections which might nor might not prove significant.

Adams tries to help with that query, but can't. He tells me that Khalifi still kept current with things in North Africa – we've heard the same from other sources and his bank records show that he's travelled as far afield as Dubai and Jordan – but he can't say whether Mortimer had any professional interest in the area.

We talk a bit longer. Adams was amazed that Mortimer turned out to have an involvement with drugs. He seemed somewhat less amazed that someone chose to chop Khalifi into several dozen pieces. No tangible suspicion or anything like that, just less amazement. No knowledge whatsoever of Mary Langton.

I leave Adams's house unsure how to proceed. Adams's grey sea has leaked into a dark night. Dark and rain-swept.

Because I'm in a mood to think, I start walking. And because I'm in Penarth, where Idris Prothero has his home, I decide I may as well drop by and have a snoop. Prothero: the owner of the place where Mark Mortimer worked and the business buddy of Brendan Rattigan.

I walk the six or seven minutes to Marine Parade, Prothero's street. I've already scanned the vehicles parked in his front drive – nothing of interest there – and I'm checking the rest of the street for the sake of completeness.

It's not a good night for it. Rain mixed with sleet and worse weather promised.

I'm wearing gloves and have to write in felt-tip pen, because it's the only thing that will mark the wet pages of my notebook. I'm trying to make notes, keep the notebook vaguely dry, and avoid getting too soaked myself. I do okay at all that, but it means I'm slow to notice a couple of guys on the street. Dark coats. Scarves. One in a woollen hat, one not. Close-cropped hair, the bare-headed one. They see me, stop, start moving along again, then stop and walk back.

I finish putting a registration number in my book, then look up, making proper eye contact.

'Hi,' I say.

The two men exchange glances. The shorter one – bare

head, slightly ginger, late thirties tough – speaks.

'You might not want to do that. People can get a bit funny about their privacy.'

'Yeah, and maybe you could fuck right off,' I suggest.

The taller man, the one who's been silent, enjoys that response. He smiles involuntarily and raises a hand to cover his mouth as though there's a law against smiling.

'Let me see that,' says the other guy, gesturing at my notebook. He has a Scots accent.

'Fuck off.'

I turn my back on them, or half-do. Take a few steps down the road to the next car. Ready to note down the next plate.

I get the number in my book, then turn.

The street is lit and is a reasonably well-populated residential street, but there's no one around, not even much traffic. Just the two men. Houses are set back from the road, so we might as well be in a dark wood or a deserted inner city alley for all the protection I've got.

I can hear Watkins's voice in my head. *Step away. Do not seek confrontation. Step away now.*

I hear Lev too. *Choose the fight you want, not the one they want. If you can't win, don't start. It's okay to say no. Sometime, is the only smart thing to do.* And he's right. He always is. Lev: my martial arts instructor, if you want to call him that, though the term diminishes him. He's not one of these fighting-as-meditation guys. He's strictly fighting-as-fighting.

I take a pace or two back. The two men take a pace or two forward. They exchange glances. Some hidden exchange of communication, I can't guess about what.

I continue to back away. Shove the book into my shoulder bag. Something drops as I withdraw my hand. A plastic-wrapped energy bar, I think. It splashes down onto the wet pavement. I don't bend to retrieve it. I don't want to make myself vulnerable. I back away another step, but hesitate, as though reluctant to part with whatever it was I'd dropped.

The taller guy, the one who's been silent, whispers something to his companion, and the mood seems to shift. Any threat seems to be vanishing. The shorter guy bends to pick up my energy bar. It is, I suppose, a gesture of peace.

Choose the fight you want, not the one they want. If you can't win, don't start.

Lev's words. Wise words.

I shift my body so that my weight falls over the ball of my leading foot, the left one. My heel comes just a little off the ground. Then I move. I bring my right leg round hard, lashing at the man's jaw. I make contact with the toe of my right foot. I'm wearing chunky winter boots. Designed for fashion, effective for combat. My toe strikes his jawline almost dead centre. Strikes it hard, smashing through bone.

I feel as much as see the man's head jerk back with the whiplash.

Feel as much as see the bone broken, the jaw sagging loose and useless from its socket.

The man sprawls backward on the tarmac, disbelieving eyes raised to the pelting rain. His companion gawps at the fallen man, gawps at me. No one says anything. No one cares about my energy bar now.

I reach into my bag. Grab something. Hold it up in the feeble orange glow of the streetlights.

'This is a rape alarm. If you fuckers, either of you, take one step closer, I'm going to let this off and tell everyone you tried to assault me.'

I move backward as I say this. Partly – mostly – to put more distance between me and them. But partly also because I don't want them to notice that it's not a rape alarm I'm holding, but a tube of deodorant.

I'm panting for breath as I talk. Nothing phony about the panting. Just nerves.

The guy whose jaw I've broken is staggering to his feet. Part of him is nakedly furious, wanting to finish this fight. The other part is bewildered. He keeps putting his hand to his jaw as though he can just slot it back into place, but pain drives his hand away. His face looks unmade. A waxwork in the process of collapse.

The taller guy restrains him, stops him doing anything, and already the energy is bleeding from the situation. I'm feeling safer already.

'Just so you know,' I say, 'I've been parking here and twice now someone has keyed my car. I wanted to know who, that's why I was looking at the number plates. I don't know who you are. I don't care who you are. Now I'm going to walk away and if either of you comes after me, I will let off this alarm and press charges for assault.'

I back away, until there are twenty yards between us, then turn and walk normally, but keeping constant watch over my shoulder. The two men stay where they are, until they too start walking, but away from me, not towards me. At the street corner I turn. There is nothing now ahead of me but sleet and parked cars and the sigh of the sea beyond.

I realise I'm shaking. Literally. Huge waves start in the soles of my feet and rise up through me. I bob on their surface like a boat at anchor.

My car is parked in the other direction. I'm not going back to get it. Buzz will bring me back to retrieve it tomorrow. I'll just have to concoct a sweetly plausible lie about how I came to leave it here.

I don't know Penarth all that well, but navigate toward the bright lights of Stanwell Road. When I get there, I find a guy waiting at a bus stop, sheltering from the rain.

I stand next to him, because it feels safer. I'm still shaking, but I think the waves have gone inside now, not visible.

'Hi,' I say.

'Hi.'

After a bit, he says, 'Are you all right?'

I say, 'I don't know.'

I want to ask him to punch me on the arm, to see if I can feel anything, but I don't.

He smiles and shifts his weight.

We stand there together until I see a taxi. I try to flag it down, but walk straight into the glass wall of the shelter instead. My bus-stop buddy does the honours, flags the taxi and sees me into it. He handles me as you'd handle a figurine of antique china.

When I get home, I start to run a bath, then get a joint from the shed.

While the bath is still running, I call the A&E department at Llandough Hospital in Penarth. I tell them I'm a police officer. Say we're looking for two men, one of whom sustained a broken jaw in an altercation. I use that word – *altercation* – wondering who would keep it alive if policemen and women didn't.

They tell me that there's no one in like that yet, but I leave my number. I turn the tap off, light my joint, and get into the warm water. Call University Hospital in Cardiff, the Morriston Hospital in Swansea, and every other hospital I can find in the semi-circle bounded by Bristol, Brecon and Camarthen.

Nothing. I get nothing. I finish my joint, the first I've had since Droitwich. My shaking is no more than a memory. I bruised my forehead on the wall of the bus shelter and I can feel a darkening circle of pain when I press it with my finger. Which is good. I'm okay, in touch with myself. I'm feeling my feelings. I press my bruise every minute or two for reassurance.

I drain the water.

Then, finally, get a call back. Bristol. Frenchay Hospital. Two men entered. One with a serious compound fracture to the jaw. He was seen immediately. An A&E nurse and junior doctor corrected the dislocation by simply thumbing the bone back into place, but prepared the patient for immediate surgery on the fracture. They placed a temporary bandage over the jaw to limit movement, then left to arrange the operation. When the nurse returned with the necessary consent paperwork, both men had vanished.

The patient had given his name as Neil Moggach, a name that will certainly prove to be false, and an address in Bristol which will be equally useless.

Damn.

Mostly I'm pleased with the way I handled things. I chose the fight I wanted, not the one they offered. My kick was good. My actions afterward rapid and well planned. Except for one thing. I'd assumed I'd be able to get at my targets in the hospital. I assumed I'd be able to get a pair of handcuffs on my guy in the post-op recovery room and interview him under caution. I'd probably have threatened him with some bullshit threatening-a-police-officer charge, which I'd never have been able to sustain but wouldn't have needed to. I'd have done enough to secure a verifiable ID, a registration plate, phone data, address. Not merely the guy I kicked but, quite possibly, his buddy too. It simply hadn't occurred to me that the injured man would simply walk into hospital, get bandaged up, and walk out again. How the hell is he even planning to eat?

I call Frenchay again, ask to speak to the relevant nurse and get her to look for any paper towels or bed coverings that might have gleaned a drop or two of blood. She promises to do what she can, but her voice tells we'll get nothing. I'll be able to secure CCTV footage from the admissions area, but I doubt if the images will be clear enough to secure a visual ID. I request the footage anyway.

It all sounds uncomfortably like a dead end, a tree without fruit, but somehow it doesn't feel that way.

I remember the cow, the leaning, the break.

When Buzz calls to chat – we always talk on the phone if we aren't spending the evening together – I'm talkative and warm and charming and flirty. I can almost feel the force of attraction that is making him fall in love with me, and I feel like a fraud. The worst girlfriend in the world, not the supergreat and perfect one I aspire to be.

What I ought to tell him is this:

'I'm only this nice because I've had a joint, smashed someone's jaw, and feel alive. When I walked into the bus shelter, it hurt and went on hurting, and in my crazy world that's good news. Beautiful news. The sort of thing that makes me want to flirt and have sex and make my lovely boyfriend fall in love with me. But I'm still a total disaster and sane boyfriends would be well advised to run a thousand miles. You, my dear Buzz, would be a million times happier with the kind of woman whose sense of adventure would be amply satisfied by baking a different type of cake.'

I ought to say that, but I don't. I just talk too much and remember the cow.

The leaning weight. The sudden break.

And jagged timber lances flashing in the sun.

17

The next day at work I can't tell anyone about the incident on Marine Parade. I'm no expert, but I'm fairly sure that the narrow minds of the Police Misconduct Panel would take a dim view of my jaw-smashing activities, particularly given the fact that I have a little history along those lines.

The Internet tells me that fixing a complex fracture of the jaw is a difficult business. Elastics are used to hold any loose teeth into place. Jaw wires are extended from the fractured bone to the line of teeth opposite, to provide stability during healing. The patient can eat only fluids and very soft foods for six to eight weeks following surgery. In days gone by, a broken jaw could often prove lethal, because you can't chew with a fractured jawbone.

The two men last night may not have been experts on these matters, but it's telling that they chose to drive an hour to get medical attention, when the nearest hospital was just a few minutes away. Telling that they gave a false ID. (I've checked it and it is.) Telling also that my victim chose to walk out of the hospital with nothing more than a bandage and a couple of paracetamol.

Trouble is, I'm not sure what to do next. I saw their faces, of course, but not for long and not in good light. Experience with e-fit technology places day-after accuracy at worse than twenty per cent. And in any case, e-fit technologies work when you have a suspect whose identity needs confirmation. I have nothing. No name, no phone, no address.

I tried running the various car numberplates I'd collected, but no joy, or no obvious joy. One car, a Mercedes, was rented by an Egyptian man, Mostafa el-Saadawi, at Heathrow Airport. Given the vague North African connections in the case so far, Saadawi's nationality rings some kind of bell, but not loudly. It's two thousand miles from Cairo to Casablanca.

On the other hand, Prothero does own Barry Precision, which does sell to North Africa, which could account for Saadawi's presence.

Or not.

My ignorance is boundless.

I don't even know why the hell the men were interested in me. Because I'd been talking to Adams? To Sophie Hinton? Or because I was on Prothero's street, looking into his front yard and collecting vehicle registrations? Or none of the above?

I don't know.

All this is a lot of ignorance, but it seems like a rich unknowing, not a poor one. Watkins's investigation has gathered lots of facts, but increasingly her orchard seems a barren one. It has neither buds nor flowers.

For example: Two more pieces of Langton have been found. A small plastic-wrapped bit of calf was found in yet another Cyncoed outbuilding. It was only found because the mother of the family concerned became worried about all the stories in the press, and organised a major clearout of her garden shed and bike store. She found a Tupperware box, hidden out of sight in the sloping roof of the shed. The box was filled with table salt, turned pink with blood, and a chunk of Mary Langton, about the size of two fists placed end to end.

The woman, Sian Phillips, used to be a primary school teacher, but now – with four active kids under fifteen – is a full-time parent, who works as a churchwarden at the local church. Her husband, Karl, works in local government finance. Neither of them seems like the slice-up-a-dancer type. Neither knew Elsie Williams, Ryan Humphrys, Arthur Price, or any of our other tremendously non-suspicious suspects. No connection with Langton either. The shed had no doors and was just a step or two away from the street, so anyone could have had access to it.

More weirdly still, a jam jar was found tucked into the spare tyre compartment of a Volkswagen Passat. The jamjar, which according to its label once contained 454 grams of Pembrokeshire honey, was now found to hold only vegetable oil and a thumb, speedily identified as Langton's. The Passat belonged to a garage mechanic, George Thomas. Thomas was Ryan Humphrys's regular garage guy, but the two men play in the same pub football team, declare themselves to be friends, and don't strike us as members of some body-part swap club. Thomas may once have handled an MOT on a car belonging to Elsie Williams, but only may have done, it would have been only the once, and the total fee was fifty pounds, which hardly suggests a transaction of any great moment to either party. Thomas also once fixed Arthur Price's lawnmower, or thought he had. No known connection to Langton.

It's the lack of any clear centre to the investigation which is freaking everybody. How do we even start to investigate?

The incident room wall now has 268 'people of interest.' The phone directory is back too, not as a joke, but as a practical resource. Stirfry/Abacus now has not one but two full time data managers. The investigation feels like it's teetering on the brink of failure.

You can feel Watkins's anger at the turn things have taken. She's like a volcano in some Nordic myth. Wreathed in smoke. Spitting fire. Concealing dragons.

I'm busy with these thoughts when the phone rings. It's Dad.

'Fi girl?' he bellows.

'Hello, Dad.'

'Morning, love, I've probably interrupted you in the middle of something important, have I? I expect you're applying the thumbscrews to some poor bugger right now.'

Dad is always like this when he calls me at work. Too loud, too jokey. That's part of the house style, of course, but it's also because he's uncomfortable with calling the station, knowing the lines are probably monitored. Old habits, dying hard.

It turns out he's calling to invite me and Buzz round to see his latest project. A city-centre bar. No pole dancers at this one – that market is saturated, Dad says – but a 1920s-themed American bar. It's a new game of his. He uses the recession to take short leases on good-quality properties at ridiculously low rates. Then he crates in some cheap junk from U.S. suppliers and, under low lighting, makes the place look great. Cocktails from £4.95. Imported beers from £3.25. If the Cardiff formula works, he'll roll the format out. Swansea, Bristol, Newport.

I check Buzz's availability. He's available. We tell Dad we'll meet him at the bar at six that evening.

I do my boring crap for Dunwoody, pester Frenchay Hospital until they get me some CCTV footage, then print off the best stills the footage yields. They're not much, but better than nothing.

A memo comes round, asking if anyone is interested in applying for the NPT Undercover Training and Assessment Course. I say yes. I don't know why.

At five-thirty Buzz comes by my desk.

'Ready?' he asks brightly, wanting me to be and knowing that I won't be.

'Almost,' I say.

I finish an email, look at the paper on my desk, then shove it into a drawer. I go to the Ladies to 'freshen up.' I never really do much there, but Buzz thinks that women need to undergo some mysterious completion process before they can go out for the evening, and I don't like to disappoint him. Bev Rowland's just leaving as I go in, so we chat for a couple of minutes.

Then I stare at my face in the mirror for a minute or two, wondering if it feels like mine. In Bram Stoker's *Dracula*, the dark count is invisible in mirrors and I often feel something similar is true of me too. I can't feel any deep relationship between the face that is mine and the person I am. Like they're two different things.

I don't know if this is something that everyone feels.

I put water on my face and wipe it off.

Then put the vaguest bit of makeup on. Lipgloss, mascara, blusher. I mostly don't buy my own makeup. I wait for my sister Kay to give me stuff for Christmas or birthdays, then either eke it out till she gives me some more, or buy exact replacements when the item in question runs out. Or, of course, just forget.

I put my hands on my hair and move it around a bit, wondering what I would do to it if I were Kay. Or sulky Sophie Hinton. Or the red-cheeked, cow-toothed Mary Langton, getting ready to spend an evening churning her hips around a pole.

Then I lose time and simply stand there doing nothing. When someone comes in, I remember what I'm supposed to be doing and go to find Buzz. It's 5:55.

He says, 'Done?'

I say, 'Done!'

He gives me one of those male expressions which says simultaneously: (A) you look great and it's going to be an immense pleasure to be with you this evening, and (B) what in *God's name* took you so long? I counter his look with a mysterious feminine smile of my own devising.

The bar is only a twenty-minute walk away and parking could be difficult, so we walk. After a couple of minutes, Buzz puts his arm around me and squeezes me in close. It's a gesture that moves me every time he does it. Like I'm not just being hooked in close to one large and well-proportioned male body, but like I'm being gathered back into the world of the living.

It makes me think of those astronauts dangling in space on the end of their tethering ropes. You think that those ropes are pipes feeding air to the space suit, but they're not. They're just ropes. If someone cut the rope or unhitched it from the spacecraft, the astronaut would be left dangling forever, hanging a thousand miles above the Earth, waiting to die. Buzz's enfolding arm brings me in from the void, through the airlock, back to the community of the human race.

I usually become girly and affectionate when I feel these things. I become that now.

The streets are dark. The shopping scrums are finished and the drinking scrums are yet to form. No rain. Buzz keeps on hugging me, shortening his steps so I don't have to gallop.

'Only twenty minutes late,' says Buzz as we get to the bar.

'Dad will be late anyway,' I say. I have my hand inside Buzz's jacket, feeling the flex of his pectorals.

'Well then, you won't mind if I put a parking ticket on that Range Rover.'

Buzz indicates a spot a little farther down the street, where Dad's big silver Range Rover is indeed illegally parked.

'I think you should give it lots of tickets,' I say. 'It would make Dad respect you.'

I nuzzle Buzz's shoulder with my head. He kisses and releases me, gently freeing himself from my hand.

We go inside.

Dad doesn't notice us straight away. The grand opening is in three days' time and the place is still a blizzard of sawdust and power tools. There are five workmen still on site. The place looks a long way from ready, but these last stages happen fast.

We stand and watch. The place is smaller than I'd realised. His pole-dancing clubs, the two of them I've seen, are big. Black, shiny, ugly things. Moneymaking machines. Turning girls into profit. Not prostitution, but it feels almost the same.

This place is classier, smaller, more intimate. It doesn't repel me.

Dad sees us and breaks into a huge smile. He comes over and has to introduce us to everyone.

'Kevin, you know David Brydon, do you? *Detective* Sergeant Brydon, no less. Make sure he doesn't see your bloody electrical work in that corner or you'll be doing time for attempted murder, eh? Murder by electrocution.'

He shouts, he introduces, he charms. He makes sure everyone knows that Buzz is a police officer, not, presumably, because anyone here is doing anything illegal but because Dad has never kicked his old habits. Disciplines of an earlier time.

We spend forty minutes admiring the bar. The place looks a mess but, seeing it through Dad's excited eyes, you can see how nice it'll become.

We end up in a room upstairs, furnished like an ordinary office, drinking Labatt's from the bottle. Or rather, Buzz and Dad do. I just fool around with my bottle and sip tiny bits of foam from the head.

'Keeping busy? That Mary Langton business, no further ahead on that, are you? Not that you can tell me, but what a horrible business, eh? Imagine that, if it was your daughter, imagine how you'd feel.'

I tell them both about going to see Langton's parents. I've told Buzz before, of course, but differently. I say how the mother cried. The father too.

'You know, I've always thought it was funny how we

112

never came across the girl. I mean, a girl like that in South Wales, you'd think she'd have shown up at our club once or twice.'

Buzz throws me a sharp look but I keep my face flat. He says, carefully, 'We interviewed your managers at the time. Inspected payroll records and so on.'

Dad says, 'Payroll! Trouble is, when you're the boss, you want everything to be done just so. Every box ticked. So you tell everyone you want it done right, but then, you know how it is, the minute your back is turned. A girl doesn't turn up when she's meant to. Someone has the flu. The night manager is short handed. What's he going to do? Probably make a few calls and pay someone under the table. I said all that to Emrys, in fact. Told him to ask around. They'll tell him stuff they'd never tell me.'

A thought strikes him.

'In fact, sod that, I'll call Em now. Think of that poor girl in someone's bloody freezer!'

He pulls out his phone and stomps off, incapable of making a phone call while sitting still. It must have been torture for him, the days before mobiles.

I smile at Buzz. He doesn't know how to read this. Is my dad genuine? Or is this all prearranged? He tries to get a clue from my expression, but my face is a smooth, clear wall of nothing.

After a few moments, Dad comes back in. 'Do you have photos? Of the girl? Mary?'

We say yes. Not on us, but we can call them up from anywhere with Internet access. Dad leaves again. Buzz and I talk about the bar downstairs for a couple of minutes, until he comes back. 'Let's go,' is all he says.

Downstairs and outside to the Range Rover.

Buzz in the front alongside Dad. Me in the back. Dad starts talking to Buzz about the Wales–Australia rugby match. We lost it apparently. There's another match against South Africa in a couple of days. Dad thinks we'll win. Buzz thinks we'll lose.

Dad and Buzz are both tall, big men. I am five foot two and hardly big. There's something about the scale of the car, the size of the two men in the front, and me all alone in the back which makes me feel about eight years old. Like I'm swinging my heels on the way to the beach while the grown-ups talk about grown-up things.

The city moves past the windows.

The rain has returned, but not much. Speckles on the windscreen. Buzz and Dad are talking about a rugby player called Jones. I listen in for a while, but there seem to be at least four different Joneses in question, which seems excessive, even by Welsh standards.

We leave town, or sort of leave town. Arrive in Saint Fagan's, a village which just about remains that rather than a mere suburb. Dad turns aggressively onto the Crofft-y-Genau Road, then right again when we get into the village. Buzz has stopped talking about rugby. Dad too.

He parks outside one of the houses. White stucco. Modern. Decent-sized garden. Garage.

'Rhys Jordan, one of my managers,' Dad tells us.

We all get out.

The rain softens the air. I feel it on my face and, for a moment, have no self-consciousness about it. I'm just someone feeling rain on my face and I like it.

Dad bangs on the door, rings the doorbell and shouts, 'Hello, Rhys?' He starts telling us that Jordan probably isn't in, although there are lights on inside and only a matter of seconds have passed since he started banging, ringing, and shouting. Then there's a shape behind the glass, and the door opens. Mid-forties. Black hair thinning on top. Dishevelled, but in a way that inclines toward handsome rather than

114

repellent. Rhys Jordan seems sleepy, but I suspect that's all part of the look.

He sees Dad and says, 'Oh, Tom, okay, do you want to –' but Dad doesn't need to be invited into places, he just needs an open door. We're already inside. The hall, then the living room. The living room is larger than I expect and looks all early seventies. A big, curvy orange sofa. A fake zebra skin. A gas fire. A couple of lava lamps. The look is so carefully retro, I imagine it's achingly hip. There's even a record player and a stack of vinyl by one of the lava lamps.

There's a woman on the sofa. Pale skin. Long black hair. Immaculately smooth, the way Welsh hair gets only with straighteners. Black sweater over black jeans. Jewellery and red nails.

'Corinne, isn't it?' says Dad, who never gets a name wrong. 'How are you, love? Rhys behaving himself, is he? You'll tell me if he doesn't. These two ruffians are police officers, would you believe? Detective Sergeant David Brydon, this one. That's Fiona, my daughter. You've met before, have you? You must have. No? That's terrible, Corinne, we must have you over. Look, sweetheart, be a dear, will you, and give us a few minutes? No problem, we just need to talk to Rhys.'

Corinne sways gracefully up from the sofa. She's going to go upstairs but a quick conference with hubby in the hall sends her out into the night. We see her vanishing down the garden path in a long coat, her hair wound up inside a woollen hat.

Dad looks at Jordan, who looks at Buzz first, then Dad. I don't exist, not in this duel of glances.

Dad says, 'Emrys has spoken to you, has he?'

Jordan: 'Yes.'

Then Dad, explosively: 'Fuck it, man! Why the bloody hell didn't you come clean? Years back. There's a dead girl involved here.'

'Look, Tom, we gave the police –'

'Don't give me crap. I never take crap.' Dad's eyes are blazing. He is either genuinely angry or giving a master class in how to act it. I can't tell. But Jordan is scared. Not pretending, the real thing. 'Fi girl, be a love, would you, and –'

But I'm already on the case. There was a laptop closed up beside the sofa. I'm booting it up, waiting for a Wi-Fi connection.

The computer processes slowly. Buzz watches the scene silently.

Then we get a connection. Jordan gives us the password. I log myself into the police portal and bring up photos of Mary Langton. Not the ones of her dead: the leg, the head, the other bits and pieces. I like those photos, the head shot especially, but my tastes aren't widely shared. I bring up the others.

Langton playing hockey. Langton at graduation. A family photo. The one of her at the party wearing her Shoes of Death. A couple of her swivelling around a pole.

Jordan nods.

'Yes,' he says. His voice is husky on his first attempt, then he clears his throat and repeats the word.

Buzz says, 'Are you able to identify this girl as a dancer at your club?'

'Yes. Or no, I'm not sure. Waitress probably.'

Dad nods, a micro-nod not intended for general consumption. I suspect he thinks Langton didn't have the physique required for a dancer in one of his clubs. Her plump hips would have been fine in a spangly miniskirt, her breasts would have nestled nicely in their cutaway bikini top. But that uniform was for the waitresses and bar staff. The dancers wore less and earned more.

Buzz goes back to his question. 'Can you confirm that you employed this girl, Mary Jane Langton, in some capacity – either waitress or dancer – at your club?'

'Yes. She wasn't employed, exactly. She was never on the payroll. But she was on our list of phone numbers to call if we were shorthanded. And ...'

And?

Buzz runs through the inevitable follow-up questions. I take notes as he does so.

How often would Langton have been employed on that basis? A couple of times a month, probably. She had a reputation for being a steady worker. Under pressure from Buzz, Jordan's 'a couple of times a month' changes to 'pretty often, I suppose.'

How was she paid? In cash, from the till. Payments weren't large, because waitresses could make up to £120 an evening in tips. On busy evenings, waitresses would be expected to work for tips alone.

Why was this information not disclosed to the police at the time of the original investigation? Because the payments were under the table. Jordan was worried about the taxman. Dad had to interject at this point, 'Fuck's sake, Rhys. A dead girl. A *dead* girl and you're worried about a stupid little tax thing.' An exchange of glances follows, which I can't read.

Back to Buzz. Over what period of time was Langton employed? Jordan offers us one answer – a few months – then corrects that to more like six – then says he doesn't know.

Dad asks him how he can find out. Jordan says he's not sure, then says there'll probably be a cashbook somewhere, so they can reconcile till takings to the electronic cash register. Then he says he's not sure if a book would still be around from so many years back. Dad gets antsy again and makes Jordan phone someone called Colin at the club. The person called Colin says he'll get straight back to us.

The room goes quiet.

Dad is still fuming. Buzz lets him fume. Outside, I see Corinne coming back, a dark shape gliding up to her own front door. I go to intercept her and we stand outside together.

'Is there a problem?' she asks.

'Not really. Rhys withheld some information from a murder investigation and we may want to give him a bollocking, but that's about the limit of it.'

She smiles. White teeth, red lips.

I ask her if she has a cigarette. She does. We stand there on her own front doorstep, smoking. I don't usually smoke tobacco, but it feels nice, this.

I ask her what she does. She says, 'Music production.' I don't know what that means, not really.

The phone rings inside the house. There's a conversation.

Corinne and I talk about what we're doing for Christmas. She and Rhys are going to her family in Merthyr. I say, 'Same here,' then have to explain my family isn't in Merthyr, but in Cardiff.

There's a crashing sound behind us. Dad yelling. Corinne and I are suddenly keenly aware that my father is furious at, what – her partner? her husband? – in the house behind us. An awkward silence. Corinne says, 'They say it's going to get a lot colder soon. Freezing, apparently.' I say, 'Really?'

They're finished inside. Rhys comes to the door, lets us in.

Dad is rolling his shoulders, eyes smouldering. Buzz stands aside, watching everything. We say goodbye.

Dad, Buzz, and I get into the Range Rover, head back into town.

'Where can I drop you?' says Dad. The first words since we left.

Buzz and I exchange looks. The three main choices: Buzz's flat, Cathays, or Dad's club. But it's no choice really.

'We'd better go to the Unicorn, interview people there. Sorry, Dad.'

'No, no. No sorries. You two have got a job to do.' He drives on in silence. The rain is back again, but more heavy

118

now. Welsh weather. 'Listen, I'm sorry I shouted.'

'That's okay,' says Buzz. 'You had every right.'

'Bloody traffic.' Dad mutters a little later, but before long we're at the Unicorn. *The Virgin and Unicorn*. A neon sign. The word *Virgin* in simpering pink, the word *Unicorn* in deep flesh red.

Buzz and I get out, say goodbye to Dad. He apologises again and drives off with a fierce sprayback from his rear tyres. My face can't feel or not feel the rain. It's already inside the club, with its girls, its cashbooks, and its secrets.

18

Later. Ten thirty in the evening. The rain gone and skies clearing.

Buzz and I leave the club. Only now is it starting to get busy. On the stage behind us, the first breasts and thighs are starting to appear, like stars emerging overhead.

It feels weird being here with Buzz. Knowing that he's a bloke. That his hormones are tugging him backwards into the bar behind us. I haven't looked down, but for all I know he's aroused. Why wouldn't he be? Why shouldn't he be? We walk out into the night, feeling weird.

Watkins is there waiting. Her silver-grey BMW, sleekly parked, sidelights on. The Ice Queen's face expresses no sign of her having seen us, but the car purrs into life and the side-lights switch to headlights.

Buzz gets in the front. I get the back again. The child's seat. Swinging my feet and thinking about ice cream.

We drive to Cathays.

Not much conversation. We've already briefed Watkins by phone. We'll have a proper debrief in her office. As we drive, she asks us to get Susan Konchesky to join us. It's an order, obviously, but first I do nothing, somehow assuming that Buzz will call her. But that's not the police way of things. I'm the junior officer in the car and anything boring is my job, anything interesting is someone else's. Buzz moves uncom-fortably in his seat. His way of reminding me to stick to the party line: We don't keep our relationship a secret, exactly, but nor do we do anything to advertise it. Him making the call instead of me would be an advertisement, albeit not a very big one.

So I jump to it. Find my phone, make the call. Tell Susan Konchesky that if she'd had any idea of having a nice evening, she could pretty much forget it. I don't put it quite like that, but I put it enough like that that Watkins's habitual air of grim annoyance thickens into something soupier.

Susan says, 'Okay, if I have to. Where are you now?'

I say, 'In a car, with DI Watkins.'

She says, 'You're joking,' but she can tell I'm not.

When we get to Cathays, Buzz, being a man, has to go and pee. Konchesky hasn't yet arrived. I find myself going to the kitchenette with Watkins to make coffee. While we're waiting for the kettle to boil, I put my hand out to feel the fabric of Watkins's suit sleeve.

'Sorry,' I say. 'Do you mind? It's lovely.'

If she does mind, it's too late. But she doesn't, or doesn't say she does. The kettle boils. Three coffees for everyone else, peppermint tea for me.

There's a stupid moment of awkwardness at the door as we're sorting out who picks up which mug and how we get out of the door without pouring boiling fluids over each other. Which is good. I've made Watkins the Badge nervous. A stupid triumph, but sometimes I enjoy stupid things.

To Watkins's office, with mugs. Buzz arrives, bladder nicely empty. Konchesky too, nervous, clutching paperwork.

All the lights are on. Ceiling tiles and that unblinking fluorescent glare. It feels wrong. Unsettling.

Watkins to Buzz: 'Okay, from the beginning.'

Buzz reports everything that happened. Or rather, he takes a series of life events and translates them into police-ese. 'The witness confirmed his identity as Rhys Jordan and that he has been employed as manager at the Virgin and Unicorn for a total of nine years.' He doesn't normally talk like a training manual, but everyone behaves weirdly in front of Watkins.

'When we got to the club, we spoke to Colin Jones, who produced the relevant cashbooks. We have them with us now. In the eight months before her death, Mary Langton received cash payments from the Unicorn on fifteen different occasions. Amounts ranging from twenty to eighty pounds.'

'Dates?'

I have a list of the dates in my notebook and pass them over.

'Susan?'

Konchesky has been doing a lot of the gruntwork on Khalifi. She's been back through his bank records for a full nine years. He was no saint. Numerous card transactions place him in clubs and bars. He's been more abstemious in recent years, but further back he appeared to have been out on the town most Friday and Saturday nights. She has the dates in front of her. Dates when Khalifi used his card in the Unicorn. None of those dates match the Langton ones.

Khalifi also used plenty of cash. He used to withdraw four hundred pounds at a time and spend it fairly rapidly. So perhaps he was in the Unicorn on one of those Langton nights, but spending cash. No suggestion that he was trying to keep himself invisible, just that he liked to use cash.

Watkins, Brydon, and Konchesky bend over the various lists and printouts trying to find a match. I lean away, wondering if it would be okay to turn off the overhead lights and just rely on the desk lamp. I don't like the brightness. The other three mutter to each other as they compare lists.

I say, 'Cash payments to Langton all fell on Tuesdays, Wednesdays, and Thursdays. The Thursday payments tended to be lower.'

Everyone looks at me.

I say, 'According to Jordan, the girls make most of their money from tips. I imagine waitresses worked for tips only on Fridays or Saturdays.'

They all look again at the lists. Langton drew no payments from late November to early January either, although she'd worked the autumn before and in the months immediately after. 'Christmas,' I say. 'More trade, bigger tips.'

Watkins looks up from the desk, staring at me. I don't look away.

She says, 'So, your hypothesis is that Langton was working for tips only on some of the nights that Khalifi was there?'

There's a prickling feeling in the room. A sense of movement or hidden life. I don't know why.

I say, 'Yes.'

Three heads bend back over the lists. Not mine. I'm trying to work out what this prickling sensation is. I can't. I try to understand the feeling. What bit of me is feeling what? I try to dissect my own sensations the way my psychiatrists once taught me to, but I don't get anywhere.

I say, 'Langton called her mam most nights.'

Watkins glares at me. A bit of jaw action, but not much. She pulls the phone records away from Susan Konchesky. The records list dates and times of calls. Langton used to call her mother briefly – a minute or two – then her mother would call back to save on the phone bill. Mostly Langton called fairly late – 9 or 10 PM mostly. On nights when Langton was working, she called much earlier, 6 or 7 PM, and spoke for less long. There were a number of Fridays and Saturdays over the right period when Khalifi was in the Unicorn and Langton was calling her mother early.

Watkins and the others have a bit of discussion about this. Langton was a student, so if she wasn't working on a Friday or Saturday, she was probably going out for the evening anyway.

Buzz says, 'Yes, but she wouldn't go out that early. A girl

like that wouldn't go out on the town until nine o'clock or whatever. It wouldn't have been cool.'

Buzz is a nice man, but he's about as cool as I am and I'm as cool as a lump of coal. Konchesky is a mother of two who works part-time. She's hardly got her finger on the pulse either, but she agrees with Buzz.

Watkins grabs all the paperwork now and bends over it, leaving nothing for the others. I'm fed up with the overlit room and turn all the lights off, except the spot directly over where Watkins is sitting. When she glares at me, I say 'Sorry,' but don't put the lights back on. It feels better now. The prickling feeling is still there, but not in a bad way.

'Isn't this nice?' I say to no one in particular. Everyone stares at me but no one says anything.

Then Watkins is done. It seems probable but not certain that Khalifi knew Langton. Watkins will arrange a full set of interviews in the morning. A load of DCs will be sent to talk to Langton's former colleagues at the Unicorn to see if any of them can connect her to Khalifi.

The meeting breaks up. Watkins says to Buzz and me, 'Good work, well done.'

Buzz says something. I nod and look like a Keen Young Detective.

In the street outside afterward, Buzz says, 'Are you okay?'
'Yes.'

'You'll be okay, driving?'
'Yes.'

'Not too fast, all right?'
'All right.'

'Back to mine?'
'Yes.'

I don't know why I'm talking like everyone's favourite village idiot, but it doesn't bother me and Buzz is used to it.

We go back to his place. I don't speed. I park neatly. We

go up to his flat. He has a glass of wine. I walk around the flat fiddling with light switches and being annoying. Then Buzz lifts me up, carries me over to the bedroom. I'm not quite in a head space for sex, but I pretend that I am. I fake it. Fake the moves, the noises. I TV-movie my way into a performance of some kind, and at some point the hormones take over and I do start to feel things. The TV-acting falls away and I become a bit more me again. When we're done, I say, 'Mmm. Thank you.'

He says, 'You're very welcome.' He's quite pleased with his sexual performance, is Mr David Brydon, but that's allowed.

'Do you think your dad was for real earlier?' he asks.

'I assume so. He seemed pretty angry.'

'I thought he was going to rip Jordan's head off.'

'Yeah, well, the old Dad might have.'

I'm lying. I'm pretty sure the whole thing was a show.

I think Dad knew from the very beginning of the original investigation that Langton had worked in his club. When the leg showed up in Cyncoed, he was aware of the possibility that the leg would turn out to be hers. That's why he changed my word 'Llanishen' to 'Cyncoed' on the phone that first night. His way of saying that he knew what he needed to know.

I don't, in fact, think that Dad has anything to hide, but if there had been any risks to his business, he would have known about them long before Watkins did. Known about them and dealt with them.

As it was, I assume Emrys spoke to Dad. They both spoke to Jordan. Checked the cash-books with Colin. Discussed possible risks to the business. Decided any risks could be controlled, so put on the entire play for our benefit. Yes, there might have been some minor tax issues arising from the way the business was run, but cops on a murder enquiry are hardly tax specialists, and if people give us good-quality information we'll overlook minor misdemeanours. I think the whole

Dad-'n'-Jordan show was aimed at ensuring that Dad was clean as clean in the eyes of the law.

Once again I'm awed by my father's dangerous competence.

I don't say any of this, however. But I do come in for some stick from Brydon for my Mortimer theory. He says, 'Looks like that one might get laid to rest.'

I don't feel like talking about that now, so I just say, 'Did you say "get laid"?' and I run my hand down his stomach until I'm all out of stomach.

He keeps my hand where it is and we fall asleep like that. Lights off. Listening to the city being the city.

But I can still feel that prickling feeling from before. That sense of something hidden.

And when I started to investigate Mark Mortimer, two men became overinterested in where I was and what I was doing. When I put one of them in hospital, he gave a false name and address and walked out as soon as he could.

As far as I'm concerned, the Mortimer connection is still live.

19

Next morning, a Saturday, I sleep in until Buzz wakes me. Back from a run, sweaty T-shirt off, shorts still on. He looks yummy, in a rough-and-tumble kind of way. I watch him getting into the shower, then watch him more as he gets out. He knows I'm watching, makes the most of it. Sits on the bed naked and lets me bite him on the back of his neck, which is both salty and soapy.

When we're done fooling around, he tells me that there's fresh juice, bacon, eggs, everything in the fridge. He's already eaten.

'You're off already?' I remember he has some family shindig today, but thought it wasn't till later.

He gives me a crooked smile. 'Watkins. She wants to work this angle. She's got me, Konchesky, couple of others coming in today.'

The news surprises me, then bothers me. As far as Watkins is concerned, the glory of the Rhys Jordan breakthrough belongs equally to me and Buzz. As far as reality is concerned, of course, the glory is shared between a triumvirate of me, Emrys, and Dad. But by ordinary police logic, Watkins ought at least to have offered me the chance to join the inner team. That's surely what yesterday was about.

I know why I'm being ditched. Watkins the Badge has an icily tedious adherence to the rules. My father owns the club where Mary Langton might or might not have met Ali

127

el-Khalifi in the months before her death. If that connection turns out to have a bearing on the case, I may have to appear as a witness in court. A defence lawyer could make merry play of some potential conflict of interest between me, my father, and the police investigation, so Watkins is keeping me well away from the epicentre. That strikes me as wildly unfair, though I also know that Watkins is making the right call.

Dammit.

'Lucky you,' I say, trying not to let my feelings show. 'A Saturday love-in with Watkins. Every girl's dream.'

'What have you got on today?'

Buzz, the sweet foolish man, has this delusional belief that if he speaks to me evenly and chirpily, I'm suddenly going to turn normal on him. That one day, I'll suddenly want to fill my life with trips to the shops, visits to friends, and a little light home decoration. I honestly think that his joy will only be complete when one day he returns from a hockey match to find that I've baked a new kind of pudding and have bought an Interesting China Ornament for the flat.

I blink at him, instead of answering. I don't know what to say.

He does a thing with his face which is hard to interpret exactly, but is his way of nudging me to give an answer that's more complete than just blinking.

So I say, 'I'm over to my family for a late brunch, then probably go shopping with Kay.'

He says, 'Brilliant. That sounds really nice.'

Most men saying that would sound sarcastic, but Buzz just sounds like Buzz. First he waits for me to get out of bed, so I can kiss him off at the door, then he realises that I'm not getting out of bed, so he kisses me where I am.

'Have a good day,' I say. 'Don't let Watkins pinch your bum.'

He goes.

The flat is empty. *His* flat.

I do get out of bed now and fidget around, getting dressed slowly. I swing open the fridge door. It's full of lovely food, very little of which I had any hand in acquiring and almost none of which is covered in interesting colours of mould. I don't eat anything, just poke the packet of bacon, then swing the door shut.

We don't have a mantelpiece, because the flat is too modern to have a fireplace, but there is a cupboard-cum-display-unit which could probably bear the weight of an Interesting China Ornament. Buzz has some photos there. Framed. A couple of us. Some of his family. One of him in his paratrooper's uniform. He looks the same, but younger. I shift the photos around a bit, then move them back again.

When I'm dressed, I leave the flat and drive over to my mam and dad's. No reason to, except I said to Buzz that that's what I would do, so doing it seems easier than anything else.

I get there not long after nine. Mam is already up, dressed, hair done, fussing. My younger sister, Ant-short-for-Antonia, is hanging over the kitchen counter protesting against some familial injustice or another. Dad's still sleeping. Kay's not downstairs yet, but I can hear her padding around upstairs and she yells down a greeting.

I arbitrate the Ant–Mam dispute, by telling Mam it's a special occasion because I'm there, so Ant should be allowed to have her way. Ant accepts that gleefully and I get a special hug. Mam accepts it with a sigh and a headshake.

She asks me if I've eaten and I say yes and so she only gives me orange juice and a croissant, taken from a packet and heated in a microwave.

Ant tells me about school.

Mam says have I heard, it's going to get cold, and I tell her yes, I've heard.

Kay comes downstairs, gets breakfast. She's tall and skinny

129

and has a way of dressing that looks completely casual but hopelessly sexy. Today, a chunky jumper over leggings and boots, which doesn't sound like much, but it's the way she wears it.

She asks me what I'm up to. I say we could go shopping if she likes. She says yes. Ant asks to come too and we say no, but say it nicely.

There's a bit more hubbub. Clamorous, intimate family stuff. Somewhere along the way, Dad gets woken up and he comes downstairs in his dressing gown, looking like a bear with its hair fluffed up. I give him a kiss and fluff his hair up some more.

Tea, coffee, more juice, more croissants. Bacon and egg for Dad. Everyone talks and everyone at least half-listens.

Dad says, 'Was it all okay yesterday?'

I say, 'Yes, there'll be more interviewing today, but no one's worried about a few cash payments here and there.'

Dad nods, changes the subject.

Then Kay and I really do go shopping.

We drive. Kay likes it when I drive fast, but there's too much traffic for any real speed. It's too cold for us to have the top down, which she also likes. We leave the car in a car park on Dumfries Place.

'Where do you want to go?' says Kay.

'I don't know,' I say. 'Maybe Gap.'

That's what I always say. Sometimes Gap. Sometimes Next. Sometimes if I'm feeling really unsure of myself I say M&S.

She makes a face at me, but that's okay. We go to Gap, the one in Saint David's. I stand in the middle of the shopping floor, surrounded by beige things.

I think of Mary Langton's head. The feel of it in my hands. The look of it, as it rose grinning from the oil barrel. The large round pebble in its mouth. The sound of that pebble as it moved against Langton's teeth: an oily clacking.

'What do you want?' asks Kay. I wouldn't say that she's patient with me, exactly, but she's tolerant. Good enough.

'I don't know. Not this anyway.'

'What kind of things? Office wear? Casual? Or you know it's going to be Christmas soon. Do you even have any party dresses?'

I think of Khalifi's grey lung bobbing on the last puddles of the Llanishen Reservoir. A Labrador retriever running over the grass with Khalifi's liver slopping from its mouth.

The prickling I felt yesterday is back, but clearer, better than before.

'Um, maybe I'll just browse. Is there anything you want?'

This is our deal. Half the reason why Kay comes shopping with me. She puts up with me. I buy her stuff.

We leave Gap and go to Howells, the department store. The streets are November streets, not yet Christmas ones. Everyone's bundled in jeans, boots, and warm anoraks. The coffee shops are standing room only.

In Howells, I hang back and watch Kay go at it. This is her territory. She understands shops the way I understand mortuaries. As I trail round after her, I see that Hobbs has an in-store concession – I hadn't known – and I say, 'Oh, look, Hobbs.'

She fastens onto that. 'Hobbs? Okay then.'

That's the other reason Kay shops with me. She likes the creativity of it. The challenge of turning me into someone who doesn't just buy beige things from Gap. And she's good. Mostly people want to turn you into someone who looks like them, only worse. Kay isn't like that. I rely on her.

She shuffles through racks, holds clothes up against me, discards most, retains some. I try to play my part. Really try. Give it steady, focused thought. But I never know what I'm doing. After a while, Kay has found three things she wants me

131

to try on. I've found one, a blue dress that I picked more or less at random.

She looks at my offering, says, 'Mmm,' but takes the plus-size item I've got in my hand and replaces it with the same thing, but in my size. 'It's a bit safe,' she admonishes.

I try things on and each time walk out of the changing room, arms stuck out like a ten-year-old boy being good for his mam.

'God's sake!' she mutters, plucking and tweaking me into shape. 'What do you think?' Before I can say, 'I don't know,' she says something which is, in my view, an insight of staggering genius. 'Don't think about what you look like,' she tells me. 'Just imagine the person in the mirror is someone completely different. Someone you're watching on a stakeout or whatever.'

We don't have so many stakeouts in Cardiff. No guys with guns, pint bottles of bourbon, and dubious attitudes to police violence. But I know what Kay means. And she's right. If I try to figure out whether I like something for me, I have no idea at all. I just see a woman with her arms stuck out like a ten-year-old. If I switch the question, detach myself completely from the person in the mirror, it becomes instantly simpler. I still don't have a like-it/don't-like-it response, but I can at least figure out what I'm looking at. For a wonderful five minutes, I feel something close to normal: a girl going shopping with her sister.

I try everything on. The star of the bunch is a dark grey suit. Woollen. Knee-length skirt. Jacket. It sounds super-safe – the sort of refuge clothing I usually buy – but working on the someone-completely-different principle, I see beyond that. The suit is sharp. Stylish.

'It's really good,' says Kay. 'Half sexy secretary, half woman of mystery.'

I don't know that I want to be either of those things, but

it feels like an excitingly bold idea that buying new clothes can make me into something that I wasn't before. I wonder if that's why other people shop.

The suit is screamingly expensive. A hundred quid for the skirt and almost two hundred for the jacket, but I buy them anyway. Dazed, but in a good way, I end up spending another £135 on stuff for Kay. She does a little skip of excitement as we leave the shop and says, emphatically, 'Fab.'

She's meeting friends in a coffee shop, so we part company there and I go back to the car. Put the Hobbs bag on the passenger seat. I doubt I'll ever wear the clothes inside, but that's not the point.

Buzz sometimes thinks I'm extravagant, but I'm not really. I hardly ever buy clothes, take vacations, or go out. I'm not even very good at buying the basics: food, cleaning stuff, anything at all. But when I do spend money, I'm rubbish at calibrating my purchases. I don't have any sense of value. I just pick something up and pay for it. Mostly that'll be some awful budget item from Lidl. Sometimes it'll be something ridiculous from Hobbs. I don't often run out of money and when I do I just eat muesli until my pay cheque comes in. I stay alive.

Meantime, Buzz and Watkins and Susan Konchesky are hunting for a connection between Khalifi and Mary Langton. A connection that I brought them.

But what's their theory?

Khalifi could have met Mary Langton at the Unicorn and they could have had some sex thing that went wrong. But then what? He decides to chop her into pieces (but why?), deposits her in various freezers and outbuildings around Cyncoed (but why?), then lives happily for five years until someone decides to take revenge by chopping him into a thousand pieces and leaving his lung bobbing on a grey and empty lake surrounded by toads, slowworms, and waxcap fungi.

The story makes a wearisome sort of sense, but falls apart

at the seams. Khalifi seems to me too sane to be a person-chopper-upper. I mean, no one is too sane to be a murderer, we could all be that, but you've got to be a fairly committed nutter to slice-'n'-dice with such happy abandon. That's not the worst part of the story, though. The bit that makes no sense is the revenge killing. Who took the revenge? Rosemary Langton, Mary's mam? Her solicitor husband with the collapsing face? The Langtons have a twenty-three-year-old son who has been more keenly investigated now than would have been the case seven years ago, but still. I remember the beige carpets and the willow tree in the garden. Some families just give off a choppy-uppy odour. Others don't. This one didn't.

Which leaves me back with Ali el-Khalifi. He of the mobile face and the glide-rail know-how. I've had my head too full of Langton and Mortimer to give Khalifi proper attention, and it's time to put that right. I want to know him better. There's a way in which police work stops you doing that, but I've got all weekend now.

I slip the car into gear and leave the car-park.

Sexy secretary. Woman of mystery.

20

First stop: Llanishen. I'm not looking for clues. It's atmosphere I want.

Because of the way this enquiry started – because I found her leg, her lovely, lovely head – Mary Langton feels vibrant and alive. She sings to me. Yet the blunt, objective truth is that Langton, poor girl, was really too boring to end her life distributed across a number of suburban outbuildings. The cow teeth and the hockey should have won out over the pole dancing. She isn't, on the face of it, the sort of victim that most attracts me.

Khalifi's different. In a way, that displaced, clever, well-connected womaniser should have piqued my interest from the very first. I should have attached to him at least as much as I did to Langton, yet he's still nothing more to me than a couple of photos and a pathologist's report.

It's time to get to know him, and I'm starting here. With the reservoir. Vacant and almost hostile. Empty of water. Empty of purpose. Clouds racing fast overhead and enough cold in the wind to feel like a threat.

I drift around, just getting a feel for the place. The fenced-off, empty lake. The rough ground around it. The dog walkers.

A good place to die, this. To lie spread out, under the wind.

The prickle I felt yesterday has settled in now. It has a feel of permanence.

135

When I get too cold to stay longer, I go back to my car and drive to the dead man's flat. A two-bedroom penthouse on Ferry Road down by the bay. Value, around half a million pounds. Half a million is a lot more than a lecturer could afford, but Khalifi bought early, when prices were lower, and he did plenty of consultancy work for private-sector firms. Overall, there doesn't seem to be any huge discrepancy between his incomings and his outgoings.

It's easy enough getting into the building: there are people coming out as I enter. The flat itself is locked.

I try knocking at the door in case there's still any SOCO activity there. Try neighbours in case any of them has a key. End up having to rouse up someone from building maintenance. Produce my warrant, sign a book, get the key. I'd prefer not to have done that, because Watkins will be angry if she learns. But she probably won't learn.

Back to the flat.

The apartment is all about the emptiness. There's a huge east-facing balcony opening onto the bay. The same grey light that Adams had. The same changeless change. Except that Khalifi has the city version of this view: the marina, the Assembly building, the patches of muddy green. Cardiff's version of an esplanade.

There is something addictive about the view, but not necessarily in a good way. Self-harm: that's addictive too.

The interior boasts blond wood floors in kitchen and living room. White walls. White kitchen units with a shiny black work surface. One wall – would an estate agent call it a feature wall? – is lined with an expensive designer-looking wallpaper that has a silky finish. Perhaps it is silk. But I doubt if Khalifi chose it. I bet it came with the flat. His own taste seems timidly restrained to a few obvious choices. A few Moroccan things: tiles, rug, photos, a framed print of some fort or other. And some engineering stuff. A cubic sculpture

136

made of interlocking pieces of highly machined metals. Half curiosity, half art object.

It's hard to find the human in this room. I move around changing the position of things, for no reason except to make a mark. The only thing that really feels personal – sentimental even – is a small wooden sail boat with heart-shaped sails cut from white-painted metal. It sits in a little alcove with a garland of fairy lights. Its lack of stylishness is almost its best feature. Like he temporarily forgot about being cool, forgot about wanting to impress.

I think of myself inhabiting the space in that Hobbs outfit. Clicking round in heels.

A woman of mystery.

I'd carry a slim pearl-handled pistol and take secret lovers.

I wonder where Buzz is. What he's found.

The bedroom offers me more. It's flash. Not in a clever way, but in a touchingly crass one. Giant bed. White duvet. A purple silk throw. Blue and red silk scatter cushions. Some expensive clothes. A large mirror and twin mirrored side-tables. In the bathroom: more of the same. The fixtures are all modern, glitzy, posh. But it's those other touches that delight me. The leather shaving set with the badger-hair brush. The bottles of body lotion from Penhaligon's. Monogrammed towels.

I run the brush against my cheek. Smell the lotion, feel the towels.

My colleagues, whom I respect and adore, neglect this kind of evidence, because it's not court-worthy. Because you can't photograph it, or tabulate it, or put it into an evidence bag. But it's solid gold all the same. There is a packet of Fetherlite condoms in the mirrored cabinet. The whole place is very tidy.

I spend an hour or two just kicking around the apartment, then leave. Hand back the key. Sign out.

I know what I'm doing now. I'm on the scent.

Khalifi had a female colleague, Jenny Harrison. About my age. Attractive. One of my colleagues interviewed her in the normal way and came up with normal answers. I've got a pile of paper somewhere that has a mugshot of her and an interview report sheet.

But normal isn't always the right approach.

I don't have her address but drive round to the university, show my warrant card, and force some poor receptionist to give it to me. She gives me an address on Ton-Yr-Ywen Avenue, just off the Maes-y-Coed Road. I drive up there as fast as I can, keeping an eye out for cameras on the North Road.

Harrison's address. Modern house. Bland as a shoebox and as functional.

I knock. She's in.

Brown hair. Blue eyes. Nice eyes, actually. Friendly. Jeans, boots, jumper. Some jewellery. She's every bit as pretty as her photo, maybe prettier. Also pregnant. And, after introducing myself, I ask the obvious question.

'Six months,' she says. 'It's our first.'

I don't know who the 'our' is, but I don't care. We sit down in the kitchen. Postcards stuck to the fridge. A loaf of bread proving on a countertop.

'Ali el-Khalifi,' I say. 'You and him.'

'There wasn't really a me and him. And it was ages ago.'

'I know.'

'It's not … I mean, I'm sure there's no connection between *that* and… you know.'

People are so stupid. Sweetly, irritatingly stupid. Of course there's no connection between gentle, pregnant Jenny and whoever danced around Llanishen scattering Khalifi's body parts. But that makes her an ideal witness.

I nudge her for her story and she tells it.

It was five years ago. She was fairly new in the department,

Khalifi a well-respected lecturer. He was very charming to her, very attentive. She knew that he had an agenda, of course, and 'well, put it this way, I never thought Ali was the settle-down-and-get-married type.' He invited her out one evening. She said yes. He took her somewhere expensive, ordered champagne. They ended back at his place.

'Back at his place. Meaning?'

'Well, not *that*, no. But I did go up there.'

'So you must have thought about it? Having sex with him. You wouldn't have gone back there unless you'd thought there was a possibility.'

'Yes.' Gentle Jenny has a grounded quality that's nice to be around. It makes her a steady witness too. 'I think I was curious. I wanted to see him in action. Wanted to see his place. And, you know, I was a bit drunk. A tiny bit flattered. New in town and all that. I'm not the one-night stand sort of girl, really, but – well, you're right, I was interested enough to go back with him.'

'Did he pressure you? Was there any intimidation involved? Even that creepy sort that hovers in the background but isn't definite enough to put your finger on?'

She laughs. She knows what I mean, which is more than I do. I'd miss any creepy background intimidation until someone groped my breast and I found myself displacing their kneecaps and bursting their testicles.

But that's another story.

Jenny says, 'No. I mean, there was the champagne, the nice restaurant, the BMW he picked me up in. You can call that "pressure" if you like, but not intimidation. No way.'

'And in the apartment? You get up there, and . . .?'

I can see it. The big, expensive view over the bay. Lights set to moody. Mozart on the stereo. More champagne. The place was a shag pad. A single man's idea of every single woman's dream. Gentle Jenny gives the lie to that. She's got what most women want: an ordinary house on an ordinary street. A good job, a steady husband. Bread rising on the sideboard and a bun in her oven.

'As soon as I got up there, it felt wrong. I mean –' She wrinkles her face. It's a look that manages to be compassionate and patronising at the same time. 'You know, he tried hard. It was quite sweet really. That's almost what made it feel wrong, the trying. I think he wanted me to be something I wasn't. Like he wanted me to be wearing Manolo Blahniks and was disappointed when I said I got my stuff on sale at Dorothy Perkins.'

We laugh. Share a female-bonding moment.

She resumes, saying, 'I sobered up pretty quickly, said sorry, I wasn't ready, and got out of there. He was okay with it. I mean, I *think* he was.'

She wrinkles her face again. The same expression. She'll have a wrinkly baby, I reckon.

'If you'd gone ahead and had sex, did you get any sense that the sex would have been weird in any way?'

'No.' She answers that too quickly and I make her think again and take longer to answer. She still says, 'No.' Our search of the apartment found nothing obviously kinky.

'Was there a moment, even a brief one, where you felt threatened, especially when you said you were going?'

'No, definitely not. We kissed goodbye.'

'Drugs? Did he offer you anything? A party drug, I mean. A line of coke? Ecstasy?'

'No.'

More hesitation now, which I like. 'But you're not that kind of girl, are you?' I say.

'Put it this way, I think if I'd been a different sort of girl, there might have been more exotic fare available. Looking back on it, I think he was anxious. Anxious to score, anxious what I thought of him. He tried really hard. I don't just mean in a dirty-old-man way, but in general. Working for the department. Getting his consultancy work. Dating women.'

Forensics have done the basics on the flat, but drugs were never their principal focus. They'd have been looking for signs of struggle, traces of blood, any DNA. They'll probably have swabbed the toilet cistern in the bathroom as standard, but that's not where Khalifi would have snorted his coke. He'd have done it straight from the shiny black worktops in the open-plan kitchen/living room. Mozart playing and the champagne cooling. A woman there to admire it all.

The worktop on the island unit wasn't in one piece. There were two pieces, butted together with some black silicone-type material in the join.

'The thing about Ali,' she says, 'is he never quite felt like he fit in. I mean, he did. In reality, he truly did. He was British much more than he was anything else. I don't think anyone treated him differently because he had Moroccan origins. But I think he tried extra hard to compensate. Maybe he'd have done better if he'd been more relaxed about it.'

I nod, but also notice that she said 'British,' not 'Welsh.' Cardiff is multicultural enough, but it's not London. I think of Khalifi's flat. His consultancy work. All that departmental diligence. All that effort, and what he really needed was Welsh skin, a stocky build, and a deep knowledge of the oval ball.

We talk a bit more, but Gentle Jenny doesn't have much more to offer. She sees me out.

'Look,' she says, 'can I just ask? I never told anyone about that night with Ali. It just seemed better to let it go. I know maybe you can't say, but I'd love to know …'

Sweetly stupid.

'He was career-minded,' I say. 'He knew not to try it on with students. These days, that would get him fired. But you? You were new, young, pretty – you were fair game. He seems to have been reasonably compulsive where women were concerned. I just wanted to understand his game plan. How he operated.'

Jenny nods. Almost blushes. Makes a little movement that intrigues me: tossing her head back and simultaneously flicking her hair aside with her hand. As though correcting herself. Like some old-time maiden who'd been caught with her garter loose or an ankle flashing free of her petticoats. I try to read the look in more detail, but it escapes me. I don't think it matters.

A moment later, the door is closed. I'm alone.

I go to my car, get in, call forensics. Tell them to get someone to reswab the kitchen on Monday. The silicone join. They agree to do it.

Not that it matters.

I ought really to write up notes of this interview and get them on the system. But that means telling Watkins what I've done and she'd probably be pissed off at me for going off-piste. So I won't do the write-up. Which is okay, I think. Gentle Jenny hasn't given me evidence that will help in the courtroom or the police enquiry. She's just given me a glimpse of Khalifi. A chance to get closer.

I lean back in the car seat. Allow myself to think of Langton's head. The dripping hair. The clack of the pebble.

Try to picture Khalifi. Try to find him. But get nothing. Just that prickle.

The Khalifi prickle.

There is almost no movement on the street. Down the road from me, a fat woman is loading plastic bags into an old red car. I can hear piano scales being practised indoors somewhere. Soft notes, laid over the hum of traffic.

I know what happens next, what I need to do.

When I dissociate – when I lose all feeling in my body and can't tell what's happening with my emotions – there is normally a kind of upward-spiral thing that happens first.

142

As though my soul is escaping upwards through my head. I think that's why people with out-of-body experiences so often report themselves as floating above the room, not peering up at it from below. It's why normal people sometimes call themselves dizzy, or ungrounded, or say they have their head in the clouds. Those normal people never go where I go, never experience what I experience, but it shows that our paths to dissociation are the same. The sensation is universal, even if I've carried it further than most.

I have it now.

A kind of heady uppiness. That phrasing makes it sound upbeat, even euphoric, and it can be like that at times. But not now. What I have is just a grey, upwards draining. I'm not scared by it. I don't have any feelings about it at all.

I do my breathing exercises, because I've drilled myself into doing them, no matter what, but the exercises help only when you're lost in the foothills. It's too late for that now, for me.

I'm past the treeline and heading up.

21

Home.

Bath.

A joint. A full, fat, long one. Weed normally helps me to settle, but it doesn't now. Or maybe it does. I'm too numb to know.

I call Buzz, not because I want to, but because I know we'll have to talk sometime this evening, and I don't trust myself to do it later. We have a short, stupid conversation, but I don't think Buzz notices anything. I hope not. I don't want to scare him. He shouldn't be scared.

We ring off and I'm alone.

I text Watkins. I write, DAD SAYS DO I WANT TO COME AND CHAT WITH UNICORN STAFF ON SEMIOFFICIAL BASIS. OK?

I get a text back two minutes later: 'OK'. Nothing else. But it's enough.

I'm not frightened.

Observing myself, I'm almost pissed off at my own reaction. Fuck's sake, woman, what are you worried about?

Physical safety? Not an issue. Sexual safety? Ditto, almost certainly, and in any case it's not as though I'm some dainty Victorian flower. So it comes down to what it always comes down to with me: psychic safety. And even here, I feel the same thing: Fuck's sake, woman, get a grip.

Because, curiously, I know all this is temporary. This time tomorrow, I'll be fine. As fine as I ever am.

I even realise that I've long known it was going to come to this. That first night, in the office, the one with the fireflies and the dead girl's shoes, when I made the call to Dad. Did I really not know then that it would come to this?

The bath goes cold.

It takes me time to notice. I have to concentrate hard to figure it out. Put my hand under the cold tap, the hot tap, and back into the bathwater. I used to think my senses just went numb, but it's not that. They're still doing their job. Diligently reporting their information. Presenting their little manila packets of facts and data. But the management staff are all away on leave somewhere. I'm like the last guy left in corporate HQ desperately trying all the phones and getting no more than a fading crackle and an echo of laughter from somewhere sandy.

Anyway. I figure it out. The bath is cold. I ought to run it hot again to warm myself up, but I know that I won't be able to tell the difference between warm and scalding, so I just get out.

Towel dry.

Underwear on.

My hair. I know that hair can sometimes be wet, sometimes dry. If it's wet, you have to make it dry. I don't know why that's so important, I just try to follow the rules. It's quite hard to tell, though. I think my hair is dry, but maybe a bit steamed up, and I don't know if that makes it wet or dry.

If Buzz were here, he could tell me. But if Buzz were here, he wouldn't let me do what I'm about to do. And anyway, he's not here.

I decide to dry my hair. I don't think you can make hair too dry.

A clock tells me the time. Upstairs, I only have analogue clocks, the sort with hands. I find those harder to read when I'm like, this, so I go downstairs where there is a friendly

145

green digital clock on my oven door. It says 19:15. I look at it for a while. It's nice. Then it says 19:23. A bit after that it says 19:51.

Then I go upstairs.

Usually I choose safe clothes when I'm in this place. Easy ones that aren't complicated to understand or wear, but those won't work now. I need a dress. I take three dresses from Kay – her castoffs – and put them on the bed. I've never worn any of them.

I take the middle one and put it on. Look at myself in the mirror. No, that's wrong. Not myself. I have to imagine the person in the mirror is someone completely different. I don't quite manage that, but I can tell I look more normal than I feel.

I sit down on the bed and try to remember what happens next.

Shoes. I need shoes.

I don't like putting them on, but I manage. I ought to put makeup on too, but all I have is a few disconnected words and phrases. 'Eyeliner.' 'Lip gloss.' 'Mascara.' 'Blusher.' There are some things on a bathroom shelf and there are some words in my head. I wait around to see if anything joins up, but it doesn't. Then I see a tube of lipstick and my mind goes 'lipstick!' and I know what I'm supposed to do with it, so I make my lips go red. I wait a bit more, but nothing else joins up, so I leave all the rest.

The person-in-the-mirror still looks reasonably normal, I think, though I can't be too sure. Normal enough.

I still don't like the shoes.

Downstairs, the clock on the oven says 21:38.

I spend some time looking for my car keys, then decide that maybe driving isn't a brilliant idea. So I get the phone and a card with the number of a taxi firm on it. The number seems quite long, but I manage it by dividing it up into slices of one number at a time. I'm quite pleased with myself when a man answers. I ask for a taxi. He says, 'Right away?', and I say, 'Oh no, in a minute will be fine,' and hang up. Then the phone rings and it's the man again, asking for an address. I give him my address and put the phone on the floor in the corner, because it made me jump when it rang.

I sit there waiting. Watching the phone in case it rings, watching the nice green clock on the oven door.

22:18.

I'm not frightened.

I don't know why I'm like this.

I know that it's a good idea to connect with people when I'm in this state, so I try to think of the people I love. I can only think of three. My dad, Buzz, and Mary Langton's head. I know that's not a very good list, but it's a start.

Dad. Buzz. Mary Langton.

I count them off, one after the other. After a bit I manage to add Mam, Kay, and Ant. They're blurry, but they're there.

Outside, a car swings up in front of the house. Headlights on. The doorbell rings. There is a wooden knife rack on the counter containing six knives, at least four of which would make effective weapons, but I decide the doorbell man is probably the same as the taxi man, so I decide it's safe. I leave the knives, answer the door. It is the taxi man.

I'm about to walk straight out, when he says, 'Don't you want a coat, love? It's freezing.'

I go back and get a coat and also remember that I hadn't got house keys, money, bank cards, phone, or bag, so I get those things too.

I get in the car, which is nice and warm. He asks me where I want to go and I tell him. The name of the street, not the name of the place. He says, 'Right you are,' and off we go.

His car seems very clean. It smells like bubble bath. The streets slide by very easily. Croescadarn. Pentwyn. Eastern

Avenue. There is no noise except that his radio talks quietly all the way.

The world outside looks like a film of itself.

When we arrive, the man says, 'Have a good evening, okay?' and I say, 'I will.'

22

I'm outside it now.

It. The club. Dad's beast. His first real step into the world of legitimate business.

I've been inside only three times in my life. The first time, when Dad first set it up, when it was still at the sawdust-and-paintbucket stage. The second time was when I had just passed my driving test and I swung by to surprise Dad with the news. I entered the club at around eight in the evening, well before the place was busy. I found Dad, told him my news, and we were out on the street again within five minutes, maybe ten. The third time was the other night with Buzz, when again we arrived before the place had really started to fill up, and in any case, we spent almost all our time buried in paperwork in a back room. So in a way, tonight is the first time.

The Virgin & Unicorn.

Simpering pink. Fleshy red.

The neon glow lifts the street out of Cardiff and deposits it somewhere else altogether. New York. Tokyo. Bangkok. Montmartre.

I feel like a wooden toy.

I approach the club and the two black-suited, black-shirted doormen who stand guard outside.

'Entry for one,' I say. I've no idea what you're supposed to say.

'You know what this is, darling?'

'Yes. I'm joining friends.'

They exchange glances but don't object. Just start running through the rules. No touching. No photographs. No videos. No fighting. No excessive drinking. No propositioning for sex. The dancers are dancers, not prostitutes. Yadda yadda. It sounds like some dispatch from a foreign war zone, infinitely alien. The doorman who is speaking has a head shaped like a bullet. There are three gold rings on his right hand.

Whenever there's a gap in what he's saying, I say, 'Okay.' After a bit, I'm still saying okay and he's not giving me more rules, so then I shut up and he says, 'You can go in.'

I thought there was an entry fee, but no one asks me for any money.

I go inside. Tables with shiny black tops. Chrome seats with black leather seats and backs. Dark red walls. Low lighting. Framed pictures of art-house porn.

Which is just a way of saying porn.

I can't feel anything at all.

Everything looks sleek and dark and glossy. Leering and acquisitive. Like the sort of men your mother warned you about.

I know there is music playing, because it creates a pressure in my head, but I can't tell if it's loud or quiet, or what songs are being played. There are people in the room too, but I can't look at them yet. I have fragments – legs, shoes, a man's wrist with intense black hairs and a Rolex-style watch – but I'm not yet ready to join the pieces. There is a platform, strongly spotlit, at the end of the bar. I sense it the way I sense a headache.

This is Khalifi's place. I can feel the energy of it chiming with the energy of him. His apartment and this club: They're the same thing. Different slices from the same loaf.

He feels more real to me already.

Purple silk. Black marble.

I go to the bar and order one of my non-drink drinks. Mineral water. A slice of lime. Ice. I don't care about the lime or the ice, I just don't want to look like the out-of-place person sipping a mineral water. I'm out of place enough as it is.

The barman gives me change. A man standing next to me leans in and says something. I don't hear what he says over the music and the buzzing in my head, but it was a friendly thing. Not hostile. A beery welcome.

And that's all I need. Something alters in my head, as sudden and complete as flicking a light switch. I'm still out of body. I still couldn't feel a lighted cigarette butt pressed up against my arm, but my other senses suddenly intensify.

There are about fifteen customers in the place, including one other woman. The men are dressed well enough. Jackets. Dark trousers. Shoes that aren't awful. My newfound clarity allows me to look at the pole-dancing platform too. It's got all the class of a Las Vegas casino personally styled by Donald Trump. There are three poles, three dancers. One of the girls is really pretty, the other two just thin. They're all either big-breasted or, as I assume, have had boob jobs. Also, big hair, lots of makeup, fake tan. The aesthetic is unashamedly *Playboy*. It's like these women have disassembled themselves into their sexual parts only. Remove the brain, enlarge the tits.

I don't have a moral reaction to this – not now, anyway. Those parts of me just aren't available. I can dimly feel that the glass in my hand is cold, but only dimly. The music remains just noise. It's not just the Unicorn that has made me like this. It's also Khalifi.

This thing I'm experiencing wasn't the connection I was seeking, but you can't pick and choose. You take what you're given and this is what he cares to give.

I'm confident now, know what I'm doing.

I walk to one of the best seats in the house. Close to the

dancers. I'm aware for the first time of what I'm wearing. A gold beaded dress. It's short enough on me, would have been micro on Kay. My shoes don't quite go, but almost do. Good enough. I exchange glances with the other woman customer. The unity of the sisterhood, you'd say, except that, in here, the sisterhood serves a pretty thin gruel.

When I turn my eyes back, there's a girl in front of me. Blood-red shoes. A sequinned bikini. Nothing else. She wants to know if I want her to dance. It's twenty quid. I say yes. The current song is coming to an end. In the gap between songs, she tells me that I can touch if I want to. 'Supersexy,' she says, in an accent that could be Polish or Slovenian or Finnish or Dutch. Then the next song starts and she starts dancing, lips open, eyes half shut. I don't touch her. A couple of times she tries to put my hands on her thighs, but I move them away. Halfway through the song, she turns so that I have her bum in my face. She's not performing for me now, but for everyone else. A porno-pantomime. At the end of the song, she takes my twenty quid but her eyes are already on the hunt. That's why she wanted me to touch her. Get the guys so aroused they'd buy the next dance.

It's not about the dancing, but about the hustle. That's what the tits and the hair extensions are for. There's an intensity to the sell I don't think I've experienced before. Silent. Furious. Unrelenting.

I realise I've got Mary Langton wrong too. Not completely wrong, but enough. The core of her is what I've already seen: the hockey player, the English student, the girl with the sensible mam. But no one works in a place like this just to earn some extra cash. To work here, you have to have something self-hating. The dancers in front of me slide up and down their poles like marionettes. Drug-fuelled. Drugs or drink.

The force that through the green fuse drives the flower. The poem up in Langton's room. How did she get from there to here? Why did she work here for one short year, then stop? What brought her here? What drove her away?

I don't know. My picture of her has just grown more complex, more ambiguous.

I think of her mother's sobs, her father's choked numbness. The grief that filled that house.

Because I am who I am, I tend to spend more time thinking about the dead than the living. I bond easily with Langton's head, with Khalifi's elusive shadow. But there are other victims too. Living ones. Mary Langton's parents. Her two siblings. Sophie Hinton: not my favourite person, but her life was damaged too. Ayla and Theo: their worlds have never recovered from their father's death. Perhaps they never will.

And Khalifi. Who mourns him?

I don't have an answer to that, but I do feel Khalifi now. Feel him strongly present in this room. There's a lovely unity between his lonely corpse, shredded like some macabre goulash on that empty reservoir, and this place now. Over to my right, the dancer who almost gave me a mouthful of bottom is dancing with another girl right in the face of a guy in a black jacket and dark navy shirt. A guy who looks to have all the charm of a car salesman just made Salesman of the Month. The two girls hardly make eye contact with each other. They happily stroke each other's breasts and mime oral sex, but their eyes are roving for the next target. The next twenty quid.

No touching.

No photos.

No fighting.

There isn't a difference here. No exploiter and exploited. The men are dragged here by their cocks. The women dragged by their self-destructive lives. The only person who is emphatically not exploited is my father. The man who makes money from all of this. That's the same man who put down a 30 percent deposit on my house, who bought me my car, who

153

paid the first year's insurance, who would pay for just about anything if I let him. So I'm an exploiter too.

The two dancers have finished with the Salesman of the Month, but he hasn't finished with them. He tucks twenty-pound notes into their bikini bottoms and pulls a fifty-pound note from his wallet. He's on his feet. His mates are clapping him. The place has got more crowded since I've been here, and there's a din behind me.

The two girls are leaning in close to his mouth. He's saying something. Half-shouting, half-miming over the music. But the deal is pretty clear. There's a competition for the fifty pounds. The guy's mates cheer. One is sent over to get champagne. Or rather, non-label fizz that sells for forty-five pounds the bottle. The pole dancers rest on their poles as the spots are trained on Salesman Guy and the two girls. It's a striptease. Sexiest stripper gets to go to a private booth with Salesman Guy, the fifty-pound note, and the champagne.

The two girls do their stuff. They're good. Not easy to tease with so little to strip. One girl is prettier. Blonder, skinnier, better features. But the other one, the brunette, responds with all-out technological warfare. Hair extensions. Pumped-up boobs. Lips so full they must have been collagened.

Blondie seems too casual. Like she assumes her looks will win, no matter what.

There's nothing relaxed in the brunette. She's like me. If there's a fight on, she'll fight it. *Der totale Krieg.* The doctrine of Ludendorff and Clausewitz. War without limits.

I watch keenly. Brunette's gestures are big, her miming blatant. For a while I think she's overdone it, but she knows her market. Salesman Guy makes a big show of awarding the prize to Blondie, only to pull it away at the last minute. It's not her, it's you, he tells Brunette.

The two of them walk past me with the booze. Salesman Guy is living in the moment. This is the highlight of his fucked-up car-selling month. Brunette isn't like that. She's still selling cars. Her face is still doing the spreadsheet, the maths, figuring out those cash-in/rent-out sums that will tell her if she has enough money over to feed her habit.

The sight clarifies everything.

I realise Khalifi knew Langton. That's not a definite fact, but a highly probable one. Khalifi came to these clubs often enough that he'd have seen himself as a connoisseur. He'd have wanted to know the talent, so he could appraise it. Langton's plump white hips might or might not have been his thing, but he'd have known her. When they're back at work on Monday, Salesman Guy and his buddies will talk about and dissect every dancer here.

That's not the main thing, though. The main thing was the transaction I've just witnessed. I'd thought lap-dancing clubs were about sex and it turns out they're not. They're about cash and addiction and status and anxiety. Khalifi's status. His anxiety.

He was a lecturer – good, diligent, and well respected – but on a lecturer's salary, a lecturer's perks. No Lecturer of the Month bonus for him. No bottles of no-label fizz and crowds of mates hooting him on. He had his private-sector consultancy money, but how far does that go when bad-quality fizz is forty-five pounds a bottle?

What this place tells you has to do with Khalifi's yearnings. He was a British-Moroccan guy. No amazing looks, no inherited wealth. One talent, which had to do with engineering savvy. Or two talents, really: engineering know-how combined with a flair for a certain sort of networking. He had parlayed those talents into his position at Cardiff University, where he acted both as lecturer and honeybee. Buzzing around. Making connections. Fertilizing projects.

But he wanted so much more. He had a half-million-pound apartment and wanted a million-pound one. Had a low-end

BMW, wanted a high-end one. Fooled around with lap dancers and pubs and clubs, but wanted more. The same thing,
but classier. He wanted the stick-thin model girlfriend, the
yacht in the bay, the supercar in the garage. He went out with
pretty, skinny Jenny from the office, hoping that she could be
his trophy girlfriend, but she let him down. She didn't want to
snort coke from his kitchen worktops and bought her clothes
in the sale at Dorothy Perkins. The harsh truth is that Khalifi
didn't have enough to attract the kind of girl he wanted. Not
enough of anything. Looks. Class. Glamour. Cash. The only
part of that he could change was the cash.

I spend another hour in the club.

My feelings are returning to me. I can hear the music as
music, not just as relentless aural pressure. When I go to the
loo and wash my hands, I can tell the difference between hot
and cold. If I press my forearm hard against the side of the
basin, I can sense the pressure, or almost can. I can't feel my
feet at all – I have to look down at them to even be sure
they're there – but feeling my legs and feet is the hardest thing
for me anyway.

The face in the mirror is the face of a stranger. Gold dress,
red lips. Lips that move in sync with mine. I don't even try to
join up with that face. It's not mine.

Back in the club, I spend enough time to be sure I'm not
missing anything. To make certain I'm leaving on my own
terms. Mostly, though, it's a good discipline for me. Training.
Learning to reverse that grey, upward draining. Bringing
myself down from the snow line, toward the trees, and
through them down to the valley floor.

No drugs. No doctors. No dramas.

Just me.

It helps that Khalifi is here too. His energy. His dead presence. That makes it easier. I don't know why.

I buy another drink. Go crazy. Order a white wine spritzer,

which is mostly spritz and only a splash of wine. I'm even feeling confident enough to risk a few sips.

To the barman, I say, 'If the punters want to spend time with the girls – you know, get to know them, have a kiss and a cuddle, a proper chat –'

He interrupts me. 'Not here. Strictly *verboten*.'

'But then where? Is there a place where people go after?'

'Yeah, well, maybe. Different places.'

He feels uncomfortable saying what he's said and I don't push it.

I spend my hour in the club, then leave.

Taxi home.

By sheer chance, it's the same taxi driver as before. He says, 'Did you have a nice evening?'

I say, 'I did.' And before we even get as far as Croescadarn Road, I find that if I drive the end of my house key hard into the upper part of my foot, I can feel it bruising muscle, injuring bone.

It hurts. I can feel it hurting.

I stay that way, pushing with the key, feeling the pain, until the taxi's headlights wash up against my own front door.

23

Undress. Wash a bit. Brush my teeth. Put Kay's dresses back on hangers that they'll probably never leave again.

It's long gone midnight. On Planet Buzz, we'd have had sex and fallen asleep by now. On my planet, things aren't so simple.

I think vaguely about having a joint, but only because I think about them quite often. But I had one earlier, a big one, and a non-emergency smoke now would be a serious violation of my own house rules. The only rules I never break.

Go down into the kitchen. Leave the lights off. I like the dark.

The streetlights outside and that friendly green oven clock give enough light for me to find my way around.

Swing open the fridge. Have I actually eaten anything today? I can't remember.

My fridge is more interesting than Buzz's. Less food, yes, but more going on at the microbiological level. There is a half-eaten nut yogurt, whose mould has now grown higher than the carton itself. Long filaments of moss-brown hair. I drink a bit of orange juice, then swing the door shut.

I'm barefoot and I can feel the floor.

I'm not tired.

Other people get tired predictably. Buzz is wired up like some old-fashioned bomb. When the hands of the clock reach a certain point, something triggers unstoppably. By ten, he's yawning. By eleven or eleven thirty, he's in bed and fast asleep.

I sleep okay most of the time, but I don't have those rhythms. That predictability.

I slept better when I kept a gun in the bedroom.

For no particular reason, except to do something, I make a cup of peppermint tea. Take it upstairs.

Get into bed.

No lights inside the house. The glow of streetlights through gaps in the curtains. I imagine lying here with a gun in my hands, a firing grip, barrel pointing straight at the bedroom door. Chest height. Lethal, at this range.

The thought game relaxes me. I don't know why.

It's half past one in the morning.

I reach for the phone and call Ed Saunders. A clinical psychologist who once cared for me when I was a teenage nutcase. Who became my lover – not then, but later. Professional boundaries all very much respected. And who is now my friend.

The phone rings and is answered.

'Yes?'

The voice of a sleepy man.

'I just wondered whether you've checked your smoke alarm recently? Did you know that a working smoke alarm halves your risk of death by fire?'

'Oh God, Fi.'

'In a strikingly high proportion of households, smoke alarms are present but nonfunctional, because the batteries have either been removed or are dead.'

'Look, is this about something or did you just want to chat?'

'Um, we could just chat, if you liked. Since we're both awake.'

There's some grunting on the other end of the line, then, 'Look, I'll call you back.'

A few minutes go by.

I try pointing my pretend gun at a pretend person behind the bedroom door again, but this time it doesn't do much for me. Then Ed calls back. He'll have slapped cold water on his face, rinsed his mouth, got himself something to drink.

'Is it tea or whiskey?' I ask.

'Tea.'

'Good.' Whiskey indicates that he's having a rough time or I'm being extra awful. Tea is good. 'How was your day?' I say. After one o'clock, people are bad conversationalists, I find. They need warming up.

Ed sort of answers, but doesn't say anything interesting. I try again, but Ed's not Mr Sparky no matter how much I try.

Eventually, he gives up and says, 'How was your day?'

'I went to a lap-dancing club and bought a dance for twenty quid.'

'You did what?'

'She had her bum in my face. She told me I could touch her.'

'Well, for twenty quid –'

'And when I was there, I was completely dissociated. When I ran a bath beforehand, I couldn't tell if the water was hot or cold. I couldn't feel a single thing.'

'Bloody hell, Fi.' He's awake now. I can see him sitting up in bed, gripping the phone.

He comes over all Clinical Psychologist. How long was I dissociated for? How completely? Do I have anyone with me? Have I remembered my Survival Plan?

Survival Plan: one of the things that idiots with clipboards get you to do when you're locked up in their care. But Ed wasn't an idiot. And I needed all the help I could get.

I answer his questions. Degree of dissociation: very complete. Duration: very short, a few hours. Presence of Buzz: negative. Survival Plan: don't need it.

Then he asks the Big One, the question he's most worried

about. 'Negative affect? How was your mood?'

'Negative affect, Ed? Fuck's sake.'

'You know what I mean. Were you depressed? Did it go dark?'

'Not really.' I try to explain how it felt, but it's like describing red to a blind man. Or a blind man describing a watermelon to the sighted. You can shuffle partway across the bridge of meaning, do your very best to link hands through the darkness – but in the end, the effort only serves to prove that you're you, they're them. You might brush fingertips, but you'll never merge, never join.

I know what he's asking, though, and why he's asking it. My *thing*, my Cotard's, arises when two lethal forces come together. Dissociation plus depression. Dissociation removes me from my feelings. It numbs me. Depression paints the entire world in charcoal greys. Put the two together and you have the teenage me. A girl who couldn't feel herself existing. A girl who saw the worst, assumed the worst. In herself. In everything.

For two years, I believed myself, quite literally, to be dead.

And because I know what Ed is asking, I know what he needs to hear. I say it.

Yes, I dissociate a fair bit still. But I'm not depressed these days. I stay positive. It's very rare that I creep even up to the edge of full-blown Cotard's. When I lose touch with my feelings, I remain okay. I remember my exercises. I stay close to Buzz. I keep it together.

I also grow marijuana in my potting shed and have an illegal handgun stashed in a Pembrokeshire sheepfold.

I don't say that last bit, though.

I do say, 'Ed, why do you think it happened? I mean, I was okay. I was having a nice day. My version of nice. A bit crazy, but no crazier than normal. Then I realised that the logic of my investigation would take me to a lap-dancing club.

161

Dad's club, in fact. For some reason, that did it. I drained away. Emptied out. I haven't been that nuts since I was at Cambridge.'

Ed doesn't like it when I call myself nuts but, yah-boo, it's allowed. Like when gay people call themselves faggots.

Ed doesn't rehash that argument, just says, 'Do you think it was the sexual aspect? Or the fact that your father owned the club?'

'I don't know.'

'What was it like when you were there? Did seeing the lap dancers bring up anything for you?'

'No.'

'Did it get worse once you were inside?'

'No.'

There's a pause. I don't know who started it, Ed or me. But I know why it's there. Cotard's Syndrome, my illness, is the big, ugly mother of all psychological conditions. It's usually lethal. A large majority of those who suffer from it attempt suicide. Many succeed. I came very close, not once but often. Forget the logic of it – why do people who think they're dead need to kill themselves? – just stay with the fact. Cotard's is generally lethal. And I had Cotard's. And the condition is almost always associated with early childhood trauma. And the first two and a half years of my life are a total mystery.

'Look,' I say, 'early childhood trauma. What does that mean? Really?'

'Fi!' Ed's voice is warning me. Cautioning me.

I don't feel cautious.

'Okay, let's just pretend I'm a copper. Let's just say I might have some expertise in criminal investigation. We normally try to make connections. Sift through piles of data and see if we can make something in Pile A match something in Pile B.'

'Yes, and let's just say that *my* day job involved clinical psychology ...'

I interrupt. 'A girl with Cotard's. You'd probably guess that sexual abuse had been involved somewhere along the line, right? Only a guess, but a pretty damn strong guess, right? Then – bam! – twenty-something years later, that girl enters a lap-dancing club and experiences a very powerful, temporary increase in her symptoms. A fucking *lap-dancing club*, Ed. Tell me what the other options are!'

'You really want to know?' He's heated now. Not angry exactly – Ed is a bit too English to get properly angry – but heated. He says, 'You have no idea. You think you do, but you don't. Sexual abuse is one way to screw up a child, yes. But there are others. Neglect. Drug addiction. Physical abuse. Injury to the brain or brain stem. Inflammation or infection of the brain or brain stem. You. Just. Don't. Know.'

'She had her bum in my face, Ed. And I was nuts. Totally dissociated. Not like some rinky-dink teenage self-harmer who screws around with razor blades and listens to Kurt Cobain. The only reason I wasn't playing with blades myself is that I was way beyond that point. I was so far past that point that I wouldn't even have got a kick from cutting myself.'

'Oh, okay, so that's your argument, is it? And yes, you can present as evidence the fact that you had a weird evening to-night. But then again, *I* could present as evidence the fact that you do not seem to be very screwed up around sex. When we were together, the sex was about the most normal thing about you.'

I'm about to respond. Pressured speech is the clinical term. Where the speaker is so driven to talk that they can't listen. Can't even get their own sentences out properly. I'm there, in that place – and then I'm not. As though I'm worn out by the day, the night, the argument. By myself.

So I just say, 'Yes.'

'Those things cut both ways, you know. You don't know, Fi. You really don't.'

163

'Okay.'

I'm not normally this humble. This submissive. But he's right. I know he is. I could find five facts that argued for the sexual-abuse theory. Five that argued against it. An unresolvable argument.

'I think I've always been waiting for The Clue,' I say. 'I wanted some kind of eureka moment, one that would unlock the past.'

'Fi, do you remember Brian from the hospital? The guy with the beard and the acid burns.'

Yes, I remember Brian. A schizo. He was always having eureka moments. Two or three a day when he was fizzy. He'd lean in, with his bad teeth and stinky breath, and explain his latest vision. One of those visions resulted in him pouring battery acid down his face. Hence the burns.

Ed goes on talking and I say stuff back at him, but I know he's right. The eureka moment won't come. And if it does, it can't be trusted.

We talk a bit more. Ed yawns. Maybe just a yawn, maybe a 'shut up and let me go back to sleep' signal. Either way, I'm good as gold. I say, 'You sleep well, Ed.'

'Thank you. You too.'

We say good night and hang up.

I let the room drift back into silence. I raise my nonexistent gun at the nonexistent intruder and fire off six rounds. Two groups of three. Chest and head.

Lower the gun.

Why do I miss having a gun with me? Why does the possibility of violent response to intrusion feel good? Why did my brain go AWOL today?

Ed's right. You can't trust eureka moments. But that doesn't make the questions go away. The questions are real.

I fire off another five rounds. Gently, though. Accuracy, not speed. Squeezing the trigger, not pumping it.

Then call Ed back. He mumbles something into the mouthpiece.

'Don't talk, Ed. I don't want to wake you up this time. Not really. Just thank you. Thank you for being you. Sweet dreams.'

He mumbles a mouthful of nothing and I hang up.

And Ed has taught me something. These last few months, I've believed myself to be actively investigating my past. Those missing two and a half years. The presumed cause of my teenage Cotard's Syndrome. But my investigation has been half hearted. I've not really tried: haven't tried the way I normally would on a case I care about.

I've wimped out for two reasons. Partly, I've been waiting for that eureka moment, a *boom!* of recognition. And that's not how it happens. Not how it ever happens.

But I've also wimped out because of fear. Why did I go nuts tonight? Simple: I was afraid. I've chosen never to look under the lid of how my father makes his money, and tonight I did. I took one tiny step into my father's world – and instantly, my system was so washed through with fear I could hardly move.

I'm afraid to know who I am. Terrified. That's why I haven't really tried.

The knowledge soothes me. I feel calm and integrated in a way I seldom do. I don't know what I'll do with this insight yet, but that's a question that can wait for another time.

The room is full of silence now. The hall full of dead intruders. The streetlights glow their unprotesting orange.

I go to sleep.

I know what I'm doing tomorrow.

24

Barry.

In the 1880s, the place was nothing. Two or three villages on a muddy shore. Population in three digits. Then those bustling Victorians built docks to carry the coal pouring out of the Valleys. From Senghenydd, Abercarn, Risca, Rhondda, Cwm Cynon, Tondu, Aberbeeg, Aberfan, Morfa. A black tide pouring south. At the outbreak of the First World War, Cardiff was the world's foremost coaling port, Swansea its foremost steel port. Barry, in between the two, shipped every damn thing it could.

The black tide built and the black tide killed. It built the Empire. It built Barry. You can hardly find a house here older than 1890. But it also killed. Every mine had its fatalities, every village its memory of disaster. In 1901, the mine at Senghenydd suffered a major blast when gas and coal dust ignited. There were eighty-two men down the mine at the time. Eighty-one of them died. Twelve years later, same mine: a second blast. Four hundred and thirty-nine men lost their lives. A second generation: gone.

Our cities are built on corpses. Perhaps they always are, but ours are recent.

Cardiff and Swansea have both found new purpose since the death of King Coal. But Barry – what is it for? The past blows like rubbish in the air, sags like a collapsing door. When we were kids, my dad used to take us to Barry Island, a place of rides and ice creams and fierce Atlantic winds. I used to love it, but somehow even then I felt the air from Senghenydd. Coal-black and a smell of gunpowder.

The place I want, Barry Precision, is down by the docks. Industrial sheds tamped round a rectangle of water. Slate-green and restless. I park. It's Sunday and the place is closed. Gates locked by a padlock on a fat chain. Wind, rain, and cold. I've got gloves but my coat isn't particularly warm and I don't fancy getting out of my car in order to jangle uselessly at the chain. I think I ought to do that, though, so I do. Jangle uselessly. The cold from the padlock penetrates my gloves within seconds.

Some people, Buzz for example, would know exactly what to do. He has an almost instant mechanical intuition. Say something like 'See what the silly buggers have done? All we need to do is slip the split pin out of the O-socket, then bend the hasp back – no, the other way – and the hinges should just lift off, like so.' Mechanical intuition and that unfussed masculine strength. All I see is a tangle of cold metal that hurts my hands.

I get back in the car. A black and yellow sign on the fence gives the name and number of a security company. I call it. Police, I say. Reports of a break-in. The phone operator, apparently overwhelmed with boredom, says she'll send someone.

I wait.

There's enough wind that I can hear it whistling in the fence. Over the roof of my car.

This northern climate is hostile to life. If you fell in the water, how long before you died?

I make a call to Rhys Jordan.

'Hi, Rhys, are you okay after Friday night? Dad was a bit over the top.'

'Oh, that's okay. He's allowed, I suppose.'

'Look, funny question. But a few years back, where did the

girls go at the end of their shift? To get something to eat, have a chat, whatever they did to end the evening off.'

'Oh, well, the club finishes around four in the morning. A lot of the girls just go straight home.'

'Right, but if they do stick around? Have a ciggy. Get something to eat?'

'There's nowhere really good anymore. A few years back, the big place was Macca's. An all-night café. It opened early for the truckers and the market traders and people. But we used to pour in about four fifteen, four thirty, whatever.'

He starts laughing and telling me some story, the gist of which has to do with a trucker getting a full strip from two of the girls in return for a plate of egg, chips, and beans. The place is closed now, but he gives me the name of the person who used to run it, a guy called Gavin Watson.

I tell him thanks and ring off.

The wind still chatters in the fence.

I wonder if I could pick the padlock. I probably could. I've got the tools, but not with me here. Instead, I listen to music. Radio 2. Radio 6. Classic FM. Settle on Brahms. Unhappy violins and plenty of them.

Then the security guy comes. He's got a proper coat. Warm, rainproof, and covered in fluorescent strips in case I have difficulty seeing him.

I show him my warrant card. 'It's probably bollocks,' I say, 'but I need to take a look round.'

He nods. Bored. He's got a dog in the back of his van that wants to come out and play. Either that or eat me. The guard unlocks the gate and we drive through to Barry Precision. A blue shed, fairly new, and large. Ten thousand square feet or more. A stock-holding yard behind. Security cameras.

The guard has keys to the unit but needs to call to get codes for the alarm. More waiting. Then we're in.

We flip some lights on. There are some thin-partitioned

offices at the front of the building, but the main space is a factory. Some fancy machines. Steel gantries. Forklifts. The place is ordered, tidy.

No break-in.

The guard looks at me. I say, 'Look, can you just take a look round the perimeter? I'll check around in here. Meet you outside in five minutes.'

He walks off. I spend a bit of time in the factory. Running my hands over complex metal objects. Things I don't even know how to describe. Compressor blades. Cylinder heads. Turbofans. I don't know what any of those things are, but for all I know I'm surrounded by them now. Rods and bars of specialty metals. Tungsten. Copper. Low-density steels.

Mark Mortimer knew about this stuff. So did Khalifi.

Both dead.

I like factories, but it's not the factory I need. So I go back to the offices, which just look like offices. Holiday calendars. A coffee machine. Grey invoice files. Red swivel chairs. Mouse pads with adverts on.

The executive suite isn't much – an office with glass windows that look out only to the reception area. A fancier type of desk lamp. I go inside.

It's all weirdly normal. Neither thronged with the spirits of the dead nor even particularly bland. Not obviously hiding anything. It just is what it is. A not very smart office inside a middling-sized engineering company located in a decaying port town in an unimportant part of the United Kingdom.

I crawl under the desk. Burgundy nylon carpet tiles. That smell that comes from electric wires and office carpets. I fiddle round to the back of the computer. Pull at various cables until I've figured out which one belongs to the keyboard. Should have brought a torch. Didn't. Pull out the lead. Take a thing like a memory stick from my pocket. Fit the keyboard lead into one end of it. Fit the other into the keyboard port of the

PC. Shove the computer back to where it was. Get up.

Everything's the same as it was, except that my gadget now sits between keyboard and computer. A keystroke recorder. Bought for thirty pounds from Amazon and so simple to use that even an idiot like me can use it.

It doesn't collect mouse clicks.

It doesn't store images.

It doesn't record web addresses or emails or copy files.

But it does collect keystrokes. And people use keystrokes to enter their passwords.

I root around until I find a stash of stationery and nick a few envelopes. Find a memory stick and take that too.

Outside, I ask the guard about the perimeter fence. He shrugs. I shrug. I pretend to call the office while he resets the alarms.

Then we leave.

Outside the estate, the gate again locked and padlocked. The guard goes back to wherever he ought to be. I don't leave straightaway. Wind the windows down. Get cold.

I'm feeling good. Send a text to Rhiannon Watkins, telling her about Gavin Watson and the place called Macca's.

Ali el-Khalifi liked sex with pretty girls, but I think Ali was also desperately concerned about his status. He wanted money, the better apartment, the girl with Manolo Blahniks. I don't know where Mark Mortimer comes into that and perhaps he doesn't, but my little keystroke recorder is about to tell us either way.

I'm feeling good, but not quite satisfied. Buzz and I are spending the afternoon and evening together. A couple of his old friends are coming round to dinner. These normal boyfriend-girlfriend days used to terrify me. I assumed that the effort of playing normal for that many consecutive hours would blow a fuse somewhere. Yet that's not been my experience. I find the whole thing a challenge, but an okay one. I

170

feel about it the way yachtsmen must feel about crossing the Great Southern Ocean. Not a voyage to undertake lightly, but one which mostly repays the commitment.

Still, I feel a bit too jiggy to dive into full-on girlfriending yet. I need something to take the edge off my energies.

In the car, driving slowly, windows still down, heater to full but the air still cold. From Barry to Swansea. I hug the coast instead of blasting straight down the M4. I want to see the seas as much as possible. Slate-green water and Atlantic winds. The waves foam-topped, with that foam that's never really white.

When the Ice Age comes, it'll start like this.

I drive to Swansea, because I want to connect with Mary Langton. I seek out her old haunts. Places she lived as a student. Cafés we know she frequented. End up down by the sea, in the blast of the wind.

Five years ago, Mary Langton left a party in a quiet part of Cardiff and walked away to her death. A few days ago, Ali el-Khalifi walked out of a coffee shop, out of CCTV range, and also ended up dead. The two corpses strewn across Llanishen in a muddy unity.

Last night's insight still seems true to me now: The two of them knew each other, were more than strangers. I don't know where these reflections take me, but you can't rush these things. I feel like I'm getting to know them, though. Mary Langton and Ali al-Khalifi. My all-too-human dead.

When I'm too cold to brave the seafront anymore, I zip back to Cardiff, to the office.

Up to my desk. Computer on. Enter the police database. In the 'search for persons' box, I type 'Thomas Griffiths.' My father. There are a few different Tom Griffithses available, but my pa's folder is eight times longer than all the rest put together.

Click it.

View All. Select All. Print.

My paper tray starts filling with printouts. I realise I'm shaking. But this is a huge step for me. A step towards knowledge.

Frightening knowledge.

And as the print tray fills, I get a call. It's Buzz.

'You're late,' he says.

'I'm on my way, Buzzling. I'm on my way.'

And I am. On for an afternoon and evening of high-intensity girlfriending. An afternoon during which I won't think or talk about work at all.

Supergreat and perfect. What I aim to be.

25

Monday. Rhiannon Watkins. The briefing for Operation Abacus, aka Stirfry. An event which used to be daily and is now only twice weekly, with additional helpings of Watkinsian sunshine served as required. Kirby floats on the margins now, distancing himself. Our 'persons of interest' board now has 275 names.

But this morning Watkins is in the closest thing to a good mood as she ever gets. Close the way Antarctica is to Cape Town. It's not that she cracks a smile or anything anatomically dangerous like that, just when she ejects nails, the nails fly out at slightly lower velocities than usual and aren't always aimed at the eyes.

Good mood – good news. Intensive enquiries over Sunday afternoon and evening succeeded in tracing one of the waitresses from Gavin Watson's now-defunct greasy-spoon café. The waitress, one Sandrine Cooper, currently working as a server in her uncle's fish-and-chip shop in Tongwynlais, was shown eight photos of different women, including Mary Langton and another dancer who worked at the Unicorn over the relevant period. Cooper picked out both girls immediately, and correctly named them both. She also picked, from a group of eight photos, a picture of Khalifi. She didn't know his surname, but named him correctly as 'Ali.' She thought that he and Mary had a relationship of sorts, but she wasn't sure. She knew they 'hung out a bit,' but didn't know any more than that.

It's not much, but enough. Watkins finally has her connection.

To any copper, a connection like that is like a point of weakness in a fortification, a vulnerable angle on an unguarded wall. It's where you train your artillery. Where you concentrate your fire.

Watkins must know that the Khalifi–Langton connection brings as many questions as it answers, but she redeploys the manpower she has to focus aggressively and intensively on this new line of attack. She wants people who saw Langton and Khalifi together. Anyone connected with the two of them. We've done some work on that in the past, but we've never brought all our resources to bear on that single question.

The enquiry has found its centre.

Watkins starts to dole out assignments and interview schedules. I vaguely notice that Watkins didn't mention it was my text to her that gave us the Sandrine Cooper connection. I don't really care, but it's a breach of senior officer etiquette. They're meant to give patronising little public accolades to us baby detectives when we manage to do something a tiny bit right.

But that's not what concerns me most. What concerns me more is this bit now. What happens next.

And what happens next is that people are paired up. Given targets. Buzz and Jon Breakell will be interviewing or re-interviewing current club employees. Bev Rowland, Jane Alexander, Jim Davis, and Angela Yorke are going to re-interview as many dancers as they can find – not the current generation of dancers, obviously, but those that were working in Cardiff or Swansea five years ago. For the first time in what seems like ages, there's a stir in the room, a sense of excitement. A fire trying to fan itself back into life.

I wait for my name to be read out. Relieved to hear I'm

not with Jim Davis. Sorry that I'm not with Bev Rowland. Then realise the meeting is ending and I've been excluded completely. Kicked off the whole damn operation. My eyes are widening with indignation. The normal charge for the coffee machine passes me by, led as ever by Jim Davis, and I don't even take the opportunity to say something pointlessly offensive.

I'm still standing there, appalled, when I realise Watkins is at my elbow.

'My office, Constable,' she says.

She walks away and I follow. Other senior officers would make small talk. How was your weekend? Cold, isn't it? If I was a bloke, they'd be talking rugby. Normally, I like Watkins's bluntness, but I'm feeling pissed off with her, so right now I don't.

On the way upstairs, my phone rings. I don't answer it. A couple of moments later, a text comes through. I don't look at it.

We get to her office. I close the door behind me and sit down without invitation. We face each other over her desk. Storm grey eyes from her. A fuck-you face from me. Lines of battle.

'Okay,' she says.

'Okay what?' I should probably add a 'ma'am,' but don't remember in time and might not have added one even if I had.

'Your semi-official conversations. Who, where, when, what?'

'I spoke to some of the barstaff, without gaining any real information. I subsequently called Rhys Jordan and asked him if there was a place where dancers and bar staff used to congregate after hours.'

'And it was Jordan who told you?'

'Yes.'

'Have you made a note of that conversation for the records?'

'No, ma'am.'

'Do so. You should have done so immediately.'

I nod.

She needs something on the system to document how the enquiry came to bang on Sandrine Cooper's door. Like every good copper, Watkins always has an eye on how an eventual prosecution case will play out in court.

'Right. Now this Langton connection. According to DS Brydon, your father simply volunteered the information without prompting.'

'Correct.'

'Correct, meaning that is what Brydon reported? Or correct, meaning that that is in fact what happened?'

I'm tempted to fudge the issue, but I don't. A sudden burst of honesty finds me saying, 'I nudged my father for information, yes. Not directly, but via a trusted colleague of his. What my father did with that nudge was up to him.'

'You didn't offer any kind of protection or amnesty?'

My mouth falls open at that. If Watkins is asking that question, it'll be because the entire high command of the South Wales force is uncertain about my ultimate loyalties. I'm genuinely astonished and I think I look it.

'That would be beyond my pay grade, ma'am.'

'It would be a *very* long way beyond your pay grade, Constable.'

'I offered my father nothing. The day after DS Brydon and I went to interview Rhys Jordan, my father asked me if there would be any comeback. I assume he had in mind any tax irregularities. I said I didn't think there would be an issue. That was the entire extent of our conversation.'

Watkins's does her storm-grey thing at me. I stare back.

Eventually she sees what she needs to see. Or just moves on. Either way, she gives a sharp nod. 'If the Unicorn is involved in this case in any way, I can't have you connected with it. Not that aspect of it.'

'My father isn't –' I begin, feeling angry again.

I don't get far. Watkins interrupts, 'Your father has been repeatedly investigated for serious offences. He's been prosecuted five times –'

'And found not guilty.'

'Don't be stupid. At least two of those trials were farces.'

She doesn't complete the thought, but she doesn't need to. Dad's prosecutions comprised two armed robberies, one possession of a firearm with intent, and one each of kidnap and arson. A well-balanced portfolio, if you ask me. The crimes of which he was suspected but for which he was never tried would have made a vastly longer list. Handling stolen goods was – as far as I know, at least – his particular forte, but my good and worthy predecessors on the force never collected enough evidence to mount a prosecution.

The intelligence that they *did* collect is currently weighing down the bottom drawer of my desk. I feel its tug. Its undertow.

And I know Watkins is right. Our investigation has to be whiter than white. If the Unicorn connection becomes central to a prosecution case, I need to be nowhere close to it. I feel angry and disappointed.

'I don't want to leave the case,' I blurt out. I'm not being strategic. Not figuring out how best to get what I want. It's just the truth. I say, 'Mary Langton. Al Khalifi. I feel I know them. I don't want to be reassigned.'

'I'm not reassigning you.'

'You're *not*?'

I'm stunned. If I'm still on the case, then what's the problem? My look must reveal my confusion.

'I need you off the Langton–Khalifi connection, that's all.' Watkins says that almost gently.

Her version of gentle: one that leaves the skull intact.

'Okay.'

'I wasn't asking for your permission, Constable.'

'No, ma'am.'

'I'm guessing there are aspects of the case you have an interest in exploring?'

'Yes.' Then, as she glares, I add, 'I think there continues to be merit in exploring Khalifi's engineering connections. Reason one, the nature of any connection between Langton and Khalifi remains very unclear. Two, even if he killed her, his own death is completely unexplained. Three, he *did* know Mortimer, who *did* die violently. Four, there is a consensus among Mortimer's family, friends, and colleagues that he was not a drug-smuggling type. And five – well, why does anyone kill anyone, if it's not just a pub brawl type thing? It always comes down to sex or money, doesn't it? And there is money floating around at the edges of all this. Mortimer's drug smuggling. Khalifi's work for the university. Those private-sector consultancies. His taste for the expensive.'

Watkins nods. 'I agree.'

She doesn't seem to be angry with me now, which always feels weird. If I spend too long alone with a senior officer without them reprimanding me, I'm not quite sure what's going on. Watkins nods. Something happens to her lower face which could be a muscle spasm or could be an attempt at a smile. She's about to say something when her phone rings and my phone vibrates again with a text. She answers her phone, only to say that she's not taking calls. I use the interruption to look at my phone. When Watkins turns back to me, she's ready to restart from where we were.

I'm not.

I show her my phone. My text, the second one, is from the duty medical officer at Cardiff Prison. It's about Brian Penry.

He's been attacked. He's in hospital. He's asking for me.

178

26

A ward on the fourth floor. Squeaky hospital trolleys on overpolished vinyl floors. Medication and bedpans. Nurses in starchy uniforms and sensible shoes.

Penry is in bed by a window, looking south. He's in a good mood.

'I can see my wing from here,' he says, pointing south at the prison.

I pretend to look, but I don't really. I prefer the light beyond the city. I like the way it reminds you that the universe is huge and that we humans dance on its surface, briefly, and without sound.

Penry's head is swathed in bandages. Recently done, so blood hasn't yet had time to soil the nice white linens. He hasn't shaved for a day or so, and he's one of those men who looks almost instantly grizzly.

'Making friends, then?' I ask.

He grins. 'Yeah. In prison, everyone loves a copper.'

I sit down. The squeaky leatherette chair is designed to be comfortable for long visits, but it's too big for me and the synthetic fabric immediately starts gluing itself to my legs.

'DI Watkins is outside.'

'Watkins?' Penry spent most of his policing career with the Met in London, but he's a Welsh boy at heart and knows most of the older hands at Cathays. 'I get a visit from the Ice Queen herself, eh?'

He chuckles at that. For him, being out of prison is as good as a trip to the seaside, even if the local tourist attractions involve the A&E department and Cardiff's scariest detective. But it's also information. DIs don't chase around after every lead. The fact that Watkins chose to come is partly police-solidarity – Penry is a former officer, even if he's also a convicted criminal – but it's mostly because Watkins doesn't have complete confidence in the Langton–Khalifi connection. Or indeed, complete confidence in me.

'She's off checking your records with the head nurse. Wants to know if you'll live.' I look hard into his eyes. 'And you will, will you? You're okay?'

'I'm grand. It's nice to be back in the saddle, actually. I've never minded taking some knocks.' He gives me a twisted grin. It's odd the way people work. Maybe a near-death experience was what he needed.

On a sudden impulse, I say, 'Brian, before you went to London, when you were still a copper here in Cardiff, who was the best officer you worked with? The best detective, I mean.'

'Why?'

'Just let me have this one. I can't tell you why.'

He gives me some names. Most of them I don't recognise or, if I do, I discard them because they're too long retired or because their careers took them in different directions from the one I want. But one name works for me: DCI Jack Yorath. Spent his whole career in the South Wales CID. Retired only a few years back. Specialised in organised crime.

'Yorath,' I say. 'He's good, is he? You'd trust him?'

Mischief hovers round Penry's mouth, but doesn't quite take possession. He says simply, 'I'd trust Jack anywhere. He's got brains, guts, and integrity. A good copper.'

A good copper: the ultimate police-ish compliment.

'Thanks, Brian. That's helpful.'

Watkins comes in. She's got a long coat on, a warm one, and I suddenly remember that I'd meant to get myself a proper winter coat when I went shopping with Kay. Got myself an expensive and unnecessary suit instead. Ah, well.

Watkins struggles to find the right tone with Penry. She can't be horrible to him, because he doesn't have to talk to her, because he isn't a copper anymore, and because he's got a gash in his skull so bad that he was rushed to hospital, given a blood transfusion, and is being held for observation. At the same time, he's a former police officer serving a prison sentence, so Watkins can't quite bring herself to make nice.

'Mr Penry. DI Watkins.' She gives a stiff semi-bow from the neck.

'Yeah, nice to meet you. How's Gethin these days?'

Gethin: DCI Gethin Matthews. Penry's only using the name to remind Watkins that he knows some of her more senior colleagues. Those little power plays are more or less compulsive with him.

'I'm sure he's fine. I understand that at the request of DC Griffiths, you were making preliminary inquiries into the suicide of Mark Mortimer?'

'DC Griffiths?' Penry sounds baffled. 'You mean Fiona here?'

'DC Fiona Griffiths, yes.'

'And *preliminary* inquiries, you say? There must have been an inquest, surely. I don't think my inquiries were exactly *preliminary* in nature.'

Watkins isn't enjoying this at all, but there's not a lot she can do about it. What could she threaten? That she'll throw him in jail? Crack his skull open?

'Maybe you could just tell us what happened?'

'Of course, but be a love, would you, Rhiannon, and fetch me a cup of tea? I'm parched, I am.'

Watkins glares at him, then at me in case I'm colluding, but

181

she can see she won't get an answer unless she submits to his crap, so off she goes to hunt down a cup of tea.

As soon as she goes, I look at Penry and laugh.

'Fuckwit,' I tell him.

'I'll send it back if it's too weak.'

'Did you learn anything?'

'No. Somebody just hit me from behind with a brick. Lots of blood, because it was a head wound, but looks worse than it is really. I'm not even sure who did it. I mean, I might have a guess, but I'm not too sure I want to. Ignorance is bliss sometimes.'

'But the attack was definitely connected with Mortimer?'

'Yes. I asked around. People knew I was asking. I wasn't trying to keep it especially quiet, because in prison you never really know who knows what. I wanted to get the word out.' Penry shrugs. There's something sad in his face for the first time. For all his macho posturing, it can't be that easy being a policeman in jail. Not that fun being half-murdered just because you've been doing a favour for a friend.

I put out my hand and rub his upper arm. Not normal for me, that kind of affection, but it feels right. He gives me grateful eyes, then adds, 'After I was hit, I was down on the floor, with blood in my eyes. Someone kicks me in the ribs and says right up close, "Keep the fuck away from things that have got fuck all to do with you." Then he kicked me again. Then after a bit he stopped. End of story.'

'That's not proof positive.'

'I haven't been asking about anything else. And it's not the kind of jail where people get beaten up for no reason.'

I nod. I believe him. It's not me but Watkins who'll need convincing. Just then, she comes back with a cup of tea. There's tightness all round her mouth and anger lines above her eyes. It's funny really. I'm with a guy who's been violently beaten while serving a four-year prison sentence and a woman, with a good income and a respected job, who's been asked to fetch a cup of tea. One's happy, the other's really not.

Penry takes the cup, peers at it all disappointed, and says, 'Oh, sorry, Rhiannon, I should have said –'

I have my hand out to take the tea before he can even finish his pointlessly needling comment. I take the cup and leave the two of them alone together. Penry will end up telling her what he told me, he'll just make sure he annoys her all the while.

I don't do anything with the tea. I don't drink it. Don't find somewhere that will serve a stronger cup. Just find a window with a view to the south.

The prison. The sea. And a pale blue light that has no limits.

When Watkins finally comes out, she looks grim and says just two words. 'Let's go.'

27

Barry again. Frigid green water in the dock. A cold northern wind has forced a floating throng of industrial refuse up against the concrete walls. Discarded plastics, chunks of polystyrene, broken pallets. Because it's no longer the weekend, there are no locked gates at the entrance to the property. Watkins parks her BMW in a free space overlooking the dock. I park next to her. We've come in two cars, so Watkins can get away quickly and I can stay on if need be. Getting out, we can hear the slap of water against the dock, the moan of wind. Barry Precision's blue shed rises like a tent against the elements.

'Nice place,' I say. 'Pretty.'

Watkins opens her mouth and closes it again, primly. We march across the car park to reception. We sign in, are offered 'refreshments', are taken through to Jim Dunbar, Barry's chief executive. He's got that Welsh physiognomy. Short, strong, dark-haired, dark-eyed. Give him a few acres of upland field and he'd look the part right away. Here, in suit and tie, he's trying to look all executive and still smells of the farm.

Watkins does the intro. Double murder. Drug deals. A prison suicide. One of the murder victims known to have had close connections with Dunbar's former employee. Dunbar takes this all with composure, but he's also careful. Vigilant. After speaking for two or three minutes – no more – Watkins shuts up and lets me get on with my questions.

Mortimer's dates of employment. His speciality. His job performance.

Dunbar's impressions of him as an employee. Mortimer's reputation within the work force.

Any notably close connections with clients or suppliers?

Any previous evidence of drug habits?

Dunbar deals with some of those questions smoothly and easily. Mortimer had been with the firm six years. He was a skilled engineer. Well respected, internally and by clients. Never known to be a drug user. Never known to have had drug issues.

When I get to the questions I'm most interested in, though, Dunbar slows down. Goes carefully.

'Did Mortimer cause you any managerial problems?'

'No. No, I wouldn't say problems. Mark was a careful man. He had high standards. But we're a precision engineering company, so we trade off high standards, and I don't have a problem with that.'

'But ...?'

'Well, in some ways, I think Mark forgot he worked for a commercial enterprise. It sometimes felt like he wanted to work in a research institute or university. Working here, you *work*. You have to hustle. If a client wants something, it's your job to deliver it, not find reasons why the client shouldn't want it.'

There's a sudden emptiness in the room. Big enough that I find myself glancing at Watkins who is simultaneously glancing at me. It's the same emptiness that I felt at the university with McKelvey, but bigger. And closer.

I push away at the silence. 'Can you give me an example of Mortimer not wanting to deliver on a job?' I bring my chair as close to the desk as I can. Partly I want to see his face close up. Partly I want him to feel pressured. Partly I want to get my leg into a tangle of computer wire.

185

Dunbar stares at me. He's teetering on the edge of telling me something. Teeters, then pulls back.

'He tended to get into dialogue with clients. They'd ask us to make something to such-and-such a specification. He'd want to know how they evolved those specs. Sometimes he'd end up persuading them they could achieve the same performance with an off-the-shelf solution. Which wasn't exactly good for our sales.'

'Did he have ethical issues with your clients?'

'Ethical? Mark would have had ethical issues with a roomful of bishops.'

'Which makes him not exactly your run-of-the-mill drug smuggler.'

'No, but he did bring five kilos of cocaine into the country. I've no idea how he argued that one to himself, but I'm sure he found a way.'

'Yes.'

I look at Watkins. She feels this thing I'm feeling. I can tell she does. A DI is the most senior active field rank in the CID. Go any higher, and you start to be a desk jockey. Marshalling paper, not interviewing suspects. Watkins is a field officer, not a bureaucrat, and she feels the withholding too. Nothing that's necessarily criminal, but an intriguing lack of openness. And Penry in hospital with an ugly skull wound.

There's something awry here and we both know it.

She says, 'Mr Dunbar, could you just give me a couple of moments with my colleague?'

Dunbar looks briefly surprised at being ejected from his own office, but he shrugs and leaves us. Goes out to talk with his secretary on the other side of the internal window. I roll back from the desk. My foot has become caught in his computer wires and I've pulled out a couple of leads.

Watkins points, unsmiling, to the tangle round my foot. I get down on hands and knees, repair the damage. As I do, I pull the keyboard lead from my keystroke recorder, put the recorder into my pocket, replace the lead. Emerge, bum first, from the desk. The way every girl likes to be seen by her boss.

'He's not telling us something,' I say as I rise to the surface.

'I agree.'

'And nothing about Mortimer makes him sound like a drug importer.'

'Mortimer pleaded guilty. Didn't even offer a defence.'

'Which could cut both ways.'

If you don't offer a defence, it's because you're either very guilty or very innocent.

Watkins nods. 'Yes. Quite. Are you happy conducting further interviews here on your own?'

'Yes.'

She calls Dunbar back in, explains I'll be staying around for a bit. There's a bit of sorting out to be done. When it's over, I walk back to the car park with Watkins. No reason really. It just seems natural. It's cold and windy and I've left my coat inside. My eyes start tearing up with the cold.

Watkins is saying something. I don't catch the first part of it, but then I do. '... well done. Your instincts here have been good.'

'It's a family thing. An interest in the criminal justice system.'

Watkins's mouth moves at that, but not in a good way. 'Don't push it,' she says, making an odd repeated hand gesture as she does so. A choppy, downward gesture, but more nervous than that sounds.

'Of course not.'

She gives me a look of iron and steel, then relents. 'Well then.' She attempts a smile, except her face doesn't really do smiles, so she just flexes some muscles in the right general area and hopes for the best.

I return her grimace with a peach plucked from my very

187

own orchard of smiles. Crinkly eyes, white teeth, plenty of dimply cheek action. And say, 'Thank you,' which doesn't make any sense, but what she said to me didn't make sense either.

Watkins is about to turn away and get into her car, when I say, 'Ma'am?'

'Yes?'

'Khalifi's family. I assume his mother or father will be coming over to deal with his personal effects?'

'Yes.'

'May I ...?' I suddenly feel weird. I don't know why. I just say, 'I assume you'll be assigning someone to look after them when they're over here?'

'You want to do that?'

'Yes please.'

Watkins nods. She turns abruptly and gets into her car. She's cold too. I go back inside.

Someone has cleared a tiny conference room for me. An interview roster is being organised. I say who I want to see and who can wait. Someone brings tea.

I ask for a few minutes to set up. Drag out my laptop. Boot up. When it's ready, I pop my keystroke recorder into the USB port. My laptop says 'New Device Detected' and asks if I want to import files. I do. There's only one file, which opens as plain text.

A complete record of Jim Dunbar's keystrokes from first thing on Monday morning to the moment I crawled under his desk just now. It's not a long file. He's not much more of a desk-animal than he looks. But all I need are the very first items of text.

jimdunbar@barryprecci ⊠ ⊠ ision.co.uk ⇦shelby57⇦

A helpful little guide that comes with the recorder informs me, that the back-pointing arrow with a cross in it represents the backspace key. The other back-pointing arrow represents the enter key. Dunbar looks like he's in his fifties, so the 57 is probably his birth year. I don't know what the 'shelby' is. A pet. His mother's maiden name. His wife's maiden name.

Don't know, don't care.

My laptop is picking up two available networks, one labelled BarPrec1. That'll do. I click the button that says connect. It asks me for a password. I offer shelby57. It makes a gracious little salaam and admits me to the network. Only two bar strength out of five, but good enough. I go to File Manager and check what the system has to offer. The answer is everything. Everything I could want, and more. All neatly filed. Accounts. CADCAM. Email_archive. HR. IT. Facilities. Invoices. Letters. Tenders. Suppliers_EU. Suppliers_UK. Tech.

I poke around for a few minutes, then start to copy everything that looks even half interesting. I select about eight gigabytes of data and hit go.

I cram in six interviews that afternoon. All uninformative, but who cares? Behind me, my laptop has finished copying.

Before I leave, I copy my lovely new data from my hard drive to the memory stick I took when I was here before. Drop the stick into an envelope addressed to Cathays. Post the envelope from the main post office in town.

Then tootle back home, feeling happy.

That night, my good mood remains intact. I had been intending to spend some lovely private hours investigating my pilfered stash of documents, but instead decide on an impulse to cook for Buzz. Properly, I mean, not something found in the fridge and dropped in a saucepan. I announce that I'm going to cook a chicken stew – an Italian version, with red wine, tomatoes and anchovies – and zoom out to get ingredients, then zoom out a second time when I realise my shopping haul somehow failed to include either chicken or anchovies.

Then get cooking.

I concentrate hard but somehow it's long past nine thirty before the food is cooked. Buzz keeps wanting to help, but I shoo him away. Won't even let him set the table or light candles. I want to show him that I can do these things if I put my mind to it. Or rather: want to show myself. Train myself into it. Real life, not TV movie.

It's almost ten when we sit down to eat. But Buzz tastes, smiles, appreciates, clinks glasses. He would do all that anyway, I know, but I think he's doing it for real and I feel a wave of warmth towards him.

Or love. Quite possibly love.

That thought is in itself somewhat stunning, so I'm relieved when Buzz – who has manfully eaten not just seconds, but thirds – pushes his chair back and says, 'We'll wash up tomorrow, shall we?' In Buzz-speak, that sentence has nothing to do with keeping order in the kitchen. It's strictly a question about my appetite for sex. Which is perfectly healthy. So we take my still-stunned brain off to the bedroom, where we find other ways to occupy it.

Afterwards, when Buzz is snoring and I've grown bored of playing with his hair, I turn my attention back to that rush of warmth I felt as we were eating.

Is what we have love? He may well feel it for me, the poor fool. But what about me?

I check he's fast asleep, then speak to him.

'Buzz, my beautiful man, I think I'm in love with you.'

It doesn't feel wrong, so I say it again, only this time without the 'I think,' and it still doesn't feel wrong, though that's not the same thing as feeling right.

Buzz doesn't care. He snores away. The city around us snores away. A cold front rides in from the north and industrial trash thrashes against the walls of an unused dockside in Barry.

Where's Penry? Still in hospital or returned to prison? And

where are Ali el-Khalifi and Mary Langton? Where is Mark Mortimer and his secrets? And what was it that DI Watkins meant with that odd, repeated chopping gesture when we said goodbye?

Lots of questions, not many answers.

I think about some of those questions for a while, but at some point, I'm not sure when, my attention shifts. To myself. To a little girl in a pink and white dress. Sitting mute in the back of an open-top Jaguar, a camera hanging round her neck. One sunny Sunday in a past beyond memory.

I haven't been fair to myself. I see that now.

I've investigated Khalifi's death, and Langton's, and over these past months I've done all the other work my duties have thrown at me. But I've neglected my own mystery. My strange origins.

Ed Saunders helped me see that I've been *afraid* to look, but the *excuse* I've given myself is that I haven't known what to do. No clues. No evidence. No witnesses. No leads. Nothing beyond that tiny distortion of the camera lens.

And I've lied to myself. It's been obvious all along what I need to do. I have a giant clue, built in the exact size and shape of my father.

Naturally, it could be coincidence that somebody chose my father's car as a place to leave me but, really, what are the odds? I guess, though I don't actually know, that my father was at that time Wales's most successful criminal. His main business, I believe, involved trade in stolen vehicles. According to those of my brother officers who were in CID at the time, my father acquired stolen cars from all over the UK. Some of those vehicles were stripped down and sold for components or scrap. Others were repainted and resold, either using false or stolen documents, or just sold for cash.

Dad operated on an industrial scale. He kept ahead of my predecessors because he was smart, cautious, and well

191

organised. His workshops were always on the move: flitting from barn to barn in the hills of South and Mid Wales. The farmers would enjoy a few weeks of tidy cash payments. A short whirlwind of profitable activity. Car transporters moving at night. Cardiff accents in the country lanes, city faces in village pubs. And Dad always kept himself one step beyond trouble. Except, presumably, at the start of his career, he kept himself remote from the coal face, always operating through lieutenants, like Emrys, never directly. He never put anything in writing. Never conducted his business on the phone. He somehow inspired such trust and love in his colleagues that he was never troubled by a single significant betrayal.

Or so I believe. That's the story as I know it, as I've chosen to know it. But the criminal underworld is an unstable place. You don't get to the top and stay there without making enemies. Without using your fists, or worse.

When I wanted a handgun on the Rattigan case, my father supplied one with a deftness that was almost breathtaking.

I don't know whose daughter I am. I don't know why I ended up in my father's car. Why I was mute so long. Or what happened in those first two years of my life. But I know these things are connected.

My past is also my father's past. My mystery is also his.

I'm still sitting up when I fall asleep, left hand thicketed in Buzz's sand-blond hair.

I dream of Theo and Ayla all night long. I keep telling them I'm going to find out why their father killed himself, but I can see they don't believe me.

28

The next day the morning news is full of the coming cold spell. It's been predicted for a while, but the forecasters are more confident now, their prognostications darker. Snow, ice, blizzard and freeze. I hope they're right.

Buzz says, 'Do you have an emergency kit in your car?'

I start to say yes because of the chocolate and the joints, then realise that he means things like shovels and torches, so say, 'No.'

'I'll get you the basics. You ought to have them.'

'Thank you.'

He doesn't approve of my coat, so I tell him I'll get one.

'Right then,' he says.

He has already been for a run, shaved, showered, made breakfast, washed up both his breakfast and our supper from last night, is dressed and ready to go into the office. I've showered and am sitting around in one of his T-shirts. I haven't eaten anything and don't know if I'm going to.

'Right then,' I say.

Buzz gives a military nod, we kiss, and he marches out. He'd like it if I were a bit more like him. Up early. Off for a run. Quick to attend to those little domestic duties. On the other hand, if he truly wanted someone like him, he's chosen the least suitable girl in the world. So I don't understand. His choices don't make sense.

By way of experiment, I try being a bit more like him. I

193

don't do anything drastic, like go for a run, but I do eat something, wash up, get dressed, make the bed. In the same spirit of investigation, I even hoover the living room, which doesn't need it as far as I can tell, but my mother always seems to be hoovering rooms that seem perfectly clean to me.

By the time I've done all that, I realise I'm going to be forty minutes late for work and bolt out of the flat, leaving the hoover in the middle of the floor.

Cold is whitening the streets and I'm stuck behind a lorry scattering grit. There's a white-blue sky above, paling to frost at its edges. I spend too much time looking up at it and I almost run smack into the back of the gritter when it stops at the lights. Only the metallic patter of grit against my bonnet alerts me in time.

From the car park to the office. I can feel the shift in temperature. Buzz is right that my coat – a blue woollen affair – is too thin to keep out any real cold. Then again, we live in a world that has doors, walls, and central heating, so Buzz's survivalist anxieties seem a little out of place.

When I get to my desk, there is no knot of senior officers angrily demanding explanations for my absence. Indeed, it looks like no one has noticed at all, which doesn't say much for my impact on world affairs. The mail will have arrived in the post-room but hasn't yet chugged its way over to my desk. I can't quite bring myself to sit prettily and wait, so I make tea and spend ten minutes chatting to Amrita, who wants to know all about my day out with Watkins yesterday. I'm feeling uppy today, so I tell her that Watkins was lovely to be with.

'Honestly? Oh my God, you are too nice, really!'

I make up for my gossip-failings by agreeing to criticise Watkins's cold-weather coat, a padded green affair which makes her look like a pensioner of indeterminate gender. It's meagre fare, but Amrita seems pleased with it.

Then I drift over to Bev's desk. She's not instantly happy to see me, which normally means that she has some actual work to do. Delightful company as I am, I don't always help create a purposeful working atmosphere. This time, though, I'm good as gold.

Bev has been allocated the tedious task of collecting Khalifi's bank records from five and six years back and seeing if she can match them against anything that crops up in Langton's record.

The Langton end of things is easier to work with. Because she earned essentially all of her income in cash, her bank records show a few college-related items – charges for rent, a parking permit, a bookshop account – settled by bank card or standing order. Little else shows up. Investigation is also made simple, because we still have the entire data set from the earlier investigation. Everything filed and boxed, nothing missing. Because we're now reaching far back into Khalifi's past, the data we have for him is patchier. A tidy-minded engineer, he was pretty good at his record-keeping, but not perfect.

'There's nothing here,' Bev complains, once she's decided I'm not here to waste time. 'I mean, I've started listing all the places where Ali spent money, but since Mary hardly ever used her bank card, I don't know why that helps.' Bev isn't normally complainy, but the spectre of Watkins's icy disapproval is making her anxious. She's the only copper I know who always refers to victims by their given names. 'Half these places don't even exist anymore.'

I see her point. She's tried the Internet for help, but businesses that have changed their name or gone defunct in the last few years are hardly likely to have web pages still operative.

'The library should have some old Yellow Pages,' I say and a couple of phone calls proves they do.

A prissy-voiced person on the other end of the phone starts listing their collection in date order.

'That's wonderful,' I interrupt. 'My colleague, Detective Constable Beverley Rowland, will be over in a few moments to pick them up.'

I scrunch my eyes at Bev to check she's okay with me saying that, and she is. She's relieved. That's part of how our friendship works. She links me to Planet Normal. I do the bossy, conflictual stuff which her sweet-as-milk personality recoils from.

Prissy Voice tells me that she can't let reference material leave the building. I tell her that she will if we send a van full of uniformed policemen to seize it. She says something betokening sour surrender and I grin at Bev when I replace the phone.

'Get the volumes for Cardiff and Swansea,' I tell her. 'Check any dead businesses against the directories, mark them on a map, and see if any of the places are close to Swansea Uni or places where we know Langton or students hung out. You'll get a map of those from the notes on the first enquiry.' I scrutinise Bev's list of Khalifi's credit card payments. He was always mobile. A good proportion of his charges were made in what look to be Cardiff-based businesses, but plenty weren't. 'You might want to make sure you get Yellow Pages for the whole of South Wales,' I say. 'Better safe than sorry. And Bath and Bristol, if the library has the information. Langton was a Bath girl, after all.'

Bev nods. 'Thanks, Fi.'

She starts winding herself into enough woollen outerwear that she starts to resemble an accident in a knitting factory. The library is a bare ten-minute walk away and we live in Cardiff, not Stromness or Tromsø. And the cold front, the real one, has not yet arrived.

'You'll be all right, won't you? You can have my scarf too if you want.'

Bev looks puzzled, then anxious, then decides I'm joking

and laughs. I would go with her, except that I've spied the lovely internal-mail cart tootling past my desk and want to sup of its bounty. Bev leaves but, instead of going to my desk right away, I spend some time studying Khalifi's spending habits. Not just the historical data which Bev is interested in, but the more recent stuff too. Dates. Places. Figures. Orderly columns that might offer a peep into murder.

They certainly offer a peep into his personality. Whenever his spending was essentially invisible, he held the purse strings tight. We know, for example, that he used price comparison websites for his utility supplies, his broadband service, his home and car insurance. He had no private health care. He wasn't mean, but he was careful. And yet, when it came to spending money that people might see, that flashy edge was always there. A spring break in Dubai last year. A week spent in Jordan this year. Paul Smith suits. City-breaks to Lausanne, Doha, Vienna, Cairo.

That prickling feeling I've had off and on recently intensifies again. It's a good feeling. A sense of being in the presence of the dead.

I print off all the data that Bev has compiled, then fiddle around on the system until I find his tax returns too. Print those.

The way I saw things once, Mary Langton had nothing to do with Khalifi. Khalifi had, as I saw it, plenty to do with the violent death of Mark Mortimer. I still think the latter, but I'm less sure about the former. The fact that Langton once danced in a bar where Khalifi drank is, as far as I'm concerned, the weakest of weak evidence. There must be literally thousands of people in South Wales who saw Langton in her itsy-bitsy little bikini. That Khalifi was one of them is hardly more remarkable than any other big-city coincidence you could think of: sharing a bus route, having the same postman. But still, it's the angle that Watkins is bombarding with her massed artillery. It's the angle that is sending the much-bescarved Bev out to do battle with sour-voiced librarians. Is it maybe the angle that is making me prickle now?

In the incident room, we still have the 275 'persons of interest,' but all the papers in the centre of the board have been moved aside, to be replaced by a photo of Langton, a photo of Khalifi, and a thick black line running between them. Someone has adorned that black line with a little red cutout heart. Mark Mortimer's name isn't on the board anywhere.

Paper pours from the printer until the output tray over-flows. I grab the pile and take it to my desk, where on the top of my regular mess and clutter is a plain manila envelope with a small bulge at one end and a postmark from Barry. I open the envelope, remove the memory stick, bring up the documents it contains. I can't conceal a grin. The joy of investigating.

I call Watkins and tell her about my treasure.

She comes down to my desk and stands beside me, looking at the documents on the screen.

'Someone wants us to know something,' she says.

'Yes. Someone does.'

I'm not lying. Ayla and Theo. Maybe Khalifi. And then there's Mary Langton. Her, her parents, her brother and sister. I feel the pressure of these people, the living and the dead, clustering round my desk. I feel crowded by them, and Watkins's bad-tempered presence doesn't make it easier.

We stare at the list of file names on screen.

An incomprehensible amount of data. A mountain of secrets.

29

Police work always moves in circles. The witnesses stay the same, but each time round you drive a little closer to the target.

In one way, the archive from Barry Precision has been disappointing. In another way, it's been a game changer. It's been disappointing because it's hard to see anything awry. Neither I, nor Susan Konchesky, who has been assigned to help me, is an engineer or an accountant, but the material we've looked through so far seems exactly what you'd expect from a mid-size engineering company. Tedious, orderly, baffling.

On the other hand, any real secrets aren't going to be blazingly obvious. If, for example, the company has been running drugs from Gibraltar, they'd presumably ensure that any related documents were encoded in some way. So for all I know, Susan and I have been looking at a mountain of highly incriminating data that we don't yet know how to interpret.

One thing we *have* found is that El Saadawi, the Egyptian businessman whose car was on Marine Parade that time, is one of Barry Precision's buyers. That's an interesting fact to me – because I know about the Marine Parade incident and no one else does – but even so, it's elusive. Saadawi was, presumably, visiting Prothero. But why shouldn't he? There's nothing wrong or even underhand about a major buyer visiting a company's owner. I know nothing about business, but presumably those sort of contacts are part of how stuff gets done.

In any case, the main thing is that Watkins is now certain that there's something here worth investigating. From her point of view, she has three pieces of evidence all pointing in the same direction. In mounting order of importance: that weirdly unproductive interview with Dunbar, the memory stick, the assault on Penry. I know the memory stick doesn't quite mean what she thinks it means – but still: Penry *was* assaulted and my little altercation of Marine Parade *did* take place. There's something here, and Watkins knows it.

So committed is she to this new line of enquiry that it was she who ordered the reinterview with Sophie Hinton. Susan Konchesky and I are to conduct it, and tape it. We discussed taking Hinton down to a police station for a formal video interview, but instead settle on requisitioning a patrol car so that Hinton's neighbours will see the police presence. It's the sort of non-intimidatory intimidation that can work very well. That can sometimes force disclosures from people who are reluctant talkers, not hardened criminals.

We arrive at the appointed time.

Same kitchen. Same sulky, pretty Sophie Hinton. She's in a grey pinstripe skirt, boots and a camel-coloured polo-neck. The police car is visible through the kitchen windows. The kids are not back from school yet, but I'm wearing Ayla's shell bracelet just in case.

She makes coffee, which neither Susan nor I wanted or asked for, and bangs things around to show how petulant she can be. Which is fairly petulant.

'I've put milk in. There isn't any sugar,' she says.

I don't respond directly. Just turn the tape recorder on, give names, place, and date. Because I've interviewed Hinton before, I'll lead this one. Konchesky is here so that we can confer if anything unexpected arises.

'Ms Hinton, are you happy for us to call you that? Or should we call you "Sophie"?'

'Yes. Either.'

'We're here in connection with the suicide of your former husband. With his conviction on drug charges. And with the murder of Ali el-Khalifi.'

She doesn't answer, just pulls her sleeves down over her hands, tucks her chin into her polo-neck and gives eyes that smoulder. If I were a guy, I'd probably roll over onto my back and drool with desire. As it is, I want to slap her.

I continue with the basics. When she met Mark Mortimer. When they married. When he joined Barry Precision. She gives her answers resentfully and briefly. After a while, she says, 'I should probably have a lawyer here. Aren't I supposed to have a lawyer?'

'Why? We're not charging you with anything. Do you think you need a lawyer?'

'No.'

'Was your former husband threatened at any time by anyone for any reason?'

'No.'

'And you would be prepared if necessary to swear on oath to that effect?'

'Yes.' Mumbled.

'Your former husband. Prior to his arrest on drug charges, were you aware that he had any involvement with the drug trade?'

'No.'

'Did he seem like the sort of person to be involved with drugs?'

'Well, obviously.'

'What do you mean?'

'Well, he was arrested, wasn't he? He pleaded guilty.'

I'm not getting the sulky kitten eyes anymore. I'm getting a woman's eyes with tears in them.

Better. I feel Susan glancing my way, and I give her a little micro-nod to let her know that I've observed the same things as she has.

'That's not what I asked. I asked about your impressions of him prior to his arrest.'

'He didn't seem like that sort, no.'

'Then he was arrested and ...'

'And everything went to shit. *Everything.*' The tears are spilling now. Hinton's self-absorption is exposed. She's not crying for her husband, but for herself. The girl she was, the woman she's become.

And it explains something too, this reaction of hers. She must know her husband was an improbable drug dealer, yet she seems oddly ready to see him as guilty nevertheless. But in her world, he *was* guilty. Of hurting her. Of spoiling her cocooned little life. Of getting into some dark and dangerous little corner with no regard for the possible consequences. Hinton is still angry at that betrayal. Angry enough that she'll treat him as a drug smuggler, though part of her knows he wasn't that. Angry enough that she'll airbrush him from his children's lives.

'Did he have any concerns regarding his employment at Barry Precision? Concerns about the legitimacy of any aspect of its business?'

I get a shrug, not an answer.

'Sophie, we need a "Yes" or a "No".'

'Look, Mark didn't talk to me about any of that. There's a cottage he used to go to. He shared it with his brother and sister. We used to go as a family, in summer mostly. It's a bit ...'

She makes a face. A face which says, 'I'm too precious to

deal with anything muddy, or wet, or rustic, or basic.' It's a face the English have used about the Welsh for fifteen centuries. Fifteen centuries, during which they stole our farmland, murdered our princes, and scattered castles, a giant Saxon *screw you* across the country.

Wales is the world capital of medieval castles, the world's most conquered nation. Either that, or the most belligerent.

'*Twll din pob Sais*,' I say.

'Pardon?'

'Doesn't matter. The address of the cottage, please.'

She gives it to me. A place in the Black Mountains, only just inside the border.

'He used to work in this cottage?'

'Yes.'

'On a project that he kept secret from you but which, to the best of your knowledge, was connected with Barry Precision?'

'Yes.' Her answer is so mumbled, I make her repeat it. Not so much for the tape recorder's benefit as to remind her that she's in the presence of two police officers, who can mess her life up if we choose to do it.

'That project. Are there papers or computer files connected with it? Yes or no?'

'I don't know. Not here.'

'In your former home in Barry? In the cottage?'

'Not in Barry. In the cottage, maybe. I *said* I don't know.'

'We may need access to the cottage.'

She shrugs, says nothing.

My voice hardens.

'Sophie, we're asking for permission to enter that cottage. If you say yes, we will go there discreetly and investigate discreetly. If you say no, we apply for a search warrant, in which case we will force entry and we won't attempt to be discreet. It's your call.'

'You can look around, I don't care. I don't *go* there.'

We talk about access. There's a key left there somewhere. In an outbuilding, Sophie thinks. She's either being obstructive or genuinely doesn't know.

Outside, I see the kids arrive back from school with their grandmother. They're shepherded into the living room, away from us.

I ask a few more questions. Go back to the issue of whether she, her husband, or her children have been threatened. But she's got the hang of this interview now. Her answers get ever sulkier and briefer and the line of her polo-neck is now level with her lips.

But we've got what we need. I snap the tape recorder off. Confer briefly with Susan, then say, 'Thank you, Ms Hinton. You've been remarkably helpful.'

And I think, despite herself, she has been.

We don't leave at once, though. I go through to the living room. Theo and Ayla want to see me, I can tell. They want news. They want an answer to Theo's question: *Was it a mistake?* They know their father is dead, of course – whatever way a child can know that. But they want him rescued. They want a hero dad, not a suicide-criminal one.

I don't know if I can deliver the former, but I've stopped believing in the latter.

I show Ayla the shell bracelet. 'We're still trying,' I say. 'We haven't stopped trying.'

We say our goodbyes and Konchesky drives us back to Cardiff. As we pass the Gloucester junction on the M5, I say, 'It's probably worth taking a look at that cottage in the Black Mountains.'

Konchesky shrugs and says, 'I suppose.'

30

Buzz has been as good as his word. The back of my car now boasts a snow shovel with a giant red plastic scoop, a torch, a tow rope, a sleeping bag, bottled water, chocolate, biscuits, and a spare can of petrol. Also some snow chains, which I promise him I will practise putting on before I drive off anywhere, but which I can't see myself using under any circumstances. I have also promised again to buy a proper coat. Also to take gloves and so on, but most of my clothes, including all my cold-weather gear, are at home, not Buzz's flat.

My promises aren't always worth much.

I pick up the shovel and wonder what it would be like to use it. It looks like an object designed by men for men. And in any case, I am standing in a car park by Cardiff Bay with no snow visible anywhere. The temperature is chilly but hardly arctic.

Nothing feels real.

I slam the boot down and get behind the wheel. Switch the engine on.

My exhaust plumes briefly in the air behind me. Ahead of me, a row of leafless trees and the slate water of Atlantic Wharf. A man dressed in a dark coat worn over a suit comes out of Celerity Drive, looks at me, gets into a Volvo saloon and drives off. I wonder if his boot is full of giant red snow things.

Just for a moment, I have no idea why I am here, where I am going, or who I am.

It's not a disconcerting failure, like that night in the Unicorn. It's more a temporary lapse. Like an elderly lady mislaying her glasses or a garage mechanic groping for a wrench. And sure enough, I find the missing knowledge before much time goes by. I'm Fiona Griffiths. I'm driving up into the mountains to investigate murder. My boyfriend is Buzz. Detective Sergeant David 'Buzz' Brydon, no less. I am working on a murder investigation run by DI Rhiannon Watkins and she has authorised this trip.

I lay these pieces of knowledge in front of me. Some of them make sense, others don't. I understand about driving up into the mountains. I understand about the murder, the investigation. I can feel Khalifi's chuckling interest in my labours, Mortimer's sad despair. I find it harder to connect with Buzz, or even with myself if it comes to that, but those things come and go at the best of times. Not something to worry about. I put the clutch in, drop the car into gear, and glide out of the car park.

The journey out of Cardiff is fine. No snow. No ice. No multi-vehicle pileups or lines of shivering refugees reenacting the retreat from Moscow. The radio reports heavy snow in Scotland, Northern Ireland, North Wales, and Pembrokeshire. Eight inches of snow over the Pennines. But I don't live in those places. I'm not going to them.

I take the motorway to Newport, then turn off to Cwmbran and Pontypool. Scars of coal mining above me. Pit explosions and dead miners.

Town built on corpses.

Then through the mining belt to Abergavenny and the mountains beyond. Mortimer's cottage is in the Llanthony Valley, the most easterly of the valleys that divide the Black Mountains. Not far past Abergavenny, I make the turn left for Llanthony.

A different world.

The valley narrows as it climbs. Pasture and snippets of woodland on the valley floor. Green fields pasted as high up the mountainsides as technology and climate can take them. The flanks of the hillside are grizzled with the rust-brown of bracken, humped with gorse and hawthorn, slashed with the rocky-white of mountain streams. There's not much on these roads. A tractor carrying a roll of hay. An agricultural four-by-four with a couple of sheepdogs panting in the back. An old Rover 25 driving twenty miles an hour.

Just for once, the pace suits me. I'm not in a rush. I can feel Khalifi and Mortimer, of course, but I think about Buzz too. Why, of all the girls in the world, should he choose me? Is he simply making a mistake or does he see things that have eluded me? Human relationships aren't my strong point, so I genuinely don't know the answer to that. And that warmth I felt toward him the other night is here now. All that nonsense in the boot of my car was placed there by hands of love. I feel grateful and humble and loving all at once.

I think this is how other people feel. How they feel if they're lucky enough.

At Capel-y-ffin, the way divides. The main route heads up to the valley head and the pass over the mountains to Hay. My fork cuts to the other side of the stream and runs up a side valley to a dead end. Both roads are real Welsh mountain roads. A car's breadth wide, no more. Hedges almost brushing you on both sides. If you meet a vehicle, one of you has to reverse back to the mouth of a gate or a field turning. And when the fields end, the transition to open moorland is abrupt. Exposed and dangerous.

Mortimer's cottage, Pen-y-Cwm, is one of a straggle of houses linked by the dead-end road. Once, I suppose, each house would have been its own tiny farm. A few bony acres yielding a scant living in good times, a starvation diet in times of hardship. These days, the fields are probably all operated from one big mechanised hub farther down the valley. These houses, including Mortimer's, are relics of that earlier age. Adapted now for holiday rentals in the summer. Vacation cottages. Dinosaurs.

I drive slowly, searching for the right place. I would ask someone, but there's no one to ask. On the far side of the valley, I can see a farmer on one of those four-wheel-drive mud buggies rounding up sheep, but he's three miles away through the crystal air.

I get all the way to the farmstead at the end of the road. Talgarreg. There are sheep shuffling in a barn and a dog barking somewhere inside, but no one to ask the way. I turn back down the valley and this time see the entrance to an unpaved track, with a carved wooden board marked PEN-Y-CWM. My car is a city car, poor dear. A coupé cabriolet. I point its wheels at the alarming slope above us and cautiously, in low gear, start to floor the accelerator. The surface is atrocious. Grey aggregate laid over rock. Streams have formed in the path of the tyre tracks, washing away any smaller grit and leaving the occasional violent hole in the path. The car's bottom hits rock deafeningly once and there are a couple of other scrapes, but we get to the top in one piece.

Pen-y-Cwm. In English: the end of the valley.

Up here, you can see why it was named this way. The land flows away from the house in one long liquid scoop. It's closer to the buzzards above than the cluster of houses down valley in Capel-y-ffin. Cardiff feels utterly remote. A myth. A rumour once heard, never believed.

Cardiff, Swansea, Newport, Barry.

Mortimer's house is built of local stone, hard and grey. No whitewash. No snuggling into the mountainside behind. There is a little stand of rowans, mountain ash, but nothing larger. Nothing offering shelter. A stream pours off the hill behind the house. The crash of water onto rock.

No lights on, no car outside.

I was expecting neither. When Konchesky and I discussed this visit with Watkins, the main question was whether to arrive with a brace of uniforms and a forensics specialist, just in case. We all agreed that that didn't make sense. Not yet anyway. We don't actually know that there's anything here. Susan Konchesky was meant to have come with me today, but she never really wanted to, and found an excuse to cry off. Watkins let me come on my own, because there wasn't much reason not to. My job is simply to ascertain if the site holds any secrets, if it calls for a major deployment of resources. It's the sort of task that will take forty minutes, if that.

I try the door to see if it's unlocked. It isn't. Then turn, so I'm standing with my back to the grey house, looking out at the fall of the hill. Ravens bicker in the valley. The distant farmer has his sheep gathered in a flock and is headed down. I look out for the black-and-white dots that must surely be there too, and finally see them. Sheepdogs loping in bracken. A friendly sight.

The rowans cluster around a low outbuilding. A pigsty once? A small barn? The key is there, according to Sophie Hinton, so I get the torch from my car and peer around inside. The place contains some gardening tools. A bit of kidstuff: toboggans, a paddling pool, the limbs of a plastic climbing frame. I heave junk around looking for the key, without joy, then turn back to the doorway. The wall is rough stone, in poor repair, but there's one that looks looser than the rest. Looser and more polished. When I put my hand to it, it slides out easily. Something glimmers in the shadows. I reach in and take the key out.

The front door unlocks easily. I wasn't certain that there'd be electricity up here, but there is. The lights flick on. The place is as cold as a tomb. The main heating is provided by night storage heaters – which means that by this time tomorrow, the house might be getting warm – but in the meantime, I find an oil-filled electric radiator and turn it on, thermostat turned up to maximum. For good measure, I go into the kitchen and turn the electric stove on as well. Already I'm regretting not having bought that coat.

Silly girl, sensible Buzz.

But a bit of cold won't kill anyone. I start to explore.

The living room has a mustard-coloured carpet laid over old stone flags. A black wood-burning stove, two red sofas, and a non-matching armchair. Some cheap pine bookshelves filled with books. Windfall from past bestseller lists. Some tatty boxed board games. On a windowsill facing down the mountain, a pair of binoculars and a bird-watching guide.

The kitchen is similar. China and glasses, plentiful but cheap. Some plastic picnicware. A mismatched assortment of pots and pans, but enough to cook with. The cupboards have some basics – salt, sugar, oil, some candles, a bag of tea, a scrunched-up packet holding some penne pasta, a bottle of malt vinegar – but nothing more.

A downstairs toilet smelling of some chemical pine freshener. A bootroom for coats and spare wood.

The vibe is comfortable enough, but low budget. Sophie Hinton's worst nightmare.

I mess around for just long enough to get used to the space, but it's not downstairs where any secrets will lie.

I head upstairs, where everything is carpeted and feels newer. Three bedrooms – bland, neutral – and a tiny bathroom tiled in blue and white. The bathroom has frosted windows, though the nearest neighbours would need a telescope to see anything. That plus a change in the curvature of the earth, because as far as I've been able to tell, the house is out of sight of everything else. You don't get much farther from people than this.

The room I'm after, however, is none of these. The 'study'

that Sophie Hinton referred to is really little more than an alcove on the landing. A small desk. A laptop. Lamp. Books. Files. There's a little bit of corkboard behind the desk pinned with photos of military hardware. Boys and their toys. Soldier porn. Buzz doesn't keep anything like that. He doesn't even like most action movies, probably because he once served himself. Served and saw action. If you've had the reality, I guess you don't need the fantasy.

I turn the light on, get the laptop fired up.

Back in Cardiff, Watkins has a team exploring the data dump from Barry Precision. She's confident, I think, that it holds some answers, but so far as I know, nothing suspicious has yet been found. I wonder if I should be there instead of here. But I'm pleased I'm not.

Because if anything it's colder up here than downstairs, I rummage round in the bedrooms until I find a huge Aran wool jumper and put it on. It's a man's jumper, XL, and it hangs around me in swags, as though a hot-air balloon has collapsed and died on me. I'm as cold as I was before. I've got hiking boots in the car instead of my stupid office boots, but can't quite face going to get them.

The laptop is ready for action and I sit in front of it, expecting a torrent of secrets to come pouring forth.

The first things I try yield nothing, however. There's no Internet connection up here. Mortimer could have brought a mobile broadband dongle with him, perhaps, but the only web browser I can find is years out of date and the pages stored in History don't seem of any special interest. In any case, my phone doesn't get a signal up here. Perhaps other networks have coverage, but likely not. It's not the kind of territory that gets phone executives hot and sticky with excitement.

So next, I try any documents stored on the hard drive. There aren't many. Some letters. What look like some school projects. Ayla and Theo are too young to have authored these, but their cousins, Mark's nieces and nephews, are presumably the right age to have compiled 'reports' on the Tudors, fossils, and the Battle of Britain. A giant history sandwich.

More interesting, in theory, are some technical documents, but I don't understand the language involved. The document headers are effectively in code. Not secret-agent-speak, just a combination of engineering-speak and office acronyms. The documents are headed things like 'MC Shpt 110305.' They contain mostly compilations of technical specifications. Stuff that seems broadly similar to the data I abstracted from Barry Precision. Same sub headings, same layout. I should really have brought that other data here, so I could compare, but I think I was expecting something simple, not some arcane technical conundrum.

I'm not immediately sure what to do, so go downstairs and fill the kettle. Turn it on. Make tea. There's nothing herbal here, so I make do with a regular tea bag. No milk either, so just brew a pint of hot, black tea in a huge pottery mug. Contrary to my usual habit, I add sugar, to take away the taste of the metallic mountain water, the strongly tannined tea. It tastes like sweetened bog water, but is nevertheless somehow welcome. A comfort against the cold.

And as I leave the kitchen, for the stairs that rise directly from the living room, I notice what must have been obvious from the kitchen window. It's snowing. Big heavy flakes. Falling with a calm insistence, a sense of purpose

Against the grey sky above, the flakes look black. Like imperfectly burned coal ash settling back over a mining village. But the ground below gives the lie to that. It's already covered. Sheeted in white while I was at the alcove upstairs. Every field, every hedge, every stroke and line of moor and mountain. The rowans stand black-fingered against the white. Farther down the hill, little stands of oak and hawthorn seem to have contracted into two dimensions. Given up colour and volume for the purity of shape. The naked essence of tree.

I stand at the window for a while, watching.

Because I am who I am – and because I am *where* I am – I can't help but feel the terrible peacefulness of death. It's as though the world has given up on life. As though the sky is shredding itself and scattering its remains. One giant burial, robed in white.

It's not a bad feeling at all. On the contrary, it's calming. Under other circumstances, I would allow myself to sink into it. Relish it. And I do. For a while I do. Just stand at the window and watch the landscape disappear. Cardiff is no longer even a rumour. Abergavenny lies on the outer edge of the world. The storm and fury of Watkins's police investigation means nothing up here. The rules, the files, the tasks, the duties. All that stays real is this whitening mountainside and the presence of those who died. Mary Jane Langton. Mark Mortimer. Ali el-Khalifi. The two halves of the human race joined by this snow. A temporary unity.

I don't know how long I stare out at the scene, but the untidy realities of the present summon me back.

It's four in the afternoon and the light is failing. I need to leave now or spend the night here. There's no option really. The lane is already under two inches of snow and the temperature is below freezing. There are steep hills and sharp turns on the road back into Capel-y-ffin, and I don't trust either me or my car to navigate them. Still less do I want to attempt it at the onset of more than fifteen hours of darkness.

So I leave my bucket of tea and bustle around trying to be sensible. Buzz-style sensible. Very cautiously, I turn my car, then take it, skidding, to the bottom of the drive. There's another hideous encounter with a rock about halfway down, but the car still seems to be in one piece. I'm guessing that there will be tractors or four-wheel drives moving in the morning. Once they've dug out the road for me, I should be able to

213

slide down their tyre tracks into the valley bottom. And if the worst comes to the worst, I can always walk. If I allow myself enough daylight, I can't see myself getting seriously lost.

I check my phone again so I can text Watkins, but there's still no whiff of a signal. It's annoying, but not the end of the world. Buzz will worry a little, but he knows I'm likely to be out of signal.

So much for that. The next issue is getting through the night as warmly and safely as I can.

I change into hiking boots and grab Buzz's biscuits and chocolate. I wonder about taking a joint as well, but I don't need one. Joints are mostly for when I get stressed and I'm not stressed. I'm happy.

I plough my way back up the hill to the cottage. Hard work. Not just the steepness of the hill and the uncertainty of the track, but the snow is already thick enough that I can feel it dragging against every movement. I'm panting by the time I reach the front door.

The next thing is heating. I'm wearing the ridiculous Aran jumper with my coat buttoned over it. The jumper's sleeves are so long, I use them like gloves. There's not a glimmer of warmth from the storage heaters, but they'll presumably start kicking out heat in the morning. The oil radiator is ridiculously underpowered for the size of the property, but I suppose it's only there to top up the storage heating. I do, however, manage to rustle up paper, firelighters, wood, and matches and get a fire burning in the stove.

I think how little Sophie Hinton would have liked this way of life.

The room is still cold, but between the stove, the radiator, and my unerringly fashionable outfit, I'm warm enough. I throw out the tea I made before and make a fresh mug. I bring the laptop down from the alcove, along with a heap of Mortimer's files. Thinking about it, I go up and drag down a couple of duvets. The only room in this house that's going to be even half warm is the living room, and I can sleep well enough on one of the sofas.

Food is the next puzzle, but one with a refreshingly simple solution. There is nothing to eat except the stuff I brought up from the car, plus the pasta, oil, and sugar from the kitchen. So I'll eat that. I won't starve.

I make a nest of sofa cushions and arrange the duvets around me like some Ottoman sultan. The laptop snuggles with me in the centre of my nest.

This is good. How it should be. I realise that there's something about the way police officers work that's utterly inimical to real investigation – or at least, inimical to the way I like to work. The office is about institutions and procedures and all the false realities of any large organisation. None of that stuff makes any sense up here. All I have is words that a dead man wrote, here in the place where he wrote them.

I light a couple of candles and turn the living room lights off. I'll work by candles, the light of the laptop screen, and the red glow from the stove.

Turn my attention back to Mark Mortimer. Already I know I'm going to find what I came for.

31

Outside the cottage, the early evening darkness hardens into something blacker. I can see a single light from my window, from a barn miles away in the valley. Aside from that: nothing. A black sky, no moon, a million stars.

The cold is intense. It's chilly enough inside the house, with the stove burning nonstop, but I venture outside a couple of times – simply to see and feel the diamond hardness of the night – and the cold has a physical presence I've read about but never previously experienced. It's like the entire world is being tightened up. Waterfalls are being frozen into place, trees stiffened, the air clarified, the ground plated over with iron.

I like it. It's easier to feel myself at times like this. In opposition to something, not just wading through Cardiff's too-ordinary air.

When I get hungry, I eat Buzz's biscuits. When I get hungry again, I cook the pasta and eat that.

Most of my time, though, I spend with the laptop and the files. The answer lies here. It's up to me to find it. I decide I will read every piece of paper, examine every computer file. By eleven in the evening, I've more or less accomplished that. No joy. I've got a notepad filled with little questions to myself. Things to check later. Things to check when I'm in a warm office with access to the Internet. But nothing screamingly obvious. Nothing that feels like the secret for which Mortimer died.

I make more tea. I probably haven't drunk as much caffeine as this in my entire life. It feels okay though. Part of the experience. I'm feeling clear, not buzzy.

Back at the laptop, I'm uncertain what to do. I've tried every Word document. Every spreadsheet. There aren't many emails and those that there are are very old – presumably dating from the period before the laptop was brought to this cottage. I don't really know my way around Powerpoint, and Mortimer doesn't quite strike me as slick-presentation man, but I can't find any Powerpoint files anyway.

I'm puzzled.

There *is* a puzzle here. Hinton's silences virtually confirmed it. Penry's head wound and the incident on Marine Parade Drive certainly do. But what's the mystery? Had Mortimer hidden some documents somewhere in the house, or loft, or outbuilding? I even spend an hour or so rummaging around everywhere I can think of. Examining floorboards for loose nails, that kind of thing. I don't venture into the outbuilding, because it has no power, and I would need daylight to search it, but mostly I end my search more certain than ever that the laptop must have the answers. You don't come up here to hide stuff. You're hidden just by being here. And it wasn't as though Mortimer was on the run from anyone. He wasn't. He lived in Barry and had a good, ordinary job. Until things went pear-shaped with his prettily petulant missus, he probably had a regular, happy family life too.

So the computer is the answer. I heave more logs on the fire, resettle in my nest, and go back to the screen.

File Manager this time. I want to make sure I understand where all the files are. And as soon as I do, I realise what I've been missing. It's a *doh!* moment. Mortimer was an engineer. Of course he used Microsoft Office from time to time, but that wasn't the centre of things for him. There's a program on the computer called Solid Edge. I open it up. It's a CAD program: computer-assisted design. It has heaps of files associated with it. In terms of memory usage on the hard drive, there is almost fifty times more data associated with Solid Edge than with everything else put together.

Here. The answer is here.

I'm not an engineer, have no training in Solid Edge, and don't know exactly what I'm looking for. But I fool around, learning how to open files, how to look at what they contain. It's slow work – and I'm starting to feel tired, hungry, and cold – but I start to get the hang of it.

Shapes appear from the computer. I find I can revolve them, inspect them. Virtual steel turned by virtual hands. Tubes, rings, flanges, gears. Countless things whose names and uses I don't know. A mass of associated technical data and computations. There's a kind of beauty in it all. A flowing exactitude.

In my next life, I'll learn maths.

A lot of this looks like the data I took from Barry Precision. I haven't yet looked at the technical drawings in any detail, but presumably the two datasets have a lot in common. On the other hand, the Barry data was far more copious than just this. This is an oldish laptop and its hard drive is barely one-third full. This data was carefully selected. Those selection criteria will, I'm certain, be key to the riddle, but how to know what they were? How to guess?

Then I realise that Mortimer *worked* up here. That is, he didn't just examine documents brought from work, he did creative modelling work of his own. By tracking back on the document histories, I can find the documents that he either worked on or created up here. I go through my notes marking documents that seemed to have had extensive work, and those that didn't. The files divide into two sets. If there's a forged hollow tube in the set of files brought up on disk from Barry Precision, there'll be an analogous file created up here. If there's a gear coupling in the Barry dataset, there'll be a gear coupling created up here. Pinion rods. Moulded steel.

I understand something else as well. The Barry dataset comprised only the volumes themselves. That is, a virtual metal shape floating in a 3D cyber-void. But that was all. No technical data, no calculations.

Then it clicks. Mortimer wanted to understand those shapes for himself. He needed to understand them the way any engineer would: through maths, through design. So he rebuilt them. From the ground up. Reverse engineering the technical data from the shapes.

The Barry dataset was impoverished. It contained pictures, but not the maths. Up here, Mortimer reconstructed the maths. And the maths taught him something which would end up killing him.

Six in the morning. I make more tea and take it outside with the rest of the biscuits.

The stars are gone. Someone has come along in the night and stolen them all. Cloud has rolled in again and it's snowing again. I've come out in the giant jumper, my coat and a duvet over my shoulders, and it's still cold.

I wonder if anything will drive down the lane in the morning.

I wonder how long my wood will last.

I go back into the cottage. My eyes need a rest from the computer screen, so I prowl the house, still wearing everything, including the duvet.

In the living room, I top up the stove. There's a weak heat starting to come from the night store heaters. In the kitchen, I boil the kettle again, not because I want more to drink but to create a little heat. In the bootroom, I inventory my wood stack. There's not a lot there, but if the storage heaters work properly, I shouldn't be so reliant on the stove during the coming day.

Upstairs, the bathroom is so cold there is ice on the inside of the window. The bedrooms are bland and dull. I'm about to go back downstairs again when my eye falls on the alcove.

Tanks. Artillery pieces. Rocket launchers.

Soldier porn.

Ich bin ein fuckwit.

This is what I've been looking at all night. I've been looking at weapons. Not the whole assembly, but individual parts. One of the photos is of a tank firing in a desert somewhere. The gun barrel has a distinctive shape. It's not a single smooth tube, there are areas of greater thickness, parts that move. And I've seen that exact object downstairs, floating in a 3-D void. I didn't recognise it because I didn't know what I was looking for. Maybe also because I'm not a guy. My mental attic doesn't have much soldier porn kicking around its dusty spaces. All the same, there's not much doubt in my mind now. Another hour's work and there's no doubt at all.

From the photos pinned to Mortimer's wall, I can identify at least six different weapons parts, plus three maybes. That still leaves numerous files without an obvious linkage to weapons, but no doubt if I put the whole lot in front of a procurement officer at the Ministry of Defence, I'd learn exactly what those links are. The unlicensed export of weapons is a serious offence. And, though I'll need to check when I'm back at the office, Barry Precision holds no export licences, I'd bet my life on it.

Sophie Hinton's words from that original interview come back to me. *He had this Saint Mark thing going. Butter wouldn't melt, and all that. Then what is he, really? A drug dealer who was busted and sent to jail.* She couldn't have been much wronger. Her children's silent belief in their father couldn't have been much righter.

And this, I bet, is the story. Barry Precision decided that the manufacture and export of weapons parts would be a profitable – if illegal – sideline. Mortimer found out what his employers were up to. Made certain that he was correct before levelling any accusation. No doubt discussed the whole thing with Khalifi. No doubt, in his patient engineer's way, became remorseless and obsessive in documenting the entire profitable, lethal scam.

He pissed off his wife. Neglected her. Nudged her just enough to get her started on her path of sulky self-pity. The one ally he might have been able to trust was increasingly lost to him.

His employers somehow found out. Or perhaps he told them. Either way, they decided, fuck you, we'll destroy your life. And did. Framed him on a drug-smuggling charge. Something so clumsy, so crass in design, that if he had wanted to fight it, he probably could have. But I bet they also threatened him. His wife, his kids. Told him that if he didn't accept his time in jail, his family would all be killed or injured.

So he took it. Saint Mark took the drug charge. Lost his job, his wife, his means of making a living. Accepted that he couldn't take the risk of divulging what he knew. A martyr to his own purity of purpose. The suicide, I guess, was simply the outcome of all that. When your life is completely fucked, what's the point of continuing?

Other parts of the puzzle start clicking into place too. Some clearly. Others dimly. Like water trickling under ice or a weight of snow settling on a roof.

And that's fine. I don't need the whole thing now. I have what I need.

I'm still wearing Ayla's little bracelet. I touch it and promise her and Theo, once again, that we're going to drag this whole mess out into the open.

Their father: not a criminal, but a fighter for justice.

How much difference will it make to the children to know that? I think it'll make all the difference in the world. I imagine

Theo's serious dark-eyed little face when I tell him, *Yes, it was all a mistake.*

But back to me and back to now.

It's past 7 AM. It's still dark. Nothing has moved on the lane. Nothing will until full daylight. The snow is above my boots now. Still falling, still beautiful.

I decide I'll get two or three hours' sleep, then get down the hill early enough that I can walk it if I really have to. I've enjoyed my night up here, but there's almost no food left and not much wood. I'm exhausted, I realise. Bone-tired.

Pull my nest closer to the stove. Add logs to the fire. I'm asleep within the minute.

32

Wake up. Achy and cold. It's dark.

Dark and it shouldn't be.

Cold and it shouldn't be.

Check my watch: it's half past two in the afternoon. I've slept almost eight hours, rare for me at any time, no matter now tired I am.

The room is dark because more snow has fallen and the window is occluded. A dim white light filters in. The room's not supposed to be cold. The stove is long gone out, but the storage heaters should be burning the place up and they're not.

A moment's experiment shows that the electrics are all dead. None of the switches have tripped. It must be a full-scale power outage. Hardly surprising, I suppose, and up here there won't be engineers racing to restore power.

Oh crap. I need to get out of here and my brain is feeling muddy after too much sleep. There's half a packet of biscuits left. Otherwise only oil and sugar. I shove the biscuits in my pocket and go carefully down the drive to see if my car will start. The poor lamb is completely buried in snow. At first the door is frozen shut, but when I yank it hard enough, it opens. Key into the ignition. A quick prayer to whichever god protects sporty little cabriolets of dubious mechanical reliability, then turn the key. The engine fires up on the second attempt. Quick thank you to the god in question.

And there have been vehicles moving on the lane. There are tyre tracks already part filled in, but at least they point me in the right direction. I'm a little uncertain as to whether I'll be able to get my car out of the drive and onto the lane, but I set to work with Buzz's precious shovel. It is indeed ridiculously oversized, but what the hell. Needs must when the devil rides.

I work hard until the car stands clear of its snowy curtains. Clear enough that there is, at least approximately, a way through onto the lane.

Then nothing for it but to try. Get in the car. Put it in gear and try to get it out onto the road. It needs to clear a little ridge of snow and turn hard through ninety degrees, if I'm not to ram the hedge opposite.

Buzz, I know, would have an instinctive feel for how to do this. 'Back up a little, Fiona. Rock it, don't let that wheel spin. Easy now. No, no, half-lock only. Don't try to force it.' Buzz would ease that car out onto the road and make it look as easy as pie.

Me, my technique is different. I try easing the car over the ridge, but nothing doing. Then I start panicking and start revving the engine and gritty snow flies in a gale of fury from my front tyres. Then I stall. Then restart the car and leave the engine running as I hack away with the shovel again.

I wish Buzz was here.

Wish, but also don't. When your head has been as muddled as mine, for as long as mine, you see things in a different way. Right now, I'm alive. I don't just know it with my head. I feel it in my painfully cold fingers. Feel it in my sodden boots. Feel it in my racing heart. I even feel it in these intricate little computations of survival. A dead person wouldn't care, and I do. I really do.

Anyway. I'm done digging. Back into the car. Try again. First nothing happens, then the car shoots forward out of its rut. I turn the wheel, skid, slide straight into the bank opposite, bounce off and end up pointing downhill, the right way, square in the tyre tracks. I drive a few yards, just to check the car can do it. And it can. The clever beast. It can.

My thinking now is completely clear. I know what I'm doing. I go back up to the house as quickly as I can. Unmake my nest. Put the duvets back on the bed. Wash anything I've used in the kitchen. Dry it. Replace it. Watkins is a stickler for these things. Hinton gave me permission to enter the house, not to eat all the food in the kitchen and sleep there overnight. I don't want to provoke complaints. For the same reason, I take off my supersized Aran jumper and leave it back in the drawer were I found it.

I do take the laptop, though. It's evidence in relation to a major offence, and if I don't take it, there's a risk of data being lost. I'm operating well within police powers here, so I don't care if anyone complains or not.

Leave the house, lock up, return the key to its resting place. Back down to the car.

I wish I hadn't left it so late – the light is dimming behind thick cloud – but I'm not too concerned. I'll follow the road down to Capel-y-ffin, then either stop there for the night or, if the roads are okay, get out to Abergavenny or even back to Cardiff.

If for any reason the car gets stuck, and it might, I'll simply follow the tyre tracks by foot. It's no more than a few miles to Capel-y-ffin. Probably not even as far as that to the first inhabited house. It's cold, but hardly murderous. I have a torch. I'll walk fast. And if that really doesn't work for any reason, I'll spend the night in the car. I have a sleeping bag, water and chocolate – my chocolate, that is, not the stuff Buzz gave me, which is already gone. My petrol tank is nearly full. I'll run the engine through the night if I have to.

You'll get through this, Griffiths. No worries.

And it's true. I will get through this. I'm not worried.

I change my wet hiking boots for my dry office ones, which are in any case easier to drive in. Then, proceeding with extreme caution, headlights on full beam, I start to creep down the hill.

33

It goes okay. I'm not likely to win prizes for extreme-cold-weather driving, but I don't have to. Admittedly I do get stuck early on. I'm going so slowly that when I come to a slight rise in the road – it mostly curves steadily down – I don't have the speed or the traction to ascend.

Silly girl.

What would Buzz do?

He'd ramp it up. I reverse back up the road as far as I can. The snow is cold enough and hard enough that the existing tyre tracks nudge me back onto the road if I start to drift off. I move forward with more speed. Get higher up the hill this time, before coming to a stop, wheels spinning purposelessly on ice. So reverse back again, farther than before. Move forward faster. It's exciting, actually. This time, I sail up the hill no problems and am so pleased with myself that I have to stop the car to enjoy the moment. In the valley far below me, I see the first lights twinkling through the twilight.

I feel a rush of something. I'm not always good at naming my feelings – it's something I used to practise by rote with doctors – and pride isn't something I feel often enough for me to feel very confident about spotting it when it comes. But this feeling – warm, happy, a bit excited – is pride, I think. I spend a few moments letting myself feel it, what it's like. It's partly, of course, the computer I have on the back seat. The fact that I was right to explore Mortimer.

But it's not mostly that. I know my detective work is good. It's not something I worry about. But driving a car in the snow? That's something I've never done and would expect myself to be plain useless at. This whole twenty-four hours, I've lit fires, cooked pasta, made tea, kept warm, shovelled my car out, got it out onto the road. That doesn't make me Buzz. Still less does it make me Lev. But a girl's got to start somewhere and right now I feel pleased with myself.

Slipping back into gear, I drive on.

Get to a fork in the road. I don't remember this from before, but I was driving the other way, looking forwards. One way looks a bit more roadlike, but there are no tyre-tracks – or no recent ones anyway – and the other route looks freshly driven. Peering cautiously down the slope, I see, joy of joys, a pair of red lights. Lights attached to that thing of beauty: a Land Rover four-by-four. Not caring now, I turn down the hill and drive up to the back of the Land Rover. As it sees me coming, it ploughs off into the snow to let me past.

I don't especially want to pass it. I want to stick close and let the Land Rover watch me all the way down to Capel. So I pass the Land Rover, then stop.

Stop for two reasons.

One, to stay close to my saviours. Two, because the track ends at a low barn, standing just above the rise of a stream.

This isn't the road, it's a field.

It's not the way to Capel-y-ffin, it's a dead end.

Sod it.

Not a big *sod it*, mind you. A small one. I'm pretty certain that my sporty little town car isn't going to have the muscle to climb back up the hill I've just come down, but I can either get the Land Rover to tow me or I can just dump my car, come and get it when I can. The bright edge is taken from my pride, but not too badly.

I'm about to change back into my hiking boots, go and

talk to the farmer, when I see that the farmer has swung his car round, pointing back up the hill. He probably knows he's going to need to tow me out of here.

The Land Rover cuts its lights. Two men tramp towards me through the snow. I can't see them. It's not fully dark now, but almost.

One of the men comes to the passenger side of the car. One to the driver's side. I've wound my window down to talk to them, letting the cold air in.

Only they're not a farmer and his mate. And they're not here to rescue me. They're my friends from Marine Parade. Jaw Guy and Silent Guy.

The men who, I'll bet, killed Khalifi.

Fear has a colour. A taste and feel. Cold, mostly. That's mostly what I notice. The chilly touch of adrenaline finding its way into those places I never normally feel. The very tips of my fingers. The soles of my feet. A cold burning in my ears. The taste is like an absence. I'd say like a mouthful of cotton wool, except it's emptier than that. My mouth feels both choked and as if it's biting down on a vacuum. That same vacuum fills my stomach. I feel scooped out, empty. Like one of those corpses on the pathologist's table that look vaguely normal but whose cavities have been filled out with pipe insulation and Sealed Air plastic bags.

These people have come to kill me.

'Evening, gents,' I say.

Silent Guy gets into the cramped little back. Jaw Guy gets into the passenger seat beside me. I let them because I can't stop them. Because I don't know what else to do.

I'm not sure how they knew I was at the cottage, but then I realise they *didn't* know. I'm sure they – or their employers at Barry Precision – do have some kind of hold over Sophie Hinton. They've either threatened her or paid her. In any case, Hinton must have felt worried enough by my visit to contact them. To mention that I seemed to have an interest in the cottage. That was likely enough the first they knew of the cottage, so they came here to clean up. When they arrived, they found me here too. Two birds, one stone.

When Hinton called whoever it was she called, she probably didn't mean to kill me, but she also wouldn't have bothered to think through the possible consequences of her actions.

One loose word, one dead body. Not her concern. I can hear her voice in my head now. 'I don't want to sound awful. I'm very sorry and everything.'

Petulant cow.

I should have given her that slapping.

But Silent Guy and Jaw Guy don't kill me. Don't hurt me. Don't even seem to want anything from me. Sure, they take the laptop. Just walk it over to their Land Rover, drop it on a back seat, then saunter back again. Mostly, though, they just sit in my car. I keep the engine running for warmth. I've got loads of petrol and I do remember to check. Headlights on, because it would seem too weird sitting there in the dark.

On my left is Jaw Guy, Scottish guy. The broken jaw looks both normal and not quite. Like something's askew, but in the poor light it's hard to see exactly where the problem lies.

Behind Jaw Guy is the other man, who hasn't yet said anything audible in my presence. My car is a three-door convertible and though there is space in the back, it's not really the sort of space designed to accommodate reasonably large, reasonably well-padded contract killers. But that's not really my issue.

I wait a bit for them to say anything or start anything, but they don't.

'This is fun, isn't it?'

No response.

To the Scotsman whose jaw I broke, I say confidentially, 'How's the jaw? Bit sore, maybe?' Since I still get no response,

I push a bit harder. Turning around to the guy in the back, I say, 'Did he have to drink through a straw? Or did you have to bottle-feed?'

The guy in the back chuckles, and says, 'Something like that.'

He's wearing hat and gloves. So is the other guy. They're not removing them even though the car is warm. I guess they're being cautious about DNA. I like to see that in a contract killer. Professionalism. Attention to detail.

But they're not killing me.

'Dunbar,' I say. 'Jim Dunbar at Barry Precision. He's sort of got the motivation, but does he really have the pizzazz? I mean, you're a fairly top-end pair of murderers. I don't think Dunbar is quite in your league.'

No response.

'But maybe you don't know about things like that. Why you kill the people you kill. Maybe you're just given a name and a face. Ali el-Khalifi. He lives here. He looks like this. Go kill.'

No response.

'Whose idea was it to copy the Mary Langton killing?' To Silent Guy, I add, 'I'm guessing that was you. I think your friend might be a bit stupid, yes?'

Still no response and the silence is getting tiresome, so I change the subject. 'Okay, shall we play I Spy?' There's nothing in the sweep of my headlights except snow and some trees. The barn too, dimly. 'I spy with my little eye something beginning with *S*.'

No response.

I give them two minutes by the dashboard clock to think of something, but they don't manage it. I give them the answer. 'It was *snow*. I'm slightly disappointed, to be honest. I was trying to start with something easy.'

'*Ja*, I thought of *snow*.' The guy in the back. He has an

231

accent of some sort. Not British. Scandinavian, I guess, and he looks Nordic. His eyes are dancing with amusement. He's enjoying this. His Scottish buddy just glowers at me or avoids my gaze. I don't think he likes me.

'I don't know your names and it seems a bit weird doing this without them. You are ...?' I ask this question of the Scottish guy, but get no answer. 'Hamish, is it? Hoots mon and och aye the noo.' My Scottish accent is crap. 'You know, your jaw looks a bit funny.' I turn to the guy in the back. 'It *does* look funny, doesn't it? I'm not making it up.'

The guy in the back shrugs, but it's a gesture. A communication of a sort. His eyes are laughing.

'What shall I call you? Bjorn? Ulf? Sven? Mikkel? Olaf? Jakob?' My well of Scandinavian-names-suitable-for-contract-killers is beginning to run dry, but the guy rescues me.

'Olaf. We'll go with that.'

'Hamish and Olaf. Olly. Okay. This is nice, isn't it?'

We sit around some more. I switch my lights to sidelights only. The engine is still running. The car is warm.

When I cut my headlights, I sensed, or thought I did, a ripple of alertness from my two silent companions. There's no point in having lights up here, except as a signal. Are we meeting someone here? Now, that *is* an interesting thought. If so, I'm guessing Prothero. Or – more interesting still – maybe Mostafa el Saadawi. Dunbar might be another possibility, but what I said to Hamish and Olly about him is true. I bet he knows what's going on, but he's too small-time to hire killers. Not enough skin in the game.

I say, 'Just so you both know, Detective Inspector Watkins knows where I am and why I'm here. So does the entire chain of command. And if anything happens to a serving police officer, there will be a total shitstorm.'

And as I say those words, I feel them. Feel their truth. I know Watkins doesn't know what I found up there in the cottage.

232

She sent me there. She debated sending a team in and decided against it. It was meant to be me and Susan Konchesky, but when Susan weaselled out, Watkins sent me anyway. I agreed with that decision – lobbied for it – but Watkins isn't one to shirk responsibility, legal or moral. If something happens to me, she'll be on the case.

I realise something else too. That I do now belong to the police. Part of the family. I'm far from being Cathays's favourite copper. We don't have an employee-of-the-month contest, but if we did, I'd never win it. I've had more than my share of bollockings, more than my share of office feuds. Truth is, there's a fair-sized kernel of people who actively dislike me. But none of that matters. I'm part of the family, a wayward daughter. If anything happens to me, there truly will be a shitstorm.

I feel a pricking in my eyes.

I know what that pricking means. Not tears, but whatever comes before tears. I've only cried once since I was a very young child. This moment now isn't the second time exactly, but it comes close. It's the best feeling in the world. Dead people can't cry. I bet their eyes don't even prick.

I'm sitting there, thinking these things, when I notice that the lights on the dashboard seem dimmer than they were. I flick the headlights onto full beam again and now I'm pretty sure. There's a loss of power somewhere.

Olaf says, 'You need to turn the engine off and on again.'

So I do. It seems logical enough, but I'm not very practical about these things and in any case I'm still cuddling up to that lovely pricking feeling in my eyes. Result: I'm not thinking about the electromechanical aspects of my situation.

Which is an error.

I turn the engine off, then turn the key the other way. The starter motor chokes weakly. That's all. My first thought is,

That's stupid, the engine is warm. My second thought is, *Ah, so this is how they intend to kill me.*

Olaf, reading my mind, says, 'I think there maybe is a small electrical fault with your alternator.'

I don't know what an alternator is. I assume the thing that recharges the battery. In any case, it's clear what they've done. It was they, not the snow, that cut power to the cottage. They wanted to drive me out of there and they did. At the same time – while I was sleeping, presumably – they sabotaged my car. They drove down into this lonely patch of nowhere and kept their tracks fresh enough and deep enough that they could be sure I would follow. How sweet. How beautifully simple.

I try the engine a couple more times, but each try is weaker than the last.

Hamish has opened his door. The car's temperature drops immediately. Both men are dressed in heavy boots, down jackets, gloves, hats. They've probably got thermal undies on too. Me, I've got a thin blue coat and opaque tights.

Olaf says, 'Can I have your coat, please?'

I think about that. I could fight, of course, but they're ready for that. There are two of them and they're miles stronger. I could try running, but I couldn't outrun this pair. Not uphill, not in snow, and not while wearing slippery-soled boots.

So I get out of the car, take off my coat, fold it, hand it to Olaf. He says, 'Thank you.' I'm wearing black trousers that I normally wear to the office. Tights. Woolly socks. A long-sleeved T-shirt with a poloneck over the top. That's all. It's minus whatever and the cold is already starting to bite.

'And maybe your pullover.'

That's harder for me to remove. Scarier. But I hand it over. Olaf says, 'Thanks.'

I wonder if there is going to be a sexual attack here. It's funny, as a woman, you can't help but wonder. Even when you're about to die. But this pair seem too professional for that. They want the emergency services to find a hypothermia victim, not a rape victim.

Hamish meantime is patting down the car. He's found the torch, the sleeping bag. The things that might keep me alive. He does something to the torch in the snow and kills its light. There's a brief discussion with Olaf about the sleeping bag, which I gaze on with longing. I can't hear their muttered conversation, but it ends with Hamish taking the sleeping bag to the Land Rover. I imagine they'll take it back up to the cottage and leave it there. Buzz, the only person who knows that it was in my car, will assume I just forgot it at the house. Typical Fiona, he'll think. And he would, most of the time, be right to think so.

Poor Buzz. This will be very hard on him. Not supergreat and perfect at all.

'The last part,' I say to Olaf. 'The very last part. I'd like to be left alone, if that's okay.'

He thinks about that briefly, but nods. 'Sure.' He holds eye contact with me. 'It's quite fast, you know. And after a while you don't feel much.'

He's trying to be nice. The contract-killer version. I say, 'Thanks.'

Hamish comes back. The two men complete their check of the car. They're looking for blankets, tools, anything that might help me out of this. They don't find anything. The car battery is pretty much dead now. There's a dim spark left in the headlights, but almost nothing.

'Can I get back in?'

'Sure.'

We get back in, though mine is the only door that's closed. The other one is wide open and a convertible isn't exactly the most heat-proof conveyance at the best of times. A faint breeze – a whisper of air, no more – wanders through the car.

It is profoundly cold.

We're sitting in the same configuration as before. Me on the driver's side. Hamish to my left. Olaf behind. He has my coat and jumper folded on his lap. He takes my phone, checks it for signal – which is registering zero, *null points*, forget-about-it – and hands it to me.

'You can write texts if you like.'

So I do. Write my last words.

To Buzz. To Mam and Dad, Ant and Kay.

I tell them I love them. That they've been my most important people. That I wish every good thing in the world for them.

None of it is original or clever or witty. Not one word of it. But it is real. My eyes are pricking again. If I weren't so cold, I might even cry.

I love those people. Love them with all my heart. Nothing else matters. Not really. I hope Buzz and the others know that. I wish I had more time to communicate. More time to express those thoughts.

I'm shivering now. Shaking with cold. As I was completing my texts, my fingers were jittering on the keys.

I hand the phone back to Olaf, who wordlessly scrutinises my texts. Checking I haven't said anything about how I came to die here like this. I haven't. Maybe there's some clever code I could have used, but I'm too cold to think of anything like that. In any case, that's not the most important message for me right now. Olaf says, 'Okay.' He gets out of the car – Hamish has to pull the seat back so he can get out – then he walks up the track into the darkness, comes back a few minutes later without the phone.

'They'll find it. I've made sure they'll find it.'

'Thank you.'

We sit in silence.

These are the minutes in which I die.

Temperature isn't a feeling anymore. It's not like a spectrum of colour, a range of smells. Cold and pain are the same thing. They've merged, become one. Colder means more painful. A pain that expresses itself in every part of my body. My now compulsively shaking body.

'Hamish?' I say.

He turns to me. His stupid, gingery, violent face. I shoot my right arm out and strike his nose as ferociously as I know how. Heel of my hand. Shoulder backing up the arm. All of Lev's good teaching in the blow.

There's a spray of blood. I think I've broken his nose. He thinks so too. He claps one hand to his face. The other hand wants to get right on and murder me now.

Might even do so except that Olaf physically restrains him.

'To match his jaw,' I say to Olaf. 'Even things up.'

Olaf's somewhat amused by that, but mostly pissed off. I've broken our lovely little murder-in-the-snow compact. Taken the sweetly amiable edge off it. More to the point, there's blood all over the car and they have to clean up. Olaf releases Hamish's arm but growls at him not to touch me. There's a fierce authority in his voice. He always felt like the boss of these two.

He orders me out of the car and guards me as Hamish wipes down the surfaces. But there's a limit to what he can do. There will still be blood in the seams of the leather seats. Blood on my trousers. Blood on my T-shirt. And they can't take those things if they want this murder to look like an idiot-girl-gets-lost-in-snow death.

Truth is, I don't know if anyone will order forensics on this crime scene. Why would they? There's little enough that will look suspicious. It would be totally like me to get stuck in the snow. Like me to be underdressed. Like me to set out at night in an unsuitable car. Like me to forget my sleeping bag. That spray of blood is a lovely little clue that could lead straight to the murderer and no one may ever find it.

But maybe not. Watkins will be the grim angel of this investigation and she's not one to undercook things. She sent me here. She'll do this right.

I stand in the snow as Hamish does his business. Olaf keeps me standing there long after he's finished. Partly punishment. Partly just wanting to get on and finish the job.

A T-shirt in this weather.

I am practically naked.

These are long, freezing minutes.

The cold is bewildering now. My feet are burning with the cold. A fire I can't step out of. My hands are the same. But what's worse is the shudders from within. I can feel my body retracting into itself. Like the last warm ember in a dying fire. I feel myself get stupider. I try to say something to Olaf and I hear myself slurring the words. Like my tongue is lolling about in my mouth, useless as whale meat. Any movements I make are gross, clumsy. On the edge of failure.

I don't know how long I stand there. When I'm too cold to stand anymore, I fall over.

More minutes pass.

I'm not even shaking now.

Finally Olaf says, 'I think it's time you had your clothes back.'

He hands them to me, but I can't put them on. That's not me being tactical or obstinate or anything else. I simply can't co-ordinate my movements.

I think there might even be tears in my eyes now, but not real ones. Not like when I was thinking of Buzz and my family. Just eyes watering with the cold.

I find myself being lifted by the two men. Bundled into my clothes. Hamish holds my arms behind me, twisting unkindly, while Olaf does up the buttons on my coat. They lift me into the car. I press myself into them as they do so. Wanting to snatch any glimmers of warmth from their bodies.

They're not returning my clothes to me to keep me warm. The clothes wouldn't be sufficient to protect me on a night like this, even if I had any body heat left to conserve. They're just setting the stage for this final act.

I don't object. I prefer having my clothes back.

And it's close now. My death is close. Olaf was right. It's a kind death, in a way. You expect a lot of things from dying. Coldness. Stillness. Silence. Pain. What you don't expect is this great clumsy stupidity. A blanketing idiocy. Brought about as blood retreats from the inessential organs – like the brain – to the only two things that ultimately matter right now. Heart and lungs. I don't know which of those two things fails first. I only know that I won't be conscious when it happens. Any pain I've felt is receding now. I'm too cold for that.

I'm so cold, I hardly feel the cold anymore.

I say to Olaf, forming my words as carefully as I can, worried that I've already lost the power to form coherent syllables, 'Please. Go. Now.'

He studies me. He's Swedish or Norwegian, I assume. Knows his snow, anyway. If he has had any military experience – more than likely in a professional killer – he'll have done plenty of arctic survival training.

He knows hypothermia. Knows the passage to death. He's looking to make sure that I am on a path from which there is no return.

And I am. In his expert eyes, I am.

He says, 'Okay.'

He and Hamish walk off back to their car. They are leaving me here to die.

34

I've spent more of my life with death than almost anyone. Not the shoot-bang sort of death. I haven't had Lev's kind of life, not even Buzz's. I don't know exactly what my father got up to in the dark days of his past, but I haven't had his kind of life either.

All the same, for two years as a teenager I lived with death. It wasn't something external for me. Not something encountered on the point of a gun, the tip of a blade. It was internal. I didn't confront death, I *was* dead. I lived it. That doesn't make sense to people who haven't been where I've been. To the tiny handful of those that have – well, there's no other way to describe it. We have been dead: lived it and breathed it. Some very few of us even survived it.

You don't encounter something like that and emerge again normal. For long years after I was no longer officially sick, I still saw death's yellow teeth grinning at me from every corner, every shadow. Those years, in some weird way, were even worse than the ones that came before. I found the struggle for life harder than being dead.

That struggle does, now, abate. This year, in the arms of my beloved Buzz, I have sometimes known what it is like to live without struggle. Sometimes almost without fear. But I've never thought I would plant my flag permanently on Planet Normal. That planet is not my own. I might perhaps acquire papers permitting residence, even naturalisation, but its gravity – its soil and atmosphere – will always be alien. They will never be mine.

Until maybe now.

I'd never thought about it before, but there is no more powerful statement of being alive than the business of dying. Plenty of lifeless things have the power of motion. Crystals grow and viruses replicate. But to die – actually to die – that's an honour only granted to the living. The cost of admission.

And I'm about to be so honoured. The stupid thing is, I *feel* honoured. Insofar as I retain any sensation at all, I have two things in my head. The love I have for Buzz and my family. And the stunning assurance that I am truly alive. I couldn't be dying if I weren't. I don't want to die, but a strange way this is the best moment of my life. Something precious. Something longed for. There are worse ways to die than this. Many worse.

I'm too fuddled to think anything quite so clear, but these thoughts hang there in the middle distance like the golden background on a Chinese painting. Gently illuminating. Not interfering.

Which is just as well, because I'm not planning to die.

I roll over onto my back in the driver's seat and lash my booted feet at the window. Not once, repeatedly. I can't coordinate my movements at all well, but there's something in the abruptness of the action which seems to work for me. The first few times, I achieve nothing. Then I do. I don't even realise that I've broken the window until I lash out a couple more times and can't even find the window. It's gone.

While I'm in the position I'm in, I grope for the levers that release the bonnet and the petrol cap. I pull them both.

Then I roll over and forward to find a splinter of glass – only to find nothing usable at all. The stupid, stupid window is made of safety glass. It's crumbled into a million tiny granules. None of them are usable as a cutting tool.

I stagger back to the rear of the car. I'm not thinking any of this through. I'm just acting out the plan I made as I was standing, dying, in the snow.

Open the back. It takes me several goes but I do it. Buzz's spare petrol can sits in the way of the little hatch that protects the tyre irons. I heave the petrol can out onto the ground behind, fumble the hatch open, and grope for the tyre iron. I have to do all this by moonlight because there is no other source of light. But I know where the tyre irons are: they're where I keep my cannabis.

Leaning against the car all the way, I stumble back to the broken window. Feel for the wing mirror. Find it. Smash it.

The mirror, the little darling, shatters beautifully. Long, dangerous shards, reflecting starlight. I take the most dag-gerlike of those shards and start ripping up the seats. Foam rubber bursts forth.

It's hard getting it out. I keep failing. My shard breaks and I have to find another. There is blood on my hands. Blood everywhere. The stitching on the seat resists my cutting. And everything I do is done through this dull soup of stupidity.

Somehow, though, it happens. Beautiful sheets of foam rubber. I get the first out, stuff it up the inside of my coat. Then, because my technique has improved, get more foam from the other seats. Enough to stuff down my back, down my trousers. Anywhere I can, I stuff it in. I wrap foam over my head. Tie it with the belt from my coat.

None of this will stop me dying, I know that. The slow leaking of heat from my body is still happening, but not as fast. When Olaf and Hamish left, they drove up to the top of the hill, to get back onto the road proper. But they're pros. They won't have left immediately. They'll be parked there, looking down.

They'll want to be sure I don't magic fire from somewhere, don't summon the airborne cavalry using a microtransmitter hidden in the sole of my boot. But then, once they're confident that I'm done for, they'll leave. Exit the crime scene as swiftly and noiselessly as they can. Start to build an alibi in some other part of the country altogether. I don't know how long they'll watch me, but I need to outlast their watching.

When I've done all I can to insulate myself, I force the car bonnet open. There is still some residual heat in the engine block. Not much, and I lie over it pulling my arms and legs in for whatever warmth I can find. In the old days, drovers caught out in the snow would sometimes get through the night by sheltering in the opened guts of newly dead animals. Forget the smell, feel the warmth. I'm the same. Sheltering in the guts of my Peugeot. For the first time in what seems like an eternity, I can feel my midriff. It's cramping with cold, but that's better than no feeling at all.

I find myself daring to think the unthinkable. *Go on, Griffiths. You'll get through this.*

I need to keep alert. It would be all too easy to drift into unconsciousness.

I try chanting to stay awake. Counting up to twenty, then back down again. Listing all the people I know, all the people I love. Some of my words are out loud. Most, I think, aren't. My tongue is made of wood. My cheeks are walls of bone.

I try to notice whether the engine is still warm, whether it's still giving me any kind of sustenance.

Weirdly, I think I have an advantage over ordinary people in all this. They're so used to having their sensations arrive in the regular way, they wouldn't know what to do under these unordinary circumstances. But these cloaked and unreliable feelings are what I'm used to. The world I've lived in. Figuring out how to manage them, how to make decisions despite the fog, is my own particular expertise. My sphere of excellence.

I last as long on the engine block as I can. When I can't any longer count up to ten, not even in my head, I realise it's time for the next phase.

If Olaf and Hamish are still on the hill waiting for me, I'm dead.

If they've gone, I've got a chance.

I go back to the boot of the car. I'm shocked to find that I can't walk. Not at all. I have to hit my legs to find out if they're there or not. I have some stupid idea in my head that they've fallen off. I can't feel myself hitting myself, but somehow my brain catches up with reality and I stop worrying. In any case, I don't need to walk. Crawling is fine.

I get to the boot. The little tyre iron hatch. Find the little tin that contains my joints and a cigarette lighter. Somehow, on the third or fifth or tenth try get a joint in my mouth.

That's the easy bit.

Cigarette lighters – cheap, disposable ones like mine – are hard to use. You need strong fingers and a clear action to get a light. My fingers are weaker than milk and I live in a world where I think my legs have fallen off.

I try I don't know how many times to force a light.

Can't do it.

Summon all the concentration I have. All the will. All the effort.

Nada. Nothing. Sweet fuck all.

Mostly it's that my movements are just too uncontrolled, but I think my hands are still bleeding from the glass. They are slippery with blood. My fingers aren't strong or adept enough to turn the serrated double wheel of the lighter. I am dying because I can't turn that wheel.

Think, Griffiths. Think, bitch.

And I do. I change my grip, press the wheel into the fake-wool interior of the boot and roll it along.

Flame.

Instantly flame.

244

Because I'm so excited, I drop the lighter and it goes out immediately, but I know what I'm doing now. Three or four more goes and I get it.

Flame. Blue-yellow. Steady. Life-saving.

I light my joint.

I want to do more than that. Want to press my face up against that beautiful steady light. But I'm in control now.

This time I don't even try to walk. Just edge round on my knees, leaning up against the side of the car to the petrol cap. It's hard work getting the petrol cap off, but I just lit a lighter. A petrol cap is child's play.

I take the joint out of my mouth and throw it into the petrol tank.

There is a tiny gap of time in which absolutely nothing happens. One of those relativistic moments, where my clock is running at warp speed and the rest of the universe seems to be locked in super slo-mo. Just me. A car. A frozen snowfield. And a hillful of nothing.

Then it changes.

There's a *woof* of flame, so hot and intense I'm stunned by its arrival. I jerk instinctively back from the blast, but find I can't. My cheek has frozen fast to the side of the car. For some seconds, the flame is still not merely pouring from the tank opening, but actually jetting, flame-thrower-like. I'm still wrapped like Michelin Man in foam rubber and I can hear and feel the bubbling crackle of the foam as it burns back toward my hair. I rip my frozen cheek from the car. In other circumstances, I think it would have been a painful thing to do. Right now, I feel nothing at all.

And then – I'm free. Standing in the glorious heat of my burning car. Still utterly hypothermic. Still much more frozen that not. But, for a few magical minutes, I am not getting any colder. I can feel the texture of the air change. It becomes alive, expansive. The torrent of flame is no longer just confined to the petrol tank. The car itself has begun to burn. Seats. Matting. Paint. Lining. I stand much too close to the delirious flame and simply welcome its presence. Its consuming, destructive, life-giving presence.

I don't know how long I stand there, but my returning brain kicks back into gear. My hiking boots are still in the back of the car. I try to rescue them. Make one attempt and am pushed back by the density of the blaze. Try again and come away with one boot.

I think the other's lost.

I've already thrown the spare petrol can into the snow, but I shift it farther away to protect it.

As I do this, I realise that my coat is on fire. I'm not sure how that happened or even how long it's been burning. I fall over and roll in the snow until it's out. I can't feel any pain. There is a huge hole in the single best survival garment I have, but I'm still winning this particular game.

Or I assume I am. I do take a moment to look back up the hill. Looking by firelight now as well as moonlight. If Olaf and Hamish had seen this, they'd be back for me now, wouldn't they? And the hill is empty.

I've only the cold to battle now. Hamish and Olly are long gone.

So for a while, I just relax. Explore my burns. Embrace the heat. I can feel its crackle changing my skin. Like when you bring your hand close to a grill. Intense, but good. I try hard not to set myself on fire again and seem to perform that task without further hiccups.

My brain is warming up too. I'm thinking more freely again.

Hypothermia is about core temperature, not surface temperature. Close as I stand to this blaze, a few glorious minutes won't bring me back to life. I'm gaining breathing space, nothing more.

But I don't care. Breathing space is all I need. This girl is going to make it.

I check repeatedly that I still have my cigarette lighter. I do. My fingers still can't operate it, but they will as they start to warm.

But there's no rush. I take a little more time to roast in the heat of the car. The gale of flame from the petrol tank is subsiding now, but everything else is burning beautifully. The flames are starting to shift from the back end of the car to the front. The engine still seems untouched, but I hope it starts burning too.

Once I'm warmed enough to have approximate control of my limbs, I jog over to the barn. A corrugated iron roof supported on long wooden pillars and trusses. Beneath it, hay. Gathered in those big round bales. The barn is two-thirds empty, but that's still one-third full. Winter fodder.

The hay is tightly packed and frozen hard. I can twitch out a few loose handfuls, but my hope that I could just burrow into a pile of warm hay is a forlorn one.

Oh well. Arson it is.

Jog back to the car. The engine is on fire now too. Wonder vaguely about the insurance. I'm covered for fire damage, but presumably they don't normally pay out when you start the fire yourself. But maybe they have to if you started the fire to avoid dying. Who knows? And who cares? I can measure the state of my body by the suppleness of my mind. And I'm warming up: I can think again. Not well, admittedly, but I'm beginning to clamber out of that great deathly idiocy that had threatened to bury me.

I spend another few minutes by the car. Adjust my foam rubber padding so it's as well distributed as possible. Then, when the car blaze is starting to trickle down, head back to the barn.

Lighter. Petrol. Hay.

It takes me a minute or two to make it work, but I get there. Before long, I have more lovely flames licking up the side of something flammable.

This fire will be a big one. A long one. It will burn for long enough to warm me properly. And once I'm warmed through, I'll jog up the hill, back to the road proper, and follow Olaf and Hamish's tyre tracks down to Capel-y-ffin. Their tracks can't lead anywhere else. There's only one way out of this place.

A barn fire makes a car fire look like nothing. A child's toy oven next to a catering-scale range. There are flames now reaching the full height of the building. The raging intensity of this heat forces me back, then back again.

I spend happy minutes by this blaze. Fuck Olaf. Fuck Hamish. Fuck Prothero and the whole stinking lot of them. I'll kill 'em or jail 'em. They've messed with the wrong girl.

I'm thinking these happy, arrogant thoughts when something heavy strikes me from above. I fall sideways onto the ground. I can't move. And though the air is warm, the ground is frozen hard. I hear the fire blazing beyond my feet, but feel the heat leaching from my body into the frozen earth. And the night is still freezing, with hours to run until dawn.

I try again to move, but can't.

There is blood on my head.

I don't know what's happening.

The last thing I'm aware of is a rumble of machinery grinding away and light descending from above.

35

Newport. The Royal Gwent Hospital.

I'm swaddled like a cartoon character. Bandages on my hands. Dressings on my head and arm. I'm on a drip. Antibiotics. Painkillers. But I'm in one piece, even if the piece itself has seen better days.

The thing that knocked me down in the barn was a timber falling from the roof. It struck me on the back of the head. Could have been fatal if I'd been standing farther back. I don't know how long I was lying there, but as it turned out, it didn't matter. The farmer whose barn it was came out in his tractor to see what was going on. Found the wreck of his barn. The loss of his hay. And me. Hauled me semiconscious into his cab and drove us down to his farmhouse. His wife dialled the emergency services while the farmer – Arthur, as I subsequently learned – picked me up, carried me upstairs, and dropped me in the bath.

I was in and out of consciousness at this point. I remember I kept saying 'tepid, tepid,' because I was worried that hot water would be bad for my burns, cold water terrible for my hypothermia. But Arthur had hauled enough sheep out of snowdrifts that he didn't need any advice from me. He dumped me in that bath and kept me there while his wife – Mary – bobbed in and out offering tea and kindness. For some time I could talk only with extreme slurring and used that slurring to apologise for having burned down his barn.

We even, I think, got into one of those stupid courtesy-fights. Me saying I was a terrible person to burn his barn. Him practically telling me the damn thing needed destroying.

They couldn't get an ambulance up the hill and any helicopters were in use elsewhere. But a pair of coppers fought their way to me in a police Range Rover, with a paramedic and a case of equipment in the back.

Jouncing down the hill was an agony. They took me to the hospital in Abergavenny, where the duty staff took a quick look at me before rejecting me. Some of my burns are third-degree: that is, penetrating all the way through the skin. Abergavenny didn't have the capacity to deal with that, so they sent me straight on to Newport. Lights flashing all the way but still never creeping above fifty on icy roads.

The radio told us that temperatures in the hills were fourteen degrees below zero.

T-shirt weather.

The burns unit at the Royal Gwent enjoyed the clinical conundrum that came gasping in from the Range Rover. Not every day they deal with hypothermia and burns on one and the same patient. A junior doctor told me with barely concealed delight that he thought some of my toes might have frostbite. The doctor who patched me up told me that *on average* I was in great shape. Medical humour: a beautiful thing.

It took most of the night for them to repair me. Some skin was removed from my left buttock cheek and grafted onto my left side. There'll be some scarring on my bum. My side will show some marks, but should be okay. The areas involved aren't huge. No bigger than the palm of my hand. The doctors didn't regard the procedure as especially complex. They just got on with it.

Everyone was very kind.

Hospital trolleys and lidocaine. Surgical instruments flashing under lights.

Doctors with masks. Nurses with smiles.

Surgery was carried out under a twilight anaesthetic, so I was aware of things, but not very. I tried to say that the sensation was like that of advanced hypothermia. Like being curled up on that car engine counting to twenty as stars wheeled in a distant sky. But it wasn't really like that. Here, there were people around me. Friendly ones. Creating life, not causing death. In any case, no one could understand my mumbling and they told me, politely, to shut up.

A frozen dawn was greying the sky when I was finally wheeled to my bed.

I'm staggered at how cold it is even here, at sea level, in the wash of the Gulf Stream. I've never known it as cold as this in Wales.

Part of my brain is still standing in that field, in that snow.

Handing my coat and jumper to the men who want to kill me.

Wearing a T-shirt, but feeling as naked as starlight.

When I arrived at the hospital, I refused to let anyone notify my family. I didn't want them woken, but it'll be time to make that call soon. A nurse comes round with a breakfast trolley. I haven't ticked any menu, so get given the hospital default meal. Rubber eggs. Sausage. White toast, which is both a little burned and a little soggy. It is all delicious. Every morsel.

The nurse asks if I want more, and I do.

She asks if I am ready to use the phone, and I am.

I call Buzz. Call my family. Call Watkins. Those three, in that order. I tell Watkins not to get here before midday. I want time with the others first.

I haven't slept at all. Not a wink. I've been unconscious at times, but that's different. I can feel a gathering exhaustion, ready to whack me with its great rubber mallet. I'll accept that when it comes, but my loved ones come first.

I want to tell them what it said in those texts. Say it face-to-face. Say it properly.

Buzz comes first.

His expression is jaunty when he enters the room, shocked when he sees the scale of the damage.

'Bloody hell, Fi!'

He wants to kiss me, but kisses aren't so good right now. One of my hands is less bad than the other, so I let him hold that. The fingertips.

I tell him, through cracked lips, what happened. He gets the abridged, expurgated version. The version that includes idiot-girl-gets-stuck-in-snow. The one that makes no mention of Caledonian-Nordic contract killers. He says, 'Bloody hell, Fi,' again, but this time there's a tint of how-*do*-you-get-into-these-scrapes? in his tone.

I say my thing.

I say, 'Buzz, when I thought I was dying, I wrote you a text. It said "I love you." It said more than that, in fact, but that was the main thing. When I thought I was dying, I wanted you to know that I love you with all my heart. That was the thing that mattered most to me then. I wanted to say it to you properly now.'

Buzz is profoundly moved. His eyes tear up. Mine don't, but they do prick again. We stay there like that, not quite holding hands, not quite crying.

There are other ways to be alive. Ways other than dying. This is one of them. I am alive now. I am with Buzz. I cannot adequately express how grateful I am that he is here. That he is with me. That he loves me.

I cannot adequately express these things, but I do try.

A grey sun shines on a frozen world.

I sleep a bit with Buzz beside me at the bed. Sleep briefly, because it is not long before my family pours cacophonously through the ward.

Dad has brought a mountain of flowers, a basket of fruit wrapped in tissue paper and clear plastic and tied with a ribbon.

It will take me a fortnight to eat it all and I don't particularly like fruit.

Mam has brought a clucking anxiety, some home-baked brownies, and a mild, implicit rebuke that getting stuck in the snow and burning upland Powys to the ground isn't something that nice girls should do. She doesn't seem very surprised that I did, though. She makes it seem like I make a habit of it.

As for Ant and Kay: they are both shocked but excited. Kay is worried that she won't get any more rides in my car. Ant half wants to see under the dressings but is half scared at what she might find there.

Buzz stays with us to begin with, then tactfully vanishes to fetch hot drinks for everyone.

While he's gone, I say to Dad, Mam, Ant, and Kay more or less what I said to Buzz. They're worse listeners. Mam keeps interrupting and saying, 'Well, of course, dear.' Dad is better. He cries openly and tells me how much he – and they all – love me. He's a sentimental pig, but his sentiments are loving ones. And he speaks for them all. We all hold hands. Then that's not enough for Dad, so he grabs Ant and Kay in his giant embrace and pulls them down onto the bed for a group hug.

Which is a nice idea. And the good thing about third-degree burns is that the nerve endings are burned off with the skin, so you feel nothing at all. Aren't even meant to. But there are enough other parts of my body that do feel things, and that have been variously cut, bruised, burned, frozen, or surgically removed, that I don't particularly appreciate having three hefty bodies falling on top of them.

I scream.

Everyone leaps off the bed, but the leaping involves more

pummelling. A nurse comes rushing to see what the commotion is. Buzz comes in with a cardboard tray of drinks. Order gradually returns. Ant and Kay are sent to scrounge seats from around the ward and we have a kind of bedside party, with me cast as the white queen of Ward Six. The Bandage Princess.

It's nice. Noisy, but nice.

And after a bit, it's enough. I tell them all to go.

Dad, inevitably, resists. He's got a load of alternatives. He'll just wait in a seating area outside. Sit in the car. Hire a private ambulance to take me home – his home, he means. Bring in nurses to give me private care. And I don't want that. I want peace. I want sleep. With Buzz's assistance, I persuade them all to go.

I sleep for a bit. An hour maybe.

Then a doctor comes by and talks to me about my skin graft. I don't really listen. I'm sure he knows what he's talking about. The doctor goes and I sleep a bit more.

Then I wake and somehow become aware that I'm not alone. Watkins is there, in the chair that first Buzz, then Dad were sitting in. She's got her face in her hands. Bowed down. Grey hair. Grey light.

When she's aware of me looking at her, she straightens up. There's a lot going on in her face. Worry. Stress. Concern. Other things too. I don't know what they are. I'm not her.

'Fiona.'

I nod. 'Bit of a mess.'

She shakes her head at that. 'I've spoken with the doctors and –'

'I know. I'll be fine. I might lose some bits of toe here and there. They've already done a skin graft.'

'Young skin,' the surgeon had said, pinching it. 'The easiest stuff to work with.' I don't say that, though. Not to Watkins, not in this grey light.

Watkins isn't in ogre mode, but her other settings are rusty

254

from underuse. She's having difficulty with her range-finding. So I help out.

'There's a bag under the bed.'

The doctors had wanted to throw my clothes away. They looked like trash. Are trash. But they're trash with blood spatters.

I tell Watkins the whole story. The laptop. The engineering models in Solid Edge. The weapons.

I tell her about what really happened in that field. About Olaf and Hamish. She asks how come I didn't die, so I tell her that too. The whole thing, except I say 'cigarette' instead of 'joint.'

'Does anyone else know this?'

'No.'

She spreads the coat out until she finds some marks. There's plenty of my blood on that coat, but there's some of Hamish's too. The forensics people will find both.

I memorised the Land Rover's registration number too. I give her that and she makes a note.

'You think they killed Khalifi?'

'Yes.'

'Because he knew? Because he was going to spill the secret?'

'Maybe. I suppose so. I'm not sure about that part yet. There could be other reasons.'

'And the method? The dissection of the corpse? That's ...'

I shake my head at that. As I've always said, the case has always had coincidence at its heart. Whichever way you look at it. If Khalifi was killed as some kind of revenge for his murder of Mary Langton, it was an extraordinary coincidence that his death coincided so neatly with our discovery of Langton's corpse – a discovery which was essentially random in nature. On the other hand, if Ali el-Khalifi was being coolly murdered by a pair of contract killers, their decision to scatter his corpse *à la Langton* was simply an inspired piece of improvisation suggested by the news spreading on radio and TV.

I say that. Not very clearly, but I mumble something along those lines.

Watkins doesn't hide her disagreement. 'Why do that? If, as you say, they're professional killers, why not just make a clean disposal of the corpse? Quite likely they've done it before.'

I'm not strong enough to argue with her, but Watkins is wrong. Scattering Khalifi's corpse was *exactly* the right thing to do. The way we found the corpse sent us chasing after connections between Langton and Khalifi instead of concentrating our firepower where it was most needed. If Khalifi had simply gone missing, we'd have been forced to look at his activities in the round. Instead of being obsessed with his sexual and romantic past, we'd have been drilling away at his business contacts, among them Mark Mortimer and Barry Precision. As it was, if it hadn't been for my perverse insistence on following that line of attack, the investigation might never even have touched those things.

Even Watkins sees this logic. 'Of course, it *did* push the investigation toward the sexual angle.'

I nod. Yes. It did.

But Watkins's thoughts are already moving on.

'On the other hand, we don't *know* that any of this Barry Precision stuff is connected to Khalifi. To Mortimer, yes, but not necessarily to Khalifi.'

I shrug. I don't agree with that either. The two men knew each other well. Were buddies. Fellow engineers. Both died violently. What more connection do you want? And if it comes to that, the two men who tried to kill me did so with a bit of grace. A little flourish of invention and quick thinking. It seems to me that the same house style is apparent with Khalifi's death too.

Watkins stares at me. I don't look away.

She doesn't say so, but I can tell she agrees.

'Why try to kill you? That's another question. But presumably they didn't go to the cottage to kill anyone. They learned – from Sophie Hinton, I suppose – about that laptop and they went there to retrieve it. They found you there. They didn't know how far their operation was compromised, so decided to kill you, take the laptop, hope for the best.'

I nod. I agree, but it is odd to be spoken about in this way.

'There's no phone signal up there,' I add. 'They probably figured there was a reasonable chance I hadn't managed to communicate my find to anyone – which indeed I *hadn't*. If you'd found me dead in a field from hypothermia, you wouldn't necessarily consider foul play. That's why I broke the guy's nose. I wanted to leave a clue at least.'

'I'd have found it. I'd be sure to have found it.' Watkins looks severe and authoritative when she says that, but she tries to jam a smile into the expression too. The smile doesn't work. It looks clumsily out of place. A child's pink party bow stuck onto a formal business suit.

I say, 'Yes.'

I tell Watkins that she should get a log of calls to and from Sophie Hinton's line. I assume the Olaf-Hamish-Dunbar-Prothero axis is careful about calling from untraceable numbers, but you never know.

She nods and makes a note. 'And Mortimer? Any theories on him?'

'I don't know. Perhaps he thought he needed to kill himself to protect Sophie and his kids. Perhaps he just thought that his life was fucked anyway. Either way, he was pushed into it.'

Watkins doesn't like the word 'fucked,' but she doesn't rebuke me.

Instead, she picks up my hand, the one nearest her, and turns it over. There is some blood leaking from the bandage. Her touch is oddly gentle.

257

'How did you hurt your hands?'

'When I was cutting the seats up. I don't know exactly how.'

She turns my hand over again, to leave it as it was, but she keeps holding it. We are hand to hand, fingertip to fingertip. We stay like that for a bit. I'm not that far from going to sleep again.

'Dennis told me about this,' she says after a while. 'The things you put us through.'

Dennis: Dennis Jackson. My boss on the last big murder case. Apart from that, I don't know what she's talking about. She doesn't elaborate.

For a while we just drift on the silence. But there's something else I need to say.

'We won't get a conviction for what happened last night. Not a chance.'

'We might.'

It's all very well having Hamish's blood on my coat. That proves that he and I were in contact at some point. But we've got no way to prove when or where that contact happened. We can't even show that a *crime* took place. The word of a police officer: that's all. And it's not enough. For a modern jury, under modern rules of evidence, it's not remotely sufficient.

'They're good,' I tell Watlans. 'They were careful last night. Gloves all the time. Hats. Wiping the car down. They didn't touch me even when I smacked the Scotsman. They'll have been professional about Khalifi too. Very clean. Careful about CCTV, numberplates, forensics. All that stuff.'

Watkins nods. 'We'll see.'

There's not much more to talk about. The world outside is still very grey, very cold. Watkins says they are talking about the coldest winter on record.

I fall asleep with her still holding my hand. I lean my head

258

against it, because it is nice having the human contact. I say, 'Thank you,' or I dream I do.

When I wake, darkness has fallen and I'm on my own.

36

A cold world spins. Time organises seconds into minutes, minutes into hours, hours into days.

I'm released from hospital. To Mam and Dad's, because Buzz needs to be at work and because I'm still not much good for anything.

I have my old room back. Mam has filled it with flowers. Dad has ordered special support pillows from a supplier in London and a contraption that fits under the mattress to raise and lower it like a hospital bed. I laugh at him, but it's nice to have. He puts a TV in there too, and Mam and I watch recordings of *Downton Abbey*. Mam is so absorbed in the show, I think she half lives it.

I spend hours with Ant and Kay too. Kay buys me a phone, which is really nice of her, even though I know she'll get the money back from Dad. She also goes round to my house with Mam and brings back clothes and my laptop. Mam goes shopping and buys a winter coat for me which is weirdly similar to Watkins's granny coat, the one Amrita so despised. Kay takes it back and brings me something from Monsoon instead. Fur-trimmed. It looks nice. She also gets, at my request, a proper padded coat, the sort of thing people go skiing in. It's going to be a while before I walk out underdressed for the cold again. That's not logical: Olaf and Hamish would have removed any coat I'd gone out in. But somehow it makes sense. Even the idea of cold is frightening now.

Ant just likes snuggling with me. She'd worm right in alongside, except that there aren't many bits of me that want a wriggly thirteen-year-old bumping up against them. So I pile pillows up against my side and let her bump against those instead. We do a school project of hers together and she tells me stuff about what's happening on Facebook and the music she's into.

Buzz visits too. Office gossip and low-intensity snogging. He wants to know, a bit upset, why I didn't tell him what I told Watkins. He feels that I didn't trust him.

I look at him like he's an idiot. 'I didn't. Of course I didn't.'

I explain: if Buzz had known how come I ended up in hospital that morning, he'd hardly have been able to keep his feelings under wraps.

'Fi, you know it's okay to have feelings –'

'Yes, my dear Buzz, but your feelings would have ended up letting my father know what happened. You might not have meant it that way, but –'

'You think he'd –?'

'Well, what do you think? How do you honestly think my father would react if he knew someone had tried to kill his daughter?'

Truth is, I don't know the answer to my own question, but nor do I want to find out. I don't think Dad is involved in his old games anymore, but he still has his friends from those days, his contacts, his resources. If he wanted to find a couple of underworld figures, he'd have a fighting chance of locating them before we do. And if he did, I don't think they'd ever see the inside of a jail, which is where they belong.

Buzz sees this logic. His mouth falls open with it. 'Bloody hell, Fi. Your family!' It must be strange for him. A well-behaved boy from a nice family. Finding himself dating the more-than-slightly crazy daughter of one of Wales's best-known criminals. Probably not what he imagined for himself.

261

Life's like that: It never serves up what you think it will.

He's also seen my name on a list of people down for the undercover training thing. He's upset I didn't run that by him first. He reckons, probably rightly, that undercover cops – the real ones, the long-termers – never manage a successful relationship. I agree with him. Say I don't see myself doing anything like that, not really. I just fancied adding some new skills.

Which is almost true. But it's not really the skills I want, more that I don't like the idea that I might be prohibited from doing something I want to do. Any police officer can go undercover in small ways – buying drugs from a dealer, seeking to sell stolen goods – but you're not allowed to go *deep* undercover without special training. And what if, one day, a case needs that kind of tactic? I don't like the idea of being barred from something just because I haven't been on some stupid course.

Buzz accepts this, or sort of does, and the conversation moves on. We watch a bit of TV and cuddle. After a bit, I want to sleep and Buzz takes himself off. It's been a nice, peaceful, contented time.

But I'm not ill. I'm a bit knocked about, that's all. My burn wounds need gentle treatment for a few weeks. My cuts are already healing. The tips of my toes are, in some cases, looking black, but the cheerful junior doctor at the Royal Gwent told me that the rule was 'frostbite in January, amputate in July.' So: my toes might need surgery at some stage. Or they might not. In any case, there's nothing to stop me working, so – when I'm not watching *Downton Abbey* or protecting myself from a wriggling younger sister – I work.

Although I shrink from what I might find, I force myself to start reading those police reports on my father. Though I can't ask anyone to get the printouts from my office desk, I can access the same material via the force intranet.

And I do. I read. *Thomas Griffiths known to have ... Thomas Griffiths believed to be ... Telephone interception reports on Thomas Griffiths ... Thomas Griffiths, formerly of ... Thomas Griffiths was identified by ... Prosecution case for Thomas Griffiths ... Anonymous caller reports that Thomas Griffiths ...*

It's endless. It feels endless. The language, criminal law, and police procedures have all changed since then, but not so much. Twist the lens a little, and I'm seeing myself – or rather, my brothers and sisters on the force – on my father's trail. Doing everything they can to secure a conviction. Earlier on in the paper trail, you can see the cops expecting victory: securing a conviction for one of those banker offences, achieving one of those ten-year-plus sentences that every good copper loves to see.

The first prosecution was for armed robbery. Two eye witnesses. Both reliable. Nice clean statements. No awkward alibis. Identity parades all tickety-boo. The sort of case that the CPS can manage in their sleep. Then the damn thing came to trial, and both witnesses retracted in full. Their retractions were stumbling and awkward, but they made them. Insisted on them. The case collapsed.

In the years that followed, you can see my colleagues getting tighter, sharper, willing to run with any little offence they thought they could pin on him.

And all the time, I see my father waltzing through the shadows. Laughing at his pursuers. I try to imagine how deft he must have been. How constantly cautious. What must it be like when you can never use a phone without assuming that someone is listening? Never send a letter, never trust that innocent-looking stranger?

I don't think I learn much from the files, not directly, but I do start to break that sense of fear I have. My sense that I can't investigate these things, that it's better not to know.

And of course there are leads: so many leads, it's hard to

know where to start. Known associates. Associates not known but suspected. Friends. Associates of those friends. At one stage, the Serious Crime Unit put together a chart trying to trace major associations between the South Wales underworld. The chart is a whirlwind of circles, arrows, interconnections, with my father standing at the very centre. A Mr Popular of the criminal fraternity.

I try to do two or three hours each day I'm in bed. I get through about a third of the material, no more. There's far more to be done, but I'm already certain that my father's past holds the clue, in some way, to the mystery of my origin. I'm just daunted by the scale of the investigation.

When I need a break, I retreat to the sweet enchantments of Operation Stirfry. I'm missing the briefings, and the incident room all aflap with paper. But I have the intranet and I have my phone. Watkins is now investigating, as well as Langton and Khalifi, the matter of possible illegal arms export, the possible framing of Mark Mortimer, and any threats that may have been made against Sophie Hinton. Oh yes, and the small matter of the 'attempted murder of DC Fiona Griffiths,' on which a team of three is now labouring full-time.

It's clear that the dramas of Capel-y-ffin have revived Stirfry. Interest from senior command has revived. There's a new intensity about the operation. And part of that is for my sake. I appreciate it. I get a home visit from none other than Detective Superintendent Kirby, who sits awkwardly on the edge of my bed and praises me for my courage and resourcefulness in the line of duty.

I don't think it's seeing one of his young female officers in her nightdress that makes him awkward. More that he's in the home of Tom Griffiths and speaking to his daughter.

I look at my hands and say, 'Thank you, sir.' The weird thing is that I mean it. Then my mam brings in tea and biscuits, and we all sit around and talk about the weather.

I'm still involved in interesting stuff too.

Watkins phones to ask if I have any suggestions about reviewing those engineering drawings from Barry Precision. I do. I know a guy called Stuart Brotherton, an engineering lecturer at the University of Leeds. I knew him when he was a junior research fellow at Cambridge – he was my first ever drug dealer, in fact, though Watkins doesn't need to know that. I tell Stuart what we need and why we need it. I say he can charge us a consultancy fee if he likes. He says he'll be happy to do it.

I also log into the secure network and keep up to date with what's been going on while I've been adventuring. Less than I'd hoped, in truth. Although Watkins's demand for more manpower is now being treated sympathetically by those above her, the cold weather has drained the force of resources. Officers are managing blocked roads, failed power lines, and abandoned vehicles and supporting a programme that aims to protect the elderly against the cold. Until the weather relents, we're struggling to cover what we need to do.

But progress is slow, not absent.

I click through to Bev's researches. She's listed, with true Rowlandian neatness, every payment made on Khalifi's bank card, every payment on his credit card. The same for Langton, though her transaction record is so meagre as to be almost silent.

Bev's work is wonderfully literal. When Khalifi bought stuff from Tesco, her notes report, '*Tesco: large supermarket.*' When he spent seventy quid at the Swansea Bay Yacht Club, her notes say, '*Swansea Bay Yacht Club: primarily a yacht club. Also windsurfing and similar social/recreational activities.*' I can see why, if you're a Watkins or a Jackson, you want plenty of Bev Rowlands on your team, not so many Fiona Griffithses.

But still, I've got my uses. I spend hours studying Bev's spreadsheets. They are things of beauty. A life photographed in data. The commercial imprint of a man. And these things are strangely informative. I check some websites, phone through to the yacht club. Call up and study as many photos of Langton as I can find.

My orchard of knowledge grows another apple.

Langton and Khalifi. The leg and the lung.

Her grinning blonde head rising from its barrel of oil. His freshly scattered parts gleaming in the Llanishen mud.

I still feel close to Mary Langton, but I've got a better relationship with Khalifi now too. That mobile, ambiguous face feels friendly, not just evasive. I realise too that I think of them as a pair, Langton-and-Khalifi: the way you think about friends who are dating steadily.

My colleagues are excited because Khalifi might have led them to an arms-smuggling ring, as though that's where the glamour and the excitement really lies. For me, all corpses count the same. One dead body might lead to Barry Precision. Another to nothing more than a love poem lost down the back of a sofa. There is no eminence here, no lowliness. We are all equal under Death's scythe.

I silently apologise to Mary Langton for my colleagues' mood of indifference. Promise her that it's temporary. I've been a little neglectful myself, in truth. Because I've had to work hard on Khalifi–Mortimer, I haven't quite given Langton the attention she deserves. But time enough for that now. I think we'll get her killer too.

Meantime, I research Saadawi. Some of the websites I need are in Arabic, but the English-language *Egyptian Gazette* has a story which seems to identify Saadawi as a businessman with trading and construction interests. Whose brother is a procurement officer in the Egyptian defence ministry.

What you might call a smoking gun.

I also research Barry Precision's other overseas buyers. The company boasts a Libyan buyer. Also Lebanese, Moroccan,

Saudi. I can't yet find obvious connections between those names and defence or security services, but there's a limit on what you can do with Google alone, and I've not been on the case for long. I mention these things to Watkins, who tells me brusquely that she has a pair of DCs on the case already.

Stuart phones me back the afternoon after getting my data – my third day at home. He tells me I'm right. Barry Precision makes bits and pieces for all manner of people, but a sizeable portion of its business appears to be manufacturing parts that are weapons-suitable. Blast protection equipment for trucks and armoured cars. Gun barrels for tanks. Probably a whole lot more besides.

I ask him to put his preliminary conclusions in an email.

He does. Although the email is carefully circumspect, we don't need proof to secure a search warrant, just reasonable suspicion. I forward the email on to Watkins.

I spend more time on Bev's spreadsheets. They speak to you differently, depending on what you know.

Four years ago, before Mortimer started having his suspicions, before anything irreversible had happened, Khalifi took his holidays in Spain. Later on, Khalifi's holidays changed. Dubai. Jordan. Lausanne, Doha, Vienna, Cairo. It doesn't take long to figure out. A few mouse clicks.

I'm still grinning when Watkins calls.

'I'm going to raid Barry Precision tomorrow morning.' She briefly spells out her intentions. Five vehicles. Two dozen coppers. Arrive at 6.30 AM, an hour before dawn. Gain entry. Seize files. Seize computers. Interview all members of staff. Interview top management under caution.

She asks if I want to be there. I say, 'Yes.'

'Are you okay to move? I don't want –'

'I'm fine. I just won't kick any doors down, if that's all right.'

Watkins responds to that with her normal lighthearted

grace and wit. She wants to send a car for me, but I don't want that.

Instead I say, 'Idris Prothero owns the company. He lives on Marine Parade in Penarth.'

She thinks about that, then says, 'Okay. We'll take Prothero in first.' She gives me details of where and when we're meeting.

I say, 'We'll need to interview him, of course.'

'You want to?'

'Yes.'

She thinks about that a moment. 'All right. Mervyn Rogers leads. You support.'

I nod. Then, because nodding isn't a brilliant telecommunication technique, I say, 'Yes, ma'am.'

'And you both stay in close touch with me. No flying solo, Constable.'

I can't quite say 'Yes, ma'am' again, so instead I say, 'Did you know Swansea Bay Yacht Club doesn't do boat hire?' which might not be the best way to put it but was how it came out.

'What?'

'Nothing.'

Watkins says something growly and hangs up.

I think that's interesting, even if she doesn't.

I get out of bed.

Apart from short visits to the bathroom, I've mostly avoided moving around. That's partly because my healing skin is still fragile and so wants to be moved as little as possible. But also, bed has been the most comfortable place to be. Since I've not needed to be anywhere else, I've not forced myself to move.

Time for that to change.

I pull off the T-shirt of Kay's that I've been using for a nightie. Examine myself in the mirror.

I'm okay. A bit bashed around, but okay. Walking feels a

little strange, because toes turn out to be oddly important when it comes to balance and I still don't have full feeling anywhere that's been blackened by frost. But still. I'm on my feet. I'm not falling over. I feel achy and sore, but I felt achy and sore in bed too.

It's odd examining myself like this. Back when I was staring into a shop mirror with Kay, I couldn't connect with my own visual image. I seldom can. But I have no difficulty with that now. My face doesn't seem particularly to belong to me, but the rest of what I see prompts a feeling of belonging. Of recognition. This is me. This petrol-scorched, frostbitten, snow-burnt, glass-lacerated body is mine. We feel a kind of kinship – the thing in the mirror, the brain in my head. When I move, the mirror-beast moves and it makes sense. It all makes sense.

I stare at the mirror until not just the body but the room behind starts to blur into unreality.

I run the taps and do stuff with water and soap. I don't know if it makes any difference, but it's what you do. Chomp some aspirin.

Get Mam upstairs to help change my dressings. Shoo her away when we're done.

I dig through the clothes that Kay has brought me. Opt for leggings and a jumper. Boots. I check the mirror-beast to see if I recognise myself but I don't. Not really. I'm not especially disconnected, just normal. My version.

Call Buzz. He tells me he'll pick me up once he's done at work.

I'm back in the saddle and it feels good. Me and Penry. Two sides of the same copper coin.

37

The next morning. Long before dawn.

It's still astonishingly cold. Astonishingly snowy. This isn't Wales as I've ever known it. It feels as though South Wales has somehow cut loose from the mainland and drifted north. We're bumping shorelines with Baffin Island and Spitsbergen. Polar bears on Queen Street and penguins clucking in Bute Park.

I like it. When I'm not being left to die in it, I like it.

The alarm goes off at four fifteen. The rendezvous is at Cathays at five thirty. Because of the snow, we can't just scream down to Barry in a blaze of sirens. We'll need to creep there. And because Watkins is in charge, no one will dare be late.

Buzz gets up, showers, gets dressed. He chooses the sort of clothes you'd want if you were about to see real action. Boots. Thick trousers. Ski jacket. Combat wear. It's hardly necessary, of course. We're hardly expecting armed resistance. Indeed, we're not expecting anything beyond an empty building and some unguarded computers. But still. The drama of a dawn raid seizes the imagination. Even for Buzz, who's presumably kicked down a door or two in his time.

Bosnian doors. Doors with scarier things behind them than anything we're likely to find in Barry.

But the mood is contagious. Instead of lying in bed and saying annoying things, I get up too. I don't shower – I'm still wearing too many dressings to make that particularly easy – but I clean myself with a flannel. Do something to my hair so that it looks like I've done something to it. Buzz is in the kitchen, singing to himself and making a fry-up. Bacon and eggs. Probably a heap of other things besides.

I get stuck in the bedroom wondering what to wear. I'm not normally girly about that sort of thing. I just choose something and wear it. I never buy anything complicated, so the choices are easy.

But I already have a reputation in the office. A bit wild. A bit strange. My mountaintop adventure was always more likely to happen to me than to anyone else. So I want to downplay it. Make it seem smaller than it was. I want to diminish the gossip, not inflate it.

Buzz comes through to see where I've got stuck. I explain my dilemma.

'You could wear that new outfit of yours.'

What new outfit? I can't remember anything. He reminds me. There was a Hobbs bag in my car. He took it out when he loaded the back with snow shovels and sleeping bags. It's now in my corner of the wardrobe.

'You could wear that,' he says.

I blink.

Yes, I could. I'd never really expected to wear it at all, if I'm honest, but nothing says 'I'm not the almost-victim of a hypothermic contract killing' like a three-hundred-pound suit from Hobbs. And, strangely enough, it's not a bad choice. It's loose over the parts of me that will welcome looseness. It's comfortable enough to wear, chic enough to deflect attention from the way I spent my weekend.

So I put it on. My face has some minor burn marks and there's still some abraded skin where I pulled my cheek from the frozen car panel, but I play around with makeup until I look presentable.

'Bloody hell, babe, you look gorgeous!'

He gets a kiss for that, despite his tone of surprise. A kiss, but not a long one, because we have a fry-up to eat and a raid to attend. He clears away. I put on socks and boots, coat and hat, scarves and gloves. It's a cold world and I don't want to feel it.

The rendezvous at Cathays is a thing of headlights and car exhausts. Men in black jackets and knitted hats. Feet stamping on icy pavements. Snow in heaps along the North Road. The dirty grey-brown of city snow. Darkness overhead, battling streetlights for control of the city. Watkins, in her granny coat, bustles in and out of view.

She's good at these things. Certain and in command. There are six vehicles now, and more than two dozen cops.

We leave Cathays before dawn. Drive back down to Cardiff Docks, then across the bay. I'm in a Transit van with Watkins and two uniforms whom I know by sight and by name, but no more.

There's not much conversation.

When we hit the end of the bay, our own vehicle and a patrol car make the turn down into Penarth. The other four vehicles continue on. We creep down the frozen roads into the sleeping town. Headlights shining off ice. An occasional breeze sends a scurry of ice crystals across the road. Between the tyre tracks, there's a hard ramp of snow and ice.

Penarth. Marine Parade. You can't see the sea from here, but you feel it. Cold waves nagging at cold sand, cold rocks.

Six fifteen. Prothero's house. Pulled back from the road, a gravelled driveway in front.

We sweep straight in. Headlights shining full-beam on the front door. Partly for lighting. Mostly to disconcert and frighten the occupants. There are six of us all told. Four in uniform. Myself and Watkins not.

The knocker is a big heavy cast-iron thing. Lion's head,

or something like it. One of the uniforms smashes down on it. Not once but repeatedly. A din that, briefly, becomes the centre of the world. The only thing that matters.

Watkins stands back. She's on the phone to the leader of the other team. They've gained entry to Barry Precision. Bolt cutters will have been used to cut the chain guarding the property, then a steel ram used to gain access to Barry Precision itself. 'The Enforcer'. That's what those rams are called. The boys love 'em.

The uniforms are having another go with the knocker and beginning to yell 'Police' and flash torchbeams around, when the hall lights go on. The front door opens.

Idris Prothero stands there – I recognise him from the photos I've studied. In a dressing gown and half asleep, but also composed. A kind of silvery indignation.

The uniforms don't put cuffs on him. We will if we have to, but for now we're not making arrests. If Prothero comes with us voluntarily, that's good enough. We have a search warrant too, however. We'll enforce that all right.

Watkins flashes her warrant card. Prothero takes it. Steps inside, puts the porch light on, studies the card, returns it.

He didn't care about the card, though. He's just staging a little show for us. The Idris Prothero I'm-not-flustered show. He's about five foot eleven. Lean. Tanned. Handsome too, I suppose, though I don't see him that way.

He's a wanker and I want him in jail.

He agrees to come with us.

A uniformed officer escorts him upstairs, where he'll be allowed to dress. He won't be left alone for a minute, not even to pee. Prothero's wife – Millie – appears briefly on an upstairs landing. Frightened. Pretty. Wifely. That's what money buys you. The kind of woman who plays the part of loving wife so fully, she's forgotten it's all a part. Above her, one floor up, two moon shapes appear, peering over the banisters.

273

Prothero's kids, I assume. He's twice married. This is his second brood.

There's an odour of fear in the house. One we sought to generate.

Watkins doesn't notice any of this, or if she does, she doesn't care. The remaining officers are ordered to search the house top to bottom, including attic and outbuildings. Almost immediately, they locate two mobile phones, an iPad, a couple of laptops, a desktop, some boxfiles, a games console, but all those things were left hanging around in plain sight, in the sort of places you'd expect them. Prothero might be stupid enough to leave incriminating materials there, but he might not.

Watkins snappishly supervises the operation. I'm left out of things. Possibly because Watkins knows I'm still in a fairly delicate state. More likely because she thinks I wouldn't be much use anyway.

Prothero is dressed by now and downstairs again. Grey suit. Pale blue shirt. No tie.

Watkins has a search warrant and orders the removal of the electronics and the papers. The standard play for someone in Prothero's position is to argue with the warrant, demand a lawyer, start negotiating over precisely what is being removed and what not. He does none of those things. Just says, with a half smile, 'I suppose I can use the coffee machine?'

He can. Goes into his gleaming kitchen. Polished wooden boards, hand-fired cream tiles. Coffee for six. Him, his wife, the four of us. Tiny white espresso cups with a blue pattern on the lip. Millie Prothero wears a bathrobe over a long cotton nightdress and keeps flitting in and out of the room. I'm not sure if that's to look after the kids or to stress over whether the uniforms are grinding dirty snow into the pure wool carpets on her living room floor.

Watkins downs her coffee in a single blast. Woman has a

throat made of fireboard. She leaves to supervise the removal of Prothero's effects. I'm left in the kitchen guarding him. He looks at me with as much interest as he'd look at a new secretary at work. A vague sexual curiosity. Nothing else.

I look at him like he's an arms dealer who murdered Ali el-Khalifi, caused the suicide of Mark Mortimer, and who almost murdered me. A cold sense of anger. Nothing else.

He looks at his watch and sighs.

But my anger is tempered with uncertainty. I strongly doubt that Prothero is innocent of arms smuggling, but what about what happened to me? I try asking, *Did this man order my death?* It seems highly probable that his firm, his arms dealing, sent Hamish and Olaf up into the hills to find that laptop. Given his choice of messenger, the murder of any police officer they happened to encounter probably lay well within their rules of engagement. But my question is more specific than that. What precisely took place? Was there an explicit instruction, a phone call, from this man to Hamish and Olaf, saying 'Kill the copper'? And if so, did he make that call with this same calm demeanour, wearing this same elegant suit, this same air of slight impatience? Is that, in fact, how arms dealers conduct their business?

I don't know, but in a way, it's a side issue. His arms dealing has created plenty of corpses already. Not in the U.K., but abroad. Egypt, Libya, Syria, Iran. How much blood is there in this impeccable kitchen? How many bones beneath these polished floors?

He says, 'Will this take very much longer?'

I don't answer. It takes as long as it takes.

There's a minor commotion out in the hallway. I stand where I can see and listen better. One of the uniforms has just found a stack of boxed-up mobile phones in the wardrobe of an upstairs bedroom. Eight boxes. All unopened. Eight cheapie phones.

Watkins marches from the living room to view the haul. She reaches for her phone, summons another six officers. Then she does a thing which I've seen her do, but no one else. A kind of 180-degree rotation of the head, stare fixed outward, like a steel spoke aimed at anything in her path. The steel gaze stops when it reaches me. She jabs her chin in my direction, her hand at Prothero.

'Cathays,' she says.

And I nod.

38

'*Eight* mobile telephones.'

Mervyn Rogers has one of the boxes in front of him. He's broken the seal, opened it up, is playing with the little gadget in front of him. It looks small in Rogers's hands. Like the buttons would be too small for his big fingers to operate.

'You like phones? My daughter has two.'

We're forty minutes into the interview. So far our interview tapes have recorded Rogers mostly, and me occasionally, asking questions. Prothero answered questions about name, address, and so forth with swift, clipped accuracy, and that's about as much progress as we've made.

He phoned for a lawyer from the car on the way into Cathays. A London man, from a big firm of solicitors. The lawyer promised to come immediately, but that's still three hours' driving, even if the roads were okay, which they're not.

And in the meantime, when we ask a question, Prothero mostly just smiles at us or waves a hand, as if languidly batting the issue away. It's a gesture he probably uses a lot.

The formula we're required to use by the 1994 Criminal Justice and Public Order Act is intended to give us a little leeway. Right at the outset of the interview, Rogers said, speaking directly into the microphone, 'You do not have to say anything. But it may harm your defence if you do not mention when questioned something which you later rely on in court. Anything you do say may be given in evidence. Is that clear?'

Prothero gave us one of his I'm-richer-than-you-are smiles, then leaned forward and said, also speaking directly into the microphone, 'I'm perfectly happy to answer every one of your questions, but given that I'm suspected of what sounds like a very serious offence, I'd prefer to have a lawyer present throughout. You'll understand that, I'm sure.'

Then leaned back and asked for coffee.

Rogers slams away at his current line of enquiry.

There is no innocent reason for Prothero to have these phones. Gangs, drug dealers, and serious-fraud-type criminals have modernised their communications. None of them would consider saying anything incriminating on a landline, and most are exceptionally careful about texts and emails. The gold-standard form of criminal communication is disposable mobile phones. You use them for a day or two – perhaps only a call or two – then ditch them. There's a kind of organisational complexity in making sure that people have the numbers they need to reach you, but that's it. Manage that, and you have an untraceable, untappable communications network.

I decide it's highly improbable that Hamish and Olaf chose to kill me without getting instructions first. Apart from anything else, they'd have wanted to confirm a fee. So they rolled up the hill to get the laptop, found they were too late, and drove far enough down again to get a phone signal. Called Prothero on whichever phone number he'd given them. Got their orders. Drove back to do the deed.

Quite likely, these phones almost killed me.

Quite likely, the man sitting opposite me ordered me dead.

I think of myself standing in the snow and the starlight. My feet in a basin of white fire as I froze, slowly, almost to death.

Rogers beats away at the phones. Gets nothing. Literally nothing for the most part: Prothero remains largely silent.

This is the third major tack that Rogers has tried. The first had to do with Barry's products. The second with Mark Mortimer's history at the firm.

And then, Rogers steps back and asks a straightforward question which, with hindsight, is where we should probably have started.

'Okay. Let's go back to some basics. You are the owner of Barry Precision, correct?'

'Yes.' But there was a hesitation there, which Rogers picked up on.

'Yes, but ...?'

'But nothing. I own a hundred percent of the shares in Barry Precision. I do, however, have a cross-ownership arrangement with a partner of mine, David Marr-Phillips.'

Marr-Phillips: another one of Rattigan's buddies. Another name on my A-list of people to investigate. A guy who inherited twelve hundred acres of Glamorgan land from his father. Used his business savvy to trade up to a property empire worth seventy million or more.

I'm semi-surprised to hear the name in this context, but only semi. South Wales isn't London. All our rich guys know each other. Most of them have probably done business together. But neither Rogers or I know what a cross-ownership arrangement is. Rogers asks. Prothero explains.

'The company is legally mine, one hundred percent mine. But I have a contractual arrangement with David whereby he picks up twenty percent of the risks and rewards from the company. In exchange, I have an equivalent interest in some of his properties. It's an arrangement which simplifies certain tax issues and which diversifies risk. It's common enough and perfectly legal.'

His tone adds the words *you pig-ignorant, piss-poor, provincial cretins.*

My look sticks a seven-inch steel dagger between his eyes

and twists it around. Mervyn Rogers is probably wondering how fast he could beat this guy to a pulp.

We all enjoy a little moment of silence.

Rogers and I don't immediately know how to respond. The ownership structure creates a weird little wrinkle. Unanticipated. Maybe a so-what thing, but one that needs investigation.

'Risks and rewards,' says Rogers. 'Would that include the risk of prosecution for illegal arms export?'

Prothero gives a smile so thin it was probably manufactured in an Apple design lab. '*Financial* risks and rewards. David has no vote on operational matters. He trusts me to do my job.'

'We'll need to see the agreement.'

Prothero shrugs.

'And,' I add, 'we'll need to understand what you got in return. The "equivalent interest" you mentioned.'

If Prothero was disconcerted by having revealed more than he's intended, that moment is over. His glossy, disdainful confidence is back. Prothero's figured out that I'm the junior cop in pretty much any gathering. I'm so unimportant, he doesn't even deign to sneer at me properly. Just raises a hand in a 'fine, who cares?' sort of way. His look doesn't get within two feet of my face.

Fuckwit.

Rogers starts again with his questions, but Prothero has pushed his chair back. A gesture which indicates, I think, that he's irritated with himself for having made the Marr-Phillips disclosure. If Prothero stays like this, which he most likely will, we'll get nothing until the lawyer comes, at which point we'll get a glossier, shinier version of nothing. Reading the interview the same way, Rogers shoots me a glance and says, 'Take over a moment, would you?' He steps out. He'll want to get on the phone to Watkins, see if she has any bright ideas.

The door clangs shut. My arse hurts where the skin was taken for the graft. I take out some painkillers and swallow them without water.

I already know we'll get nothing from this interview. We'll get nothing in the morning, less than nothing in the afternoon.

I hold Prothero's supercilious gaze and tell him, carefully, 'Fuck you.'

Then I get up and leave the room.

39

Leave the room, find Rogers.

We quickly agree that there's not much point in pursuing the interview until Prothero has his lawyer. For form's sake, Rogers and another DS will put in shifts, one hour on, one hour off, asking the same battery of questions. There's no evidentiary purpose in doing so. Prothero will say nothing. But you get more from suspects if they're tired and angry. Plus you piss them off. Both good reasons to keep at it.

But Rogers doesn't need me, and I don't want to stay. It's not much fun sitting opposite your probable would-be murderer, unless you're sure of nailing the bastard. And we're a long way short of that.

'You could always go down to Barry,' Rogers says.

So I do. Find a patrol car going down there and hitch a ride. We arrive around nine thirty. A civilian vehicle, an Astra, enters the car park with us. The woman who gets out of the Astra wears a red-and-white bobble hat and says she's an Export Manager. She doesn't look like a dealer in illegal arms, but maybe she didn't know that's what she was. Or maybe arms dealers like to wear Christmassy bobble hats.

We escort her into the building, which has grown mountains of computers, wires, printers, laptops, phones. Boxed or in stacks. Yellow police stickers marked with reference numbers. Every item logged and signed for. And not just electronics. Boxes and boxes of paperwork too. Personnel records, employment contracts, bank records, invoices, technical drawings, visitor sign-in books. Everything.

And it's not just a question of lugging the stuff out of there. A CID IT specialist wants to map the network architecture, whatever that means, so there's potentially hours of fiddling around before we can carry off any booty. Whatever excitement there must have been when they forced entry earlier in the morning has long gone now. It's like a massive furniture removals project, only with lots of data complications and the risk of massive legal liabilities if we fuck up. The mood is simultaneously tense and frustrated.

DI Ken Hughes, who led the Barry raid this morning, is overseeing interviews with the bad-tempered snappishness that is native to him. There's a swirl of confused surprise around his desk as employees are paired up with officers.

But it's surprise, I note, not fear. It's as though our presence here is like the snow. Unexpected. A disturbance of the normal order. But somehow also accepted, a freak of the climate. An IT guy helps our CID specialist with the network architecture. Someone shows an officer how to get the coffee machine to produce hot chocolate.

Watkins is in with Dunbar, giving him the third degree. She'll be a good interviewer, I bet. Naturally scary. Dunbar has a lawyer sitting in with him, but Dunbar's budget doesn't run to some arsehole from London. His guy is local. A cheap grey pinstripe and a voice that's higher pitched than Watkins's.

I greet DI Hughes and offer my services. He doesn't much like me, which makes for a neatly symmetrical relationship, as I dislike him. He assigns me to interview a spotty boy from sales, who looks eighteen but claims to be nearer my age. We make a space for ourselves on a workbench under the windows that overlook the dock.

The kid knows nothing. He keeps asking, 'How are we going to do our work?'

Not my fucking problem, matey, I want to tell him. *If you want to work, you probably shouldn't have started dealing in illegal arms. Shouldn't have framed Mark Mortimer, shouldn't have killed Khalifi, shouldn't have left me to die in a fucking snowfield.*

I don't say that, though. I act like a copper out of a training video. 'We will keep any disruption to a minimum, sir. We do have a warrant to impound items that may be required for our inquiry.'

The kid looks at me blankly with eyes the colour of peat water. I run my tape recorder and write my notes.

Finish that interview. Do another. There's a flavour here that's missing. A fear.

I think of Theo and Ayla. Theo's question: *Was it a mistake?* Yes, Theo, it damn well was.

The atmosphere tastes like potatoes boiled without salt.

The lads who, earlier this morning, broke open a door with a steel battering ram are now reduced to figuring out schedules for the return of property. The vending machine runs out of coffee. A couple of uniformed coppers drive into Barry to get supplies.

I do another interview.

At midday, Watkins takes a rest from the business of throwing hostile questions at Jim Dunbar. She goes for a prowl so she can blast anyone who offends her.

By this point, I'm not doing anything at all. I don't think the interviews are helping us, so I've stopped doing them. I don't want to load paperwork into boxes, so I don't. Nor can I be doing with the whole logistical mess of figuring out what stuff Barry needs to continue in business and how soon we can get it back to them. As far as I'm concerned, we should take everything, without apology or excuse, keep what we need and dump the rest in Cardiff Bay.

So I drift around, make stupid jokes, and try to stop other

people from working. I'm sitting on a desk chatting with a couple of uniformed officers when Watkins heaves into view. She lasers a couple of people, just to demonstrate her weapons are in order, then rolls over to us.

Gives us the glare.

We look like what we are: two people trying to work, one person being annoying.

Watkins does that circular jaw action thing she does. The uniformed cops don't know her well enough to be terrified. But that jaw action is normally a prelude to launch, a countdown to detonation.

I give her a sunshiny smile, all tropical beaches and swaying palms.

She says, hoarsely, 'How are you feeling?'

I say, 'Fine. Mending up.'

She nods. Makes a half gesture at my outfit. 'You're looking smart.'

'Hobbs,' I say.

She makes some incoherent noise in the back of her throat – probably a glitch in her missile ignition system – and trundles away without remembering to reprimand us for existing. I turn to my two workmates with a grin, but they're not impressed. They don't know how close they came to incineration.

And after a while, I'm bored.

I quite like the factory hall itself. The incomprehensibly complex machines. The manufactured parts and works in progress. The precision of surfaces whose form and function is entirely beyond me to fathom. Aside from that, though, the place weirds me out. The offices at the front of the building are poky and lightless. Even worse than ours. We're here, barrelled up in a metal shed, close by the black water seething in the docks, the ice hardening its grip on walls and roads and ironwork, and we see none of it.

I need to get out.

Need to get out, but don't have a car.

Think about bothering Buzz, but his car is at the station and he's busy being a good, dutiful copper. So I call Jon Breakell in the office. No joy: he's on something and can't talk. I'd normally try Mervyn Rogers, because he quite likes me and because his attitude to work isn't always rigorous either, but I don't want to get sucked back into interviewing Prothero, so I avoid calling him.

Instead I try Bev, and am instantly in luck. Watkins has her driving round the various businesses that Khalifi patronised all those years ago. Not the Tescos or the SWALECs, of course, but those businesses small enough and personal enough that they might just remember a repeat customer. Watkins's hope is that if Bev flashes photos of Khalifi and Langton in front of enough people, she might just jog a memory or two. It's not even clear how that would assist the investigation, but Watkins is remorseless. She'll keep going till there's nothing more to do. I like that about her. Bev is in Penarth, just up the coast, feeling anxious that she's doing something wrong.

I start sweet-talking her into coming to pick me up, but she agrees right away and I ring off, smiling.

I'm bored no longer.

Ayla and Theo.

Al el-Khalifi.

Mary Langton and her grieving family.

Different victims, different remedies. It's good to act.

40

'The yacht club?' Bev sounds dubious. 'In this weather?'

I know what she means. The Swansea Bay Yacht Club is hardly likely to be humming with life. But it won't be closed either.

Bev is wearing a padded coat in sky blue. She has unnaturally blue eyes anyway and a clear complexion. In this weather, she has the clarity and perfection of a china doll. When she blinks, she looks like Bambi in pursuit of a butterfly.

She says, 'Wouldn't it be better to work more systematically? Go back to Penarth, finish up there, then do Barry, and so on.'

She's suddenly worried that she made an error in coming to get me. She wanted me in Penarth with her because she thought I'd help protect her from any Watkinsian rage. Now she worries that I'm going to lure her off-piste and end up bringing that rage down upon her.

I say, 'Bev, did Watkins specifically ask you to start in Penarth?'

'No, I just thought it would be logical to –'

'Then trust me. Let's go to the Mumbles in Swansea Bay. Start at the Yacht Club. If we don't have any luck there, we'll do it whichever way you like. And Watkins won't be pissed off with you. If she's pissed off – and she won't be – I'll tell her it was all my idea.'

'Okay then.' Bev sounds uncertain, but compliant. That's all I need.

I'm sitting in the passenger seat next to Bev. Like her, I've still got my coat on, but have shed my hat, gloves, and scarf, which lie on a woolly pile on my lap. Reaching round for my seatbelt is difficult – I don't want to stress the skin starting to grow back on my burn – and there's a moment where a small gasp of pain escapes me.

'Are you sure you're okay?'

'Yes.' I try to sound nonchalant. Try to make my *yes* sound like a *yes-and-why-wouldn't-I-be*.

'I thought you were going to be more, I don't know, more ...'

'Char-grilled? A bit crispy?'

Bev is shocked at my flippancy, but also reassured. She gives me a smile, puts the car into gear, and drives cautiously out of the snowy car park. The roads ease once we get into Barry proper. Still more so once we're on the A48. Channels of brown slush gouged into banks of dirty snow. Cars drive with their lights on. Snow doesn't just whiten a landscape, it quietens it. Sounds are deadened, speeds reduced. Bev drives sitting forward, hands on the wheel in the ten-to-two position.

When she's confident with the driving, she starts asking me about what happened up in the mountains. I give her my downsized version of the truth.

'Goodness gracious, Fi.'

That's just about as close as Bambi ever comes to swearing, so I work a bit harder to tone things down. I think it mostly works. She ends up saying, 'You do look okay. Really fine actually.'

'Hey, thanks.'

'No, I didn't mean it like that.'

We shift the subject to the weather. When I see Amrita, I'll give her the same super-low-key version of things, and with a bit of luck my weekend adventures won't have added too much to my reputation. Funnily enough, I think Buzz was right. The suit helps.

Swansea looks nothing like itself. It looks like some town in Norway, remade with Welsh-language road signs. The sea chafes all along the seafront. A contest of salt and ice.

The yacht club is disappointing. The Mumbles is Swansea's nicest suburb. I was expecting its yacht club to have a little moneyed swagger to it, but no. It lives in one of those buildings created when grey was the only colour, rectangles the only shape.

A white iron balcony daggered with icicles. Single-glazed windows in iron frames.

From the roof, a row of flags stick frozen to their flagpoles. In the yard next door, boats sit on metal trailers, each one swaddled in its winter tarpaulin.

There's only one person inside the clubhouse, an older man repinning notices to a corkboard. We introduce ourselves. He's Gwilym Jenkins and he's happy to help. He asks if we want tea. Bev starts to say no, because she is still worried about not having accomplished enough today. Not having ticked enough rows on her spreadsheet.

I say yes, because I want this man to relax and confide.

He makes tea, very slowly, but he finds us chairs and handles the china with a courtesy that amounts almost to chivalry.

When we're all done, sitting at a Formica table by a radiator, Bev lays out her photos. She starts to ask her questions.

'Are you able to identify either of these people? Did either of them use the facilities here?'

I interrupt. I say, 'Gwilym, these two are Mary Langton and Ali el-Khalifi. We think they took out a joint membership in March 2003. She was murdered a few months later.'

'Good heavens. Well, I'll certainly take a look ...'

He goes off to fetch some records. Soft footsteps on

wooden floors. Bev does Bambi eyes at me. I answer her unspoken question.

'Bev, it was your data that gave us the clue. According to your spreadsheet, Khalifi spent seventy pounds here. Seventy pounds *exactly*. That doesn't sound like a drinks bill. It's too large and too exact. It's not for boat hire, because they don't hire boats. So it seemed to me like it had be some kind of membership fee. I called the club here and asked them about their prices. The prices have changed since, but back then the charge for a double membership of the club was seventy pounds. The price for a single was forty-five. For a family, ninety.'

Bev's mouth has dropped open and her eyes, if possible, have widened.

We don't, of course, know that Khalifi was necessarily buying the membership for himself and Langton, but the dates would fit with everything else we know about them. That plus, if you look back through the photos we have of Langton, she looked fit and tanned that spring. An outdoorsy sort of tan, that doesn't reach to the neck. The sort of tan you'd get, almost inadvertently, on a boat out on Swansea Bay. That wasn't how she looked in her year of exotic dancing. You can never be sure about those things from photos, but it was confirmation of a sort.

Gwilym returns, with a membership ledger. He leafs through the years. Finds the right year, the right month. There were only three new memberships that March. The first of them belongs to Langton and Khalifi. Two signatures side by side on the page.

Evidence.

Bev is awed and relieved in equal measure. Relieved because she's escaped the Wrath of Watkins. Awed because she credits me with some sort of divine inspiration. A divinity I don't possess.

I say, 'Gwilym, we're not sure how often Ali came here, but I'm guessing that you don't have a huge North African membership ...'

Not huge, no. Gwilym phones a colleague and we hear him talking about a 'brown gentleman.' The colleague – Delyth – says she'll come on over.

She does. She's forty-something, knows everything, remembers everything. Ali el-Khalifi never owned a boat, but he used to borrow one from a Swansea-based friend of his. He and Mary Langton used to come every weekend or so, 'for a while' – we think probably a couple of months. Then less often. Then not at all. Khalifi and Langton were definitely a couple. 'Oh, they were quite sweet on each other,' Delyth tells us. 'He was a terrible sailor, to be honest. And she wasn't any better. They'd get into trouble if there was any breeze up.'

She recounts a hard-to-follow story about a time when the pair of them brought their boat back with a spinnaker only, after lowering the mainsail because the wind was too much for them. That sounds sensible enough to me – and to Bev – but Delyth and Gwilym are laughing hard.

I ask, 'Do you think they stopped coming because they weren't cut out for the water. Or because their relationship ended?'

Delyth isn't sure. Gwilym has no idea. But there's an upcoming Christmas dinner at which there'll be plenty of old hands. Bev says she'll aim to be there. I evade.

We don't really need to take a statement, but Bev wants to get all the main points in writing. I leave her to do just that – sitting there with Gwilym and Delyth over a police notebook and cooling tea. I get a glass of water from the kitchen and swallow a couple of aspirin. While I'm still in the warm, I find a number for Marr-Phillips's office and call it. Arrange an interview. His secretary takes the call in an efficient, unflustered way. Then I walk outside and over the road. There's a little car park. A clutter of food and tourist kiosks which might be busy in season but are deserted now. A concrete ramp leading down into the water. The slope is thickly armoured in plates of snow and ice. I don't step onto it. Walk instead to the end of a little pier to the right. Blue iron balustrades. An orange life buoy.

I try to feel Khalifi and Langton here. The lecturer and the student.

He: a little uncertain. An immigrant who never quite settled. Who never quite realised that the uncertainty he felt didn't come from others, but from within. Who kept on trying to prove himself because he never quite had the confidence to be himself.

Langton was different. I don't know what made her turn to exotic dancing, but the spring that she went sailing with Khalifi was surely the time when she turned things around. Quit the clubs, stopped dancing. Remembered that she was a middle-class English kid who rode horses, chased hockey balls, and wrote essays about Dylan Thomas. Out here, by these grey waters and chattering halliards, those spangly mini-skirted nights must have seemed a million miles away.

You'd say that Khalifi's was the relationship which saved her life. Rescued it from that adventure into darkness. You'd say that, except that within a few months Langton was dead. Not much of a rescue if your leg ends up in a Cyncoed freezer, your arms in a plumbers' merchant's roof, your head in a barrel of lawn mower oil.

I've been missing Langton, I realise suddenly. I like the thought of her and Khalifi together. It's like when two people who are special to you shyly tell you they've been on a date, that it went well, that they're seeing each other again.

I want to reward her with the only gifts I have to offer. Investigation, arrest, prosecution, conviction.

The girl who chased hockey balls and was crap at sailing.

I'm smiling at that thought when I hear Bev walking over the yard toward me. I turn to her, still smiling.

'Got what you need?'

She nods, waves her notebook contentedly at me.

We drive back to Cardiff and night has fallen long before we arrive. It's been a long day for my tired body, and I ask Bev if she minds driving me all the way home. She doesn't mind and drops me at the door. I ask her in, but she says no. I'm relieved to be alone.

This is the end game now.

Langton.

Khalifi.

Mortimer.

Their ghosts are bustling now. Restless. Their satisfaction rests with us, the living. I make a cup of peppermint tea and drink it in my dark kitchen. Lights off, heating off. I'm still in my warm clothes. Crunch some aspirin with the last of my tea.

This is the end game now and I have scores to settle.

41

The night is a strange one. Buzz wants me to spend the night at his place. Mam and Dad want me to go back there. I know that I need to be on my own. Need it for many reasons.

One, I want a joint. The last time I even had a joint between my lips was the moment just before I threw it into a tank of petrol. There's some strange way in which I need a long uncluttered smoke to vanquish the memory of the blaze that followed. The memory itself I can handle, but I need to soften its edges. Smudge it into something a little less than real. There are probably better ways of doing that, but marijuana is my way.

Two, and on a related point, this cold weather won't have been any good for my marijuana plants. The poor things have been trying to get by with heat lamps set to come on for just twelve hours a day. They'll need more than that in these temperatures. I go to my potting shed, check water levels, adjust the timers on the heat lamps, and help myself to a little cube of hash by way of reward. My plants aren't too happy with me, but they're not at death's door either. They'll survive.

Three, I need space. Need to feel myself in control and alone. It's thinking time, but it's also being time. Being constantly with other people places a pressure of normality on me that I can't always bear. Here, alone, I can be the way I am. My version of ordinary.

And finally, tonight, I can feel the clamour of the dead. The restless ghosts. Tonight, they must have their proper share of my attention. The living can wait.

I crumble resin on tobacco. Plenty of the former, not much of the latter. I'll smoke only one joint tonight, but I'll make it a rich one.

Rich and fat.

Lights on, heating up. Start running a bath. Talk to Buzz by phone. He knows I need time alone, but wants to know I'm okay. I say I am.

He tells me that Watkins was angrier than anyone had ever seen her after interviewing Prothero this afternoon. The guy had brought not one, but two solicitors up from London. Two glossy solicitors from some magic-circle law firm. Fuckers with money. They both seem to have been well briefed, long in advance of our raid.

'Apparently they're going to sue us if we don't have everything back at Barry Precision within forty-eight hours.'

Removing data takes much longer than that if you do it properly, recording where it's come from and how it fits together. Even a week would be good going.

'They'll lose if they sue us,' I say.

'Yes. But we'll still be sued.'

He's right. If we're sued and we lose some portion of the case, or are adjudged faulty on some narrow technical point, we may end up having to pay costs. Legal costs can quickly rip huge holes in our budgets. A couple of stories in the local press about overzealous cops recklessly placing Welsh jobs at risk could be a career wrecker for Watkins.

Buzz chuckles. I don't.

We talk twenty minutes more, affectionate nonsense mostly, and hang up.

My bath has grown cold, so I run half of it out and start refilling it with hot water, when my phone rings again. Not Buzz. Not Mam or Dad.

Watkins.

I turn the tap off and answer.

'Fiona Griffiths.'

'Fiona. It's Rhiannon.'

I had no idea that we were on first-name terms now, but I don't pass comment. In any case, Watkins has news. Nothing about Prothero. Nothing about Dunbar. This is about Hamish.

'The blood on your coat. We've got a DNA match,' she says. 'No address, but we've got a name and a picture.'

I know what she wants to know, so I tell her. 'I'm happy to look at photos.'

'The light can't have been great.'

'It wasn't. But we had lights on inside the car most of the time.' Before they faded, that is. Faded into the night I was never meant to leave. 'I'm certain I can identify him. If the photo is even halfway like him.'

'It's a 2005 photo. He's been on the run since then.'

Watkins is deliberately not telling me much. It would be easy to nudge me in the right direction. Give me enough information that I could be sure to pick the right candidate from a parade of photos. But Watkins isn't that kind of copper. I tell her again that I'll be sure of fingering him. And she's already told me to expect the photo of a man looking five years younger than the man whose nose I broke. I'd quite like to ask about facial hair – the Hamish I saw was clean-shaven and might not always have been – but I don't.

Watkins says, 'Good. Is eight thirty tomorrow too early?'

'No.'

'Good. Then come down to the interview rooms first thing. Don't go to your desk first.'

'Okay.'

If I went to my desk first, the office grapevine might well find a way to prime me with the name or the face the moment

I got there. And if Watkins wants this clean, that's fine. We'll do it clean. We may or may not be able to secure a conviction for what happened to me on that mountainside, but it's still better to do these things and to do them properly. You never know.

'I've checked Hinton's call log. She received a call from a mobile, pay-as-you-go, used once, then apparently discarded.'

'They're good. They're very careful.'

It's sort of nice to know that they called Sophie, not vice versa. Hinton needs a slapping, maybe, but not necessarily jail time.

'Yes. Look, I've been having words with my SIO.' SIO: Senior Investigating Officer. In this case, Robert Kirby. Watkins sounds stressed, but I already know what she's going to tell me. That the team tasked with investigating my attempted murder is coming up with no meaningful leads. That Kirby wants to shift resources away to Stirfry proper.

I say, 'I don't care. I mean, I want the men arrested and jailed. But we're more likely to get them for the Khalifi killing. We've got more to go on there.'

'Yes.'

'We can't even prove a crime took place.'

'I've told Kirby to give me more time. He's agreed.' She pauses in case I want to say thank you, but I resist the temptation. Then, 'I appreciated your help today.'

'I didn't really help. I mostly sat around.'

There's a moment's silence. One of those shared telephone silences that seem to expand forever. As though you have your ear pressed up against some instrument that lets you listen directly to the emptiness of space. A background crackle that reminds you how little you can truly hear.

That's how it is for me anyway. I don't know what it's like for Watkins.

Then she says, 'You can help tomorrow.' There's a line of steel in her voice when she says that. Watkinsian steel.

We ring off.

I finish running my bath.

Get in.

I'm still wearing dressings but they can get wet. The hot water is painful on my more battered surfaces, but good over-all. I take a moment to adjust, then start to relax.

I'm about to light my joint, but I don't. Someone – Mam, I think – gave me a scented vanilla candle in a glass jar. I didn't know what to do with it, so I put it by my bath. I've never used it before, but I light it now. Get out of the bath, dripping, and turn the overhead lamp off.

Light my joint. Take the first puff or two. Long inhalations.

The sweet, sweet weed.

I call Buzz. I say, 'We should have some candles by your bath. We could take baths together.'

'I don't have a bath, remember? I only have a shower.'

Oh yes. I'd forgotten that. 'Well, maybe we should get one.'

'Maybe we should.'

We say good night again.

I finish my joint.

Go to the kitchen, hunt down some food.

Slim pickings, it would appear, but I have a jar of pesto sauce and some crackers. I put pesto on the crackers and eat until I can't be bothered to eat anymore.

Clear up.

Do my teeth.

Bed.

I sleep easily for once. The bath and the joint probably helped. That, plus a long day in pursuit of a short night.

I sleep easily and without dreams.

Then, after maybe two or three hours, something wakes me

abruptly. The sudden, jolting wakefulness that arrives with a wash of adrenaline. Of fear.

At first I don't do anything at all. Just listen into the silence, seeing if I can detect the thing that woke me in the first place. I can't.

Aside from the candle that's still burning in the bathroom, there's no light on anywhere in the house. A street light outside beyond curtained windows. I can see the shape of the windows. A glimmer of mirror.

I breathe through my mouth. I don't move a muscle.

There is someone in the room with me. Someone here now.

I don't know where they are. I don't know how they woke me. But there is someone here now and I am terrified.

I don't sleep with a gun anymore. I'd like to, of course, but part of Miss Griffiths's Be-More-Normal Project involved hiding my gun in a Pembrokeshire sheepfold. The 460 bullets I have in a locked drawer of the ops room are as useless as tinsel.

Whoever is here isn't moving. He's being very silent.

Perhaps I made a sound when I woke up. Perhaps he's waiting for me to move. And I'm not fond of waiting games.

Although I gave up my gun, I didn't leave myself defenceless. In a holster made of sellotape and kitchen towel behind the brass bars at the head of my bed, there is a knife. The knife was originally an ordinary kitchen knife. A paring knife with a four-inch blade. Black-handled. Not particularly expensive.

But there are a couple of Gypsies who knock on doors round here from time to time. They have a grinding wheel in the back of their van and sharpen stuff for cash. Pruning hooks. Lawn mower blades. And knives.

I got them to sharpen my knife till it had the devil's own edge, the devil's own point.

I got, from a place online, a rubber finger loop that allows you to attach the knife to your finger, so even if you lose your grip on the handle in the course of a fight, you don't drop it. It remains attached. Ready.

So I slide my bare arm through the bars of the bed to reach the knife. Find the handle. Find the finger loop. I come back with the knife in a fighting grip. Ready for whatever follows.

I remember Lev's words.

Don't trust the stab. The blade isn't long enough to do reliable damage, and in any case, the heart is trickier to reach than you think. Shielded. You have to go in at the right place and angle to stand a chance.

Rely on the slashing movement. The face or neck ideally, but really it's okay to land the stroke anywhere. *Draw blood.* Stay out of reach. Let the bleeding do your work. You need a lot of blood. Much more than you think. A person contains four or five litres of blood and you might need a litre of that splattering your home furnishings before your antagonist is seriously weakened. So be patient, take your time, wait for the moment.

And I do.

I hold, as far as possible, my original sleeping position, my original posture. Keep my striking arm clear of the bedclothes. Listen and watch.

Listen to silence.

Watch emptiness.

Something's strange about this silence. I'm still completely certain that there's someone here, but silence of this intensity is unnatural. No creak of a floorboard, no suppressed breathing.

The energy in the room feels weird too. As though the space has acquired a chilly pressing quality. A solidification of the emptiness. A cold incandescence.

I don't know how long passes like this.

Not long probably. When you watch with this intensity, each second seems to stretch forever.

And then I realise.

Realise and laugh.

My laughter is silent and I don't let go of my knife, but I understand what's going on. Yes, there is someone present in my room. But the person in question is a dead one. Khalifi. It's his spirit that I'm feeling here.

If my first response is relief, my second is terror. It comes to me as sharp and fierce as I've ever known it. Sharper and fiercer than anything I felt up on that snowy mountainside.

It's not fear of the dead. Far from it. I *like* the dead. I'm comfortable in their presence.

Rather, it's a fear of my own head. A fear of craziness.

Ghosts and dead presences don't exist. What I have here isn't a spirit from the other side, it's psychosis. Madness. And that madness, the sort I had as a teenager, killed me – pretty literally killed me – for two years. I'm terrified that that illness is returning now. And that if it does, I'm not strong enough to stop it.

For a few minutes – five? ten? – I lie trapped in my own alarm. *Is my Cotard's returning? Am I going mad again?*

Then logic, the sweet cold stream of reason, starts to wash those fears away.

When I was a teenager, I lost all bodily sensation. I couldn't really feel hot or cold. I couldn't really feel my heart beat except as some repetitive tapping from an adjoining room. I never felt my feet. Never. They didn't belong to me at all. Some sufferers with Cotard's report 'seeing' their flesh crawl with maggots. I never had that, but I used to turn my hand over again and again, scared I would find that seething crawl of decomposition.

It's not like that now. I feel like I always do. Maybe even a bit sharper, a bit clearer. That might not be very sharp or clear by the standards of others, but I am who I am. And as far as *I'm* concerned, things are okay. I feel my heart beat. Feel the

301

knife in my hand. When I move my feet, I feel them too.

Khalifi, though, is still here. I feel that cold intensification. His chuckling laugh, the pressure of his gaze.

Feel it too much, too intensely.

This isn't real. It's illusion.

This isn't real. It's psychosis.

In my bathroom cabinet, I have a bottle containing about a hundred and fifty 100-milligram tablets of amisulpride. A second-generation antipsychotic. During my time in hospital, I must have taken pretty much every psychiatric medication known to man, but amisulpride was the only one I ever had much time for. It didn't conquer my illness, but perhaps it took the edge off it. Introduced some flickering note of doubt. Perhaps that little advantage was what my body and mind needed.

In any case, long after my shrinks thought I was cured, long after they thought I had completed my course of medication, I kept those pills as a safety precaution. Bought more from an Indian pharmacy on the Internet when it first became possible to do things like that. I haven't touched them in years, but I still know exactly where they are. I carry some in my bag. If I travel, I take a bottle.

I could take a pill, maybe two, and watch Khalifi fade away. Drive away this flash of craziness. Let the world return to normal.

I put my knife back, sit up in bed, breathe deeply. *In*-two-three, *out*-two-three. Reach down and massage my feet, until I'm sure I feel them properly. My cuts and burns and bruises help.

I am who I am.

I am all that I am.

And in the process – the breathing, the massaging, the movement – I no longer feel afraid. At least for the moment, I won't touch those pills. Perhaps if the psychosis gets worse – if

Khalifi starts speaking? If I start to see him? – I'll change my mind. I don't have a stupid pride about these things. Survival is all that matters. But for now, I'm okay. I'm just me. A kooky detective with an unreliable brain. If a corpse wants to come and visit me in the night, he's welcome to do so.

I grin at Khalifi, welcoming him for the first time.

He grins back.

The room trembles with laughter. It reminds me of that lovely moment I had with Langton's head. That lovely, spacious moment. That black and gaping mouth. The feel of bone.

Time passes. I feel comfortable. With Khalifi. With my crazy brain.

I realise too that this particular psychosis isn't as new as I first thought it. In a way, I've *always* connected too much with the dead. Felt them too much. Felt them in a way that runs far beyond reality.

Strangely – but I *am* strange – that thought settles me. I feel myself welcoming them all. Mary Langton. Mark Mortimer. Ali el-Khalifi. And others too. Cases from my past: Janet and April Mancini. Stacey Edwards. A night for all souls. The faithful departed.

Me and my crazy head in an empty room.

I get up and go to the bathroom. I fashion another joint, lighting it from the burning candle. Then go back to bed. Plump up the pillows. Sit there smiling in the company of the dead.

Finish my joint.

The chuckling quality in the room has faded to something quieter and more peaceful. But it's a good sort of peace. A special one. The sort you only get from the dead.

I wonder what Khalifi wants from me, but the truth is I already know. He wants to be with me. He wants me to complete my acts of justice on the men who killed him. And he wants to see me do right by Mary Langton. The only girl he ever truly loved.

I want those things too. We grin at each other, enjoying the communication. At some stage, I don't know when, I must fall asleep. When my alarm goes off in the middle of a grisly December dawn, I am still sitting up. I ache like hell. And I am all alone in my room.

42

I don't make it in by eight thirty. Some of my wounds need their dressings changed and it takes longer than I expected. So I text Watkins to tell her I'll be late and do the job properly. One of the cuts on my hand opens up any time I move it too much, so there's fresh blood on the bandage by the time I've finished. I'm fairly sure that even the Watkinsian Handbook of Personnel Management prohibits you from ripping someone's head off when they are newly wounded in the line of duty.

I dress with more formality than normal. Skirt, shirt, jacket. Not quite Hobbs-posh, but still. All part of my gossip-suppression strategy. Put a handful of aspirin in my jacket pocket. A couple of amisulpride tablets as well, just in case.

I'm with Watkins in the interview room by eight fifty. She glowers, but doesn't give me a bollocking. The room is bare. There's a video camera, a computer screen, a table, a couple of chairs. The place ought to look like the movies, where everything is painted battleship grey and maverick cops beat crap out of the suspects, but mostly it just looks like the sort of thing you have in local government. Budget cuts and equipment compromises.

A technician whose name might be Michael hovers around until Watkins shoos him away.

'When you're ready,' she says to me.

I nod.

Watkins turns the camera on. Gives place, time, names.

She's a little senior-officer awkward about these things. It would have been a routine part of her job once, but the rules and the camera will have changed since then. She's only doing it now because violence against a police officer is treated more seriously than violence against anyone else.

I look at the photos on-screen. Sequentially, not simultaneously. The evidence you collect is stronger that way, less prone to challenge. If, for example, you identify photograph number three from a group, where you haven't seen the later photos, it's strong proof that you're picking the right person, not merely the person who's the best-fitting candidate from the ones on offer.

I don't react to the first three photos. Hamish was a gingery blond. The first three don't even come close. I just say no decisively and move on.

The video camera makes a difference. You're always aware of it. You act for it. Auditioning for the courtroom drama which may one day follow.

Number four I need to look at twice. He's bearded and there's something about his face shape which is approximately correct. But the eyes are wrong. The face is wrong. I say, 'No.'

Then number five.

It's Hamish all right. Younger. Longer haired. But Hamish.

I say, 'This is one of the two men who tried to kill me. When I saw him on November 27th, his hair was shorter than in this photograph. Additionally, since this photograph was taken, his jaw appears to have been broken and badly reset. At any rate, there is some disturbance to the jawline not depicted in this photo. On that night of the twenty-seventh, I struck this man in the face and I believe, but cannot be certain, that I broke his nose. I would expect his nose to retain some sign of the injury, but cannot be confident of this. I am, however, completely certain of my identification. I do not need to see any further photographs to confirm my opinion.'

Watkins shows me more photographs anyway. Ten more. I say no to them all. She shows me Hamish again, a different photo this time. I repeat my identification.

Watkins nods. 'Good.' Turns off the recording equipment. Then, 'I take it that you *are* sure, Constable?'

'Yes. No question. His jaw has been injured since that picture. I'm not sure about the nose, but I thought it worth mentioning.'

I took care to do so that would bring us courtroom brownie points if I was right, but wouldn't lose anything much if I was wrong.

Anyway. Watkins is satisfied. She tells me what I want to know. 'His real name is Callum McCormack. He's got a conviction for armed robbery. He's wanted for an assault on a police officer in Aberdeen. But he's been on the wanted list for five years now, so we have to assume a new identity.'

She passes a wodge of paper to me. McCormack's record as it appears on our system. There are a couple more photos. Foster homes or institutions for much of his childhood. Joined the Army aged seventeen. Served three years. Then a drink-related assault-and-battery incident, for which he served time and was discharged from the Army. Then in and out of trouble, until the Aberdeen assault, at which point he dropped off our radar completely. No mention of any Scandinavian partners in crime.

'The car registration number,' says Watkins. 'The plates were stolen from a car in Glasgow a week ago.'

She doesn't spell out the rest because she doesn't have to. McCormack and the man I still have to call Olaf will have stolen the plates off a car locally, but driven to South Wales with their own legitimate registration plates showing – the stolen ones would instantly have been flagged by cameras and passing police cars. Once they were deep into the Llanthony Valley, beyond the reach of police surveillance, they'd have switched to the stolen plates. Then, if any local had noticed any abnormal activity, they'd have only the wrong plates to report.

'Where in Glasgow?' I ask.

Watkins gives me an address. Drumchapel. The name doesn't mean anything to me.

I shrug.

It's a dead end. That's what this is. My killers were professionals who have successfully protected their identities for five years. I'm certain they killed Khalifi, but we have not a shred of evidence to prove it. Although I know damn well that McCormack tried to kill me, we have no evidence that any crime even took place.

A dead end – yet I can't help but smile like an idiot. I can feel Khalifi's laughter in the room with me now. So I sit in the interview room, alone with Watkins the Badge and the chuckling spirit of Ali el-Khalifi. And I smile.

Watkins, I imagine, doesn't realise she's in here with Khalifi, so she probably assumes she's here with an idiot. She smiles awkwardly, then says, 'I hear you and Beverley Rowlands made a breakthrough yesterday.'

For a second or so, all I can remember is the snowy pier jutting out into an empty sea. The breaking of waves and a hover of gulls. I can't remember what the breakthrough was.

Then I do.

'The yacht club,' I say. 'The two of them signed up together.'

'Rowlands tells me that you knew beforehand. I gather she wanted to start in Penarth and work her way west.'

'They were her spreadsheets. I just made one phone call. And I didn't *know*. We were lucky, I suppose.'

Watkins makes a noise at that. Not a noise with words. Just a noise.

I say, 'Khalifi took a holiday in Dubai. Spring 2009.'

'Yes?'

'And a holiday in Jordan, May 2010.'

'Your point being?'

'He used to go to Spain. His holiday destinations changed.'

Watkins's face says *so what*? She's on the edge of angry, but her tents are never pitched far from that fierce edge.

'Maybe it wasn't Dubai he was interested in. Maybe they weren't holidays.' Watkins doesn't do or say anything much, so I continue. 'Dubai is just down the road from Abu Dhabi. And his holiday dates happened to coincide with IDEX 2009. That's the International Defence Exhibition. The biggest arms fair in the Middle East.'

Watkins finds her voice now. 'And Jordan?'

'SOFEX. The Special Operations Forces Exhibition. The dates match.' He also travelled to Doha, the scene of another major arms fair. The dates for that trip didn't coincide with the fair, but presumably the city remained a good place to meet the middlemen and buyers. I'd guess that Lausanne, Vienna, and Cairo see their share of Middle Eastern arms traders too.

'So your theory is that Mortimer wanted to expose illegal arms trading, but Khalifi wanted to indulge in it? Mortimer was framed for a drug bust as a way to shut him up. Khalifi simply set about building his own contacts. He wanted to do what Barry Precision was doing, but take the profits for himself?'

'It's a *theory*, yes. Khalifi had everything he needed: the technical expertise to replicate anything that Barry was doing. Engineering contacts all over the UK. Fluent Arabic. He'd have been perfect. Better than Barry Precision, in fact. They attracted Mortimer's suspicions because so *much* of what they made was dual use. In the end, there was no innocent explanation available.'

Watkins thinks about this. Draws the same conclusions I do.

'He'd have been perfect, wouldn't he? One of the fattest contact books in the industry. An academic job which would give him cover. And as you say, the Arabic.'

I nod. 'If I'd been him, I'd have placed one order here, another one there, a third one there. Not even all in the UK, necessarily. He had dealings with manufacturers from further afield too. Perhaps he was hoping to build his own virtual arms company. Anyone looking at the output of any single firm would never have identified the trade that was taking place. But from the end user's point of view, what's not to like? British- and European-engineered components with all the hassle removed.'

'That's speculation.'

'Yes, but verifiable.'

And easy to verify. We simply track every firm on Khalifi's contact list. Ask if he was involved in any recent orders. Get the data on all such orders and pass it over to Stuart Brotherton. If Brotherton says the orders look suitable for armaments, then our current speculation will turn to solid fact.

Watkins makes some notes. 'Good. That's easily done. I'll get that actioned immediately.'

I say something neutral. My theory remains to be proven, but I'll be surprised if I've got it wrong. Good Saint Mark came to his engineering buddy Ali worried about an illicit trade. The bad man Khalifi thought he saw a route to making his fortune. Neither of them realised the dangers they were getting into. Clever fools, the pair of them.

And it's odd. I like Khalifi as a corpse, get on with him very well. But I'd have detested him when he was alive. Loathed him. He was no better than Prothero. Selling guns to dictators, because he wanted a more expensive car.

Watkins's thoughts turn back to the murder itself. 'Let's assume your idea proves correct. You think that when Barry

Precision found out what Khalifi was up to, they decided to have him killed?'

'Maybe. Yes, I don't know.'

Khalifi was in competition with Barry Precision, certainly, but he was also in competition with Saadawi and his peers. Either of those forces might have ordered the killing. Or the two of them acting together. Or something else. We may never know.

Watkins nods as she traces through the logic of this.

'But Prothero *did* have eight mobile phones,' I point out. 'There's no way he's just an innocent businessman.'

'And Dunbar? Khalifi's other colleagues and contacts?'

Dunbar, I guess, is not much more than a fuckwit. As for Khalifi's other contacts, I doubt if any of them knew much. Perhaps McKelvey guessed something, but I doubt if he knew the whole thing. I don't think he knew about gunrunning or murder. His wasn't that sort of silence.

I say these things, adjusting vocabulary as necessary.

Watkins nods again. She's been sitting on the table while we've talked. Now she gets up. She's wearing a pinstriped jacket, trousers, and a shirt in some kind of aubergine colour. Some sort of shiny fabric, which might look nice, but only if it was worn by somebody completely else in some completely other way. I prefer Watkins when she's fierce and monochrome.

She says, 'That's very good work.'

She says more than that too. Words of praise. I nod and look down at my hands. It's what I do when I'm getting a bollocking, but the technique is adaptable. It works both ways.

Eventually she stops, changes tack.

She tells me that Khalifi's mother is coming to Cardiff soon, and did I still want to see her? I say yes.

Then she says, 'How long have you been a Detective Constable?'

311

That's one of those tricky questions. It means arranging my life into years and dates and reading them off, like figures from an electricity meter. But I figure it out.

'I joined the force in November 2006,' I say. 'I switched to the CID as soon as I could.'

Taking account of my training period, that means I've been in the CID about a year and a half.

'You'll take your Detective Sergeant exams when you can, I imagine?'

Another tricky one. A question about the future. I've never quite understood normal people's relationship to time. Most people seem riveted by questions about what might happen to them in a year or two or twenty. Not me. Most of the time, I find it hard to get my head round what might happen next week. I don't remember much about my past. I've certainly never given a moment's thought to my Detective Sergeant exams. Why would I?

I don't say that, though. I say, 'Yes, ma'am.'

'You ought to.'

'Yes.'

'Have you discussed your career direction with anyone? At a senior level, I mean. DCI Jackson? DCI Matthews? DCI Howells?'

'No, ma'am.'

'Well, we ought to do it. Lunch maybe? Are you free today?'

'Yes.'

'Good. If you come by at twelve thirty, we'll go somewhere.'

I nod. 'Okay. Thank you.'

She nods. Gestures at the bandage on my hand. 'You're healing up?'

'Yes.'

'Good. Well. I'll see you later then.'

She stomps off. She probably has to be extra horrible to someone, because she's been nice to me. She's left me with the bundle of paper on McCormack. My copy, I guess. There's nothing very useful there, but I take it anyway.

I finger the pills in my pocket. Crunch up an aspirin. Check that the amisulprides are there, which they are.

Khalifi's presence hasn't gone exactly, but he's not here the way he was. I remember the time on the stairwell round at the Engineering Faculty. When I stumbled. Wondered about morning sickness. It wasn't that. It was Khalifi. The first jostling manifestation of his presence. He doesn't need to jostle now. He's just tagging along.

This psychosis: this presence of corpses. I realise I've always had it. Certainly ever since I got better from Cotard's. There was a student in my year at Cambridge who committed suicide. I'd bumped into him occasionally at lectures, but wouldn't say that I knew him well. I remember now that he felt somehow brighter after his death than he had done before. There was some way in which I felt it easier to relate to him dead than him alive. Having Khalifi's presence come barging into my room at midnight isn't really so different from that. It's craziness for sure, but not new craziness.

Just me being me.

I go to find Amrita, to start my gossip suppression campaign. I show her the dressing on my right hand, but make it seem that that's the worst of my injuries. Amrita doesn't even hide her disappointment.

'They were saying you almost died out there,' she says contemptuously.

'Well, the hospital *was* worried about tetanus,' I say. 'I needed two injections.'

Amrita looks at my hand again, but her disgust is evident. Quite soon we're discussing whether Owen Dunwoody is going to be headhunted for the Gwent Police and whether Jane Alexander is pregnant again.

After Amrita, I go looking for Bev, but she, bless her cotton socks, is going to every other business listed on her spread-sheet. There's a note from her on my desk, saying she looked for me earlier in case I wanted to come.

I'm at work, but no one is giving me anything to do, because they're not quite sure whether I'm well enough to work or not.

I chew another aspirin.

My bum hurts where they took the skin graft.

The wound on my hand has opened up again. I can feel the trickle of blood under my bandage.

Callum McCormack stole some car number plates in a place called Drumchapel and the Strathclyde police won't find him because they've been trying for five years already.

We don't know who Olaf is.

Although we seem to have busted an arms-smuggling ring, not only are they not rolling over and playing dead, they're threatening to sue us, which is not a welcome behavioural trait in criminals.

And Idris Prothero, who has been collecting his fat little dividends from Barry Precision's murderous endeavours, is still a free man of unblemished reputation despite the fact that he very likely sought to have me killed. Which is not a welcome behavioural trait in anyone.

I get my phone out. Send a text. To Lev.

It says: 'DON'T KNOW IF YOU'RE INTERESTED BUT I MIGHT HAVE A JOB FOR YOU. FI.'

Sometimes I hear back quickly. Other times I don't hear back at all. I don't know if Lev has a home, but I assume not. I don't even know how much time he spends in the UK. He once spent three weeks on my sofa, smoking weed and listening to twentieth-century Russian music, all sweeping strings and self-created sorrow. Then he vanished and I didn't see him again for eight months.

I poke around on the network.

Bev's spreadsheets are now things of beauty, with items underlined and coloured according to some runic coding I can't be bothered to fathom.

There's a mass of data coming in from the raid on Barry Precision, but it's way too early to see what we've got.

Nothing more from Stuart Brotherton and it's too soon to start hassling him.

I need to know more about pruning techniques. I need to check that I'm right in remembering a cherry tree on Elsie Williams's drive. That and other things. I get stuck into my research and these things are always more interesting than you think.

I'm six and a half minutes late for Watkins.

I don't want to be a Detective Sergeant.

I haven't heard back from Lev.

43

Lunch.

Oh my God. Lunch.

It doesn't start well. Me late. Watkins shivering on the brink of something nuclear – perhaps only the tactical-battlefield version of nuclear, because six and half minutes late is only six and a half minutes, even in Watkins-land – but still on the brink of detonation. I mutter something. She works her jaw and says never mind. She's added a gauzy scarf in pale blue to her outfit, which doesn't suit her. Chain mail would be better.

Anyway. We tramp outside and head toward Queen Street. She asks if I like Italian food. I say yes. It's still ridiculously cold. We don't talk about the case. It's as though Watkins has been on some weekend course in Being Nice to Humans. She's got all the tricks – the gauzy scarf, the small talk, the asking where we should eat – but she's missed the somewhat essential element of actually being nice.

This new Watkins disconcerts me. I never do well with the nicey-nicey stuff. I like Watkins best when she's most up-and-at-it. Disguising fair nature with hard-favoured rage. At least you know where you stand.

But we get to the restaurant intact.

Breadsticks. Ciabata. A little tiny dish of olive oil and some fancy vinegar. A bottle of water.

Watkins says, 'Still or sparkling?'

I have no answer to that. Like I give a fuck. Like she does.

316

Neither of us gives a fuck about the water and yet we're supposed to have a conversation about it.

She says, 'Sparkling then.'

The waitress nods and goes. Returns with water. Asks if we've chosen. We say almost. Watkins says something about scallops. I nod. Then she says something about how to cook tuna. I nod again. Think of Langton's head. Khalifi's lung. I try to concentrate on my breathing.

This isn't going well.

Then Watkins says, 'Look, Fiona, I did want to talk to you about your career. I mean, you have talent. You must know that.'

I probably say something to that. I definitely blink.

'But I also wanted ... Look, I think it's time we spoke about our feelings for each other. Not as police officers, but as ...' She doesn't finish her sentence. Just lunges across the table. Takes my unbandaged hand in hers. She's bright with emotion and her eyes are full. Her lips move but nothing comes out.

I don't know what to say. No idea. Don't know what to say, where to look, how to react.

Just keep hold of that image of Langton's head rising up through the oil. The twilight lustre of her scalp. The sudden weight and the dripping hair and the pebble clacking against her teeth.

Back in this world, I keep my feet on the floor. Count my breaths.

I don't think I say anything, but maybe I do.

Watkins says, 'Have I got this wrong?'

I nod. Humble. Embarrassed.

I had no idea this was coming.

Watkins's face is a mixture of everything in the world. There's love and pain and anger and, I think, shame. It's only the last bit which makes me uncomfortable.

I say, 'I'm sorry. I wasn't ... I'm not ...'

'Are you with someone?'

I nod. She doesn't know about Brydon. We don't make a big deal of our relationship, but almost everyone knows about it. But Watkins isn't almost everyone. Too scary. Too senior. Too driven. She's probably less connected to office gossip than anyone at Cathays.

'I thought. I just thought ...' she says.

And I know what she thought. I messed around with her because she gave me a bollocking. Gave her a physical compliment, which probably no one had done for twenty years. Then went on doing with it, deliberately keeping her off balance, entering her space, giving her compliments, for no reason at all except that I was feeling scratchy.

'In the hospital, when I held your hand ... I assumed you'd pull it away, but you didn't. You did the opposite.'

'It was nice actually. I liked it.'

'And that suit from Hobbs. Almost identical to mine. I thought you were signalling something. And this morning, in the interview room, you seemed so ... so ...'

So happy. Which I was, because Khalifi was there with me. And because I realised something about how my crazy brain operates and because I felt comfortable, at last, with that knowledge.

'I'm an idiot,' I tell her. 'You need to know that. Everyone else does. The safest thing, honestly, is to ignore me completely. I'm good at detective work. That's about all. Actual life – it's not my forte.'

She half-smiles at that. She's the same. 'Can I ask? Your current partner ...?'

'Is a man. David Brydon. I assumed you'd know.'

Watkins looks grim and she looks hurt, but more like the Watkins I used to know. I know that I am confusing to people. When I was at Cambridge, I had a couple of brief

318

lesbian encounters. Back then, I wasn't too sure which way I swayed – wasn't sure about almost anything in those days – and somehow I gave off signals which alerted all those lesbian gay-dars. I suppose I still do.

We spend some time analysing stuff. The stupid things I did. The inferences she drew. I tell her I'm a fuckwit and this time I don't adjust my vocabulary.

She cries. Briefly and with embarrassment, but it seems to me like a clean thing to do. Truthful.

I tell her I'm sorry and I mean it.

And after a while, something changes.

Things feel easier and lighter. The waitress comes with food, and messes around with cutlery, and asks us if we have everything we need, and goes away again, and soon everything suddenly starts to move again.

Watkins says she's not very good at the dating game. I say she can't be worse than me. I tell her she should be more confident. I also tell her to throw away that horrible little scarf. Forget the shiny aubergine shirts. Just be herself.

And somewhere, somehow, all the bollocks drops away. We don't judge ourselves or each other. We're just normal. Normal-weird, I mean. She allows herself to be what she is: a fierce old dyke who would welcome some companionship. I let myself be who I am: a half-crazy police officer who quite likes scary old dykes and who definitely enjoys the release from all those narrow office conventions. I imagine she still fancies me, but it doesn't bother me if she does.

Over pudding, Watkins does try to talk to me about becoming a Detective Sergeant, but I shake my head. 'Some other time?'

Watkins nods. She wants me to call her Rhiannon. I'm not sure about that, but I don't call her 'ma'am.'

She's obviously been looking at my file, because she says, 'I see you put your name down for the undercover course.'

I shrug. 'Just a toe in the water, really.' The same line as I gave to Buzz.

'Is that all? Some officers get addicted to danger, you know. The thrill of it. I wouldn't want to see that happen to you.'

I say the right things. That I'm not addicted to danger. That I want to build my professional skillset. Yadda yadda.

Watkins accepts it, maybe, but I had to sit a psychometric test for that course recently. Sat down. Sixty questions to complete. An hour to do it. No right or wrong: they just wanted to find out what kind of person I was.

Five questions in, I realised that if I responded honestly, I wouldn't have a prayer of getting onto the course. So I figured out what kind of personality they were looking for and adapted my answers accordingly. It wasn't hard to do. It was probably easier for me to invent a personality than figure out the one I have.

Watkins listens to me for a while, then changes the subject. She says, 'I got Kirby to speak to Strathclyde. We want them to make McCormack a priority target.'

'Thanks.'

'It might work, you know. If Strathclyde aren't completely useless.'

'Yes, but they've sort of had their chance, haven't they? They've been looking for five years –'

'He wasn't wanted for the attempted murder of a police officer. And they didn't have a Detective Superintendent demanding regular progress updates.'

'Right, but how much of our resources would we put into this if things were the other way round? No leads. No recent photos. No address. If the guy does something stupid, they'll pick him up. If not, they won't. On the other hand ... well, there are other ways to catch people.'

'Meaning?'

Watkins glares at me. She thinks I'm talking about my

320

father and doesn't like it. The ferocity of her look makes me laugh. She's being herself.

'I can find people to ask. Not policemen. Not criminals. Just there may be alternatives to waiting for Strathclyde.'

Watkins doesn't understand what I mean, but she nods. She doesn't approve. Doesn't like it. But she doesn't rip my head off.

'If they've been careful about DNA ...' she says.

'If they've been careful, it may not do us any good even if we do locate them.' I shrug. 'But we can't not look.'

'Yes.' Watkins's face moves in a way I can't interpret. 'It's a strange sort of justice, isn't it? Khalifi kills Langton and does that to her corpse. I hope it *was* to her corpse. And then, years later, he gets the exact same treatment from McCormack.'

She'd expand on all this, except that I'm shaking my head. Big, wide, breezy shakes.

'You don't agree. Clearly.' She's laughing at me.

'He loved her. Khalifi and Langton. He never stopped loving her. That's what we've been investigating here. A love story.'

'A love story with two murders.'

'Well, yes.' That doesn't seem like an interesting objection to me. The murders only make the love that bit more real, the flame that bit brighter. 'In his apartment. Khalifi's. There was a sailing boat lit with fairy lights. It was the only really sentimental thing he had. If I had to guess, I'd say she was the love of his life.'

'When did you go to his apartment?' Watkins, typically, remembers I was never detailed to go there.

'I wanted to see it,' I say with a shrug, and she accepts the evasion. I add, 'And, as it happens, I think he turned out to be the love of Langton's life too. That wasn't how it was meant to be, not for her. She was moving on. She'd presumably have found someone else, settled down, lived the kind of life she

321

was always meant to lead. But the way I see it, he set her on the path to that new future. Took her from a world that was destroying her. Given that she never reached her future, Khalifi was the best thing she ever had.'

I want to say that I'm pleased Khalifi was chopped to shreds and scattered on Llanishen's empty mud. Him and her, united at last. But the happy atmosphere of our Weirdos United love-in might buckle at that particular insight, so I keep it to myself.

Watkins, I know, doesn't necessarily agree with me. She sees this the way any police officer would. We have a link between Langton and Khalifi. We suspect that she moved on, he didn't. On Watkins's reading of events, it's quite possible that he hassled Langton. Demanded to see her. Wanted to restart things. She said no. A struggle. Then either a deliberate killing or a gruesome accident. Either way, he killed her and in some kind of weird, angry ritual scattered her parts across a part of the city they had once made their own.

The case began with two victims and a million suspects. To the police mind, Khalifi now looks like being the one in a million. The guy who did it.

Nothing I say will convince Watkins otherwise, and indeed I do realise that she might be correct: At this stage, we're all still speculating. But as she signals for the bill, I realise that the truth feels suddenly closer, a golden apple glimmering in the darkness. I have the strange thought, *I know who killed Mary Langton*. And that's not true. I don't have a name, don't have a theory even. But it's as though I know I have all the pieces I need. That I've seen the pattern, just haven't seen that I've seen it.

'There is a cherry tree at Elsie Williams's house,' I announce. 'Cherry-coloured poo.'

'What?'

'And those espaliered fruit trees, the ones trained to grow

flat against a wall, they're clipped in summer.'

'What you are talking about?'

'Mary Langton,' I say. 'If Khalifi *didn't* kill her, then some-one did. Probably one of our two-hundred-and-whatever people of interest. I'm just trying to …' I have nothing, I realise. Nothing tangible. Nothing even that gets as far as a theory. So I end weakly, '… trying to think laterally.'

In the restaurant around me, I feel Khalifi's spirit bubble with joy. I can't help but smile with him.

Watkins smiles too. 'It's a shame you're not a lesbian,' she tells me. 'You'd make some girl very happy.'

'You too,' I say. 'You just need to get out more.'

She nods. 'I'll try. I really will.'

'A bit of confidence. That's all you need.'

'I'll give it a go.'

'There are websites, you know.'

She nods again. When we go outside, sunshine blazes over snow and ice. The streets are almost empty.

I say, 'Rhiannon,' and she stops. Looks at me with that twisted expression of hers. I tease the scarf from her neck and drop it in a municipal rubbish bin. She smiles at me. Mouths, 'Thank you.'

We walk back to the office as Khalifi whoops above us in the frozen air. I am going to find out who killed Mary Langton. I am going to find justice for Khalifi.

All shall be well, and all shall be well, and all manner of thing shall be well.

44

The week ends.

Warmer weather returns. The polar bears leave Queen Street. Bute Park is empty of penguins. Except where the ploughs have left banks of coarse brown snow, the streets and pavements are mostly clear again. Dirty water gurgles into a million drains and gutters. The gritty salt remains.

We don't get sunshine. We just get the pre-Christmas Cardiff we've always known. Cloudy. Chill. Threatening rain.

The sun sets at 4 PM. We have a scant eight hours of daylight and those hours are seldom bright.

My body gradually recovers. My cuts are sore, but healing. My skin grafts are doing fine.

Buzz and I spend plenty of time together. I'm not up for any very energetic sex, but Buzz has an impressive variety of gentler alternatives. We tell each other that we love each other. I know I said that before, in hospital, but it's different saying it now, without the drama of calamity.

And when I say it, I try to figure out what I feel. Is this love? Do I feel as a person ought to when they're in love? And if I do, does that mean that Buzz and I are forever? That we need to get married, have children, buy a nice house in a pleasant district, and, in general, that I need to model myself on Gentle Jenny with bread on the sideboard and a bun in the oven?

Those thoughts make me dizzy. And some problems

don't need immediate solution. Buzz, I hope, knows me well enough not to force the issue.

I haven't told him, or anyone, about my lunch with Watkins. Nor will I. I hope she finds someone.

Khalifi's mother does come to Cardiff. I guess there are forms to sign and things to organise, but she speaks almost no English. I pick her up from Heathrow along with a police interpreter. The mother, Fatima, is veiled and wears sandals over bare feet. I doubt she's ever seen a northern winter. Her face is lined with the sort of wrinkles that go beyond age into some kind of other state altogether.

When we cross the Severn Bridge into Wales, her eyes stare out over the estuary, with anxiety, or sadness, or astonishment, or maybe something else altogether. I say, 'Welcome to Wales,' and the interpreter doesn't bother to translate.

I'm with Fatima about two days all told. Lend her a pair of socks and a thick cardigan. I'm with her as she enters her dead son's apartment. With her as we drive up to Llanishen. With her as we go to the Muslim graveyard, where the graves lie perpendicular to Mecca and the headstones are as simple as possible, because orthodox Islam frowns on excess adornment. We have a bunch of flowers bought from a local garage. Carnations, a mixture of white, pink, and yellow. Fatima lays them reverentially. We stand by the grave for about fifteen minutes, until the cold drives us away.

A few times, I try to have a conversation with her. Never get far. At first I think this is a failure on my part. Only later do I realise that this is maybe what Fatima needs. To spend these days in silence. A pilgrim visiting the monuments of her son's lost life. On the afternoon of my last day with her, I drive her down to the Mumbles. To the yacht club. The grey, uneasy sea.

'He used to go sailing here. With a girl he liked. They were happy together,' I tell her.

The interpreter translates.

Fatima says nothing, but she gazes out to sea, the fringes of her headscarf pulling in the breeze. As we get in the car to drive away, she pats my hand, then squeezes it. Her brown eyes find mine. She says, in English, 'Thank you.' Then again, 'Thank you.'

I hug her. And that evening, when I drop her off at her cheapie hotel, I say it'll be someone else looking after her the next day. She tries to say thank you again, but she can't, and this time there are tears in her eyes.

And when I'm back at work, I make a call I've been putting off. One I'm slightly scared of. But I do it anyway: phone Jack Yorath, the DCI whose name Penry gave me. Trustworthy Jack, Brian Penry's pick of the old-timers.

I say who I am and ask if I can meet for a drink.

'Fiona Griffiths? *The* Fiona Griffiths? Tom Griffiths's girl?'

'That's me, yes. It's my father I wanted to talk about.'

'Bloody hell. Okay, yes, I'd be happy to talk.'

We agree to meet that evening. His house, because it's more private than a pub. I tell him that he needs to not mention this to anyone. Not even any former colleagues. Not for any reason at all. He says okay.

We meet that evening. Yorath lives just outside Caerphilly, a nice house, nicely looked after. We sit in a little snug-come-office off a tiled hall. From a room somewhere behind us, someone plays scales on a piano, interrupted now and again by a snatch of briskly delivered Bach.

Yorath offers whiskey or tea. I say water. He gets that and drinks whiskey himself.

'Bloody hell, Fiona Griffiths,' he says.

I let him inspect me. He thinks what everyone thinks: I don't look much like my dad. I suddenly realise I want to trust someone. Maybe Yorath could be that person.

I say as much. 'Chief Inspector –'

'Jack. Just Jack.'

'Jack.' He's sitting in a green leather chair. I'm on some kind of upholstered bench, which is more comfortable than it sounds. The room has low lighting, some lever arch files, plenty of books. 'I don't know if you can guess why I'm here.'

'Not exactly. But a daughter of Tom Griffiths in the CID? That's not exactly your standard police background.'

'No.'

Professional interrogators – as Yorath and I are – don't get uncomfortable with silence. The empty moments can be as revealing as everything else. Yorath just sips from his whiskey, while Bach skitters behind us.

I say, 'You probably know that I was adopted.'

Of course he does. The adoption process created plenty of paperwork. All that paperwork ended up in police records, and Yorath's career was spent combating organised crime. He could hardly not have known. Quite likely part of his curiosity in seeing me was to find out what I looked like.

'I know my father had his issues with the police, to put it mildly –'

'You can say that again –'

'But he was a good father to me. He and Mam, both of them.'

'I don't doubt that.'

'I'm not here to – I'm not looking to nail my father for some offence he may have committed twenty years ago.'

'No, I wouldn't expect that.'

'But I need to know where I came from. Dad's story has to do with me appearing mysteriously one Sunday, just found sitting in his car.'

'Outside chapel,' adds Yorath, smiling at the thought of my pa in the house of the Lord.

'I don't believe that story. I think Dad knows much more than he lets on.'

'I bet.'

'I can't ask him direct, or if I do he'll just give me his standard patter. If I ask any of his old friends, they might be helpful, but they'd always let Dad know I'm asking. And if Dad hears I'm digging, my chances of finding anything out will disappear completely.'

Yorath nods. 'You haven't been in the job that long, not yet. But when you have been, when you've put in the years, you get to know your quarry. Your dad was the most talented criminal we ever chased. I shouldn't say this really, but me and some of the older guys ended up admiring him. It wasn't just his organisation, though that was always amazing, it was the way his associates never dropped him in it. Those things go beyond discipline. It was a kind of love he inspired. Funny word to use, that, but I'm sure I'm right. I think people loved him.'

I nod. They did. I'm sure they did.

'You're also right that if the truth is out there somewhere' – Yorath waves his whiskey glass somewhere in the general direction of Cardiff – 'it'll disappear the instant your dad hears you're on the trail.'

'So I'm here to ask if you have any thoughts at all. I've read most of the files. I've got some more reading to do yet, but I also know that there's stuff that never goes into the files. Things you know, things you might think, even wild speculation.'

Yorath raises his eyebrows. 'This was twenty years ago.'

'More. I'm twenty-six now. I was maybe two and a half when I was found.' Yorath's face starts to do the maths. 'August 1986. That's when I appeared.'

Yorath's face is a mask, but a mask that conceals thought. He's still for a moment or two, then puts aside his whiskey, grabs a pad and pen, swivels the light.

'Nineteen-eighty-six. Tom Griffiths. Everything from hard truth to wild speculation. Okay?'

'Okay.'

'His car business. Stealing cars. Giving them makeovers. Selling them on. That was in full flow back then. Turnover? I don't know. I'm going to say five million. Profits? Don't know. Let's say one million. Total people involved? Don't know, but must have been dozens all told. Inner circle? Not many. Five, six. Probably people you know. He always kept them close, people like …'

'Emrys Thomas,' I say softly. 'He used to babysit for us.'

'Emrys Thomas as your babysitter.' Yorath laughs and shakes his head. 'He was a kind of chief-operating-officer type. Not the strategist. Not the general. But the guy who made everything else tick.'

He starts listing other members of the inner circle. Names I'm familiar with. Dad's intimate friends. Familes I know, homes I've visited.

'I know them. Dad's still close to them all.'

'I bet.'

Yorath has been covering his pad with the basic data as he's been speaking. He strikes a thick line under it as his pen hovers over the next section of the page.

'Then the sidelines. Drugs? It'd be the obvious thing. We always assumed there'd be some kind of drugs activity and I think there was. Ecstasy? Possibly. The drug was just starting to become big then. Your pa would have had the infrastructure needed to distribute it. We're pretty sure he distributed cannabis. Buying from the international smugglers, taking care of local distribution. But we never found links to anything harder than that. We looked certainly, but –'

'Dad hates hard drugs. He wouldn't have touched them. Mam would have killed him if he had.'

Yorath laughs again.

'Okay. But mid-eighties, he'd have been at his peak, just about, so I'm going to say your pa did one or two big deals at

329

least. Maybe it wasn't a regular thing for him, but you know if someone approached him, needing to offload a big supply of cannabis coming in, I don't think he'd have refused.'

I nod. 'You're right. He wouldn't have said no.'

'Okay, so you want to know names. Associates, the inner circle? Same as before. But then there'd have been the international end of things too, the Howard Markses, those guys. But he probably didn't know distributors elsewhere. The way the international sellers operate, they don't want their buyers to know each other. Safer for everyone. So he'd have had some offshore contacts, but not many and not close. Turnover involved? I don't know. Let's say two or three big deals, worth a million or two each. Profits on those things maybe fifty percent of turnover.'

I nod again, but thoughtfully. Dad is rich, but he's not as rich as Yorath's numbers would imply. He's always spent money freely, but that means changing his Jag every couple of years, building swimming pools he never used, buying single-malt whiskey back when he drank the stuff, buying huge bunches of flowers for Mam. But that's not the kind of stuff that eats a million or two a year. I would say Dad must have a pot of money stashed away somewhere, except that Dad has never been a save-for-tomorrow kind of guy.

Yorath isn't interested in my reservations. His pen continues to walk across the paper.

'Construction. Municipal contracts. Development permits. There was a lot of money in Cardiff back then. The construction business was always dirty. If anyone was skimming something, then your dad was. We had a big investigation into it. There was one guy, some middle-management type, who came to us as a whistle-blower. We took him seriously, did what we could, came up with nothing.'

'Did he name my dad?'

'No.'

'Links to Dad's inner circle?'

'No. Wild speculation, remember?'

'Okay. What else?'

'Prostitution? We drew a blank.'

I agree with that. 'Mam would have killed him. She almost killed him when he opened the lap-dancing clubs.'

'Handling stolen goods? Definitely. Any fence in Cardiff would have needed your father's say-so to operate. He'd have had his cut. We even had little bits and bobs of evidence. Almost enough for a prosecution. At the time, we decided against it because the top brass wanted to get a conviction for something big, and thought they'd achieve that by keeping your dad in play. That was the wrong decision. We should have gone with anything we could.

'And then, the bits and pieces. Let's say someone wanted to send a warning to someone. Or wanted to extract protection money. Anything like that. I think your pa would have seen Cardiff as his turf. If people didn't go via your dad for that sort of thing, they'd have regretted it.'

'Yes.' It seems strange here, sitting with Yorath, in this comfortable room, talking about my dad in this way. There's a question sitting alongside us now, one that I have to ask. 'In terms of really serious stuff, I mean the worst things ...'

'Murder? That wasn't his house style. When he was younger, working his way up, who knows? We never had anything on him. Never heard rumours. But that was the point in a way. No one ever told stories against Tom Griffiths. It's like everyone knew he was at the centre of things, but you'd never get anyone on the stand to actually say so.'

'How much violence was there?' I whisper.

Yorath shrugs. 'Enough.'

'Meaning?'

'Meaning exactly that. If your father or the guys around him decided someone needed their legs broken or their kneecaps smashed, it would have happened. A routine operational decision, I imagine. But in a funny way, those things cut both ways. We never had a huge violent crime problem in Cardiff. Never any real gangs. Your dad *was* the gang. People knew what they'd get if they crossed Tom Griffiths, so they didn't cross him. If I had to guess the total number of punishment-style beatings we handled through the eighties, I probably wouldn't get to more than a dozen. If that. Most big cities had a far worse problem than we did.

'I mean, don't get me wrong. He was a criminal, your dad, and belonged behind bars. But he wasn't … I don't know, he wasn't a savage.'

I smile lopsidedly at that. *Not a savage*. That's not much of a compliment to the man who was raised me so lovingly for the past twenty-four years, but maybe it's the one he deserves. A sentimentalist, who used to go to chapel and who still always cries at weepies. A man whose affection for me and my sisters is entirely genuine and always full-hearted. Who has been a steady husband to my mother. Who built the biggest criminal operation in South Wales. Who handed out punishment beatings the way corporations hand out stock options. Who might or might not have committed murder while he was 'working his way up.' Whose prosecution witnesses melted away on the witness stand.

This criminal, my father.

Yorath and I talk for another ninety minutes. By the time we're done, I have a huge wodge of yellow paper, covered with Yorath's thick scribbles. Almost none of what he's given me is verifiable. But that's the point. The reason why you need to talk to the cop, not just read the notes.

At the end, I blunder out onto the street.

There are crusted ridges of snow still, to remind us what we had, but mostly the town looks like it always looks at this time of year. A new weirdness this, the weirdness of the normal.

And even though I know nothing, have no tangible fact to walk away with, I feel like I've really started. Begun an investigation whose target is me. I drive away from Caerphilly certain that my father's secrets are my own. That he knew my biological father, knew my biological mother. That he knows – or guesses – the reason I turned so crazy in later life.

Perhaps he's been a better father for that knowledge. More protective. More loving. More strategic and more thoughtful.

I'm not angry with Dad. Whatever I find out, I think I won't be angry. But his secrets are mine too. And I intend to find them.

45

Stirfry trundles on.

When I get back into the swing of the morning briefings, I find things have changed. Kirby is there every single time. Adding the senior officer gloss to Watkins's parade-ground bark.

The 'people of interest' have been swept away into a single corner of the noticeboards – all 288 of them. The photos of Khalifi and Langton still dominate. The red love-heart too. But now there's a whole slew of material being generated by the Barry investigation. More names, data files, lists of statements and interviews. The operation now has a third full-time data officer.

Some key facts are pouring in.

The biggest: Stuart Brotherton has sent a preliminary report which confirms that Barry Precision was, beyond doubt, manufacturing arms. Not entire weapons systems, but spare parts for other people's systems. Gun barrels for heavy artillery. Firing pins. The gears and calibration equipment needed for range adjustment. Laser-cut ballistic-grade steel of the sort used for tank armour. Self-sealing fuel tanks. IED blast protection gear. Suspension and chassis systems built to the kind of specifications you'd need for an armoured car. The hydraulic gear needed to raise a multiple rocket launch system to its firing position. Anti-blast screens that just so happen to fit the multiple rocket launch systems in most widespread use across the Middle East.

There are still a handful of suspect items where Brotherton hasn't been able to track down their likely use, but his investigations continue. Equally, in some cases, it seems that the items sold would have needed some modest reengineering to make them fully functional as weapons-parts, but the sophisticated work had already been done.

By Barry Precision.

Which has no export licence.

Watkins has also had a trio of DCs investigating the firm's buyers, who existed all across North Africa and the Middle East. Its biggest customer was Saadawi, whose eldest brother buys weapons for the Egyptian military. And whose family owns a slew of construction and trading interests, primarily in Egypt, but operating across the entire Middle East.

Numerous other buyers also look as dodgy as hell. The Libyan buyer was an affiliate of the state-owned Libyan oil company. Its purchases were theoretically all drilling-equipment related, but Brotherton says that at least 50 percent of the items involved had clear military use.

The Lebanese buyer: a trading company with links to the Syrian regime.

The Saudi buyer: a probable intermediary for a putative Yemeni end buyer.

My hunch about Khalifi is also proving to be right. Watkins has had officers contact every firm on Khalifi's sizeable Rolodex. We've sought information about what he talked to them about. In particular, any orders he helped arrange for them.

It's slow work, but the indications are that Khalifi was indeed building a virtual arms-manufacturing network. We'll know more once we have more data and once Brotherton has had a chance to analyse it, but it's already pretty clear what the answer will be.

And I regret that, in a way. I've got on so well with the corpse of Khalifi, it's sad to find how much I'd have detested him in real life. His little enterprise was no more ethical than Idris Prothero's. Some people are better as corpses. They're easier to like.

It's not just the Barry end of things where we're making progress. We're making progress on the Langton–Khalifi link too.

We know for certain now that they had a relationship. It's not just Swansea Bay Yacht Club that confirms it. The couple also went boating on the Llanishen Reservoir, before it was emptied. A guy who used to work there, renting boats, was able to recognise the pair.

Re-interviews of Langton's old friends and a new analysis of material generated by the original enquiry all tends to confirm our general suspicion. That Langton, for whatever reason, got herself into a bad place when she started pole dancing and waitressing. The dancing was both an effect of that bad head space, but also a perpetuating factor. Langton was spiraling down. Then, her friends seem to agree, she got happier. Though she kept quiet about the details, it was assumed she had a man. She stopped dancing. Drank less. Got healthier.

As her old life got back on track, she no longer needed that rescue relationship. Again, we can't be sure, but it does seem like she was the one who ended it, not him.

Some of these things aren't beyond doubt, but most things aren't. We work in a world of competing uncertainties. But for the first time since the enquiry started, it feels like all our effort is paying off. We're moving towards arrests, prosecutions, convictions.

My own role in the hubbub is nicely ambiguous for a change. Partly because of that lunch and partly because of my little adventure on the hill, Watkins gives me considerable discretion in what I do.

And, as far as I'm concerned, it's time that Mary Langton had more of my attention. It's partly that I'm intrigued by the testimony of the boat guy at Llanishen. Previously, it was assumed that any normal girl leaving a party early and wanting to return to town would simply walk direct from the party to the station and await her train. She's have had no reason, in failing light, to detour to a largely deserted reservoir.

Only, if you had recent romantic associations with that spot, mightn't you do just that? Mightn't, in fact, it be part of the reason why you left the party early, so you could commune with the spirit of your ex? Your past happiness?

I pile my desk with printouts and start to work. When Elsie Williams thrust her walking stick into a small boy's bike, it was the August of 2007. I check against her daughter and son-in-law's travel dates. They were visiting that summer. They were there when Elsie did it.

I check weather records too. When we sent an officer round to caution the old lady, it was a hot day. Sitting-outside weather. Bee-buzzingly, heat-shimmeringly, summer-lawn-beckoningly hot.

There was a door at the back of the garage, so if the front was open, you could simply walk straight from the street, through the garage, into the garden.

Or of course vice versa.

A hot day, a vicious widow. The things we coppers deal with.

The officer who cautioned Elsie Williams is away on holiday. Which is frustrating. I want to talk to him now. But that's not the main thing, not by any means. I can feel myself convalescing, working more slowly than I normally would. And that's okay. Slow is okay, it's the outcome that matters. Mary Langton has waited so long, another week or two won't bother her.

Her leg was in a freezer, her head in motor oil, her thumb

in vegetable oil, a bit of leg packed in salt. Her arms were packed in polythene, but didn't deteriorate as much as they should.

I click around on the Internet for a bit and discover that supermarket salads are bagged up in nitrogen. The exclusion of oxygen preserves the food that much longer. I poke around on the Internet and find that I can buy a nitrogen cylinder on eBay for seventy-two quid. Or get helium for not much more than twenty.

But who would do a thing like that? I wonder.

Wonder – but other bits and bobs of work keep pulling me away.

Mervyn Rogers and I have been down to David Marr-Phillips's glitzy waterfront office to interview him about his arrangement with Prothero. He had a copy of the shareholder agreement waiting for us: the one that gave him a slice of Barry Precision, Prothero a slice of some of Marr-Phillips's property assets. Also a report from an accountant stating that the valuations had been determined at fair market value. Some stuff on tax treatment. Accounts for the property companies. Financial data on Barry Precision. Blah, blah.

Marr-Phillips was both completely open with us and visibly irritated at the time we were consuming. Neither Mervyn nor I really knew how to play things. Mervyn's best at frightening the tough-but-stupid criminals we spend most of our lives chasing, and we both felt out of our depth interviewing Marr-Phillips. We ended up asking repetitive, circular questions for twenty minutes, then let ourselves be escorted politely from the office.

We gave Watkins a full report of everything. Like us, she doesn't know what to do with the Marr–Phillips–Prothero connection. We decide not to pursue it. If we can nail Prothero, other things may start to emerge. But maybe not. It doesn't look to me like Marr-Phillips has done anything much wrong.

And nailing Prothero seems well within our grasp. Dunbar too. Watkins and I share a grim determination to see both men destroyed. Personally, I'd like to see how much they'd enjoy a prison in Libya. Or taste the pleasure of Bashar Assad's hospitality in an Aleppo jail. Smashed ankles and a scream that echoes forever.

That won't happen, of course, but I'd be happy enough if they do a long stint in Cardiff Prison. We may or may not get Prothero on murder, but there's a maximum ten-year offence for weapons export offences. That's twenty years too short, in my unhumble opinion. But still, it's enough to fuck up a life. It would fuck up Prothero's very nicely. He could try out his silvery indignation on his fellow prisoners, see how well it worked.

I think of Ayla and Theo. What does it do to children to learn that their father is a criminal and a suicide? What kind of abandonment is that? The jailing of Prothero might seem like redemption of the best sort. *Yes, Theo, it* was *a mistake. We're putting it right. We're sending the bad people to jail.*

These things run slowly, however. Barry Precision's lawyers are working to impede the investigation at every turn, claiming unreasonable interference with the operation of the business. So far the Chief Constable and the county court have swatted aside every objection. I don't think Barry's lawyers expected anything else. I think their strategy relies on pushing up the cost of our investigation to a point at which we start having to scale back our effort. I've seen perfectly valid cases fail for purely budgetary reasons. But Watkins has the total support of top management. She thinks, and I do, that we'll secure our conviction.

Slow is okay, it's the outcome that matters. What I tell myself and my injured body.

One week ends. Another one begins. It's now two weeks before Christmas and even Cathays starts to feel a little

Christmassy cheer. Secretaries wear tinsel earrings. Jon Breakell attends the morning briefing in an elf hat. Jim Davis goes out to lunch at twelve fifteen and returns four hours later, barely able to focus. A fake memo is circulated seeking the apprehension of a well-known criminal, thought to operate an unlicensed flying vehicle, to be in breach of multiple immigration regulations, and to force nocturnal entry to millions of homes. Believed to operate out of Lapland. Aliases include Saint Nick, Santa Claus, 'Father' Christmas, etc.

Everyone circulates it to everyone. I receive five versions. Delete them all. Ho, ho, ho.

Tuesday night is usually my night. That means in theory an opportunity to clean and iron things. In practice it means an opportunity to smoke a joint without worrying that Buzz is going to find me. An opportunity to moon around my own house, in my own way.

Most nights now that I spend on my own, Khalifi comes to see me.

He's not always chuckling. He has a sadder side, I see. There was something unsustainable in his earlier mood. Something skittish, excitable.

I like his visits. If this is the form my psychotic side takes now, I welcome it. Better the occasional visit from a corpse than feel myself to be one of their number.

I don't take my amisulpride. The pills go back to the bathroom cabinet.

And one night, I come home from the office. It's six thirty. My night for being alone. Only, as I let myself in, I hear someone moving about upstairs. There is a black bag on the landing. I shout up a greeting, but get nothing back.

Go to the kitchen, put the kettle on.

Go to the potting shed, get some weed.

Start rolling joints. I didn't leave the house unlocked but some people don't need keys. There isn't much in the fridge,

340

but there's probably enough. Lev is like me. He eats random-ly. And it's not my job to feed him.

Make peppermint tea for me. Put black tea out ready. Look for jam. Put that out too.

Then Lev appears. The unremarkable Lev. Old jeans and a jumper. Brown hair worn longish. Brown eyes like a spaniel's.

We don't kiss, hug, or shake hands. I don't know why not. We do smile at each other, though. I make Lev's tea. Push the jam jar and a teaspoon across the table at him. Light a joint.

We talk.

I never ask Lev much about his life. I used to, but then I realised he either said nothing or made stuff up, so I stopped asking. When he wants to tell me things, he does.

I tell him my news. About Buzz. About Langton and Khalifi. I tell him about Barry Precision: how a small Welsh engineering firm figured out it could make big money by ex-porting weapons parts on the pretext that they had innocent industrial purposes.

'This company is where?'

'In Barry. Down on the coast, just beyond the city.'

Lev's face is dark. He's been in war zones. He knows what modern weaponry can do.

'Okay,' he says, meaning *Go on*.

I tell him about Hamish and Olaf. About being made to stand outside in the snow, wearing nothing more than trou-sers and a T-shirt. About how I escaped and how I almost didn't.

Lev mutters something in what might be Russian but could be Lithuanian. Then he says, 'You know this people?'

'We've identified the Scottish guy.' I give Lev his name, photo, and the fact that he stole a numberplate in Drumchapel. 'There's money in the drawer,' I say.

I first met Lev when he was an itinerant martial arts teacher.

I used to pay him for tuition, then stopped. I'm not sure whether this is the sort of thing that requires payment. But I've put three thousand pounds in cash in the kitchen drawer. Lev can have as much of that as he wants.

He takes the documents, studies them briefly, then he says, 'You want me to find him? Or what?'

I don't know what the 'or what' means exactly. I don't know how far Lev would go. But I say, 'No, just find him. I need an address, that's all.'

'Okay.'

He nods. A dismissal. We talk about other things. Smoke. Make more tea. Lev has an iPod now – he never used to – and uses it to bend my hi-fi to his will. Russian music. The wild steppe and an infinite melancholy.

At some point we get hungry. There are peas and oven chips in the freezer. The fridge and cupboards yield up pesto sauce, crackers, some slightly bendy carrots, two eggs, some bacon that is turning an oily purple with age, and a jar of lumpfish caviar which my dad brought me thinking it was the same thing as caviar-caviar.

I say I'll make supper. Lev says he'll take a shower.

I don't think there's a recipe which involves the ingredients I have, so I just cook the things that need cooking and put everything out on the table.

Get another bag of weed from the potting shed in case we're set for a long night.

Lev comes down. Wet hair. Jeans. T-shirt sticking to his back and chest because he hasn't dried himself properly. Bare feet.

And then – we're not alone.

In the opening to the living room, a man is standing.

It's Buzz. Storm clouds rolling round his head. A deep-bladed anger between his eyes.

I've never seen him like this.

He does drop round from time to time, even on my nights off. He never stays for long and only drops by if he's in the area, but there's no rule that says he's not allowed here. I'm sure he'd have knocked before using his key, because he's a polite boy and because he knows I like my space. But I've only just come in from the garden and though Lev would certainly have heard any knock – Lev is vigilant even in sleep – he wouldn't necessarily have thought that someone's arrival demanded any action on his part.

Lev dips a bendy carrot in lumpfish caviar and eats it.

His eyes are watchful, but they always are. He is completely calm, but he always is.

Buzz studies Lev. The evidence of his recent shower. Our obvious intimacy. The bags of weed on the table. Marijuana smoke and violins.

And suddenly, there's an ugly biology here too. The biology of rutting stags. Silverback gorillas battling over harems. Wolves snarling for supremacy.

And I know what Buzz is thinking. He's figuring that he's taller, stronger, younger, fitter. That's he's an ex-paratrooper. That he could give Lev a kicking.

And he can't. He really, really can't.

I follow the template of my own biology. Stand up. Say, 'Buzz, no. This isn't what you think it is. Buzz, this isn't anything.' I can hear my own voice high and shrill. Too high and way too shrill.

'Really? Because I was thinking that there was a Class B drug being consumed on these premises.'

'Fuck's sake, yes, I smoke dope. Buzz –'

'And little Mr Pretty here –'

'Buzz, please –'

He steps up close to Lev. I don't think he is going to hit him, but he's certainly threatening to do so. He's being deliberately invasive. Testosteroney.

343

And Lev reacts. Effortlessly. Sweeps Buzz's legs from under him. Gets a shoulder underneath Buzz's falling chin. Rams Buzz's body hard against the wall. The move ends with Buzz in a neck-and-arm-lock, and I find myself thankful that Lev chose to moderate his reaction to this extent.

He can do worse than this. He can do very much worse.

I dance around being uselessly feminine, but this isn't about anything I do or don't say. The male hormones need to find their balance first.

Lev, retaining a grip on Buzz, says, softly, 'Please be a little careful and we can all talk like respectable people.'

Then he steps away. Buzz is shocked and has probably taken a bruise or two, but he's not injured. Not really.

I say, 'Buzz, I smoke dope. Not often, but I do. This is Lev. He's a friend. My martial arts teacher, or used to be. He has just taken a shower. That's all. We have never had sex. Never. Not once and I've known him for six years now.'

We tiptoe back from the precipice.

Buzz gets up, rubbing his neck and his knee. He is still furious, but there's a bewilderment here, which may yet be just as injurious. He looks at Lev with different eyes. Wondering what kind of man this is.

Looks at me differently too, I expect. My colleagues at Cathays love to tease me about a couple of incidents in my past. A man whose knee I dislocated and whose testicle I ruptured. Another man whom I kicked in the head and threw off a cliff. It's been assumed that I achieved those things by accident almost. That a petite woman of no great strength or fitness could do these things only by fluke. Some fleeting combination of time and circumstance.

Now that Buzz has met Lev, he might just revise that opinion. And this was Lev gentle. Lev the peace-maker.

I say, 'Can we talk? Can we all just sit and talk?'

My voice sounds unreal, even to myself.

Lev ignores me.

Talks to Buzz and says, 'Come.'

Takes Buzz outside, shows him the potting shed. My marijuana plants. My heat lamps. My bags of weed. My cubes of resin. The little seedbank which allows me to grow the sweetest weed in all of Pontprennau.

I don't go with them. Just sit at the kitchen table wondering if I still have a boyfriend.

When Buzz comes back, his eyes are filled with questions.

I say, 'When I was in recovery, half in Cotard's, half not, marijuana was one of the few things I could rely on to calm my mind. I don't smoke very often these days. Maybe once a week. Two or three times if I feel my head is in a bad place. And one day, maybe, I'll give up completely. But for now, I still need this. Maybe I always will.'

'So it's medicinal?'

Buzz's voice is hoarse. Like he lost it in an attic somewhere, and has only just found it, rusty and cobwebbed, like an old key.

'Well, not always, obviously.' I gesture at the table. At Lev. 'It can be social too. But not often. I grow my own so I don't have to buy it. And I never sell it.'

I add that last bit, because Buzz's police mind needs that information. A police officer who sells drugs deserves jail. A police officer who purchases drugs needs to be dismissed. An officer who grows her own drug supply for primarily medicinal reasons – even Buzz has a separate category for that.

'You could have told me.'

'Really? Do you really think I could have done?'

Buzz doesn't answer. He's no idiot, but in the last few minutes he's uncovered an assumed infidelity, discovered that his girlfriend is a drug user, been slammed painfully against a wall, and is now starting to wonder just how

345

much violence his possible future wife is herself capable of.

Gentle Jennies don't go to these places. This is not the Fiona Griffiths he wants me to be.

The possible future mother of Buzz's possible future children stands waiting to hear their father's verdict.

It doesn't come. Lev says, 'You are David Brydon, yes?'

'Yes.' The same rust. Cobwebs.

'David, I think we go to the pub now. You and me.'

And all of a sudden, the biology flips again. To a place I'd not thought possible.

I'm standing in the room, not two yards from either man, and I'm not there at all. There's some male-to-male thing being exchanged which bypasses me completely. I think Buzz is trying to make sense of Lev. To find the fighter in that unremarkable exterior. Lev is figuring out Buzz. Both men have been soldiers and they are soldiers again now.

Their eyes are military and I am not really here.

I think I say something, but my voice is without sound. Unimportant.

Buzz says, 'Okay.'

He puts out a hand. Lev takes it. Shakes it. Their eyes are still hard, but it's that masculine hardness which carries no personal implication. Which just is.

Buzz, remembering that I exist, half-turns to me and says, 'You'll be okay, babe?' but it's not a question and my nod isn't an answer.

They leave.

I eat bendy carrots and throw away the bacon because it's too old to eat.

Eat some egg and some caviar and some crackers with pesto. Throw away everything I haven't eaten.

Tidy up a bit. Smoke, but with no real pleasure. Turn off Lev's music, which is driving me nuts. Put on Annie Lennox, because that'll drive him nuts.

They're still not back. How long can it take to drink a pint of brown liquid?

I'm bored enough and agitated enough to clean the kitchen. Then hoover the living room. Dust it, for heaven's sake. Then decide I have to stop cleaning in case I pop an artery and turn into my mother.

Start to text Buzz, but cancel without sending.

What the fuck can they be talking about?

I think about ironing something.

I don't, but do remove limescale from the shower screen.

Pluck my eyebrows.

Walk downstairs, then walk back up again.

This is not going well. I am having feelings, but I don't know what they are. I've got exercises for times like this – breathing exercises, mindfulness – but I'm too agitated to do them. And maybe I don't want to do them. Maybe I want these feelings. Want to let them be whatever they are.

I'm just walking downstairs to fetch the hoover when I hear Lev and Buzz outside. I sit on the stairs waiting for the door to open.

I am the possible future mother of Buzz's possible future children.

Sitting on the stairs. Waiting for the door to open.

46

Buzz and I. We're okay, I think. I'm not sure, but I think so.

When he and Lev came in, they were best buddies. Backslappy and beery in Buzz's case. Quiet but emphatic in Lev's.

I realised I was desperate for a joint. Needed to sit there and smoke with both of them in the room, but I wasn't at all sure that wouldn't break the mood. But Lev just sparked up as normal. Buzz watched, lips compressed, but not saying anything. When Lev passed me the joint, I sucked on the damn thing like it was an oxygen line dropped to the sea floor. Both men laughed at me. When I realised what they were laughing at, I laughed too.

They arrived back hungry and I'd thrown most of the food away. But I hadn't thrown the oven chips away, so I cooked them. There was also some tinned mackerel, a jar of korma sauce, some stale mini-pretzels, a tube of tomato paste, any crackers I could plausibly rescue from the bin, and some more bendy carrots. Lev inspected the feast I laid out and said solemnly to Buzz, 'You're a lucky man.'

More laughter. I redden, but with pleasure. That is the first time I think maybe this could all be OK.

They eat oven chips, tinned mackerel, bendy carrots, and Buzz sportingly puts korma sauce on his fish. He pretends to like the result.

It's okay. It feels okay.

But then I want them both to go. I want them out of my house with an urgency I don't dare express.

Luckily, Lev, he's a nutcase too. Like me. He knows what it's like to have problems with your head, doesn't need me to tell him. After a while, he just gets his things, takes a couple of bags of weed, and leaves. I wave a weak goodbye from the kitchen table.

'I will send you text,' he says.

I give him a thumbs-up.

Buzz wants to take me back to his place and give me a good seeing to. He needs to assert his own proprietorship. And I want that too. In an only slightly different universe, that would be my choice too. But I need space and say so. Put my arms round his lovely neck, find the muscles of his lovely back, and say I'll see him tomorrow.

He understands. I think he does. He says so anyway.

I ask if he's all right. I mean emotionally. I mean him-and-me. I mean weed on the kitchen table and a cannabis plantation in the potting shed.

But Buzz just rubs his head where Lev slammed it against the wall, and says, 'You might have told me the guy was Spetsnaz.'

Spetsnaz: the umbrella term given to the Russian special forces. I think Lev worked in their Vympel counter terrorist unit. First as an operative, then as a trainer. But I don't really know. Lev has never told me much. It took me four years before I even knew for sure that he was Spetsnaz. I bet Buzz got there before he found the bottom of his pint glass.

I say, 'You didn't give me much of a chance.'

'No.'

And then we kiss.

And then kissing isn't enough.

And then Buzz is carrying me upstairs and dumping me on the bed and before very many seconds pass he is indeed giving me a good seeing to. And, I like to think, I reciprocate in a way likely to generate few complaints.

Afterward, we lie panting beside each other.

'Any more secrets?'

I think about the gun in Pembrokeshire. The knife behind the bed. My special relationship with Rhiannon Watkins. My visits from Ali el-Khalifi. The amisulpride in the bathroom cabinet. The full story about McCormack's jaw and the data leak from Barry Precision, and all the other details that can matter a lot to people like Buzz. But none of that stuff seems very significant. Not right now.

'I think it is possible that my father used to be involved in some kind of crime.'

'Really? You think?'

'And I haven't yet got you a Christmas present.'

He has his hand on my belly. Buzz is a fit lad and he eats his greens. He's been known to recharge, reload, and fire, two or three or even (once) four times in the same night. I can see him wondering whether tonight might be one of those nights.

But it isn't. I need my space and say so.

And after Buzz leaves, and the house is empty, and when silence returns to the kitchen and creeps like moonlight over the garden and steals upstairs like the last breath leaving a body, I become aware of my mind finding its peace.

I don't smoke more – I've already had more than enough – but take a shower, darken the house, and drink peppermint tea. I'm sitting upright in bed. Castled in pillows.

I've been expecting Khalifi to come, but all I sense of him is a prickle of energy. The same sensation I first felt that night in Cathays with me, Buzz, Watkins, and Konchesky. I hadn't known what it was then, but it was Khalifi making contact.

I think this dimmed presence is him fading out.

I'll miss him, of course, but you can't hang on.

They grow up so fast.

I wish I'd got closer to Mary Langton. I would have, but chasing after two murders limits the time you can give to either. I regret that, but I'm sure she forgives me. The dead are always forgiving. And I will give her what she needs.

I don't know whether I sleep or not. All I do know is that I am still sitting up when dawn arrives to reclaim the streets. My peppermint tea sits empty beside me. And my paring knife is in my hand. Finger through the finger loop. Blade pointing upward and outward at the lightening sky.

47

Later that same morning, Watkins comes by my desk.

She's in a severe dark suit. Rumpled white shirt. Iron-grey hair that's been recently cut. I like her this way. I want to smile at her, but don't. She looks tired. I probably do too.

'Fiona.'

'Ma'am.'

'I wanted to update you. The investigation into – your attempted murder. We're not getting very far.'

She updates me, brusquely. Number plate recognition: nothing helpful. Forensics: nothing at all. Eyewitnesses: less than nothing.

'As you thought, it's going to be all but impossible to bring this to court, even if we find the perpetrators.'

'I know.'

'And we haven't found them.'

I don't know what to say to that. Unless today is the day where we go up to people and tell them stuff they already know. I move my face and hands, just so it looks like I'm doing my bit.

'The team I've had looking into things. They're on stand-by. They're available if anything comes. But otherwise …'

Kirby has had his way. The troops are being redeployed. And quite right too. I'd do the same if I were him.

But Watkins isn't finished. 'The other day. You mentioned there might be ways of finding McCormack.'

'There might be. Yes.' I stop, because I'm not sure where she's going with this. Then add carefully, 'I'm making enquiries. I don't yet have anything concrete.'

'Yes. I see.' She raps down on my desk with her knuckles. Moves a yellow notepad which wasn't in anyone's way. Glares over my shoulder at the sombre grey stones of the Crown Court across the street.

Then she comes to a decision. Pulls something from her pocket. A small clear polythene evidence bag. 'This is material attaching to the Khalifi enquiry. Would you please return it to the forensics lab? It shouldn't have been removed.'

She hands it over. There are three dark hairs in the bag. Body hairs, I guess. From a hand or arm or leg or chest. Specks of skin at the root.

'Yes, ma'am.'

She's about to say something else, but thinks better of it and says nothing. Turns abruptly and stalks away. She is swallowed by the glass doors that lead to the lifts. A swinging monochrome reflection is all that remains.

That, and these three hairs. Perversion of the course of justice, if you look at it one way. Justice itself, if you look at it another.

I put the bag in my pocket.

No one needs to know about this.

When I looked this morning, there was only two grand left in my kitchen drawer.

48

Nothing happens.

The cold weather returns. First the cold, then the snow. There are satellite photos shown on the news. Britain re-created in ice. A white island floating on a sea that's dark teal close into shore, a deep, inky aquamarine farther out.

There are close-ups of South Wales too, shown on local news, reproduced in local papers. The Bristol Channel is its usual dirty brown. The forests south of Ystradgynlais are white, but pricked through with evergreen. Holly and ice.

I've never seen anything like it. Nor has anyone. Temperature records tumble again. Night after night I revisit that field above Capel-y-ffin in my dreams. Trousers and a T-shirt, worn under starlight.

My dad doesn't quite accept that I'm well on the road to healing and keeps putting pressure on me to go back and live with him and Mam, 'at least until after Christmas, love. You don't want to worry about cooking and that.' I tell him, truthfully, that I don't spend much of my time worrying about cooking, but compromise by spending more time at home than usual. Mam spoils us with huge meals. Kay has boyfriend troubles and wafts around, wearing black, an iPhone always glowing at her palm. Ant is on the verge of being a proper teenager, but her natural sweetness keeps popping out to overwhelm any incipient moodiness. Her Christmas list is already two pages long.

Dad's not always around, of course. His work often claims his evenings. But he's around enough. Enough that, one evening after we've eaten, as the family starts to scatter – Mam and Ant to watch TV, Kay to nurse her woes upstairs – Dad scoops me up and takes me through to his lair, his giant, cluttered studio. He clinks around with glasses, because he likes the whole palaver of the lead crystal tumblers and the heavy decanters, but neither of us drink much, me almost not at all. When I have something peaty and expensive in my glass, he shows me his latest toy. A chunk of rock, a meteorite supposedly. 'Three and a half kilos,' Dad says with awe. 'Just imagine where that's come from, how many miles it travelled to get here.' He whirls the lump of rock through the air to show me how a meteorite travels. I've no idea whether the item is genuine or not, or how much you have to pay to get a three-and-a-half-kilo space rock sitting lumpenly on your coffee table, but I make the noises I'm meant to make. And if the meteorite is for real, then Dad's right: It is an extraordinary thing.

Then Dad turns serious. Worried, even. I don't know how to read Dad these days. Whether any expression can be taken at face value. I can't tell the difference between him acting and not acting.

'Listen, love, I should probably tell you.'

He composes his features, but I interrupt. I think I know what he's going to say.

'About Capel-y-ffin?'

He nods.

'It wasn't an accident,' I say. I explain briefly what happened. 'They were professionals. I was unlucky to get caught. None of us had any reason to suppose there was a risk. But I was lucky to get away, so it all evened out.'

Dad is sitting by a heavily shaded lamp. His face intersects the angle of the light, so his face is a jigsaw of shadows. It's not surprising to me that he's already heard the story. He'll still have contacts in the police. He'll still hear the talk.

'You shouldn't have been there alone,' is all he says.

'No, I shouldn't really. There's an internal enquiry into whether we judged the risks appropriately. Someone was supposed to come with me. At the last minute, she couldn't come. I chose to go anyway. No one made me go.'

I shrug. And if Susan Konchesky had been there with me? Olaf and Hamish might well have gone ahead anyway.

In any case, I don't think we did judge the risks inappropriately. The police service was under massive pressure because of the weather. In the end, I was just going to an empty house where there might or might not have been useful evidence, relating to a line of enquiry which was still highly exploratory. I've said all that to the in-house review team, who, I think, accepted it.

But Dad isn't an in-house review team.

'Love –' he begins.

'Really, Dad? Really? You're going to say I should have told you that first day in the hospital. When you were most worried about me. Most likely to act on impulse. Let's say I *had* told you. That day. Or the next. The first time we were alone together. If I'd said, "Hey, Dad, two professional killers did this to me and I'm lucky to be alive," you tell me: what would you have done?'

'I'm not ... I'm not a young man anymore. I don't just do the first thing that comes into my head.'

'I know you're not.'

'And my business activities these days ...'

'Are one hundred percent legitimate. Yes, I know. But you haven't answered my question. *What would you have done?*'

Dad moves his face out of the light. It darkens, but simplifies. He hasn't touched his drink.

'I don't know. I'd have made some calls. Have you located the people?'

I shake my head.

'I could still make the calls.'

'Dad, I'm a police officer. We'll find the people, arrest them, and jail them. It's what we do.'

Dad's face flickers with a smile. 'It's what you do if you manage to catch them.' He likes this: his unblemished record of having escaped our clutches.

I smile right back. 'But back when you were doing your stuff, I wasn't a police officer, was I?'

For a moment, our smiles hang in the air together, pushing at each other. A flickering contest, then a truce.

'Tell you what, love. I *will* make some calls. If I find out anything, you'll be the first to know. I won't take any other action. And if they're local, I'll definitely –'

'They're not local. One of them is Scottish, one of them Scandinavian.'

I give him a bit of further information: height and build, that sort of thing. I don't mention Drumchapel. I don't give him McCormack's name. I don't want Dad to be the one who locates them first.

He nods. Dad never had national reach. His contacts and buddies are, as far as I know, mostly Welsh or West Country. He doesn't make any promises.

We talk a bit more, then the conversation switches to other things, then I yawn and Dad drives me home in his big silver car. We say good night at my door.

It was a nice evening and I'm pleased that Dad raised the subject with me. I'd been worried he might act without talking to me first. But though I came away feeling reassured about his immediate intentions, I realise he said almost nothing to reassure me about his current activities. *I'm not a young man anymore. I don't just do the first thing that comes into my head.* Read it one way, and it's a statement of current innocence. Read it another, and it's a fancy way of saying that he no longer commits criminal or violent acts without careful advance planning. And it wasn't him but me that stated his current business activities were all legitimate. And when I asked him what he'd have done, he said *I'd have made some calls*, without saying what he'd have done with the information received.

I still think I was right not to have told him straight out. Still want to pursue this my way, not his way.

I don't hear back from Lev.

I wear my woman-of-mystery suit into the office and get loads of compliments.

Aside from the frostbitten spots on my toes, which will be there for some time, my skin is returning to normal. I hardly ever need aspirin now.

I am getting on okay with Buzz. We still live in a world where Buzz's current and actual girlfriend and the mother of Buzz's possible-future children might be one and the same person. That first person isn't sure if she wants to be the second one – isn't sure if that second thing is even achievable – but she's very sure that she wants to carrying on being the first of those things. And so far, Buzz seems to be okay with that. One time, I cook him a meal and get all the ingredients right and the cooking just right and the candles just right and everything just right and we even sit down to eat on the right side of nine o'clock.

Whenever I have free time, which is quite often, I work on investigating my father. I don't know what to explore first, so I start by simply trying to make a map of his connections. Try to figure out who he knew in 1986. Who he was close to. Who owed him something. Who might be afraid of him.

I make lists and write notes, but the centrepiece of my work is a mind-map-style diagram, with my father's name in the middle, everyone else radiating out from there. People like Emrys Thomas are there, of course. Others too, all those who formed Dad's inner circle back in my early childhood. Family connections. Friends.

Also criminals, major and minor, convicted and merely suspected. Not just ones in the same line of business as Dad, but anyone really. Anyone who was a pro criminal, who was a player.

Businessmen too. Dad had a golf-playing phase, which came to an end in the early nineties according to Mam. I doubt if he ever really liked the game – it would have been too slow for him – but it would have given him an excuse to spend money and rub shoulders with business types. Money always attracted him, and the moneyed have always had a fascinated attraction to Dad's supposed glamour.

And cops, I don't exclude them. Cardiff has never had a terrible problem with police corruption, but we weren't as clean in the 1980s as we are now, and in any case you never really know these things for sure. So I list Yorath too. Jack and his colleagues.

It's slow work. These days, you can Google around and find connections quite easily. But both online and public sources have far less dating back a quarter of a century. I use microfiches from local papers. Photo archives. Land Registry records. Business registries. Police files. Family photo albums. I've spent a couple of lazy evenings with Emrys, and towards the end of the second one, flipped through his photo album, reminiscing. Emrys was relaxed and chatty. I took care not to appear too interested, but noted every name down as soon as I was out of his house.

I don't have any leads, exactly, but I'm learning the territory. I feel as I do at the start of a case. Eager. Alive.

Every now and again, alas, I'm expected to do my real work. Stirfry stuff.

We've investigated Idris Prothero's stack of mobile phones. None of them have been used but – an interest tidbit, this

– we do know that the whole lot were purchased as part of a batch of fifteen from an Internet retailer. One of the phone numbers sold as part of that transaction received a call from the Capel-y-ffin area on the day of my almost-murder. That's not remotely strong enough evidence to secure a conviction for anything, but as far as I and Watkins are concerned, it largely eliminates doubt that Idris Prothero issued the order to kill me. Hamish and Olaf asked for instructions. Prothero told them to kill the copper. They drove back up the hill and tried to do just that.

Fuck him. And fuck them.

I want to see them all in jail – Prothero, Hamish, Olaf – with a passion that takes me by surprise. Fuck them all.

My flame of anger burns brightly for Mary Langton too. I want her killer too. And now, at last, I think I'm getting closer. The officer, Dai Beynon, who cautioned Elsie Williams comes back from his time away. He tells me that he remembers the day concerned. He'd rung the front-door bell and got no answer. But the doors to the garage had been open. Both doors: the big one at the front, the small one at the back. 'So I walked straight through,' he told me. 'They were all there.'

I nod. The garden furniture was stored in the Williams's garage. It would have been easier taking it in and out via the large front opening, and it would have been natural to leave the door up. Natural too for Beynon to stroll through the garage into the garden. See if he could find his quarry there.

'And they were all there? Elsie Williams? Her daughter and son-in-law?'

'That's it,' said Beynon.

'Did you stop in the garage for any reason? Move things around? Make a noise?'

Beynon shrugs. There are limits to memory. He doesn't say that exactly, but he sort of does.

He stands at my desk answering my dippy questions, lifting up my stapler and tapping the surface of my desk with it.

And that too is an answer of a sort. The fidgety PC David Beynon. Moving through the garage, banging things around, because he's the banging-around type.

I don't have proof, or anything that resembles it, but I do have a theory.

I get on the phone, trying to locate the firm that built Elsie Williams's conservatory. It takes sixteen calls, but then I locate a builder in Llanishen who says that yes, he did the job. Ewan Jenkins, his name is.

'I need to know how you were paid. If you were paid in cash, if you fiddled your VAT, I don't care. There will be no repercussions. Just tell me how you were paid.'

'Yes, well, I do sometimes take cash. I mean, I wouldn't normally, but like I say ...'

'I really don't care. I'm not a VAT person. You can do what you like as far as I'm concerned. I need to know who paid you, Owen. Who *physically* gave you the cash?'

'It would have been the old lady, Mrs Williams. But there was a young man there too. Her son-in-law maybe? I think it was his money. I'm not sure. It felt like there was a bit of an atmosphere. Like there had been a row or something. The job had been okay, actually. The conservatory went up pretty well, considering, and there wasn't a problem in getting paid, exactly. But I didn't like it. There was something funny there. You know. Not just one thing. But other, little things.'

'Go on.'

I'm holding the phone so hard I can feel the plastic handset creak in my grip.

'Well, like I had to take tools and everything off-site all the time. I've got a lock-up, so that's not a problem, like. But normally, I'd just use the garage. Keep it tidy obviously, but ...'

Jenkins goes on talking, but I'm only half-listening.

Gotcha!

Gotcha, gotcha, gotcha.

I tell Jenkins that we'll need him to come in and make a statement at some point. Reassure him again about the VAT. Hang up.

And then – because I want a conviction, not just a story – I start to research things. Always an illuminating process. SNAXPO, for example. An entire conference in Arizona, just to discuss the humble snack. If you didn't know those things existed, you'd never guess. Not just one conference, dozens of them. Interpack 2011. Or who would believe that there is even something called the International Cheese Technology Expo? That delightful event takes place in Wisconsin – you get good cheese technologists in Wisconsin, I bet – but the UK turns out to have its own thriving equivalents.

Which is all good. I check some dates, make some calls. I can be smiley and nice when I need to be. That, plus I offer a load of money which I'm never going to pay. While I'm working on my laptop, Buzz looks over my shoulder and says, 'What you are doing?' I say, 'I've decided to move into PR.' He says, 'No, really what?' I say, 'I'm catching murderers.' He says, 'No, really what?' and I smack the laptop closed and give him a kiss long enough that he stops asking boring questions to which I have already given two perfectly accurate answers.

Other things go well too.

Stuart Brotherton submits his completed report on Barry Precision. It's lethally comprehensive, utterly devastating. We hand it over to the Crown Prosecution Service along with six files of additional evidence. Brotherton lists 188 counts of weapons export. Whether you judge it by the number of offences or the value of the items shipped, this is the UK's biggest-ever arms-smuggling case. Watkins, Kirby, Dunwoody, Jones, and a couple of other senior officers go out for a celebratory lunch. Come back drunk.

I send Idris Prothero a homemade Christmas card with a picture of Cardiff Prison in the snow. Inside I write, '*10-year sentence. Home in 6.*'

I visit Brian Penry a couple of times. He's okay now. Head down, doing his time. He asks how I've been getting on with Mortimer. I tell him that I can't say much now, but things are going well. After I've seen Penry, I don't run straight out of the prison. I linger. Feeling the walls, the cells, the bars, the keys. It's not a comfortable sensation, but it's not insupportable either. I manage it OK.

I wonder – and this is a thought I *do* run from – I wonder if I might be getting more normal.

I think the answer is probably no. But for the first time in my ridiculous life, I have a small but increasing pile of evidence to the contrary.

Item: I have a stable relationship with a proper boyfriend.

Item: I have a good job and am respected (if not always liked) by my colleagues.

Item: I can sometimes cook an edible meal in less than seven hours.

Item: I have been known, if not often, to clean, dust and hoover.

Item: I go clothes shopping with my sister and sometimes wear the clothes that I buy. I have even plucked my eyebrows.

It's not, now that I think about it, the most impressive list of achievements, but you can't measure impressive from the height of a wall alone. You have to consider the depth of the hole you started with.

I am sometimes scared by how much progress I've made.

And then I hear from Lev. Nothing much. Just an address and a name. The address is of a flat, in an area just outside Drumchapel. The name, I assume, is the one McCormack uses at the moment: Callum Frasier.

I check the place on Google Maps. Then Street View.

The building is five storeys high. Unpainted stucco. Flat roof. Either council housing or ex-council. Net curtains in most of the windows. Some washing on lines. Concrete balconies and plastic garden chairs. Skies the colour of stucco.

No visible contract killers, but Lev doesn't get these things wrong.

I've got what I wanted.

I've got what I wanted and I don't know what to do next. My most obvious option, the one any half-normal police officer would take without a moment's thought, is to call Strathclyde Police. Give them McCormack's current location. Wait for them to do the rest. That's what I ought to do. The correct option.

And yet, what would we do if we got a call like that? We'd send a couple of plainclothes detectives to the property, ready to make an arrest if McCormack entered or left. We wouldn't be able to force entry, because we have no evidence to put in front of a magistrate that McCormack even lived there. If he was away for a few days, it's unlikely that Strathclyde Police would maintain surveillance. If he was alert enough to check his surroundings for two men waiting around in a car all day, he'd be sure to wait them out, or just move on under cover of darkness.

And that would be that. He'd never come back.

Also, the Strathclyde Police do not have in their possession three body hairs taken from a corpse in Llanishen.

So, though I say I don't know what I'm going to do next, the truth is that I've only got one option. I tell Buzz I'll be away for the weekend. I haven't yet replaced my car, so buy one for three hundred pounds in cash. It's a VW Polo, a wreck really, but it works. I don't tell anyone I've bought it. I park it a mile and a half from my house. I don't insure it.

There are a few other bits and pieces I need, but I have

364

most of them already. A couple of things to practise, but I'm reasonably practiced already.

Oddly, I'm quite relaxed. I don't have big anxieties over what I'm about to do. I do bits and bobs at work without getting myself into trouble. I spend time with Buzz and my family and it all feels pleasingly ordinary. The snow remains. Each night we look at the latest satellite picture.

An ice-bound island, waiting for something to break.

49

Glasgow feels appropriate in the cold. A northern city, chained in ice. There's something industrial about the way they handle the cold up here. The gritters and snowploughs have a dirty, used look to them. A clanking brutishness in nursery yellow.

I arrive after dark, which is to say after four in the afternoon. I haven't had a good drive up and I'm in a foul mood. The GPS on my phone guides me straight to the block of flats, as awkward and graceless in real life as it was on Street View. Four apartments on each floor. My man, Frasier-McCormack, is in Flat 5B, so on the top storey.

I ring his bell, get an answer, mumble an apology for pressing the wrong button, then go back to my car.

Sit there and wait.

Three hundred pounds doesn't buy much of a car or much of a sound system. I try listening to Classic FM, but the radio picks up two signals simultaneously: Classic FM's own tedious repertoire and some strange Nordic station, all folk music and improbable, excessive laughter.

I switch off. Stay gazing at the front door of the building. On McCormack's floor, there are two apartments with lights on, two without. I'm parked as far as possible from any streetlight.

Time goes by.

I have the engine off. Sit back, out of sight. I don't know how alert McCormack is likely to be, but I don't want to do anything that could attract attention. At least I'm wrapped up warm.

Two kids pass my car. One of them raps on my window. I wind my window down and say, 'Yes?' The kid says something in an accent so thick I don't understand it. I reply in Welsh, the same thing as I said to Sophie Hinton. *Twll dîn pob Sais*. Every Englishman an arsehole. He goes off muttering. He might as well be speaking Icelandic.

Someone leaves the apartment block, but it's not McCormack. It gets past six o'clock. How long can a person take this freezing city, this darkness, before they're driven to the boozer?

Another forty-three minutes, it turns out.

The lights go off on the remaining top floor apartment. A minute or so later, a shape enters the lobby. Then the door opens and McCormack is briefly visible under the outside light. He's wearing a woollen hat and a padded coat: the same ones, I think, as he was wearing when he tried to kill me. There's not much of him to see. But everything fits. The clothes. The way he moves. The brief view I have of his face. It's him.

I feel a cold spill of excitement. Capillaries opening up to adrenaline, fingertips awakening. A sense of life.

But it's brief, the feeling. I'm here to do a job. I'm not looking for hassle and not expecting any. The adrenaline goes away. The fingertips close down.

McCormack walks off up the street. I wait ten minutes, then leave the car. I've got some cigarettes with me – bought specially, because I hardly ever smoke tobacco – and hang around outside the apartment smoking.

After a while, a couple of people approach the block. One of them is dredging keys out of her bag. I throw my ciggy away and follow her in.

There's a lift and stairs. The two I've followed in take the stairs. I take the lift. It carries me stutteringly to the top floor. A faint smell of piss travels with me.

The landing has a low-energy bulb restrained behind thickly frosted plastic. A single-paned glass window stares blankly over the city. A silent rectangle of lights, darkness, cold. The floor is some kind of composite stone. Cheap and durable.

Metal railings lead downstairs but I'm not heading down. There's a bag of rubbish sitting outside one of the apartments, but not McCormack's.

I put on an elasticated hair cover, the sort of thing they use in food preparation. Also latex gloves. Get tools out of my bag.

A set of lockpicks. I bought them off the Internet for about forty quid a couple of years back. No particular reason why. I just prefer to have that sort of thing. I bought a few practice locks, watched some YouTube videos on how to use the picks. Practised on my own locks and on any others that came my way. I became reasonably adept, reasonably swift, then shoved the tools away in a bottom drawer. I didn't forget about them exactly, but they weren't top of my list of things to worry about.

I turn my attention to McCormack's lock. My tools are probably good for about 90 percent of the locks in the UK, maybe more, but they're good for all the cheap ones. And these are cheap. Probably just five pin. Easy.

The light is poor, but in a way that helps. Lock-picking is all about feel.

I slot a torque wrench into the lower part of the lock, the part where the shaft of the key would normally fit. Work it in both directions till I figure out which way the lock normally turns, then place a little gentle pressure on it. Inside the lock, the pins will be pressed tight against a ridge in the locking barrel. That's the way I want 'em.

I take a raking tool – something whose business end looks

not unlike the grippy half of a hairclip – and slot that into the lock above the torque wrench. I jiggle it in and out, applying upward pressure all the time. I can't exactly feel any pins releasing, but there's a little give in the torque wrench, so I've probably scored a couple of successes already.

Then start the more detailed work with my picks. I've chosen a fairly basic pick, because I don't think this lock will have any real complexity. And sure enough, it's not long before I feel the first definite pin-release. I work a little more, then feel a second one go.

I rake the lock again, looking for an easy win. Don't get it, but try a couple of different picks on the remaining pin and it gives too. The torque wrench moves all the way round.

I turn the handle, open the door, and walk on in.

I haven't known what to expect. But it's just ordinary. Vinyl flooring in the little kitchen, tacky underfoot from poor-quality cleaning. Beige carpet in the living room and bedrooms. Charity-shop furnishings. A big plasma TV.

There are curtains in the flat – thin, unlined things in orange and red – but McCormack hasn't drawn them, so his windows offer more empty rectangles. Darkness, streetlamps, snow. Red tail lights, moving slowly.

The interior doesn't offer much. Some bottles kicking around. Whiskey. Vodka. Some DVDs, action movies mostly. A bathroom which could do with a good clean.

I start to probe the apartment more closely. It's all very well finding Hamish, but I want Olaf too. Hamish will have his phone with him, most likely, and I don't see a computer. But still. People commit things to paper too, even now.

I start opening drawers, searching the desk.

I don't find anything much. It's oddly hard searching like this while wearing latex gloves. They don't grip properly on paper and I can't use saliva to moisten them, so I'm obliged to work slowly.

I find things like utility bills and grocery receipts. Not filed, just shoved away in a drawer. I look through the receipts, find nothing interesting there.

I do, though, find a postcard mailed from Norway. A village tucked away somewhere in the mountains. Wooden houses, painted rust-brown and ochre. Forested slopes sweeping right down to a huddle of green fields. On the back, *Greetings from Norway!* Nothing else, except Hamish's own address. There is a postmark, but it's not decipherable. The slogan on the card says, in English, *Experience Norway.*

I want to take the card, but think I shouldn't.

Look behind one door, to find a junk room. A small boxy room, with an old bed, a sleeping bag, a heap of clothes. Not a lot.

I have the same impulse that I had in Khalifi's apartment. An impulse to make a mess of everything. Play loud music. Open the windows.

Not a good idea.

Go into Hamish's bedroom. He has a built-in wardrobe with a wonky door and an old pine chest of drawers. The wardrobe has some shirts, a coat, a couple of casual jackets, a suit. Shoes kicking around on the floor. There's a smell of something indefinable. Probably what happens when a mould-vulnerable apartment gets too little cleaning for years on end.

I look at the shoes and shirts closely. The shoes aren't overly clean, the shirts not overly new. The coats and jackets are also not new. There are marks which could quite well be bloodstains, but could quite well be curry sauce or motor oil or Glaswegian mud. They're just marks.

The chest of drawers is altogether better. Socks and underwear. T-shirts. Trousers. Jumpers and sweat shirts. And a plastic grocery bag containing a boiler suit. Also leather gloves. Also some socks and boots. The boiler suit looks washed but has plenty of stains.

Khalifi's blood, I'd bet a million pounds.

Quite likely other people's blood too.

These look to me like Hamish's work clothes. What he wears when he's on a job. A messy job, that is. Killing a girl in a snowfield should have been nice and clean.

DNA is normally destroyed by washing. Not one hundred percent guaranteed, but most of the time. If a commercial washer was used, or particularly if a high-chlorine washing powder was used, the chances of usable DNA surviving, even in a seam or zip, are pretty much nil.

That might rule the boiler suit out as evidence, but it's very hard to clean boots well enough. You need only one drop of blood in a line of stitching or soaked into the leather and that'll be enough for the forensics guys. If Hamish had dunked his boots in bleach, or microwaved them, or boil-washed them, they'd be clean but unusable as footwear. And these are usable.

So the betting is that McCormack has left enough evidence here for us to secure a conviction. But that's all it is: a bet.

I have Watkins's evidence bag in my pocket.

That, and a dilemma.

All I need to do, to make certain of my target, is to drop those three body hairs in that bag. Secrete them in a fold of clothing. Close the bag. Close the drawer. Walk away.

Then just wait. Let McCormack come back to his apartment. Wait for him to go to bed, go to sleep. Then call Strathclyde. Tell them where to find him. Watch for long enough to make sure they don't cock it all up. Let the forensics guys find those hairs.

Justice.

I feel myself watched by an invisible gallery of spectators. Ayla, Theo, Watkins. Watching to see me choose.

And I find I can't quite do it.

Perversion of the course of justice. I can't quite do it.

In a way, I'm amazed at my own scruples. After all, I don't doubt that McCormack is a killer. The fucker tried to kill me. I don't need a court to tell me that. And the blood on this clothing might not be Khalifi's. It might not be blood. If I don't plant this evidence, I might well be waving farewell to my only chance of securing a conviction.

But.

Although I hang over that damn boiler suit with my latexed fingers holding Watkins's evidence bag above it, the bag stays closed. The body hairs encased in their little plastic prison.

I can't do it.

And because I can't, I don't. I just close up the bag, close the drawer, put the evidence bag back in my pocket. It feels strange. Not bad strange or out-of-body strange, or any of those other versions of strange that have wandered through my life. It just feels weird to be in the apartment of a man who tried to kill me. To be here and not to plant those hairs. I wonder vaguely if this is Buzz's influence. Turning me into the sort of officer he would want me to be.

The blank window rectangles open onto the night and give me no answer.

They do, however, give me a view down onto the path that cuts through the snow to the road above the apartment building. A path down which two men are walking. One of the pair is, I'm pretty sure, Hamish.

Fuckety-doo-dah. Who ever heard of a Scotsman returning so early from the pub? Do killers have no drinkers' pride these days? I watch the two until they step out of sight beneath me.

What now? I could try to bolt for it, but I don't know whether to use stairs or lift. I certainly don't want to deal with two men at once.

I hesitate a little, trying to decide what to do, but because I've hesitated, I've run out of options. That's annoying, but also liberating. At least it means I know what to do.

I go out onto the landing, take the bag of rubbish and empty it out, kicking bits down the steps. If Hamish isn't a total slob, he'll pick it up.

Go back into his flat. Get out my picks. A good locksmith would probably be able to lock this door in fifteen seconds. I'm not as good as that, but I'm not awful and I've only recently picked this lock, so I know the feel of it, which tool to use.

In twenty-five seconds, maybe thirty, I've locked the door again, myself on the inside. I hear the wheezing of the lift, so could probably have just walked downstairs.

Ah well.

I take one of the bottles from the the back of Hamish's stash. A bottle of rum, mostly full.

Go into the junk room, roll under the bed. I've got a knife with me, the one I normally have behind my bed, and I get it out, just in case. But I'm not really in a knifey sort of mood. I don't think I need to be.

Hamish is obviously a tidy soul, because it takes a while before the apartment door opens. I can hear him talking to someone. Presumably the guy I saw him walking with. I'm curious to see what follows. Is it possible Hamish is gay? That his current companion is a partner picked up for the night?

I don't know why, but the thought tickles me. Prompts a silent chuckle. But I doubt it. I hear gruff voices. Someone pissing. The fridge opening and closing. Then the TV coming on loud.

That's all I hear for a while. Some kind of action thing, all chases and shootouts. The apartment walls are as soundproof as damp cardboard, so I hear every squeal of tyres, every beat of dialogue. I follow it for a while, but I'm not interested. Just drift off. Not asleep by any means, but trancey. I should have brought something to eat. Sandwiches or something. But I've got nothing at all, so just lie there, staring up at the bed, knife in my right hand, bottle by my left.

Time passes.

I remember lying on the car engine beneath the starlight. Wondering if I was dying.

That places feels very remote from me now. Other people, I think, would have feelings like anger or vengefulness. Maybe if I was more whole as a person, I'd have those feelings too.

But I don't. I wasn't kidding when I told Buzz that I hadn't got him a Christmas present. Him or anyone else. So I lie there figuring out who should get what. I decide I should cook Buzz a big festive meal and try to think of a menu that will feel Christmassy but will still be simple enough for me not to cock up.

At around nine-thirty, the movie ends and the TV switches to boxing. *LIVE from the O2 Arenaaaaa.*

I've studied fighting, obviously. Indeed, I've learned from, I guess, one of the world's leading authorities on that un-kindly subject. But my interest is purely practical. I've never watched boxing. I dislike the whole aesthetic of it. The shiny shorts. The giant belts. The boasting.

It's gone eleven before the damn TV turns off. It's given me a headache.

Hamish and his buddy stomp around a bit – there's a bit more fridge action – then the front door is opened and closed. Hamish remains behind. He's got a heavy tread. Thuggish.

He crashes through to the bedroom. There's a thump and a swearword, which are both good. The drunker he is, the better.

I roll out from under the bed. I'm stiff, so it's nice to be able to stretch. Roll my shoulders. Ease the knots.

He goes from the bedroom to the bathroom. I hear the shower run.

I stand outside the bathroom door, where I'll be concealed

as it opens. There's a tune in my head – Adele's 'Chasing Pavements.' I don't know why. It's all I can do to stop myself singing it.

I'm in a pretty good mood, I notice. Is this happiness? It might well be, but I can't absolutely tell. I often need to concentrate to figure those things out, and right now I need my attention for other things.

The shower stops. A tap runs. Toothbrushing.

He seems to take a long time in the bathroom. Longer than me, I think, and I'm a girl. I'm half minded to go in there and tell him to get on with it, but I don't have to. Hamish, finally, is ready for me. He steps, naked, out of the bathroom.

I allow myself a second – a half second actually – to be present in this moment. To enjoy the sensation of being alive, here and now, in a place I want to be.

It's not an idle moment, though.

I study the side of Hamish's skull. Somewhat above, and forward from, his ear. The pterion, is what doctors call it. What Lev called it, in his darkly accented English. It lies at the join of four bones. A major artery lies beneath. The skull wall is thinner there than anywhere else. God's little joke, as it's known. A spot so weak that blows to other parts of the skull often end up causing fractures here.

I mark the spot. Say, 'Hi, Hamish,' and, as he turns, hit him as hard as I can with the bottle of rum.

He drops, almost silently, to the floor.

50

He's not dead. It wouldn't massively bother me if he was, but he's not. And it's better like this.

I saw some duct tape in a desk drawer – one of your contract-killer basics, I suppose – so I get it out and tape his hands and forearms together. I don't piss around. I don't circle his arms once or twice but more like fifteen or twenty times. Cut the tape with a knife, not my teeth – I'm still being as DNA-conscious as I can. Next, carefully, tape over his mouth. Then, more confidently, tape round his ankles and knees. Because there's still spare on the roll, I lash his ankles to the sofa leg and stand back to admire my handiwork.

He's not going anywhere and he still has a pulse. There's some blood oozing from his temple, but not copious amounts as you sometimes get with a skull wound.

Good enough.

I roll him into the recovery position. Don't want the fucker swallowing his tongue. But even as I roll him, he starts to wake up. His eyes groggily search the room. I wait until he's alert enough to make sense of the world, then bend down so he can see my face.

'Evening,' I say.

His mouth says nothing, but his eyes say *Fuck you*. I walk round and kick him hard in the coccyx. No particular reason why. I suppose I wanted to see what I would feel, kicking the man who tried to kill me. But the answer is: not much. It's just a kick. It feels right and good to have this part of things tidied away, but I don't feel much personal triumph.

Also, Hamish seems amazingly naked. There's something about our situation which somehow emphasises that he's wearing nothing but duct tape and an air of hatred. I cover his gingery cock with a bathroom towel. His nose is crooked, which means I did break it that night in the car.

Now that I've got time, I can go through the apartment at more leisure. Don't find anything more than I did the first time, except that I've now got Hamish's phone, if I want it.

I *do* want it, only decide not to take it. Strathclyde will have access to technical specialists who can get through any password protection Hamish may have. And the phone may yield evidence that's wanted in court. Plus I'll be able to access anything that Strathclyde gathers. So logic wins out. I leave the phone.

It's time to clean up. It's already been reported that Hamish has been in recent contact with me, so any small particles of my DNA that are found would likely be consistent with that contact. On the other hand, I don't want it to look like I was physically in the apartment at any point, so I want to erase any significant traces of my presence. I set to work with a hoover, cleaning the area under the bed where I lay all through the evening. Although I kept on clothes, gloves, and hair protection, it's impossible to remain that long in one place and leave no trace.

After hoovering, I mix half a bucket of water with a whole bottle of bleach. Rinse down anything I'm worried about. Bleach doesn't guarantee destruction of DNA but it does a pretty good job. It'll do more than enough.

It's one thirty in the morning and I'm done.

I tell Hamish I'm going.

He gives me those *fuck you* eyes again, so I give him another kick. Basic stuff, I know, but it's still communication. Human contact.

I douse the parts I've kicked with bleach, just to be on the safe side.

Then go to the bathroom. Take the showerhead off its stand and drop it on the floor. Turn the cold tap on to maximum. Water starts to spray around.

I help myself to the Norwegian postcard. If Strathclyde want it, that's tough. Also the hoover. I take that too.

Leave the apartment door open.

Take the lift down.

Trudge wearily to my car.

It's not the beating the crap out of people that takes it out of you. It's the waiting around beforehand, the cleaning up afterwards. You should be able to get support staff for that kind of thing.

I drive south to Lancaster. That'd be two and a half hours normally, but it takes four hours because of the weather. At a service station along the way, I find one of those big commercial wastebins and dump the hoover. I'm so tired now that my eyes keep glassing over. I almost nod off, repeatedly, and need the vibration of the car tyres hitting the icy roadside snow to wake me.

At Lancaster railway station, I park the car, buy a ticket for cash. Wait for a train to take me south. First to Crewe. Then on to Cardiff. When the train has pulled a few minutes out of Lancaster, I throw my car keys out the window. They disappear down an embankment into a stand of blackthorn. There'll be loads of my DNA in the car if anyone were to choose to swab it. But they won't. It's just a car. Bought for cash, never registered, then abandoned. In a few weeks' time, it'll be towed by the police and destroyed.

I sleep till Crewe. Wait on a cold platform until the Cardiff train comes in, then gratefully get on board. The ticket collector has a South Welsh accent and I feel like I'm already home.

I'll do a roast chicken with all the trimmings. Roast tatties, bacon, gravy, two veg, cranberry sauce. Probably cheat and buy a ready-made pudding. I'll do a practice cook with Mam and write down all the timings.

On Monday morning, Rhiannon Watkins phones me. Orders me up to her office.

I go. She greets me and says, 'I don't know if you've heard. Strathclyde Police think they've got McCormack.'

'Oh, that's good.'

She tells me the news. Water pouring from an upstairs bathroom brought down the ceiling in the flat beneath. Then, because that flat was unoccupied, the ceiling one storey down was next to follow. The occupants of that flat called the landlord, then went upstairs to investigate. Found the door unlocked. Called the police, assuming theft.

'McCormack was found with a severe blow to the skull, but no long-term damage. He had been secured with duct tape, apparently. Swaddled like an Egyptian mummy.'

'Or baby Jesus,' I say, trying to be seasonal.

Watkins doesn't answer right away, maybe because she's not very Christmassy, so I take her evidence bag out of my pocket. The one with the body hairs.

'I'm sorry, ma'am, but I forgot to return these to the laboratory. What do you want me to do with them?'

She takes the bag. She seems moved. Moved and grateful. She takes the bag, half-closing her eyes as she does so. Nodding to herself. 'Thank you. Thank you, Fiona.'

It's strange to see her like this. I guess that never in her life has she knowingly contravened rules of evidence, or any of the other laws that govern our investigations. By returning the bag to her, I've kept her one hundred percent record intact. I realise how much it must have taken for her to have given me the bag in the first place.

'If they've got McCormack, I probably don't need to pursue my enquiries?'

'No. No, you don't.'

'Good. That's all good.' I think Watkins has said everything she wanted to say, but I'm still standing here. She's not telling me to go. There's something uniquely clear about the light in here. It's the snow, I think. Seconds and minutes float into the room, then get hypnotised by the light. Accumulating in little drifts of time.

'Have you gone on any of those websites yet?' I say neutrally.

'Yes.' She nods. She doesn't have full control over her voice, which is half husky, half whispering. 'I was going to ask, if you wouldn't mind, sometime ...'

'We could take a look at your profile together. Make sure you're presenting yourself right. I'd like that.'

Watkins nods. She's red. Scarlet. Watkins the Ice Queen in a puddle at my feet. I think this is a real friendship. Or could become one. We're awkward as hell now, but that'll pass. Her eyes say the opposite of McCormack's. No need to kick anyone in the coccyx.

I smile at her. Say, 'See you soon.' Go downstairs to start my day.

51

Humans want endings. Perhaps we need them. Tidy finishes. Christmas wrapping paper and a big red bow.

We don't get them, though, except perhaps at Christmas. Maybe that's why the festival endures. Maybe it's not only children who need the myth.

This Christmas, here on our frozen island, is a spectacular one. Hoarfrost so thick, there's as much as an inch lying on branches and twigs. Icicles four feet long hanging from gutters and balconies. Buzz tells me he's seen icicles that he measured at over six feet, and he, unlike me, always tells the truth about these things.

Christmas Eve is sunny. I'm not working that day and Buzz is, so I use the freedom to drive out of Cardiff, away from the coast, up into the hills. My dad's car. A Range Rover which isn't going to get stuck anywhere. Which flies over these icy roads with a certainty altogether lacking in my late and still-lamented Peugeot. I hadn't intended to go all the way, but I do. Up to Mortimer's cottage. Then to the field where I almost died. I want to see it again.

The place is piercingly beautiful. White hills and infinite light. A bird of prey sharpens its wings on the air overhead. The barn that I burned down is still charred and black, but its remaining timbers are jewelled with diamonds. The stream in the little dip beyond the barn chuckles at my presence. A line of footprints – fox, I think – marks little blue dimples up the slope of the hill.

Tonight, Christmas Eve, they're forecasting temperatures of minus sixteen degrees, which means minus eighteen or colder up at this elevation. That's colder than it was when I was here last, but not much. Either way, it isn't T-shirt weather.

When the Ice Age last covered Britain, these mountains lay on its fringes. Glaciated, but only just. These old red rocks, the sandstones and the siltstones, were scraped clean by moving ice. To them, this weather is just a reminder of things past.

I stay in that field awhile. The sun stares down without comment. The air flashes with cold fire.

The bird above me disappears, then returns.

And eventually, I don't need to be there anymore. It's gone. The whole car-death-cold thing has slipped from one place to another. From something that was still injuring me in the present to some other place where it no longer hurts. The past still happened, but I don't have to live there. I don't have to worry. The barn will get rebuilt. My skin grafts are increasingly looking like ordinary skin.

I drive down to the farm below. Arthur is in a barn, scattering feed for his sheep. Mary comes out of the kitchen when she sees me. I have presents for them both. A huge bottle of whisky for him. A bunch of flowers for her. Nice ones. They seem genuinely touched. And I am too. By their surprise. Their smiles.

They invite me in, but I say no. We stand a bit in the stone yard, looking out at the snow, and we agree that it's cold, that it's beautiful, that we've never had a Christmas like it.

I ask Arthur how his insurance claim is going. He says fine. I tell him that I distinctly recall the barn being at least three-quarters full of hay. I've already phoned him to say that, but I say it again now.

He shakes my hand with a grip so strong, I can feel bones starting to fuse in my hand.

And then I go. Dad's beautiful big Range Rover driving on ice like it was just diddling over a suburban street. And McCormack in prison.

His boiler suit yielded no useful forensic evidence, but his boots did. And his gloves. And, stupid fucker, the plastic bag that housed them all. Khalifi's blood. Also the blood of a Scottish man who disappeared two years ago, with suspected gambling debts. Also the blood of a third individual who has not yet been identified.

McCormack's phone use links him to Cardiff Bay on the night of Khalifi's murder. McCormack's car – the one they used the night they tried to kill me – can be tracked via the ANPR database to both Cardiff Bay and then, later, Llanishen. Strathclyde Police tell us that they have a strong murder case for the gambling-debt guy too. In short, McCormack is fucked. He'll spend the rest of his life in jail, near as dammit.

I don't think about him often now. He's history.

Watkkins wanted to add my attempted killing to the list of charges, but the CPS told us we had nowhere near enough evidence to secure a conviction. Watkins tried to argue them round, but I told her to leave it. I didn't want the publicity or the hassle. As long as McCormack goes to jail, I'll be satisfied.

There's more good news too. McCormack's phone was unlocked by Strathclyde's technical staff. The call log contained outbound and inbound calls from a pay-as-you-go phone purchased in Denmark. That phone showed use in Glasgow, in London, in Bristol, in Copenhagen, in Oslo. And also in parts of rural Norway.

I've contacted the company that produced the 'Experience Norway' card I took from McCormack's flat. They tell me that the picture was taken from a valley in the mountains about thirty miles south of Trondheim. The village in question has a population of just six hundred people. If I include everyone within a ten-mile radius, that still only gives me about fifteen hundred. And Norway, bless it, has a compulsory national register of all residents. The sort of thing you associate with the Stasi, but somehow an idea that's taken root in this little Nordic paradise too.

I sift my list of possible names to exclude women, children, and anyone outside an age range of twenty-five to forty-five. All male Norwegians are obliged to perform military service, but I have a strong suspicion that Olaf will have done more than the minimum. These people usually do. If you like violence, have an aptitude for it, you're drawn by the glamour of warfare. The training, the guns, the toughness. The Norwegian armed forces have a veterans' administration which keeps information on one hundred thousand ex-service personnel. I ask it about veterans of the right age registered to the area I'm interested in. The agency is initially reluctant to divulge its data, but I get Watkins to apply a little pressure and, after a few little bureaucratic shenanigans, the data is promised. In the new year, sometime.

Good enough.

I'm back in Cardiff by four in the afternoon.

Buzz is spending Christmas day with his family, me with mine, so this evening we're having our own private celebration. I've got everything I need. I've done a practice-cook, supervised by my mam, and I've written down all the timings.

Those timings don't just apply to the chicken. They apply to me too. I want to do everything right. Clean hair. New dress. Proper makeup. Sexy underwear. Though my dress isn't exactly new – it's one of Kay's cast-offs – it's one that Buzz hasn't seen. I can't tell if it looks nice or not, but I know it looks passable. Most of Kay's dresses don't fit me brilliantly, because of our height difference, but she likes her dresses short and some of them suit me well. This one looks okay, I think. The mirror doesn't say 'woman of mystery,' but it does say 'girl looking nice for a special date'.

Good enough: my slogan of the moment.

Inevitably I don't get my timings absolutely right. I was aiming to have dinner served by seven thirty, but it's going to be more like eight fifteen. That too doesn't matter. Buzz has strict instructions not to show up until I text him. He's out at the pub with a bunch of people from the office, so he's fine.

And then I am ready. I tell Buzz he can show up at quarter past. There are candles on the table. Wine. The table's laid. Everything is either cooked or just approaching perfection.

I'm a skitter of nerves.

I put my posh shoes on much too early, so my feet are killing me now, but I still skedaddle around, checking things I've already checked. I look at my watch five times in twelve minutes. Check myself in the mirror three times.

And then Buzz is here. My stomach flips, as though it's the first time I've ever seen him.

I feel ridiculously anxious and I don't know why.

He is about to say, 'Bloody hell, Fi,' because that's what he usually says when I'm making a visible effort. But then he doesn't. He just kisses me carefully and says, 'Happy Christmas, love.' I say, 'Happy Christmas,' too, but my voice is crooked and hoarse, like Watkins's was when she asked me to help her with the dating sites.

We eat dinner.

The potatoes are crispy. The chicken is cooked enough to be non-lethal, not so much that it's black. The gravy tastes good and there's plenty of it. The veg is fine too. I got the right sort of wine.

We clink glasses and say, 'I love you,' and that feels like a real thing to do, not a TV-movie thing. All of it does. The whole thing.

I'm still nervous, but no longer skittering. For all I know, I even appear reasonably calm. When it becomes time to serve pudding, I realise that it's still frozen hard. My list didn't

385

have an entry that read, 'Remove pudding from freezer, you numpty,' so I didn't do it. Didn't even think about it.

I must look crestfallen.

Buzz takes the pudding out of its wrapper and puts it into the microwave to defrost. He says it'll take twenty minutes to defrost, then twenty-five minutes to heat in the oven.

'I wonder if we can think of a way to pass the time for forty minutes,' he says.

But he's not allowed that. Not yet.

We sit on the living room floor and give each other presents. I give him a jumper that he looks really nice in. I give him a hockey stick with rave reviews on the hockey websites. This one is made of some special composite that's meant to be much better than the knackered old wooden one he uses. It cost two hundred pounds. I'm a bit worried that he'll have some manly attachment to his wooden one, but he doesn't, or at least, he says, 'Bloody hell, Fi, that's fantastic,' in a way that makes me think he means it. I give him some other things too. Nice things. Things I took care about when I bought them.

I have almost no money left in my account, or anywhere else for that matter. And that's fine. I'm not very good with money, but I don't starve.

Buzz gives me presents too. Girl things mostly, but I like that he thinks of me that way. Someone who wants scented candles. Who wants a cute little jacket from Oasis. I light the candle and try on the jacket and I still don't feel like a TV-movie person. Giddy, but okay.

He also gives me a small box and I have a sudden terror that it might be jewellery. It is, but a necklace, not a ring, and I feel a surge of relief. I love this man, but I'm not ready to take that step yet. I don't know if I ever will be, but more things are possible in this life than I ever thought likely.

'Are you okay, love?'

I nod. Smile. Put the necklace on.

'It's lovely,' I say. 'I love it.'

We've used the word *love* or *lovely* three times in the space of nine words, and it doesn't feel excessive.

Buzz takes the pudding out of the microwave and puts it into the oven. He does some other things in the kitchen too. Probably things I've forgotten.

I'm not looking at my list anymore.

When Buzz comes back, I give him my final present. A small box. Wrapped, with a red bow.

'This is a funny present, really,' I tell him. 'It's not something for you to keep. It's something for you to destroy.'

He opens it, smiling. The box is full of seeds, like green lentils, only paler. Some speckled, with tones of buff and slate and pale grey.

He looks at me with his big blue eyes, puzzled. He has freckles on the end of his nose that make me want to kiss them.

'What are they, sweetheart?'

'They're my cannabis seeds,' I tell him. 'The next generation. My seedbank.'

'Fi, that's amazing.' He hesitates. 'I mean, *technically*, giving an industrial quantity of Class B drugs to a police officer isn't amazing, it's criminal, but –'

I interrupt him. 'I'm not saying I'm giving up. I'm not even promising that I *will* give up. I don't know if I can. But I am promising to try. I want you to know I will try.'

He's speechless. Then his freckles move in for a long kiss. His lovely freckles on his lovely nose.

We eat some pudding, but though there's cheese to follow, we don't touch it. We head through to the bedroom and do what we do best. Then there's a muddle of showering and washing up and watching a bit of rubbish on the telly and cuddling up close as we watch it.

387

And eventually bed. Buzz says 'Happy Christmas' once more. I say the same to him, but it's still not Christmas yet, only Christmas Eve.

Before the church bells toll the midnight, Buzz is asleep beside me. I have my hand on his chest so I can feel him breathing. Then, when that's boring, I tickle the hairs in his nose to make him snuffle and shake his head.

I tickle his ears too, but that doesn't work as well.

Time passes.

As soon as Watkins told me that Strathclyde forensics had found Khalifi's blood in McCormack's apartment – as soon as, that is, we knew for certain he would be going to jail – I asked Watkins for permission to request an appeal against Mortimer's conviction. She nodded and instituted the necessary proceedings right away. There's a time lag for these things, but we'll get what we want, I'm certain.

I borrowed a patrol car and drove, with Susan Konchesky again, up to Droitwich.

Got Sophie Hinton, her mother, the two kids into one room together. Told them formally that Mark Mortimer had been wrongly convicted. Said that we were working to get his conviction reversed. Told them that, because of their father, a major criminal conspiracy had been uncovered. Said that the first man was under arrest and heading for prison.

I thanked them each personally – Sophie Hinton, Ayla, Theo – for their help.

Ayla and Theo cried buckets. Sophie Hinton cried too. I don't know if I've given the children what they needed, but I've done all I can. Given them a father to be proud of. Not a criminal, a hero.

I'd still like to give their mother a good slapping, but I can't have everything.

Afterwards, as we were driving back again, Susan said, 'Back there. You were amazing. I just wanted you to know.'

She was at the wheel and had her eyes fixed on our snow-bound motorway, but I thanked her and meant it.

I don't think Mark Mortimer was a hero, not quite. It was brave of him to look into the arms dealing. It was fucking stupid of him not to alert the police. A courageous idiot: that would be closer to the truth, but his kids don't need the truth. They needed their father back.

Somewhere beyond our window, a bell tolls midnight.

Buzz snores, his even, deep, masculine rumbles.

I'd like to find Khalifi, or Langton, or even Mortimer, but their spirits are silent. Perhaps that's a good thing. Something a bit like peace.

The weapons systems that left the Barry Precision factory filtered out across some of the world's nastier regimes. Egypt. Libya. Tunisia. Syria. Yemen and Somalia. Who knows how far those weapons travelled? In whose hands they ended up? The only thing that's for certain is that none of them were destined for the hands of democratically accountable governments, because if they had been, the firm could simply have applied for, and obtained, export licences.

Barry's weapons may never have been fired. The firm made parts for heavy weaponry and armoured vehicles. Artillery pieces and tanks, not small arms. It's quite possible that few or none of those weapons were fired in anger.

Yet the burden of guilt is horrendous all the same. Those armaments protected regimes against their peoples. The dictator's ultimate recourse. Barry Precision – and Jim Dunbar, and Idris Prothero – played their toxic little part in keeping those regimes intact.

I'd like to find the souls of those victims. To make contact, however dimly or however briefly. To touch hands with them, feel their existence.

I can't do that, though. Perhaps there are just too many of them. Or they're perhaps too distant. Maybe you can only feel the dead when you know them a little, the way I knew Khalifi.

A pity.

But even if you can't feel the dead, you can think about them. Make them a gift of your time and care. So I do. As the bells of Cardiff count towards the first light of this frozen Christmas, and as Buzz snores beside me, his nose hairs now unmolested, I spend time with the dead. The countless, name-less, uncomplaining dead.

The city clocks chime over Cardiff.

Buzz rolls in his sleep, allowing me to kiss the back of his neck, which is beautiful.

Outside, the great freeze endures, tightening its hold. Ice thickens. In a snowy field somewhere above Capel-y-ffin, a burned-out barn flashes diamonds at the moon, while owls hoot in the solitary woods.

And sometime before dawn on Christmas Day, I fall asleep.

52

The Norwegian veterans' administration comes back to me with names. There are five people in my target area who spent significant time in the armed forces. One of those was a naval officer, an improbable career choice for Olaf, I think. One of the others is just twenty-six, and I'm pretty sure Olaf is older. Of the three others, one served for seven years, most of that time in the Brigade Nord, Second Battalion, based in the far north of Norway. A place where you'd learn all about snow. About hypothermia.

I check out all five names. It's not hard. Armies like regimental photos. Ski teams. Biathlon contests. Those things need teasing out, but they're not private. I pose as a documentary maker researching a series on winter warfare. I get all the co-operation I could ask for. I get photos. I get a photo of Olaf.

His real name is Jan-Erik Fjerstad. He is thirty-five. He is, indeed, my man from the Second Battalion. He represented his battalion in long-distance cross-country skiing competition, before an ankle injury ended all that. He is registered to an address outside a remote hamlet in the mountains of middle Norway.

Olaf doesn't sound like a person I'd like to tangle with one-on-one. Hamish was just as tough, just as strong, but he was stupider. Not as careful. And Hamish's arrest will have put Olaf on his guard.

So I text Lev. Ask him if he fancies a trip to Scandinavia.

I don't hear back from him for a while, but when I do, it's a yes. We set a date for March.

In the meantime – work. Lots of it.

I've been working with a team of two on Khalifi's little adventures in the arms trade. We can track thirteen separate orders split across seven different firms, all of which appear to be for weapons-parts. There are a further eighteen suspect orders, either commissioned or planned, which probably relate to weaponry too. There's no use, however, in detailing these things beyond a certain point. Khalifi is dead and can't be jailed. I draw up a report presenting our conclusions, then I and my colleagues are assigned to other things.

Barry Precision itself is where the action is, and our battle with the firm is turning into a fuckery of lawyers. Like Stalingrad, only with legal arguments in place of mud, snow, and tank manoeuvres. But they've miscalculated, I think. If they wanted to sap our resolve, our budgetary capacity, they've actually done the opposite. Our Chief Officers and the top decision makers at the CPS are determined to proceed. There's a rare institutional unanimity in pursuing the case, and pursuing it hard.

Plus Kirby and Watkins, it turns out, are superb at this sort of thing. Kirby is wonderful at the politics, the lawyer stuff. Watkins is relentless in her accumulation of evidence. Presenting it in a way guaranteed to break down any opposition, to destroy any counter-argument. At the same time, she's scrupulous about conducting every aspect of her investigaton according to the proper standards. Every procedure followed, every box ticked.

Barry Precision's lawyers are still snapping away, but so far they've accomplished nothing at all. They're snapping on air.

Dunbar and Prothero are going to prison.

Once a week, on a random day and using different stationery

every time, I send Prothero a card. A picture of Cardiff jail. No message.

Idris Prothero made his money in private equity. Pays UK tax at a rate of 18 per cent, but keeps most of his business interests offshore, so his effective tax rate is well under 10 per cent. I say this to Buzz, who says cheerfully, 'Well, we must be mugs then,' and goes to work, being a mug.

Except we're not mugs. We do a good, honest job at a fair rate of pay. That's not stupid, it's responsible. It's an attitude responsible for every good thing in society. And though there's nothing illegal about the way Prothero pays his taxes, for someone to make that much money, and to pay that little tax, and then to make yet more money by selling weapons to dictators and to compound all that by giving, calm as you like, the order to kill DC Fiona Griffiths because she might, just *might*, put an end to your stream of profits – there's something breathtaking in that approach to life. Something so stunningly don't-give-a-fuck that, as far as I'm concerned, ten years in jail is never enough.

I hope Watkins gets her conviction. I hope a judge awards the maximum sentence. I hope Prothero has a horrible time in prison. I hope his wife leaves him and his kids hate him and his former colleagues steal all his money and some six-foot-six fucker with gnarly tattoos and strong homosexual inclinations shares a cell with him. And I hope it all happens soon.

Though I might be biased. I do acknowledge that.

But first things first. Mary Langton has waited too long already. Five years, poor lass, almost five and a half. Time enough.

On Monday 3 January, I go to see Watkins. She's deep in paperwork, but waves me into her office. She's gone back to her Watkinsian monochromes, but less rumpled somehow. I don't know if she's bought new stuff, or if she's lost a few pounds, or what it is, but she looks better. She still looks fierce, but the human sometimes peeps out anyway.

We have done some work on her website profile. Picked a photo of her that makes her look nice – nice in a scary way, admittedly, but nice. Rewritten her profile so it didn't sound like a two-page report for some corporate HR department. She's had her first emails and she's about to set up her first ever proper date.

'Do you have a moment?'

She does. I've brought coffee for her, a mug of peppermint tea for me.

'Mary Langton,' I say. 'I've been looking at the case notes again.'

Watkins rubs her face. The Langton investigation bothers her, I know. It's two failures for her, not one. The first five years back. The second now. And she's not used to failure.

But she's friendlier these days. Watkins-friendly, anyway. 'Yes?'

'I know who killed her.'

Watkins raises her eyebrows. Not angry eyebrows. Just prove-it eyebrows.

So I tell her. Who did it. How I know.

I connect up the bits and pieces. Elsie Williams's insomnia. The garage. The conservatory. The hot summer's day when PC Beynon gave the old lady her caution. I talk about the old woman's vendettas: kids on bikes, people lighting garden bonfires. Stupid things, summer things. I talk also about the man stuff. Car mechanics and pressure washing.

Watkins listens to me intently.

Nothing that I say amounts to a single grain of proof. Nothing that would remotely stand up in court. But the hypothesis almost always comes first. The proof comes after.

'You're right,' says Watkins. 'He's our man. It's him.'

I'm sure. She's sure. But our guy doesn't live in Britain, or even in a European country which will respond to a European

Arrest Warrant. We would need to show 'reasonable grounds' for suspicion. My pruning manuals and theories about bird droppings make for pretty ropey evidence.

It's not just that he could fight extradition and probably win, it's that we would lose all our advantages of surprise. Really, with a guy like that, you want to yank him off the street, run him straight to an interview room, and give him a good hard interrogation before he's had time to think through his strategies. Even if he gets lawyered up straight away, and these days that's hard to avoid, our chances of success go up dramatically if we can hit hard and early.

Watkins is thinking these things through. The light in her office has gone back to ordinary Cardiff light. No snow. No frost. No mounds of gritty snow or fistfuls of diamonds. Just low-voltage overhead lights. Nylon carpet and slatted blinds. And outside, that subdued January light that's never far from a wash of rain.

The frozen December island has already vanished into myth. Like something briefly escaped from the time of fairy-tale. When unicorns stalked the land.

Watkins is saying something. I'm not sure what. I interrupt her. 'He's coming to the UK tomorrow week. There's an industry conference where he'll be a guest speaker.'

I give her details of the relevant website. She gets up the web page and stares back at me.

'You're sure that's him?'

'Yes.'

I don't say so, but of course I'm sure. It was me that booked him. I set myself up as a PR agent. Paid two hundred pounds for a cheapie website. Got an associated email address. Bought a disposable phone. Invited our guy to a big industry conference as guest speaker. Offered to pay business-class travel in both directions. And accommodation. And a generous speaking fee. He haggled over the fee, so I said yes to his highest demand. Then contacted the conference organisers and said that this guy was going to be in the UK during their conference. Would they like him to come and speak? There'd be no fee attached, because he was in the area anyway. They said yes. And that was that. Bish, bosh. Job done. I'll need to pull the website and ditch the phone, but I won't do that until he's actually in the air.

'Do you know what plane he's on?'

I say no, which isn't true, because he emailed me his itinerary, but it's not hard getting passenger information.

Watkins's smile starts in her eyes, flickers at the corners of her mouth, then ignites to reveal a full set of teeth.

'Do you want to be there?' she says.

Stupid question.

53

Bath.

We travel there, Bev and I, in the rain. I'm driving. My new car. It's not a convertible, this one. Though I loved my little Peugeot and though it was hardly her fault that I almost died inside her, I needed to move on. My first thought was to play safe. Get something less flippant, more German. I thought about a VW Golf, perhaps. An Audi A1. But then I was seduced by the South. By an Alfa Romeo Giulietta, all moody curves and sulky power.

It still has that new-car smell. Plastic and leather. New carpets. Volatile organic compounds creating a sweetly heady mix only a shade or two off toxic.

'It's lovely,' says Bev, who can't afford anything like this.

My dad bought me the car as a Christmas present. I knew he would and he did. I told him that I would give him the insurance money when it comes through, and I will. But Dad also, I discovered, put five thousand pounds in cash in the glove-box. There's no rule which says police officers can't take money from their parents. On the other hand, police officers who accept large sums of undeclared cash from people strongly suspected of criminal activity are likely to run foul of the Bribery Act. And I'm not going to declare the cash. But then, my dad isn't a criminal, is he? And he's not asking me to perform my duties in an improper way. Or at least I don't think he is.

So I keep the car and the cash and deflect Bev's unspoken interest in my financial affairs.

There's a light rain falling again. Wipers like a metronome. I normally speed on the motorway, but because Bev is in the car I stay at a steady seventy. Sidelights on. Indicate when I change lane.

Bev is wearing the dark jacket that she lent me when I made this journey three months back. I'm wearing my suit from Hobbs. It's dark enough, formal enough, for this visit.

Watkins was right the first time. When she saw my jeans and didn't approve. There are times when clothes matter. When it matters what they signal.

We roll down the long hill into Bath. The day is drawing to its close. The city is a darkening bowl beneath us. The western sky is violet and orange. A lament for the departed. For the violently lost.

'They're expecting us, aren't they?' says Bev.

She's already asked that. I say, 'Yes. They're nice. They'll be okay. I mean, okay given everything.'

'I've got Kleenex in my bag.'

'It'll be fine.'

The traffic is clogged. Jerky. Bev is telling me about her parents' comical new puppy and I feel jabs of annoyance as she talks.

Then we're there. A magnolia tree in a front garden. A middle-class street full of middle-class lives. A black cat trots away from us under a garden door.

I park. We get out. I smile at Bev and ring the bell.

Rosemary Langton answers the door. She's in a navy jumper and a charcoal skirt. Her husband hovers behind, dark grey suit, home early from work.

We go inside. To the kitchen. Rosemary makes us tea. I don't want it and Bev isn't a huge tea drinker, but it's part of the ritual. What law-abiding people do when they have police officers in the house. It's our duty to drink, theirs to pour.

Then we're all at table. A clock ticks somewhere in the hall. Through French doors at the back, I see the long tresses of the willow tree and the same black cat motionless underneath.

'You know why we're here,' I say. 'We now know a lot about how your daughter died. We have arrested the man who killed her. He will be spending the rest of his life in jail.

'I also need to tell you that this story isn't a pretty one. It's as we thought, as you feared. Mary was almost certainly raped before she died. She may well have been physically hurt as well. There's a lot that we can't say for sure, but we can make some very good guesses.'

I stop there, trying to get the measure of my audience. I don't always have good sensors in these situations, but I can trust Bev's and I look at her for guidance. Her face tells me that I'm doing okay, so I go on.

I tell the story.

Almost six years ago, Mary Langton was coming out of the most important relationship of her life. We don't know why it ended, or even really why it started. But the relationship in a strange way both saved her life and ended it. First, it saved her. From the drink and the stripping. From that self-destructive path glazed with black marble and red leather. She found love. She found something strong enough and bright enough to change the course of her life. Her new course led her to the sailing clubs of Swansea Bay and Llanishen. She went back to her studies. She had never exactly terminated them, but during those strip-club months her commitment had dwindled to almost nothing. She found her way back to the life path that was first mapped out for her in these confident Bath streets.

I don't know why it didn't work out with Khalifi. Probably just two people with too many differences. Any case, they stopped seeing each other, but Langton still liked to haunt the places she had known with him. The Mumbles on Swansea Bay. Llanishen. Places that reminded her of those times. She left that unfortunate party early because she wanted to see the reservoir again, in the last of the light.

Which, as mischance would have it, was a bad idea.

Because Karen Johnston, Elsie Williams's daughter, used to visit her mother for two or three weeks each summer. Her husband, Derek, accompanied her. When they were over here, Karen and Elsie did whatever a mother and daughter do. Derek attended to those household maintenance chores that never get done by elderly widows living alone. He hired a pressure washer to rinse cherry-coloured bird poo off the driveway. He went down to Ryan Humphrys, the plumbers' merchant, to buy the parts necessary for whatever plumbing job needed doing. He took his mother-in-law's car to the garage for its MOT and service.

But Derek wasn't a nice guy. He was a rapist and a killer. Walking in the area one evening, he came across Mary Langton, come to sit by the moonlit waters.

She was young. Pretty. Defenceless. Alone.

He raped her.

Raped her, then, I imagine, killed her to escape the consequences of his crime.

Which left him with a dead body to dispose of. And which might, under normal circumstances, be a little tricky for a guy vacationing with his mother-in-law.

Option one, presumably the first thing that occurred to him, was simply to drag Langton into the woods, throw some soil over her, hope for the best. But the area round the reservoirs is a mecca for joggers and dog walkers, and Johnston must have felt, rightly, that the chances of discovery were way too high. Langton's body would have contained his semen. Most likely his blood and skin would have been under her nails too. He couldn't afford the risk.

So he took Langton's corpse back to his mother-in-law's house. To the garage. There were garden tools there, easily sufficient to hack up a corpse. Also a big chest freezer: an easy place to stash the body parts until a more permanent solution could be arranged. There was even a hose and water supply, assuming that he wanted to wash down the garage floor.

Here the story becomes very speculative, but I feel confident all the same. The old woman was an insomniac. Had sleeping issues. The doctor gave her pills, but those things don't always work, as I know well myself. I guess that, on the night of Langton's death, the old lady heard noises coming from the garage. Went to investigate and found her son-in-law ankle-deep in blood and body parts.

That's how I picture it, but perhaps she heard everything, stayed in bed, and investigated quietly the next morning, when Johnston was out doing something else.

Anyway. He murdered Langton, brought her home, Elsie Williams found out. With most in-laws, that kind of thing would be a problem. Fortunately for Derek Johnston, however, his mother-in-law was a vicious woman. Not a murderer, but a quarrelsome, vindictive woman of nasty mind and nasty temper. Not the sort of person to let a good corpse go to waste – and she didn't.

It was from about that point that Williams started to receive supplementary income from the Johnstons. It was a year after that she got her new conservatory, paid for by Derek Johnston. The loathsome old woman apparently didn't mind too much that her son-in-law was a killer. Not if she could wangle some extra income and a house upgrade.

We only ever found 50 percent of Langton. I'm guessing Johnston disposed of the other half the way you might. Chunks of corpse wrapped up in polythene, weighted with a brick, dropped in some remote lake up in the hills. But he didn't have much time. Langton's death took place just thirty-six hours before the two Johnstons were on a flight back to Oz. Assuming that Karen didn't know anything, he'd have been limited in what he could do. Throw in the time needed to clean down the garage, come to some accommodation with his mother-in-law, plus the time needed to pack up and generally act like everything was fine, and I think he flew away the next evening, leaving plenty of Mary Langton in Elsie Williams's freezer.

And then? Well, criminals generally feel panicky and upset in the first day or two following a killing. But soon, if police action doesn't seem to be catching up with them, those feelings often mutate. Serial killers almost never start out intending to kill multiple victims. The first one happens almost by accident. Thereafter, they start to feel a kind of superhuman untouchability. It's that feeling which creates the repeat offender.

Johnston went back to Australia. No visits from the police. No alarms coming from South Wales. Everything normal.

A year passed.

Johnston, I suspect, returned to Wales intending to finish the corpse-disposal job. But he didn't. I think Elsie Williams wanted to keep the corpse as a way to keep the blackmail money coming in. She *needed* that corpse, or felt she did.

But as well as that, I think the pair of them had a nasty pleasure in knowing that in the garage freezer, next to the bits of pork and the apple compotes, there was half a dead girl as well. Did they talk about getting rid of it? Did Johnston *try* to dispose of it? I don't know. Invulnerability does strange things to rational thinking.

Then, the following summer, Elsie Williams tumbled a small boy off his bike. PC David Beynon came round to deliver a caution. A hot day. The family out in the garden. The garage door lifted. Beynon would have come in via the garage.

Might have banged around in there. Certainly emerged into the garden from the garage.

That moment would have terrified Johnston. He'd have realised, suddenly, how thin his skin of protection truly was. If he went back to Australia, if his mother-in-law did anything stupid, or if, in a moment of senility, she started to babble about the corpse in her freezer, he was done for.

He no longer felt safe. His mother-in-law didn't want to release the corpse – her hold over Johnston would disappear if she let that happen – but he needed some way to protect himself.

The plan they cooked up was something that could only have occurred to the mentally unbalanced, yet it had a strange kind of logic to it too. The plan was to distribute the body so widely that it would be impossible to pin the blame on any one owner.

So Derek started to distribute the corpse. To anyone who had offended him or offended his mother-in-law. His targets were the people he interacted with on his various maintenance chores. The pressure washers, the garage guys, the plumbers' merchants. Maybe they pissed him off in some obscure way. Or maybe he was just a bastard.

Elsie's targets were more capricious. Arthur Price, who burned his garden rubbish. His plot was mostly devoted to vegetables, so there wasn't much rubbish to burn. But espaliered fruit trees need pruning in summer. Either while the Johnstons were making their annual visit or just before. So the old lady's rage would have been burning at its brightest just when Derek was on hand to satisfy it. It was the same story elsewhere. The churchwarden's bicycling children, for example, would have been busiest in spring and summer, offending the spiteful old widow with their youth and their shirtlessness. No doubt she found reasons to be furious with people in autumn and winter too, but they weren't top of her summertime hate list.

The combination of summertime targets and household-maintenance targets first alerted me to Derek Johnston. What clinched it was the weird way the Langton body parts were found. In freezers. In barrels of lawn mower oil. In jam jars of vegetable oil. The forensics guys were puzzled, but pretty consistent in their belief that none of this stuff had been decomposing for the full five years. And even if you date the degradation from Beynon's house visit in 2007, the rate of decomposition looked puzzling. In particular, the polythene-wrapped arms in Ryan Humphrys's roof had degraded less than their apparent age would suggest, even if you take 2007 as the date.

But that was a clue in itself. These days, any bag of salad is packed in nitrogen. It's done like that to exclude the oxygen which would accelerate deterioration. Nitrogen isn't a hard gas to get hold of. Any welder's yard will have it. Other inert gases – notably helium – are even simpler and cheaper to procure. My guess is that Johnston packed those arms in helium to make them last longer.

That's speculation, admittedly, but what isn't is Derek Johnston's background. He worked in food processing. A little investigation told me that he was a food technologist, senior enough to be on the conference circuit, talking about the latest advances in packaging technologies and the like. His day job involved preserving foods, including meat. I think he saw Mary Langton's corpse the same way. A dark joke, if you're kind. A personality disorder with schizoid elements, if you're not.

In any case, Johnston was reluctant to let his trophy wither and decompose. So he made efforts, however basic, to preserve the pieces. That was part of the reason I never really bought into the linkages between Langton's death and Khalifi's one. One corpse was preserved, the other one scattered. That always said two murderers to me, not one.

I don't say all that to the Langtons, of course. Watkins needed to know the full picture, but they don't.

'It came to our attention that Johnston was going to be travelling to the UK on business. When he came to immigration control, we detained him.'

The flight had got into Heathrow late. It had come via Singapore, been diverted by a mechanical problem en route, and had finally discharged its cargo of exhausted, cramped, and smelly passengers around four hours later than scheduled.

There was a long queue at immigration and we let Johnston get to the head of it. As soon as he did, he was asked to step aside to answer some questions for Border Control. We had him ushered to one of those small white bureaucratic rooms. So cheap and small and standardised that any sane person would want to kick the walls in after about twenty minutes.

We left him on his own for two hours, with a small plastic cup of coffee that we'd allowed to go cold.

Then we got an Asian-British immigration officer to spend thirty minutes asking Johnston pointless questions about his paperwork and punching buttons on a computer keyboard, while we watched proceedings from behind a one-way mirror. Me. Watkins. Mervyn Rogers. Our guy looked pissed off and shattered. Just how we like our suspects.

Then we made our move. We entered the room.

Watkins told him that he was being placed under arrest for the murder of Mary Langton. Rogers put the handcuffs on, none too gently.

Then we battered him. Not physically, alas, but with one of those hostile interviews that Rogers is so good at. He made it seem like we knew everything. That we were only after various final confirmations.

For an hour or so, I thought we were going to swing it. Rogers led the interview. Watkins launched occasional rocket attacks of her own. I interjected when I needed to, which was seldom. The pair of them were as scary as fuck. Relentless, well informed, in control.

Most people, I think, would have crumpled. Johnston almost did. English law doesn't allow us to give suspects the full Guantanamo treatment, but, give or take some orange jumpsuits, a Sydney-to-London flight comes remarkably close on the sleep-deprivation-and-general-craziness front. Johnston almost gave way, just so he could get himself to a shower.

But he didn't. At about the seventy-five-minute mark, he said, 'Fuck it,' pushed back his crappy little cushionless chair, and said nothing more. Our tape recorder picked up the background chatter of flight announcements but not a further word from him.

We wouldn't necessarily have been defeated even then.

Part of the problem with Stirfry all along was that we never really knew where to focus. Now that we do, we've already got the lab guys looking to link all the various body parts back to Elsie Williams's garage. We've already got one positive hit. The jam jar that held the thumb and the vegetable oil contained in the seal of its lid particles of ceramic dust that appear to match a broken vase on Williams's tool shelves. Further work of that sort may help us to build a case that's viable in court. Owen Jenkins's statement that he wasn't allowed to store tools in the garage is persuasive evidence that Williams and Johnston knew parts of Mary Langton were still in there. The financial data which shows that Elsie Williams's income suddenly took a hike after Langton's death. All the other little bits and pieces.

But perhaps we won't bother.

Because we are not now the only people with an interest in Johnston.

Our arrest of Johnston was notified automatically to

Interpol. And, as luck would have it, while Johnston was in the air over the Indian Ocean, the New South Wales police received an anonymous phone call from a young woman – a young woman who might or might not have had a Welsh accent, and who might or might not have been calling from her very sexy new Alfa Romeo – alleging violent sexual assault by Johnston.

The Aussie police obtained a search warrant. Forcing entry to the property, they found two dismembered female corpses stored, frozen, in a garden outbuilding. The corpses were incomplete, suggesting distribution had already begun. Although the house itself appeared normal in every respect, the outbuilding contained the dismembered, preserved remains of countless wild animals and even a few domestic ones. Items had been pickled, salted, dried, frozen, desiccated, vacuum-sealed, and tinned. There were fox paws in nitrogen, a human hand packed in potassium nitrate.

No one, Karen Johnston said, was ever allowed access to the building, which had no windows and a triple lock on the door. The police, so far, believe her.

Intensive enquiries are ongoing.

Our own preliminary psychiatric investigation of Johnston has revealed a withdrawn individual of low affect. In the words of the summary, 'His mood is neutral or even blank. He shows emotional activity only when asked about the reasons for his arrest and incarceration, a subject which confuses him. He gives conflicting reports of his previous mental history, but some episodes of psychosis or hallucination cannot be ruled out.'

I think back to the low-key Swansea psychologist. The guy was pretty much bang on the money from the word go. If Johnston had lived in the UK, we'd have got to him much faster, but you can't go to foreign police services on a hunch and nothing more, and we didn't even have a hunch. We had

288 people of interest and not a clue where to focus.

When the Aussie police went charging round to the Johnstons' place, I couldn't be certain what they would find, of course, but it was hardly wild surmise to send them in. A killer who kills in the ordinary cack-handed way – that could be any of us. A killer who kills someone, and chops up their corpse, and distributes it to people who've offended their mother-in-law – that person is a nutcase, one who's more than likely to be a repeat offender.

Indeed, the biggest question for me had been about when to make that phone call: whether to notify the Australian cops straightaway or wait till we had Johnston in custody here. In the end, I opted for the latter, because it wasn't too long to wait and because the Aussie cops might not have been able to obtain a search warrant on hearsay evidence alone. A failed intervention by the Aussies would have risked everything. So I forced myself to wait, knowing that by waiting I was running the risk that Johnston would kill again.

'The good news is,' I say to Rosemary Langton, 'that we have your daughter's killer. He will receive a life sentence. I doubt if he will ever walk free again. He will certainly never injure anyone again. What I don't know is whether we have enough evidence to convict him here. If you want us to, we will try. We'll keep him detained as we build our case. If the CPS, the Crown Prosecution Service –'

But the husband – John, I think – interrupts me. He clears his throat, with the hoarseness of scraping rocks.

'No. There's no need. As long as he does his time. Rosemary, are you –?'

She's crying. Tears like sand. But also nodding. 'I don't want him –' she says. 'I don't want him –'

She can't complete her sentence, but we all know what she means. She and her husband want the guy in jail. But they don't want the trauma of a trial. They don't want the trauma of a trial that might go wrong. If the police in New South Wales will take care of everything, and if he serves his jail time on the other side of the world, so much the better. The moons of Saturn wouldn't be too far, as long as this pair are concerned.

Bev and I have accomplished our mission. A mission to save our own police force and the British taxpayer some unwanted costs. But I don't have any sense that we've pushed this pair into a decision that they didn't want to make. It feels like the right outcome. A good one.

'I'm so pleased you've got him,' says Rosemary, 'so pleased.' As her tears still fall.

We don't rush off.

To start with, as a police officer, you assume that you're an intruder in this grief. Then you learn otherwise. That you're the opposite. An actor essential for this stage of things. As necessary as the vicar, the counsellor, the mumsy neighbour.

So we take our time.

'Her body,' says John. 'I assume we can have it now? For cremation, I mean.'

'Yes. There'll be one or two last formalities, I'm sorry to say, but we'll get those done as soon as we can. I'm sorry it's been so long.'

We take our time until, finally, we're almost done.

I say, 'Rosemary, would it be possible for me to see Mary's room? One last time. I feel like I've got to know her a little. I want to pay my respects.'

I don't know what she thinks of that request, but she takes me up. The willow tree. The beige carpets.

But the room is not the same. The duvet has changed. The poster is no longer on the wall. The wardrobe is empty.

My look must express my surprise.

'After you came last time, you and Mrs Watkins, John and I realised it was time to move on. We shouldn't still hold on to it all. We've kept everything precious. The photographs, of course, we could never throw those away.'

For a moment, she's on the brink of more tears. But it's been five years. Five heading toward six. And even tears must have an end.

I sit on the bed. There's a box of junk. Stuff that looks like it's for throwing away, not keeping. There's a small plastic model sailing boat. I reach out and pick it up.

'Your husband mentioned that you'll cremate Mary's remains. Do you know what you'll do with the ashes? Will you inter them or ...?'

'We think scatter them. She liked her freedom. And she didn't have long enough to explore the world. Maybe on the Gower somewhere, she liked her time there.'

'Swansea Bay,' I say, with too much speed and certainty. 'She loved it there. You should scatter her ashes on the waters of the bay.'

'Maybe ... yes, maybe.'

She gives me a look. Probably one that questions my right to have any opinion on the subject, but for a moment, I don't see Rosemary Langton at all. I see her daughter. Like they're one and the same person. The hockey-playing girl merging with this Bath housewife. For a moment I can't quite tell whose world I'm in. Rosemary's or Mary's. They seem equally present. Equally real.

I find I can't even quite distinguish myself. Can't locate my own boundary. As though the pencil lines demarcating these things have become partially erased. Where one person ends and another one begins. Who's alive and who's dead. These things seem so clear to most people and they aren't quite for me. But it's a good unknowing, this. Truthful, not crazy.

There's some more conversation between us, but I'm a bit lost. I'm not sure what either of us is saying. When we get up to go back downstairs, I see I'm still holding the boat.

'Were you going to throw this out?'

She was.

I ask if I can keep it. I can.

We go downstairs. Bev is telling John about the final processes with the coroner and the forensic people. Her tone is professional, sympathetic, competent.

She's a good officer, is Bev. I see how bad I sometimes am. How impossible for a well-run service to manage. But I have my uses.

We drive back to Cardiff in silence and darkness and the windscreen wipers keep the beat with us all the way.

54

Oslo.

It feels as I expected. An enormous sky. Sun fixed low against a pale horizon. Darkness welling up at street level as lights come on. The buildings are solid, blocky, a northern twist on classical. They could exist anywhere, almost, except for those muted Nordic tones. Lichen green. Rust brown. Ochre yellow. And, always, at the ends of streets, a glimpse of sea and the scrape of salt.

I'm due to meet Lev at a city hotel. A bland business-type place. Unremarkable. I book in under my own name. No reason why not, though I'll pay in cash.

I hired a black Toyota Land Cruiser at the airport, boxy and basic. Lev asked me to get a car. He didn't say what sort, but the Land Cruiser seemed about right.

I check in, dump my bag, stay just long enough in my room to get annoyed with it, then go downstairs so I can start getting annoyed with the whole of downtown Oslo.

As I'm stepping out of the lift, I see Lev entering the hotel. He looks like he always does, but with a gym bag over his shoulder. He checks himself in. I don't see what name he uses, but I'd be surprised if he doesn't have a few different identities.

He tells me he's got to go and see about some stuff. Takes my car keys and says he'll find me later.

I don't know what that means, so go out to explore. Walk

412

down to the seafront. Watch the boats. The waves.

This could almost be Cardiff, except those extra few degrees of latitude creep in everywhere you look. We're farther north than any part of mainland Britain. We're on a parallel with Orkney, Saint Petersburg. The sea here has a grey-blue seriousness it lacks in Wales. This sea is fed by meltwater running off granite and calving glaciers. A sea that booms with the sound of beluga whales foraging under ice.

The buildings lining the front are treble-glazed, thickly insulated.

Cold stones set by an icy sea.

The Barry Precision case is fucked.

The whole thing. Fucked.

If our battle was Stalingrad, it turned out that we were playing the part of the German Sixth Army. Watkins is our General Paulus. Surrounded, starved, frozen, tricked, destroyed.

We thought that the multiple waves of legal attacks launched by Barry Precision were there to bleed our resources. Slow our enquiry to the point of stalling. We were wrong. It was a blind, a diversion.

Prothero, it turns out, spent the winter chasing up his connections. A rich, well-connected businessman murmuring in his buddies' rich and well-connected ears. Ivor Harris stood up in Parliament, denouncing our pending case – though no charges had yet been brought – calling for ministers to intervene on behalf of 'this fine local firm.' Initially, his speech appeared no more than empty showmanship. He was speaking to an almost empty Chamber. Any response he got was evasive and placatory.

Except soon it wasn't. A senior civil servant at the Ministry of Defence issued a paper 'clarifying' the regulations on the licensing procedures for weapons export. The paper referred obliquely to 'persistent misunderstandings arising from inadequate MOD guidance.' It launched a consultation paper aiming at an intended regulatory reform.

The document was bullshit. The original regulations were crystal in their clarity and Barry was in breach. But following the 'clarifications,' the UK Trade and Investment Defence and Security Organisation – a government body designed to promote the sale of arms and one that employs, at tax-payer expense, some 160 people – called Barry Precision in for meetings, the upshot of which was that Barry signed a Memorandum of Understanding which made certain representations as to its future conduct. A small contribution was made to charity by way of recognising possible past infractions, without admission of liability. A junior minister issued an apology for poor communication.

Blah, blah, blah.

A junior minister at the Ministry of Defence and a more senior one at the Foreign Office had lunch with the Director of Public Prosecutions. We don't know what happened at that lunch – what threats, what lies, what blandishments – but, after a DPP-ordered 'review,' the CPS told us that they could no longer be certain that any prosecution would be successful or that any such prosecution would be in the public interest. They wimped out, backed down, surrendered, gave up.

Me and Watkins. Alone in the ruins. No boots, no ammo, nothing to eat but the rats, and Soviet armies surrounding us on every side.

We couldn't launch a prosecution on our own. So, like Paulus, we flew the white flag. Dropped the whole damn case.

Far from injuring Barry, we've helped it. The UKTI DSO has taken the firm under its wing. Helped it secure new contracts. The firm now plans to sell openly at the IDEX arms fair. At SOFEX. At others too. Farnborough in the UK. Defexpo in India. Defence Services Asia. The firm is expanding. Negotiating for new industrial space adjacent to its existing facility. Idris Prothero's only mistake was to have gone undercover in the first place. If he'd just had the wit to ask the British government for its specialist Selling-Guns-to-Dictators marketing support, he'd have got it. The whole nine yards. He wouldn't even have had to frame Mark Mortimer. Ali el-Khalifi, silly sod, could have won himself a knighthood for export services, instead of getting himself chopped to pieces and scattered throughout his favourite Cardiff beauty spot.

Watkins tries to cheer me up. McCormack is certainly heading for a life sentence. Johnston too.

But I'm not cheered. Johnston was a nut. A sadistic dangerous nut, who deserves jail and will get it. It's our job to put people like him away and we did our job. Nothing more. As for Olaf and Hamish: they were trivial. Units moved around the battlefield by a distant field marshal. What those two did was wrong, but you still want to hang the general, not shoot the infantryman.

I'm starting to think I'm playing a game whose rules have been tampered with. The fuckwits are winning. Perhaps they always do.

Except that the game isn't quite over. One part – Olaf – is still in play. Idris Prothero either directly ordered the Khalifi killing or was involved in it. I can't prove that, but we *do* know that one of Prothero's phones received a call from Capel-y-ffin the night I was almost murdered. We *do* have very strong evidence to suggest that Prothero's employee, Mark Mortimer, was framed for a drug deal as a way to silence him. It would seem remarkable, to say the least, if Prothero had not also authorised, or at least assented to, the Khalifi murder.

And if so, Olaf is our one remaining chance to prove it.

I hang around on the seafront long enough to get chilly, then buy sausage and mustard from a fast-food place. Eat it standing up.

I should drink a litre of beer and grow facial hair or long blonde plaits. I'd fit right in.

When I can't think of anything else to do, I drift back to the hotel. No Lev. I lie on my back and read an airport paperback until it annoys me, a process that takes all of seven pages.

When I studied philosophy as a student, one of the first topics we examined was David Hume's theory of personal identity. Hume didn't believe in a fixed view of self. He wrote that when we look inward, *'we are never intimately conscious of anything but a particular perception; man is a bundle or collection of different perceptions which succeed one another with an inconceivable rapidity and are in perpetual flux and movement.'* Look as he might, Hume couldn't find anything permanently fixed. When he searched for the pencil marks that demarcated his own boundary, he found nothing. They weren't there.

My fellow students – even my tutors – regarded Hume's theories as a kind of intellectual con trick. A game of three-card monte where the eye is always deceived into overturning the wrong card. My colleagues thought, *Of course we exist, of course our selves are permanent and enduring, so how can we prove Hume wrong?* I thought the opposite. I was honestly surprised that anyone thought Hume wasn't simply expressing the obvious. My whole teenage experience had been about trying to construct a sense of self that didn't collapse. Like trying to build a house on a raft of floating logs.

It's better than that now. I don't know why, but those logs jam together better than they used to. I can walk across my kitchen without finding myself falling waist-high into freezing water. But still. David Hume, right or wrong? I go on thinking he was right.

At half past eight, I get hungry and eat a sandwich from the bar downstairs.

At half past nine, Lev comes to find me. He taps lightly at

my door and walks straight on in. He has hash, rolling tobacco, and cigarette papers. We throw the window up, though there's a light frost outside, and smoke. There's nothing much else to do, so we get properly stoned. I get hungry again, Lev too, and we go outside for a prowl. Find more sausages and mustard. We eat ourselves stupid.

At midnight, Lev says, 'Okay. We leave now.'

I stare at him. He's serious?

He is.

I don't argue. We drive out of the underground car park. Lev wants me to drive, so I do. Lev helps me navigate out of Oslo, but it's hard to get lost. Once I pick up signs to Trondheim, I just stick with them. It's the E6 most of the way. Six and a half hours according to my telephone satnav. I could probably cut the time if I was willing to speed, but I'm not.

I drive. Lev sleeps.

The road's not like any British motorway. One lane in each direction. Tarmac creasing where the land has moved.

Water and ice on the road.

Flashing stems of silver birches. Snow. Grey rock walls and a million whispering pines.

The roads are all but empty.

At three in the morning, I stop and pee by the side of the road. There are stars overhead, more numerous than you ever see in Cardiff. A million stars. More stars than people. I spend a few minutes stretching.

As I'm doing that, I'm surprised to find Lev beside me. He stretches too, but briefly. Rummages in the back of the car, pulls out a rifle and a couple of handguns.

I don't think they were there before. They didn't come with the car.

I say, 'We're not here to shoot anyone.'

'I know.' Lev's voice and gaze are level.

417

'I just want a clean capture. Nothing messy. Nothing ...' I gesture at the guns.

'I know.' He gives me one of the handguns, the smaller one. 'That's why you need this. So no one want to be silly. Here, try this. Is for little hands.'

I fire a few rounds at a tree trunk. Lev adjusts my grip and my stance. Then nods. 'Okay.' He wants me to go on firing, though, so I do. Fifty rounds. Concentrating. Waiting for the weapon to stop feeling alien. I'll have gunshot residue all over my wrists, but I'm rather hoping no one's going to be swabbing them.

As I do that, Lev tinkers around with his rifle. He's firing from behind the car at a tree trunk caught in its headlights. Each time he fires, he checks the shot through the telescopic sights, then adjusts the calibration. He checks the settings until he's satisfied, then blazes off ten shots in rapid succession, checks the target again. He fires a few rounds with his handgun, but doesn't bother with any calibration.

He reloads all the guns and puts them back in the car.

'Accuracy International,' he says. 'Arctic Warfare type.'

I don't know what that means. I don't ask. We've made a real mess of a couple of trees, and there's a litter of cartridges on the ground. But who cares? Norway's a big place. It can afford a couple of messed-up trees.

I drive on. Lev sleeps. The din of our shooting is still echoing in my ears. For the first time, I'm wondering if I made the right call in coming here. I feel afraid.

The road unspools under my wheels. Trees, rocks, stars.

I've been pursuing my investigation of my father's past with increasing rigour. I have over eight thousand pages of documents, over forty thousand words of notes. My investigation of the Rattigan boys has been sidelined for the moment, but that's okay. A girl's got to prioritise.

I don't have a lead that means anything, but Jack Yorath's

comment about the whistle-blower still echoes for me. The notes we have on file say that the individual concerned – Gareth Glyn, a mid-ranking planning officer on the city council – alleged corruption in the award of development contracts. The complaint was investigated at the time – intelligently and appropriately, as far as I can tell – but no firm evidence was ever found. Glyn lost his job. Set up as a planning consultant, then faded from view. Walked out on his wife in 2002, who subsequently sold up and moved to Dolgellau. I haven't been able to find anything further.

I think, *I need to go and speak to Mrs Glyn.* The right time to start interviewing is when your preliminary investigation has given you a platform to work with. When you're in a position to ask the right questions. That moment has come.

But I don't think very much. The car feels different now I know there are guns in the back. Heavier. More purposeful.

The dope I smoked in the evening feels like it's left the system. I feel wrung out and cold.

After a while, it's time to turn off the E6. I glance at Lev, wondering whether to wake him, but find that he's already awake.

'Okay. I drive.'

We swap over. It's colder up here than it was in Oslo. Partly the night. Partly being higher and out of the city. But also these accumulating northerly miles.

We're in late March now. It's not spring, as I've ever known it, but this is what passes for spring up here. Although everything is hard frozen, you can see the streaks and marks where ice has melted during the day. When we stopped in the middle of the night, some of the snow had that granular, crystalline quality you get when snow softens during the day and refreezes at night.

Lev says, 'You want him alive, yes?'

'Yes.'

I want more than that. I want evidence. His phone, his laptop, his papers. Anything that might expose the line that links Khalifi's murder with Mortimer's suicide and Barry's weapons. The line that links Khalifi's corpse to Prothero's silky arrogance. Olaf might well be cautious enough not to retain anything that might connect him to murder, but perhaps not. Out here, on the very edge of the habitable world, he might figure that keeping a mobile phone wouldn't prove disastrous.

Lev drives on. It's not yet sunrise, but there's a softening of the darkness.

When we're ten miles away, Lev stops. Drinks from a thermos of black tea. Also something else. I don't know what. Maybe ethanol or something of that sort. To reduce muscle tremors. I know marksmen use it.

He offers me tea. I say no.

The guns in the back seem huge.

I want to pee again, but don't. Lev does, though. Gets out, pees against a tree. Walks a few feet away, to a patch of clean snow, and rinses himself down with it. Face, neck, hands, wrists. He's brisk and businesslike, as though washing in a basin of warm water.

I'm scared now. Not so much for myself – not with Lev next to me – but because of the scale of these choices I'm making.

Going to Glasgow didn't strike me as a big deal at the time. I hadn't expected to encounter Hamish, but was reasonably confident of managing him if I did. Likewise, the other little things I've done off-piste in this case. I'm not a Watkinsian by-the-book type, and I'm happy with the compromises and decisions I've made.

But now? I've had in my head a picture of what ought to happen. Lev and I surprise Olaf in his sleep. We tie him up. We search the house. We locate all incriminating items and

420

place them where the Norwegian police will surely find them. Then leave. Back to Oslo. An anonymous phone call to the local cops. Let the ordinary processes of justice do their stuff.

But a picture in my head is one thing. Reality is another. I didn't drive up to Glasgow with a carful of guns.

We could still turn back. I almost say something when Lev returns to the car, but when I open my mouth no words come out.

I don't know what I'm doing.

Lev does, though. He drives with alertness. I've never seen him like this. In hunting mode, not training mode. When the satnav says we're five miles from our target, Lev flicks his headlights off. The road is a channel of dark grey through ribbons of snow.

We ride uphill. Rocks on both sides of us. Grey cliffs blotting out the stars. When the road forks, we take the one that's unpaved. A rough track, leading up.

As we get to the top, Lev travels slower, searching for the crest. He drives like a man who knows the landscape. I don't think he can have been here before, but perhaps he's scoped it out on maps, on Google Earth.

He comes to a halt, just before the final rise. We get out. Lev shoves his handgun into his coat pocket. Then takes his rifle. Checks the wind. It was still earlier, when we stopped in the night. It's not windy now, but there's a whisper of breeze running down the valley. Lev feels the wind and makes a small adjustment to his sights.

I take my handgun, feeling like a girl in pigtails. Her first day at school.

We walk up to the top of the hill, but don't stop. Lev doesn't want us silhouetted against the light.

We start descending.

The track is worse on this side. Exposed rock wherever water has washed away the surface.

421

It's gently freezing. Our breaths make steam ghosts in the air that hang a moment, then disperse. Pines whisper to each other in Old Norse.

There's only one dwelling visible below us. A rust-red wooden house. Not big. Single-storey. Huddled against the cold. There's a single outbuilding, a log store perhaps. A patch of dirt with a parked four-by-four.

Beyond the house, the valley flattens into silver. The river coming down from the mountains widens out to a kind of lake, before narrowing again, bolting through a gap in the cliffs that wall off the valley end. The lake is ice. The slopes on the far side forested and steep.

It's getting lighter all the time.

We work our way farther downhill, until Lev stops us. He pulls out some binoculars. Night-vision things, I assume.

He scopes things out. There's no light in the house. No smoke in the chimney. No dog in the yard.

I let him do his stuff. I'm starting to feel better. Almost relaxed. As though this stupid plan might actually work.

And because I'm relaxed, I don't notice that Lev isn't.

He passes me the glasses.

'There,' he says, pointing. 'Also there, there, and there.'

To start with, I can't find what he's pointing me towards. Then I can. Dots that glow a bright green through the glasses. That are otherwise all but invisible in the frost.

I don't know what they are, what I'm looking at.

'Is surveillance device. All round house.'

Then I do feel fear. The real thing. A wash of cold that pricks open every capillary. I look at Lev, because this is his world, not mine.

He shrugs. 'We leave. We kill. We try to capture.' Lev offers me three options, like a waiter offering a choice of soups. Tomato. Chicken. Minestrone.

'I don't know. I mean, isn't there some way to ...?'

'Disable or evade device? Yes, is no problem. Give me six men. Counterterrorist training. Also arctic experience. Easy.'

He looks at me, waiting for an answer.

'Let me think.'

It feels weird standing out here, in the three-quarter dark, the surveillance cameras in front of us, a professional killer in the house below. A gun in my hand and Lev tooled up beside me.

I ask, 'If we go in, what are our chances of making a clean capture? No shooting, no blood?'

'Twenty prozent. Maybe ten. I don't know this man.' Lev uses the German word *prozent*, instead of *percent*. The odds are terrible in either language. 'If we continue, is better to start now.' Lev gestures up at the sky. He doesn't want it to get any brighter.

My mouth says, 'We can't leave.'

I hear the words. Understand why someone would think that way. Jan-Erik Fjeistad is a professional killer. Leaving him untouched means allowing him to continue his bloody trade. If we drive away from here now, someone will pay for that decision with their life.

But I don't move. I'm a motionless thing in a motionless world.

Lev makes a tiny gesture, asking me to commit. And this time, I say, 'We can't leave.' Not just my mouth. Me. Give a little nod of decision.

'Okay,' says Lev. 'So we try to capture. Otherwise kill.'

Minestrone it is. If they're out of minestrone, we'll go for the chicken.

I nod. 'Okay.'

My voice sounds like it belongs to somebody else completely. Nothing here feels real.

'Wait here. When I say, you go there.' He points, off the track, to a boulder partway down the slope. 'Don't run. Just walk. Gun please. Safety off. If you have to fire, aim with both hand and shoot slow.'

I nod, like I've understood anything, but Lev is already off. Down the hill. Dancing really. Rock to rock. Tree to tree. A shadow dancing through the half-light.

After a while, he stops against a tree. I'm about to follow him, when I realise he hasn't yet given the instruction to move. So I stay put. Lev checks his binoculars again, then his scope, then the binoculars.

Somewhere around us the colours shift a millionth of a shade as dawn strengthens its grip.

Then Lev signals and I walk down the hill. The house we're approaching has only a single window facing us. Lev has his rifle fixed on that window. He doesn't acknowledge me as I walk past not ten yards from him. We are within the range of the surveillance devices now. I can see the nearest one, a small black box on a rickety fencepost. Wires too, presumably, but I don't see them.

Then I'm behind my rock and Lev moves again.

He points me at a new rock. I walk fast toward it. Smear myself into its shadow.

Then Lev's turn. As he passes me, there's a sound from the house. I hear the detonation and it takes me half a second to realise the shot comes from Olaf. I don't see where the bullet strikes, but Lev hasn't stopped moving. He gets to a thin rise of ground, now just 150 metres from the house. Settles into a firing position. Lying on his belly, legs slightly spread and to the side. Fires.

I can't see where the bullet goes. Don't know what Lev is trying to do. He turns, beckons me toward him, makes a gesture to indicate I need to come slowly, then rolls back onto his belly and fires another shot. He fires three more times as I descend.

When I get next to Lev, the house feels very close indeed. I can see Olaf's gun now, a thin metal line against the angle of the open casement.

Without taking his eye off his rifle scope, Lev fills me in.

'Okay, Fjerstad has rifle, not just shotgun. From this range, very good shot can hit us, so be careful. But this rifle' – Lev indicates his own – 'is for snipers, not just for hitting big stupid animal. Also, bullet can go through wall, no problem. Fjerstad maybe knows this. Anyway, is worried.' His voice adjusts and turns posh and English. 'Right now Mr Fjerstad is shitting himself.'

I nod, as though this is all normal.

Nod, and see as I do that there is smoke beginning to rise from the house's only chimney. That's either because Olaf is starting to prepare himself a nice grilled breakfast, or because he's in the business of destroying evidence.

I say, 'He's burning evidence.'

'Naughty man. Is not allowed. I think we ask him to leave the house.'

Lev swings his rifle through ten degrees. Aims at the big green oil tank up against the wall of the house. He puts two bullets into the tank, waits for a spill of oil, then shoots another round onto the tank's concrete base.

Bullet. Concrete. Spark. Flame.

The oil tank disappears in a fireball. Intense orange and black. Oily clouds circling down around the updraught. You can feel the heat from here. The house starts to blaze.

While I'm admiring the flame, Lev puts five bullets through the timber walls. A kind of hurry-up to Olaf, as though having an oil tank explode outside wasn't enough.

Then Lev is moving again. Running for the corner of the house. I don't know what I'm supposed to do, so I follow him. I still have my gun in my hand. Still haven't fired it. The ground is rocky and sloping, but I run the way Lev does. By instinct. Letting my feet find their own placement.

Lev is twenty yards ahead of me. He's fixed, I think, on gaining access to the front of the house, to get a clear sweep of the terrain there. If he can get to the front corner of the house, his superior weaponry and his vastly superior fighting skills will give him command of the battlefield. But there's a stand of trees and low bushes between the house and the track leading back up the hill. The trees block Lev's view. Because I'm farther back, they don't block mine. The upper branches of the trees are already starting to singe and crackle with the flame.

Olaf isn't in the house anymore. He's not trying to defend his turf. He's trying to get the hell away. He's at the door of his Land Rover Defender. Gunning his engine. Heading up the hill.

I scream something to Lev, but my feet are travelling faster than my brain. I burst out onto the track. Olaf is forty yards away, thirty.

He'd happily run me down. I'd happily shoot him dead.

The car is accelerating towards me as fast as it can, given the adverse slope and the uneven terrain. I see Olaf's face, tense and white at the wheel.

Him against me.

I find a shooting stance.

Fire.

Feet planted. Hands out. Squeeze the trigger.

Fire, fire, fire, fire.

The windscreen ahead of me is shattered glass. The vehicle hits a pothole and instead of adjusting course, slews up the bank and almost overturns.

Fuck you, Olaf.

The front right tyre is exposed now and, aiming as carefully as I can, I empty the rest of my magazine into it.

The Land Rover doesn't move. Then Lev is next to me.

'Are you okay?'

He doesn't wait for my answer, just pats me down, checking me. It turns out I am okay. I only know that when Lev tells me so.

I don't know where Olaf is. I keep thinking that Lev is being an idiot, standing here in the open. I'm fumbling for a spare magazine, trying to alert Lev to the danger.

He changes the magazine for me. 'You hit him in shoulder. He's going other way now.'

Lev takes me to the front of the house, from where we can see Olaf heading down to the frozen lake. He's moving purposefully, but not running. He has a small backpack, slung over one shoulder only. A ski pole in one hand, his rifle in the other. He's good on skis, I remember, but he's not looking too mobile now. There's something about the way he moves which confirms that he's wounded.

'He's getting away,' I say, stating the obvious. My head is ringing with the gunfire. I feel slow, shocked, and stupid.

'No, I don't think.'

Lev lays himself out on the ground. His rifle has a stand made of two little folding legs. Lev opens those out, takes a moment to sight himself, then fires a single shot.

Olaf falls instantly.

I stare at Lev, amazed and furious. I know the whole idea of a clean capture has turned to shit, but since when did Lev think it was okay to kill the guy without even asking me? I shot at the man too, but in that case it was him or me. I was acting in something approaching self-defence.

Lev disregards my look. Simply folds his gun stand and says, 'Ankle.'

Sure enough, we see Olaf righting himself, flinging us a furious look, and staggering on. But not far and not fast. He's on the rocks by the lake shore now. He moves clumsily. Stones glazed with ice and an ankle shot to hell. If we want to pick him up later, we'll be able to do it at a stroll.

But we've things to do before that. The house is ablaze. Any evidence we might want is rapidly disappearing, if it hasn't already gone.

Lev runs to the house. I'm just a yard or two behind.

The front door is open. Scorching air pours out, as from an oven door. The interior is strangely lit. Nordic dawn and fireball heat. Like some carefully constructed palette of beige and grey and violet has been ram-raided with tinfuls of orange, red, and black. That, plus incredible heat.

I go inside.

A strip of dirty cotton curtain hangs over the door window. I rip it off. Lev knifes it into two. We hold the material over our mouths, keep our heads low. The house is small. Just one large living space, then presumably bedroom and bathroom leading off from doors at the end.

We make for the stove.

The door's open and there's stuff burning inside. Olaf was probably still feeding the fire when the corner of his house blew up and bullets poured in through his walls.

A small ash shovel stands by the stove. I use it to shovel everything out. There are some papers, a phone, a laptop. A load of crumpled-up newspapers and handfuls of firelighters. Fire and smoke everywhere.

I burn my hand on the laptop, trying to get it free of the firelighters.

The wooden building is burning fast now. We need to get out. I hurt my hand a second time trying to pick up the laptop, but Lev is ahead of me. He brings a cushion from the sofa. Knifes open the top and rips out the pad. We use the cushion pad like an oven glove to bundle all the items from the stove into the cushion cover. Laptop, phone. Whatever papers we could rescue.

We run out of the house, lungs screaming.

We've probably wasted our time. I doubt if Olaf wrote

much on paper, and the electronics look knackered.

The valley suddenly seems amazingly clear and cold and bright.

Above the lake, a rocky hummock rises from the fields. Lev gets there before I do. He lies out on the ground, sets up his rifle. Olaf is four hundred yards from us now. Crossing the frozen water. Moving slowly.

Lev sights up just for the sake of it. But there's no hurry now. No hurry at all.

I pull the laptop out of the cushion-bag. The surface is hot, but no longer scorching. I try to open the screen, but the whole machine is buckled. There's a mess where the battery leaked.

Lev looks at it solemnly. 'Is fucked,' he says.

'Yes.'

The phone is in worse shape.

'Is also fucked,' says my electronics guru.

'Yes.'

I look through the papers, but they look like trash to me. Literally. Stuff that Olaf pulled from the dustbin so he could get a fire burning more quickly. If we can't salvage data from the electronics, I doubt if we'll have anything useful at all.

The smoke which was leaking from the house is billowing now. A dirty grey mostly, but tongued with orange. There are gaps in the roof now. A latticework of rafters outlined in black.

Lev has his sights fixed on Olaf's back. He adjusts his posture by infinitesimal amounts. Either to keep pace with Olaf's movements or to move his aim onto different targets. Head. Chest. Leg.

Olaf, as though feeling that invisible pressure, turns and looks at us. Motionless. A black figure against the white.

I don't know what we look like to him. Don't know what

429

his thoughts are as he sees his house ablaze, his possessions gone, his cover blown.

What do you think when you're in that position? What do you think as you turn back to your direction of travel and see your future? A frozen lake. A facing slope of rock, snow, and pines. On the run for ever, uphill and alone, shoulder wounded and ankle smashed. And a rifle bead tightening on your back.

I don't know. I don't know what he thinks.

I do know that when I was alone in the snow, I didn't feel on my own. I felt myself part of the police family. Felt Buzz. Felt Mam and Dad and Ant and Kay.

I say to Lev, 'Leave him.'

'Leave? Really?'

'Yes.'

If there's salvageable data from the electronics, we've got it. If not, it's gone for ever.

And we've done enough to debar Fjerstad from his current career. A shoulder can be fixed, perhaps. The ankle, possibly not. But the physical side of things is only half of it. We've made a thorough-going mess of Fjerstad's home. His car is riddled with bullets. There are bullet casings everywhere. The Norwegian police will have to investigate hard. As they do, I'll find a way to allege, anonymously, on the Internet that Fjerstad is a contract killer. I'll link him to Khalifi, to McCormack. Publish photos, his army résumé, his address details, everything.

Contract killers need darkness to operate in. By the time we've finished, Fjerstad's face will be on every newspaper in Norway. On the radar of every police service in the world. He won't do to others what he did to Khalifi. What he tried to do to me.

I start explaining this to Lev, but he doesn't care. He lays down the gun and rummages in his pocket. Gets out a joint. Lights it. Takes a puff and offers it to me.

I shake my head. My attention is all with Olaf, who is moving differently now. Slowly and with a sudden terrible vigilance.

I turn to Lev, not sure what's going on.

Lev says, 'Is not lake. Is river.' He traces the line of the river's flow with his finger. I see it now that he shows me. A bluishness in the ice. A difference in the way it carries the snow.

Olaf is moving with acute care now.

With fear, I think you would say. With fear.

I see him jolt. His boot has gone through the ice. He recovers but proceeds.

And I don't want him to. All of a sudden, I don't want this anymore. I want him to retrace his steps. We'll share a smoke, shake hands, forget about all this. If he can give me anything on Prothero or Saadawi, I'll take it. And if not – well, we'll shake hands anyway. I don't want this.

But Olaf doesn't know what I think. Doesn't know, doesn't care.

He goes on. Stumbles once more and recovers. Then another stumble – and he's gone. The grey ice field suddenly darkens as water blackens it. Olaf's head and hat are visible above the ice. His arms. He's trying to roll his weight out of the water and back onto the ice. But each time he tries it, the ice shelf crumbles beneath him. He's too far now for us to see his movements in any detail. He's a fly struggling against glass.

It doesn't take long. We're too distant to witness the final choreography in any detail. We just see that, one moment, there is a head above the water, and the next moment, only a level silence. Black, silver, white. And moving water. A glimpse of moving water.

Half a minute passes without sign of further movement.

431

Lev offers me the joint again and I take it.

'This is first time for you, I think.'

'No. The second,' I say that automatically, because it happens to be the truth. But there are different possible truths and I've chosen the wrong one. So I correct myself, 'The second time I've killed someone, but it feels like the first. The one before went very fast. I didn't have time to notice anything.'

'You are okay?'

'Yes.'

Lev laughs at that. Takes the joint from me and draws hard on it. 'Stupid question, this one. Everybody always ask it, including me. *Are you okay?* Everybody says yes. Always this: *yes*. And –' He waves his hand at the lake of ice. 'Is still a person. *Boof!*'

'Yes.'

Olaf's house is pouring with flame now. The roof is mostly gone. You can see the roof joists still, spiderlike through the fire. They won't last. The walls are still largely intact, but they'll be completely gone too.

I don't know how much information there might have been there. But we won't find out. Olaf's property is rapidly reuniting with its owner. Entering the same dark house by different routes.

Fire and ice.

Hamish was a thug. Unprincipled and brutal. Olaf too, I assume. But he wasn't only that. In another world, another life, I could imagine sharing a drink with him. Enjoying an evening in his company. As it was, I've spent one evening with him and one morning. The latter resulted in his death. The former, almost, in mine.

Lev and I are still smoking, but slowly. A rose-gold light tints the mountaintop above us. I don't know which of us starts it, but one of us begins laughing, then the other joins in. We lie on our backs in the snow, passing the joint to and fro, laughing for no reason at all, except that we are alive and we might not have been, and the light is golden and it might not have been.

I say, 'I think I knew. I was just pretending I didn't.'

Lev, not surprisingly, doesn't know what I mean, so I explain.

'I had this picture in my head, that we would stroll into Olaf's house at dawn, catch him unawares, locate all the evidence we could possibly need. But in truth, I think I knew that was always an outside bet. I think I knew we might have to use force.'

'Always better to have gun.' Lev shrugs.

'Tomato. Chicken. Minestrone. I guess I knew I'd be eating chicken.'

Lev looks at me with those eternal brown eyes of his. He doesn't know what I'm talking about. Doesn't care. He finishes the joint and flicks it away into the snow. I pick it up.

'DNA on the saliva,' I explain.

We walk back up the hill and down the other side to the car.

Start driving back to Oslo.

Lev at the wheel, because he doesn't trust me to drive this short of sleep. It's twenty minutes before we pass anyone at all and seventy minutes before I see a CCTV camera.

The Norwegian cops will find the evidence of our shoot-out, all right, but they won't be able to place our car at the scene and have no reason to guess that a kooky Welsh cop and her screwed-up Spetsnaz buddy are the ones they need to interview.

Somewhere along the way, we stop for food. Lev fills his plate with cheese and sausage. I can't face any of that. I take a bowl of muesli, but don't make much of a dent in it.

Olaf was alive and now he is dead.

That's a pencil mark of a kind. One more impressive if you

witness the transition than if you don't. It's not that I feel myself so separate from the world of the dead. I don't. I feel no more distant from Olaf than I did before. The opposite, if anything. But there *was* a transition. One state changing to another. Something indelible.

When we get back to Oslo, I go straight to bed. When I wake up, Lev is still around, but the car has no weapons in it.

And last night never happened.

55

Three days later, back in England, I take the laptop and phone to a commercial data-recovery outfit that has done work for the Ministry of Defence, among others. I show Olaf's phone and laptop to a technician, but even before I have them properly out of my bag, he says, 'You are joking, right?' Three minutes later, I'm leaving the premises, with Lev's diagnosis amply confirmed. Is fucked.

Just like our case against Barry Precison. Against Idris Prothero.

I won't leave it there, of course. The man is an arms smuggler who tried to have me killed. But I'll leave it there for now. I've got no other option.

Two final postscripts.

The first is a weird one. I did go up to Dolgellau. Found the whistle-blower's wife: Mrs Glyn – Delia. In her early sixties. Living in a council flat, nice enough, but no spare cash. She had the angry, injured look often worn by the slightly mad. Her clothes weren't quite right either. A too-short flowery dress worn with bright red tights and heavy black shoes. Hair not very recently washed. I don't judge these things. I've been there. Ticked all those boxes and then some. Truth is, I feel comfortable around such people. At ease.

Delia made tea. Concentrating hard to do it right. Made it, poured it, complained about her back. We sat at a small

Formica table in her kitchen. Unlined cotton curtains splattered with grease from the frying pan.

'He was killed, you know that, he was killed.'

'I'm sorry?'

'Gareth. They never found him. They said he walked out but he wouldn't have done that, not that we were a perfect couple, but I know Gareth, he had an optician's appointment that week, I've got the booking confirmation right here. I've got everything, you know, I haven't thrown away a thing.'

She told her story. It felt like one long run-on sentence, all commas and not a pause for breath. She said that her husband 'wouldn't give up, that wasn't Gareth, see? Not a giver-upper, because it's not what you do, it's who you know, isn't it, and that was our problem, never knew the right people.'

At some point, she handed me three notebooks crammed with tiny writing – mostly his, but later hers – plus press clippings, receipts, photos, invitation cards. I wanted to look through the material, but Delia wouldn't stop talking, not even for a moment.

I interrupted to ask, 'Why did they kill your husband in 2002, when the allegations of corruption date back to the mid-eighties?'

I got an answer – four breathless minutes of it – but nothing that made an ounce of sense.

I asked, 'Who killed him? Who specifically wanted him dead?'

Six minutes that time, by the end of which Delia was quite upset. Repeating herself, adjusting her hair, getting muddled by her own line of thought. But her answer began, 'They all do, see, that's the whole problem ...' and the gist of her thesis seemed to be that everyone in Wales with the tiniest bit of money, power, or influence felt threatened by Gareth Glyn and sought to have him killed. Nevertheless, her rambling list of names intersects with at least six people on my mind-map diagram of Dad's connections. I realised that that's the first connection of any kind I have. A useless one maybe, but a connection. A lamp glowing dimly in the dark.

'What does your doctor have you on, Delia?' I asked. 'Buspar, maybe?'

She told me about her drug history. She wasn't on Buspar, a new-generation anxiolytic, but she was on Prozac, topped up by Xanax. She got the pill bottles to show me. Complained about her back, her sleep.

As a witness, she was terrible, neither coherent nor consistent. Prozac is a drug for depression, Xanax for anxiety disorders. The notebooks are no better, the sort of evidence that would destroy a witness's credibility in court.

But we weren't in court. This isn't that kind of investigation.

I tapped the notebooks and said, 'May I borrow these?'

She said yes.

And stupid as this evidence is, worthless as this witness will probably prove to be, I came away from Dolgellau elated. So much so that, intead of driving back to Cardiff, I drove down to the beach at Barmouth. Mudflats on the river, grey sands facing the sea. Ate a sandwich with a fitful west wind snatching at my clothes and hair.

Ate a sandwich and contemplated my past.

A little girl in an open-topped car. A little girl who, when grown to be a teenager, lost everything. Her optimism. Her feelings. Her sanity. Who lost so much that, when she inspected the ruins of her mind, found only death. A teenage girl who thought she was dead.

And now?

I don't know. My mental equilibrium is still fragile. That night when I thought I felt Khalifi in my room, I was experiencing full-blown psychosis. The sort of hallucination which plagues the homeless, which makes drunks and schizos yell at invisible beings on the street.

But a little run-of-the-mill psychosis doesn't feel too scary to me now. I've swum in stormier seas than those, stormier by far. And my investigation of my past – the mystery of my birth and the origins of my madness – feels for the first time like a real enterprise. One with substance and purpose. One that will have its solution.

Crazy as Delia Glyn may be, she's my first witness. Cramped and nutty as her notebooks may be, they constitute my Exhibit A.

I'm on the case and on a roll.

I've called that a postscript, but really it's a prologue. A statement about my future. The real postscript – the last, sad note of the bugle – sounds on a different coast, a different day.

The Langton family did, finally, hold a funeral service for their daughter. It was a private service, so I didn't go, though I'd have liked to. But they also hold a memorial service. At a little grey church in the Mumbles. A lot of Mary's student friends come along – not that they were students anymore. A group of people about my age, my sphere of life. Heterogeneous and identical, both at once.

Rosemary and John Langton are there, of course. They recognise me. Are surprised to see me, but not unhappy, I think. They say they're pleased.

I don't usually get a lot from church services. Christianity doesn't understand dead people very well, I think. It seems embarrassed by them. But this is a good service. Dignified and sad and celebratory and uplifting. Some people cry. I don't, but I like it when others do.

Watkins comes along too. I didn't see her when I arrived. I think she slipped in at the back, after it started. But I'm pleased she came.

And after the service, everyone troops down to the seashore. Rosemary Langton scatters her daughter's ashes onto a west wind and the west wind blows the fine grey dust far out over Swansea Bay. People clap. Some people cheer. It's a good parting. The right way to finish.

I don't hear from Ali el-Khalifi anymore these days, but I bet he's here now. Overhead, in the wind, in the unreliable sunshine, in the scream of the gulls. Following Mary's ashes as they spread out on the glittering water. It's a good ending for them both. I wish them well.

Khalifi both saved Langton's life and, by accident, helped to end it. But by a strange twist of events, his death ended up mirroring hers. Two men who killed him for money needed a way to dispose of a corpse. Because Adrian Condon and I happened to report the discovery of a corpse of our own, Olaf – I'll bet it was him – thought to use that discovery to throw a nice fat red herring our way. A red herring that, to a large extent, succeeded in subverting our whole enquiry.

And yet every circle closes in the end. Khalifi never quite found unity with Langton in life. But he did in death. Operation Stirfry: their own macabre wedding celebration. It's hard not to feel a sorrowful sense of completion. Like something satisfied.

As we crunch back up the beach towards the cars, Watkins walks alongside me. She says, 'Are you able to stay a little or do you have to rush off?'

I can stay, I say. I don't have to rush off.

'Good,' she says. 'That's good. Because there's someone I'd like you to meet.'

Her eyes have the luminous excitement of young love. In my pocket, I have a little plastic boat. Round my neck, I have the necklace that Buzz gave me at Christmas. On my wrist, I have the little shell bracelet that a little girl gave me.

'I'd like that, Rhiannon,' I say. 'I'd like that very much.'

Endnote

The inspiration for this book arose from a bizarre, but genuine, sequence of events that unfolded in the early 1990s.

A Midlands-based machine tool company, Matrix Churchill, was acquired in 1989 by an Iraqi consortium. Two of the company's new directors worked directly for Saddam Hussein's security services and set to work building and shipping advanced machine tools to assist with Saddam's weapons programme. Certain aspects of that programme were, it has to be admitted, more ditzy than actually dangerous. (A super-gun that could fire projectiles into space? Hmm.) But the company was still selling advanced technology to help a dictator threaten his neighbours and oppress his citizens. That sort of thing isn't supposed to be legal, so the company was duly prosecuted.

Unfortunately, during the course of the trial, it emerged that one of the company's directors was working for British intelligence. It further emerged that the government knew all about the company's activities and had done what it could to assist. The trial collapsed in acrimony and political infighting.

That's history now, but the business of selling arms is far from being history. Fiona Griffiths comes across a government outfit known as the UKTI DSO. That organisation is not an invention. You can check out its website, if you like, or download its chirpy little brochure. It employs 160 people and it is there solely to promote the export of arms, and related goods and services, many of which have ended up with precisely the regimes that the Arab Spring revolted against. A recent parliamentary report concluded that 'both the present Government and its predecessor misjudged the risk that arms approved for export to certain authoritarian countries in North Africa and the Middle East might be used for internal repression.'

Misjudged the risk? I doubt it. I suspect they knew perfectly well what was happening. The Campaign Against the Arms Trade welcomed the parliamentary report, saying, 'If the government is serious about arms control and human rights, it should stop using public money to promote arms sales to dictators.' Well, yes. Quite.

But we can't leave a charity to have the last word; this is Fiona Griffiths's book, after all. And as she would probably put it, the fuckwits are winning and they're using your taxes to do it.

Harry Bingham

A Note on Cotard's Syndrome

Cotard's syndrome is a rare but perfectly genuine condition, and an exceptionally serious one besides. Its core ingredients are depression and psychosis, which together bring about an extreme form of depersonalisation. Or, to put the same thing in plainer language: sufferers believe themselves to be dead. Patients frequently report 'seeing' their flesh decompose and crawl with maggots. Early childhood trauma is implicated in pretty much every well-documented case of the syndrome. Full recovery is uncommon, death by suicide all too frequent.

Fiona Griffiths's own state of mind is, of course, a fictional representation of a complex illness and I have not sought to achieve clinical precision. Nevertheless, the broad strokes of her condition would be familiar to anyone unfortunate enough to be acquainted with it.

LOVE STORY, WITH MURDERS

Reading Group Notes

For Discussion

- '*Hoping always to find something – a foot, an ear, a pair of fingers – shining in the mud like an autumn mushroom.*' The early part of the book, in particular, doesn't hold back on the gruesome. Did you find this excessive? Did it feel voyeuristic and gratuitous, or honest and necessary? And how was your reading experience affected by Fiona's unusual perspective? For example, when Fiona finds Mary Langton's head, she finds the moment so peaceful that it spills over into joy. How did *you* feel?

- '*Watkins – severe black suit, white shirt, the uptight-lezza look – beckons me over.*' You don't have to be a big fan of political correctness to find Fiona's commentary amazingly inappropriate at times. She can also be flippant about serious subjects ('*Some families just give off a choppy-uppy odour. Others don't.*' or '*Langton, poor girl, was really too boring to end her life distributed across a number of suburban outbuildings.*'). Yet when it comes down to it, Fiona also becomes Watkins' best friend in the police force and she is Langton's most redoubtable ally. Is this inconsistent? And how does Fiona talk about her own mental illness?

- *'Buzz real-lifes himself over to the table with his plate, I TV-movie myself over.'* Fiona has big problems in coming into reality. In what contexts are her problems here most acute? And are there times when those problems seem almost absent? And what do you think of the Buzz–Fiona relationship? Are they right for each other? How do you see their relationship developing?

- *'"Sexual relationships with other lecturers? Drugs? Global jihad? Bondage games?" "No." Kerry looks at me reproachfully, as though I'm not doing my job. Which I'm not.'* Fiona is obviously not a standard-issue policewoman and she's happy to breach procedure and even the law in pursuit of her goals. What do you think about the morality of her actions? If you were her police superior, would you promote her or fire her? Or prosecute her?

- *'I can't look at that dress without feeling dizzy. It's as though I find myself standing on the lip of a very deep well. No idea of how I came to be there, but weak at the knees and looking down.'* Just for fun: what do you think happened to Fiona in those 'missing' two years? What might account for her teenage Cotard's Syndrome and all the problems she'd had since?

- *'It's not the beating the crap out of people that takes it out of you. It's the waiting around beforehand, the cleaning up afterwards. You should be able to get support staff for that kind of thing.'* Fiona's attitude to danger is quite unusual. She seems fairly relaxed the entire time she's in Hamish's apartment, but she finds the business of buying clothes so alarming she can only do it with her sister – and even then she has to soothe herself by remembering the look and feel of Mary Langton's head. Does this make any sense to you? What is it about shopping that's so hard for her? And what is it about beating up serial killers that she finds easy?

- *'The silence is getting tiresome, so I change the subject. "Okay, shall we play I Spy?" There's nothing in the sweep of my headlights except snow and some trees. The barn too, dimly. "I spy with my little eye something beginning with S." No response. I give them two minutes by the dashboard clock to think of something, but they don't manage it. I give them the answer. "It was snow. I'm slightly disappointed, to be honest. I was trying to start with something easy."'* There's no question that Fiona is a tough cookie, but she's nothing like other crime-thriller tough guys, and she isn't even like the classic hardened, boozy, seen-it-all detective. (You can't see Jack Reacher playing I Spy, can you?) Do you find her toughness credible? How can you make sense of it given how vulnerable she is in other ways? Oh, and since we're on the subject, what did you think of *that* scene in the snow?

- *'I want to say that I'm pleased Khalifi was chopped to shreds and scattered on Llanishen's empty mud. Him and her, united at last. But the happy atmosphere of our Weirdos United love-in might buckle at that particular insight, so I keep it to myself.'* There are at least three love stories in this book: Khalifi–Langton, Fiona–Buzz and (sort of) Watkins–Fiona.

The first of those love stories is macabre, to say
the least, and the third of them is hardly standard.
Did the love element in the book move you? Did
you find yourself wanting the happiness of those
involved?

- *'We're too distant to witness the final choreography
  in any detail. We just see that, one moment, there is
  a head above the water and the next moment only a
  level silence. Black, silver, white. And moving water.
  A glimpse of moving water.'* One of the themes of
  this book is that of personal identity. Fiona quotes
  the Scottish philosopher, David Hume, who
  believed that our sense of personal identity is little
  more than a trick of the mind. Fiona herself almost
  completely depersonalises (in the lap-dancing club)
  and has a psychotic hallucination of a dead person
  in her bedroom. Who's right here? Is personal
  identity just a fake that some people – like Fiona
  – have difficulty in sustaining? Or is it something
  solid and dependable? And perhaps more to the
  point, is there anything that normal people can
  learn from Fiona's struggles? Are her challenges
  like an amplified version of our own … or is she
  just a one-off freak of nature?

- *'How much blood is there in this impeccable kitchen?
  How many bones beneath these polished floors?'* Fiona
  tries and fails to imprison Idris Prothero and it
  seems pretty clear that some UK companies have
  exported military and security-related hardware to
  a number of very corrupt regimes over the years.
  Does the revelation (published in the House of
  Commons Select Committee report July 2013) of

the British government's support for these efforts shock/surprise you? And more broadly, Fiona is on a bit of a mission – unsuccessful thus far – to imprison some rich and powerful people who (she thinks) are criminals, made invulnerable by their money. How do you see this story strand playing out in future books? And do you, in reality, think that there is any substance to the idea that the wealthiest class in our society might somehow be above the law?

In Conversation with Harry Bingham

Q Is there any part of Fiona – or Buzz – in you?

A For sure. I think that the principal characters in any book are likely to embody some part of the author him- or herself. Outwardly, I'd have to say I'm more of a Buzz than a Fiona, but I'd like to think I have at least a splash of her intelligence, her force and her attitude to risk. And although I don't have her problems with psychosis, I do think that we all have to manufacture an identity to get through life. We might not be as *conscious* of that process as Fiona is, and very few of us find it as hard, but I do think it's something we can all relate to.

Q Do you like Fiona?

A Yes, of course. I have to given that I spend a lot of time in her company. But the answer goes deeper than that, because the truth is that I *love* Fiona. I cherish her wit, her recklessness, her wicked side, her desire to do good, her vulnerability – the whole damn package. It's not a romantic love, particularly (personally, I think Buzz should get out while he still can). In the end, my love is the sort that only an author can have for a character.

If Fiona does drugs, hangs out with screwed-up Spetsnaz guys, or beats up professional hitmen, I'm not worried the way a father would be. I just love watching her do it. Attagirl!

Q Does she surprise you ever?

A Most crime-thrillers these days are written in multiple third-person point of view. So, for example, the author can switch from the cop figuring out his next steps, to the bad guy planning his next attack, to the victim as she becomes aware of a gathering threat. The multiple changes of viewpoint keep the story alive and make it easy to build tension. (So we see the bad guy plant the bomb in the café, then watch as our detective, unwittingly, strolls out for a cup of coffee . . .)

By choosing a strictly first-person viewpoint, I'm aware that I've sacrificed a lot of 'easy wins' when it comes to building and sustaining tension. But Fiona, bless her, always rides to the rescue. Her responses are so non-standard, that they remain surprising even when we're well acquainted with who she is. What's more, her responses to life's challenges are often inverted. Buying clothes? That's tough. Trapped in a small flat with her would-be murderer? Great: it's a good opportunity for her to think through her Christmas shopping. I wouldn't say that she surprises *me*, exactly, but I do relish her ever-reliable capacity to wrong-foot her readers. And her bosses. And, of course, the criminal classes.

Q Silence or music while you write? If music – who do you listen to? And how do you write – by hand? Computer? A mixture?

A Total silence. I have a soundproofed room and wear earplugs. The room gets its light from the sort of no-flicker bulbs they use in operating theatres. I do half an hour of yoga or pilates before writing, and drink only fruit and vegetable juices until I'm finished for the day. I write on unbleached foolscap pages using my father's old fountain pen. Later on, at the editing stage, I am normally blurry with drink and self-hatred, and just hack the material into shape using a laptop and gallons of Irish whiskey.

Q *Really?*

A No, of course not. All that 'I can only write on vellum' crap is self-indulgent horseshit. If you're a professional author and you live an ordinary, unsheltered life, you'll write wherever and however is most convenient. Some of the time, I write on a sofa with dogs snoring to either side of me and an enormous cup of tea somewhere close at hand. Other times, I've got twins screaming for a feed and builders mixing concrete in the garden. One way or another, the books get written. But for what it's worth: mostly silence and always on a computer.

Q Which authors do you admire and why?

A Jeepers. I'm an eclectic reader and my tastes spread widely. But as a crime writer, I think that Conan Doyle and Raymond Chandler are the two essential sources of all crime writing. Conan Doyle because the crime genre only came of age with his arrival, and Sherlock Holmes is still the best detective ever written. And I love Chandler because he kept all the beautiful traditions of the crime genre, but reset them in the real world. And his writing is wonderful. I think Chandler is a much better writer than Scott Fitzgerald, and has the edge over Hemingway, too. He's one of the first, best poets of modernity.

Other random facts. First literary crush: Becky Sharp in *Vanity Fair*. Favourite snowy novel: tie between *Miss Smilla's Feeling for Snow* and *Doctor Zhivago*. Best forgotten classic: *Rogue Male*. If you haven't read it, you should.

Q How do you hope your readers will feel about Fiona?

A Sounds odd, maybe, but I don't really care. My job is to keep Fiona 'Fiona-ish'. To keep her as authentic as possible and to hurl her into situations which are going to challenge her to the max. Thereafter, readers can make up their own minds. Some readers will love her. Some readers will get really annoyed with her. What would worry me is if some readers didn't care much either way. Fortunately, my naughty lass doesn't generate many middle-of-the-road reactions.

Q Why did you call the novel *Love Story, With Murders*?

A I'm rubbish with titles, usually. Mostly my publishers take one look at my provisional title and say, sweetly smiling, 'That's lovely, Harry, but do you have any other ideas?' This time, however, and much to my surprise, the title proved an immediate hit. The idea came directly out of Fiona's conversation with Watkins. (*"That's what we've been investigating here. A love story." "A love story with two murders." "Well, yes." That doesn't seem like an interesting objection to me. The murders only make the love that bit more real, the flame that bit brighter.'*)

I suppose I liked the title because it has a universal quality to it, and because it's almost a joke about why we love crime writing – about the reactions of any true crime-fiction fan. Love story? Nah, boring. Love story with *murders*? Ooh, now you're talking …

Q What single thing about you would surprise us the most?

A I'm not sure. It would have to be either my remarkable physique or my work for the special ops part of MI6. It's all covered by the Official Secrets Act, though, so they're not things I can talk about much.

Q Any clues about your next novel – any snippets for us?

A Ha! The clue is already in *Love Story*, actually.
There's a training course Fiona has put her name
down for, and that training is going to come in
useful for her next assignment. I'll also say this:
that the 'elevator pitch' – a brief summary of the
book that is meant to make publishing execs drool
with desire – is quite possibly the worst elevator
pitch in the entire history of crime writing. (The
book is about payroll fraud and is set in the world
of commercial office cleaning. How bad is that?)
But I'm getting some very good reactions from my
advance readers. And needless to say, everything
isn't quite what it seems . . .

Suggested Further Reading

The Field of Blood by Denise Mina

The Girl Who Played with Fire by Stieg Larsson

Waiting for Wednesday by Nicci French

Hume: A Very Short Introduction by A. J. Ayer

Miss Smilla's Feeling for Snow by Peter Høeg

Fiona Griffiths returns

'THE MOST STARTLING PROTAGONIST IN MODERN CRIME FICTION'
SUNDAY TIMES

THE STRANGE DEATH OF FIONA GRIFFITHS

FROM THE AUTHOR OF *TALKING TO THE DEAD*
HARRY BINGHAM

The latest instalment of
Harry Bingham's acclaimed series

Available now

www.orionbooks.co.uk

Also available in ebook and audio